Reality
by Other Means

The Best Short Fiction of

JAMES MORROW

WESLEYAN UNIVERSITY PRESS

Middletown, Connecticut

Wesleyan University Press

Middletown CT 06459

www.wesleyan.edu/wespress

© 2015 James Morrow

Introduction © 2015 Gary K. Wolfe

All rights reserved

Manufactured in the United States of America

Typeset in Minion Pro by Mindy Basinger Hill

Wesleyan University Press is a member of the Green Press Initiative.
The paper used in this book meets their minimum requirement
for recycled paper.

Library of Congress Cataloging-in-Publication Data
available upon request

5   4   3   2   1

Contents

Introduction

An Audience with the Abyss

James Morrow's Short Fiction

GARY K. WOLFE

At the 1999 International Conference on the Fantastic in the Arts — the most eclectic of the various academic conferences dealing with science fiction and fantasy — a panel discussion on the work of James Morrow drew such interest that it became the basis for a special Morrow issue of the academic journal *Paradoxa: Studies in World Literary Genres*. The impressive list of contributors included writers as well as critics — Samuel R. Delany, Michael Bishop, Élisabeth Vonarburg, Michael Swanwick, Brian Stableford, and F. Brett Cox among them — and the journal has since devoted only one other issue to a single fiction writer, Ursula K. Le Guin. As insightful and brilliant as some of the essays were, they also occasionally indulged in that favorite critical game of connect-the-dots. In trying to situate Morrow's unique satirical voice, the essayists came up with a dizzying list of possible influences, analogues, and sheer wild guesses — Swift, Voltaire, Twain, and Vonnegut most often, but also Philip K. Dick, Robert Sheckley, Chaucer, Dostoevsky, Kafka, J.G. Ballard, Donald Barthelme, Nathaniel Hawthorne, John Irving, Ray Bradbury, Anatole France, Evelyn Waugh, and for good measure, Nietzsche and maybe Heidegger. And all this before Morrow had written *The Last Witchfinder*, possibly his most complex and rewarding novel, or *The Philosopher's Apprentice*, or his delightful pop-culture fables *Shambling Towards Hiroshima* and *The Madonna and the Starship*, or *Galápagos Regained*, or more than two-thirds of the stories in the present collection.

One of the more bizarre of many bizarre sketches from the Monty Python troupe — whose sense of absurd juxtapositions is not entirely incongruent with Morrow's own — involved the ridiculously militaristic "Confuse-a-Cat" service, designed to rouse bored and mopey cats from their torpor. Since the beginning of his fiction career in the 1980s, Morrow has been cheerfully providing such a service for readers of science fiction and fantasy, and increasingly for a much broader readership in such literary journals as *Conjunctions*. The earliest story here, "Bible Stories for Adults, No. 17: The Deluge," immediately throws us off balance simply by virtue of its central character: what on earth is a prostitute named Sheila, a self-described "drunkard, thief, self-abortionist . . . and sexual deviant," doing on Noah's ark, let alone completely undermining Yahweh's scheme for the redemption of the human race — which scheme, as she points out, is really nothing more than simple eugenics? The range of deliberate anachronisms, from Sheila's allusion to a nineteenth-century pseudoscience to her apparent knowledge of how to freeze sperm for later fertilization, was startling enough — and maybe just science-fictional enough — to earn Morrow his first Nebula Award in 1989. (Interestingly, Morrow returns to a very secularized version of Noah's ark in "The Raft of the Titanic," in which the crew and passengers save themselves by constructing a huge platform which becomes their home and eventually an independent nation, choosing to forgo rejoining the world altogether after learning of the madness of the First World War.)

"The Deluge" was one of a sharply satirical series of "Bible Stories for Adults" that Morrow published between 1988 and 1994 (another included here, "Bible Stories for Adults, No. 31: The Covenant," hilariously deconstructs the Ten Commandments). Together with his "Godhead" trilogy of novels (*Towing Jehovah*, 1994; *Blameless in Abaddon*, 1996; *The Eternal Footman*, 1999), these stories helped establish Morrow's reputation as science fiction's premier religious satirist. It was a role that science fiction readers, who often felt besieged by the same forces of irrationality that were Morrow's targets, embraced with enthusiasm.

Science fiction had grappled with religion before, of course, but often in simplistic or sentimental ways. C.S. Lewis appropriated the machinery of the genre to construct heavily didactic Christian parables in his *Out of the Silent Planet* trilogy (much as he abducted the machinery of fantasy for his Narnia novels), while Ray Bradbury's story "The Man" used an elusive but thuddingly obvious Christ figure to construct a similar fable of warm faith vs. cold science. Monasticism is treated as a preserver of learning in the post-apocalyptic world of Walter M. Miller's *A Canticle for Leibowitz*, but the novel eventually turns on a church-vs.-state controversy and a familiar critique of self-destructive materialist culture. A few novels, such as James Blish's *A Case of Conscience* and Mary Doria Russell's *The Sparrow*, sought to engage a more complex interaction between faith and belief, good and evil, while fewer would take on the church itself as a cause of dystopia, as in Lester del Rey's little-known *The Elev-*

enth Commandment, and fewer still, like David Lindsay's *A Voyage to Arcturus*, would openly condemn the pernicious effects of belief itself. And, of course, Vonnegut had his Bokononism. But more often than not, when science fiction turned to religion, the results were uneasy fictions of accommodation, often featuring sensitive and intelligent Jesuit priests puzzling over mysterious aliens and intractable moral conundra. (Perhaps because of their intellectual traditions, Jesuits have long been favored by science fiction writers, who have seemed much more reluctant to take on, for example, Southern Baptists.)

Here, though, came James Morrow, unequivocal atheist, cheerfully profane fabulist, witty scourge of nincompoop theodicies — the one storyteller who could somehow make logical positivism play out like a battlefield exploit and revealed religion like a Marx Brothers movie. Morrow neither apologized for his humanist stance nor retreated into a clever but facile nihilism (as would sometimes happen with Vonnegut, the author to whom he is most often compared). Morrow would not only proclaim the death of God, but show us his massive corpse being towed across the Atlantic like a dead whale. Readers will find no shortage of such religious satire in *Reality by Other Means*, from the Church extending its right-to-life doctrine to protect the rights of the "unconceived" in "Auspicious Eggs" to the tiny Martian invaders who decide to conduct their own religion-vs.-reason ideological war on the streets of Manhattan (since they simply don't have room on the small Martian moons where they now reside). Appropriately, the only ones who know how to deal with the Martians are lunatics.

But focusing narrowly on Morrow's religious satire risks overlooking the considerably broader scope of his work — he's impatient with all sorts of dogma, the dogmas of academia not excluded — or the significant ways in which he has helped to expand the scope of what science fiction can do. Morrow's relation to science fiction is an interesting one, and not entirely unconflicted. On the one hand, he has long held, as he did in an interview with Samuel R. Delany in that *Paradoxa* issue, that science is "the best way we have of obtaining knowledge about the outside universe: provisional, tentative, vulnerable knowledge, to be sure, but still astonishingly substantive," and his fiction reveals a deep understanding of scientific thinking from Newton (see *The Last Witchfinder*) to Darwin (see *Galápagos Regained*) to current physics.

On the other hand, he is far from being a "hard SF" writer, and he doesn't hesitate to employ pulp pseudosciences when the story at hand calls for them; the magical "Infusion D," which turns already degenerate men into something like Neanderthals in "Lady Witherspoon's Solution," might well have been concocted by Stevenson's Dr. Jekyll, and Dr. Jekyll himself very nearly makes an appearance in the form of Dr. Pollifex in "The Cat's Pajamas," with his equally magical "QZ-11-4" substance, which somehow turns beast-men into successful local politicians by multiplying their capacity for empathy (don't ask; just read the story). There's also more than a touch of Wells's *The Island of Dr. Moreau* in that tale, but tracing the various ways in which Morrow adapts and reshapes tropes from earlier science fiction might well precipitate another essay altogether. The "science" of vibratology in "The Iron Shroud" is an equally unlikely but ingenious construction of a credible-sounding Victorian pseudoscience (the prolific British paperback author Lionel Fanthorpe also imagined such a science). In "Daughter Earth," Morrow moves beyond imaginary pseudoscience and fully in the direction of surrealism, as a mother gives birth to a miniature Earth, a global biosphere complete with oceans and a rapidly accelerated pattern of evolution (the extinction of the dinosaurs somehow becomes a moving family tragedy weirdly reminiscent of Thornton Wilder's *The Skin of Our Teeth*), while in "Spinoza's Golem" he moves in the direction of Jewish legend — though this particular golem is actually a kind of steampunk robot which "lives not by magic but by springs and cogs, ratchets and escapements."

There is also some familiar furniture from science fiction and horror in "The Vampires of Paradox," which could almost be viewed as Morrow's answer to Arthur C. Clarke's famous story "The Nine Billion Names of God," only in this case it's a philosophy professor specializing in paradoxes, rather than a computer scientist, whose visit to a remote monastery turns out to alter the fate of the world. Clarke, who often wrote himself into corners that he could only get out of by resorting to a mysticism he didn't actually believe in, is a good representative of the kind of rhetorical paradoxes in science fiction that Morrow exploits, and "The Vampires of Paradox" brings these to the foreground, beginning with a catalogue of often familiar verbal paradoxes and expanding its scope to include Fermi's paradox (regarding the apparent absence of other civilizations in the universe) and Schrödinger's cat (the famous illustration of quantum superposition). Both are among the favorite puzzles of science fiction writers, and Morrow's examination of them is ingenious — but the story also has its improbable pulp features, such as the roach-like alien "cacos" who feed on paradoxes and attach themselves to humans like Robert Heinlein's puppet masters, or the Poe-like "tarn" that oozes through a "crack in the lithosphere" and threatens to inundate the world.

Morrow rarely employs anything resembling traditional hard science fiction extrapolation, but in "Martyrs of the Upshot Knothole" — my candidate for the most gnomic story title here — he has done enough historical and scientific research to make almost convincing the longstanding rumor that one of the massive nuclear bomb tests of the 1950s (called "Upshot Knot-hole," which helps make sense of the title) took place just near enough to a downwind movie location for the actors and crew to suffer radiation-induced cancers years later. The movie in question is an actual John Wayne epic, *The Conqueror,* and Wayne himself, who shows up as a central character, may have been among the "martyrs."

This brings us to another fascinating but seldom discussed aspect of Morrow's fiction: his enthusiasm for popular culture, movies and television in particular, and *bad* movies and television in even more particular. His decision to invoke *The Conqueror*—widely remembered as one of the most egregiously misconceived movies of the 1950s, with John Wayne as a wildly unlikely Geng-his Khan—suggests that Morrow's fascination with (and considerable knowl-edge of) film is not exactly limited to the classics. Caltiki, the amoeba-like monster that the epistemological explorers encounter toward the end of "Fix-ing the Abyss," is borrowed from an actual 1959 Italian horror film, *Caltiki, the Immortal Monster,* to which the story's narrator, himself a third-rate horror director, has made a number of knock-off sequels. And when the same explor-ers encounter Kafka's Gregor Samsa in his giant-insect form, the narrator thinks of the 1954 monster movie *Them!* The narrator of "The Wisdom of the Skin" is likewise a filmmaker, reduced to boring educational films of the sort that haunted high school students in the 1950s, while the yeti who decides to study with the Dalai Lama in "Bigfoot and the Bodhisattva" displays an ency-clopedic knowledge of Abominable Snowman movies, partly due to his having eaten the brain of a dying NYU film-studies professor who was trying to climb Mount Everest. This same yeti forms an attachment with the Dalai Lama over their mutual fondness for James Bond films, and the oddly Buddhist-sounding titles of some of them (*Tomorrow Never Dies, The World Is Not Enough*, et cetera).

Nor will Morrow hesitate to employ a pop-movie cliché when it suits his purposes, sometimes inverting the cliché as a means of underlining his own satirical agenda. "The Cat's Pajamas" ends with a classic scene of enraged vil-lagers storming the mad scientist's lair, but these villagers are a more eclectic group than they might at first seem: "the mob included not only yahoos armed with torches but also conservatives gripped by fear, moderates transfixed by cynicism, liberals in the pay of the status quo, libertarians acting out anti-government fantasies, and a few random anarchists looking for a good time." This comes after the beast-folk, having ingested that unlikely empathy drug, have nearly transformed the local government into a compassionate liberal democracy. "Whatever their conflicting allegiances," the narrator goes on to note, "the vigilantes stood united in their realization that André Pollifex, sane scientist, was about to unleash a reign of enlightenment on Greenbriar. They were having none of it." The stereotypical mad scientist, in other words, is seen as mad simply by virtue of his being sane, and Morrow uses the familiar figure as a way of skewering no less than six different ideological positions in one sentence. As I mentioned earlier, uncritical dogma, no matter what its ideology, is like catnip to Morrow's imagination.

Playing with such clichés, conventions, and rhetorical reversals is one of the key techniques by which the author consistently reminds us that we are in a James Morrow tale, no matter how familiar its outward lineaments may at first appear. One of the most elegantly constructed stories here, "Arms and the Woman," which revisits Helen of Troy, is packed with such techniques. Its very opening line is a reversed cliché: "What did you do in the war, Mommy?" "Mommy" is Helen herself, telling her children her own version of the Trojan War in a frame-tale (another technique that Morrow often uses). Appropriately enough, Morrow sprinkles the story with Homeric epithets — "horse-loving Thebaios," "brainy Panthoos, mighty Paris, invincible Hector" — but soon the epithets themselves go wonky and anachronistic, as poor "slug-witted Ajax" becomes "slow-synapsed Ajax." When we first meet Helen and Paris, they are a bickering middle-aged couple who might as well be in a Howard Hawks comedy. Helen, stuck at home, keeps trying to find out what the war is about, while Paris keeps telling her "Don't you worry your pretty little head about it." He complains about her weight and graying hair and suggests that, with a combination of ox blood and river silt, "You can dye your silver hairs back to auburn. A Grecian formula." Then, before taking her to bed, he slips on "a sheep-gut condom, the brand with the plumed and helmeted soldier on the box."

Do such pointed and punning allusions to contemporary consumer products yank us out of the classical mise-en-scène in which we thought this story was located? Of course they do: they are reminders that we are in Morrow-space, as are such deliberately self-referential lines as Paris later saying "I'm sorry I've been so judgmental" or Helen herself, after figuring out a way to end the war, described as "a face to sheathe a thousand swords." But the most important use of such self-referential anachronisms comes near the story's moral center, after the "slow-synapsed Ajax" expresses doubt as to why the war should continue after Helen has volunteered to return to her husband. "Because we're kicking off Western Civilization here, that's why," responds an outraged Panthoos. "The longer we can keep this affair going — the longer we can sustain such an ambiguous enterprise — the more valuable and significant it becomes." "By rising to this rare and precious occasion," adds Nestor, "we shall open the way for wars of religion, wars of manifest destiny — any equivocal cause you care to name." The story, it turns out, recasts the most famous war of classical antiquity as a deliberate boondoggle born of masculinist fantasies of self-esteem — the invention of the idea of war itself — with Helen, taking charge of her own destiny, as the spoiler. It is arguably the most overtly feminist tale in this book, even without mentioning Helen's confrontation with the automaton of her younger self, built to replace her on the parapets as motivation for the soldiers, or her retirement to Lesbos, whose economy involves trading olives in order to import "over a thousand liters of frozen semen annually" — thus accounting for the children who are listening to the story in the frame-tale. It's an historical fantasia, but nearly becomes science fiction when it needs to. Genre, for Morrow, is at best a suggestion.

Frame-tales, journal entries, and false documents are narrative techniques common both to Morrow and to earlier science fiction. In "Spinoza's Golem," for example, the fictional Spinoza's own account of building a golem is framed by a contemporary museum curator's efforts to rediscover it, while "Lady Witherspoon's Solution," set in a post-Darwinian Victorian England, is another frame-tale with a distinctly feminist undercurrent. A scientific expedition in the Indian Ocean comes across a remote island populated by what the captain concludes to be a race of peaceful Neanderthals, apparently spared the "normal pressures that, by the theories of Mr. Darwin, tend to drive a race towards either oblivion or adaptive transmutation." But there are, curiously, no females among the tribe. Befriending one of its members, the captain is led to the grave of an Englishwoman, Kitty Glover, and shown her journal, which reveals a different sort of tale altogether. Kitty, well born but reduced to the workhouse, comes under the tutelage of the eponymous Lady Witherspoon, whose "Hampstead Ladies Croquet Club and Benevolent Society" disguises a far darker secret. In terms of literary dissonance, the story begins as a persuasive redaction of the lost-race tale, segues into a Dickensian fable of redemption and charity, and then turns — at least for a moment — into a bizarre Victorian rendition of something like Chuck Palahniuk's *Fight Club*, as Lady Witherspoon stages periodic fight-to-the-death battles between men — most richly deserving a stern comeuppance — who have been "devolved" through the mysterious counter-evolutionary serum "Infusion D." These are the creatures who, when their usefulness to Witherspoon's entertainments has been exhausted, are shipped off to the Indian Ocean to form what appeared to be the Neanderthal society in the framing story. When Lady Witherspoon asks her protégé if she would agree that "there is something profoundly unwell about the [male] gender as a whole, a demon impulse that inclines men to inflict physical harm on their fellow beings, women particularly," Kitty responds, "I have suffered the slings of male entitlement," among which, clearly, is sexual assault.

Given stories like these, it should hardly be surprising that Morrow's trenchant skewering of all forms of intolerant or merely muddled thinking — together with his erudition concerning philosophy, history, science, and even those bad movies — have made him a favorite among liberal intellectuals and academics. At the same time, however, he occasionally reminds us that he is hardly pandering to our comfort zones, and that herding behavior is not restricted to Victorian patriarchs, religious fundamentalists, or sensationalist media. "Fixing the Abyss," perhaps the most wildly freewheeling tale here in terms of its plethora of satirical targets, begins with knowledgeable allusions to Martin Heidegger and Jean Baudrillard, then quickly focuses on the potentially dire consequences of academic groupthink. When a mysterious and growing chasm opens on the Penn State campus, threatening all of central Pennsylvania, the narrator suggests that the causes include a resurgence in fundamentalist thinking, a revived international arms race, "the institutionalization of clerical rape, and the aestheticization of suicide bombing" — but argues that the immediate trigger was a lecture by a comparative literature professor who believes that "morality, truth, beauty, and knowledge are illusory notions at best, overthrown in the previous century by perspectivism, relativism, hermeneutics, and France." "It's all very well for a scorched-earth, skepticism-squared ethos to enrapture Ivy League humanities departments," the narrator (the horror-film director) muses, "but when *épistémologie noire* comes to America's land-grant universities, we know we're all in a lot of trouble."

Almost a commonplace in science fiction criticism is the idea of "literalization of metaphor," probably first suggested by Samuel R. Delany and later adopted by such equally distinguished writers and critics as Ursula K. Le Guin, in which a figure of speech that would be read as metaphorical in normal discourse can be a statement of literal fact in a science fiction text (one of Le Guin's examples is "I'm just not human until I've had my coffee"). In reality, it's almost impossible to find examples of such sentences in science fiction narratives, and one could as easily argue that any form of fantastic literature does the same thing ("He's a nice guy during the day, but a beast at night" could apply to any number of werewolf tales). In Morrow's fiction, though, we can actually see something like this literalization happening. The epigraph for "Fixing the Abyss" is a quotation from Heidegger: "Language speaks. If we let ourselves fall into the abyss denoted by this sentence, we do not go tumbling into emptiness. We fall upward, to a height. Its loftiness opens up a depth." In the world of the story, that abyss becomes quite literal, and the equally literal ways in which the world responds to it grow increasingly absurd. If the rift was caused by a kind of critical mass of nihilism, might it not be neutralized, as chemical compounds can neutralize each other, by inundating it with sentimentality? So the first strategy is to dump into the abyss "countless Smurfs and Care Bears, . . . wheelbarrow loads of garden gnomes, Charles Dickens novels, and Mother's Day cards, along with ten thousand emergency DVD transfers of Shirley Temple movies." In other words, literalized metaphors are used to fight a literalized metaphor. When that and a more conventional military expedition fail, "a team of crack nihilists" is recruited, including the film-director narrator, a *metal hurlant* rock singer, a playwright, and an avant-garde mathematician. Their quest turns into an almost slapstick *katabasis*, a classical journey to the underworld, only one in which the usual fearsome gatekeepers are replaced by Friedrich Nietzsche, Kafka's Gregor Samsa (in his insect form), and a financial-derivatives swindler named Roscoe Prudhomme. Finally, they reach the god-like Caltiki — a monstrous amoeba, who congratulates them on having "proven yourselves worthy of an audience with the abyss." The primordial roots of that abyss, the monster explains, can be traced to "the single worst idea your human race has ever devised."

And just what is that terrifyingly dumb idea? Again — read the story. Simply by holding *Reality by Other Means* in your hands, you have proven yourselves worthy of your own audience with the abyss, and it's quite an interview.

Reality by Other Means

Bigfoot and the Bodhisattva

After thirty years spent eating the chilled coral brains of overachieving amateur climbers who believed they could reach the summit of Mount Everest without dying, a diet from which I derived many insights into the virtues and limitations of Western thought, I decided that my life could use a touch more spirituality, and so I resolved to study Tibetan Buddhism under the tutelage of His Holiness, Chögi Gyatso, the fifteenth Dalai Lama.

The problem was not so much that I nourished myself through cerebrophagy, but that I felt so little pity for the unfortunates on whom I fed. Chögi Gyatso, by contrast, was reportedly the reincarnation of Avalokitesvara, the Bodhisattva of Compassion. Evidently he had much to teach me.

As far as I know, I was the first of my race to undertake an explicitly religious quest. Traditionally we yeti are an unchurched species. Our ideological commitments, such as they are, tend along Marxist lines, the natural inclination of any creature with a dialectical metabolism, but we try not to push it too far, lest we lapse into hypocrisy. After all, it's difficult to maintain a robust contempt for the *haute bourgeoisie* when their neuronal tissues are your preferred source of sustenance.

We live by a code and kill by a canon. Yes, kill: for the raw fact is that, while the typical cyanotic climber who winds up on the yeti menu may be doomed, he is not necessarily dead. We always follow protocol. Happening upon a lost and languishing mountaineer, I assiduously search the scene for some evidence that he might survive. If I spot a Sherpa party on the horizon or a rescue helicopter in the distance, I continue on my way. If death appears inevitable, however, I tell the victim of my intention, then perform the venerable act of *nang-duzul*, hedging the frosty skull with all thirty-eight of my teeth, assuming a wide stance for maximum torque, and, finally, snaffling off the cranium in an abrupt yet respectful gesture. The *sha* is traditionally devoured on the spot. It's all very ritualistic, all very *in nomine Patris et Fili et Spiritus Sancti*, to use a phrase I learned from the left cerebral hemisphere of Michael Rafferty, former seminarian, bestselling author of eighteen Father Tertullian detective novels, and failed Everest aspirant.

No matter how scrupulously he observes the norms of *nang-duzul*, the celebrant cannot expect any immediate cognitive gain. He must be patient. This isn't vodka. Two or three hours will elapse before the arrival of the *sha-shespah*, the meat-knowledge, but it's usually worth the wait. Typically the enrichment will linger for over a year, sometimes a decade, occasionally a lifetime. Last week I partook of a tenured comparative literature professor from Princeton, hence the formality of my present diction. I would have preferred a south Jersey Mafioso to a central Jersey postmodernist, the better to tell my story quickly and colorfully, but the mob rarely comes up on the mountain. My benefactor's name was Dexter Sherwood, and he'd remitted $65,000 to an outfit called Karmic Adventures on the promise that they would get him to the summit along with six other well-heeled clients. The corporation fulfilled its half of the contract, planting Dexter Sherwood squarely atop the planet, but during the descent a freak storm arrived, and it became every man for himself. I have nothing good to say about Karmic Adventures and its rivals: Extreme Ascents, Himalayan Challenge, Rappelling to Paradise, Jomolungma or Bust. They litter the slopes with their oxygen tanks, they piss off the sky goddess, and every so often they kill a customer. *My Parents Froze to Death on Everest and All I Got Was This Lousy T-Shirt.*

I shall not deny that a connoisseur of long pork occupies ethically ambiguous ground, so let me offer the following proposition. If you will grant that my race is fully sentient, with all attendant rights and privileges, then we shall admit to being cannibals. True, we are *Candidopithecus tibetus* and you are *Homo sapiens*, but my younger sister Namgyal long ago demonstrated that this taxonomy is no barrier to fertile intercourse between our races, hence my half-breed niece Tencho and my mixed-blood nephew Jurmo. Do we have an understanding, O furless ones? Call us psychopaths and Dahmerists, accuse us of despoiling the dead, but spare us your stinking zoos, your lurid circuses, your ugly sideshows, your atrocious laboratories.

This agreement, of course, is purely academic, for you will never learn that we exist — not, at least, in consequence of the present text. I do not write for your amusement but for my own enlightenment. In setting down this account of my religious education, all the while imagining that my audience is your cryptic kind, I hope to make some sense of the tragedy that befell His Holiness. And when I am done, you may be sure, I shall drop the manuscript into the deepest, darkest crevasse I can find.

I did not doubt that Chögi Gyatso would agree to instruct me in the dharma. For the past four years my clan and I had faithfully shielded him from the predations of the People's Liberation Army during his thrice-yearly pilgrimages from Sikkim to Tibet. Thanks to me and my cousins, the true Dalai Lama had thus far enjoyed twelve secret audiences with his false counterpart in Lhasa. His Holiness owed me one.

"Why do you wish to study the dharma?" Chögi Gyatso inquired, knitting his considerable brow.

"My eating habits cause me distress," I explained.

"Digestive?"

"Deontological."

"I know all about your eating habits, Taktra Kunga," said His Holiness, soothing me with his soft hazel eyes. He had a moon face, a shaved pate, and prominent ears. Behind his back, we yeti called him Mr. Sacred Potato Head. "You feed on deceased climbers, extracting *sha-shespah* from their brains."

Although our local holy men were aware of yeti culinary practices, they'd never learned all the sordid details, assuming in their innocence that we restrained our appetite until the donor was defunct — an illusion I preferred to keep intact. "Every species has its own epistemology," I noted, offering His Holiness an intensely dental grin.

"For me you are like the carrion birds who assist in our sky burials," said Chögi Gyatso. "Scavenging is an honorable way of life, Taktra Kunga. You have no more need of Buddhism than does a vulture."

"I wish to feel pity for those on whom I prey," I explained.

A seraphic light filled His Holiness's countenance. Now I was speaking his language. "Does it occur to you that, were you to acquire this pity, you might end up forsaking *sha-shespah* altogether?"

"It's a risk I'm willing to take."

"I shall become your teacher under two conditions. First, each lesson must occur at a time and place of my own choosing. Second, you must forgo your usual cheekiness and approach me with an attitude of respectful submission."

"I'm sorry to hear you think I'm cheeky, Your Holiness."

"And I'm sorry if I've insulted you, Your Hairiness. I merely want to clarify that these lessons will be different from the banter we enjoy during our journeys to Lhasa. We shall have fun, but we shall not descend into facetiousness."

"No talk of James Bond," I said, nodding sagely. Like the fourteenth Dalai Lama before him, Chögi Gyatso was an aficionado of Anglo-American cinema. Until I began my study of the dharma, our mutual affection for Agent 007 was the only thing we really had in common.

"Or perhaps *much* talk of James Bond," the monk corrected me, "though surely even more talk of Cham Bön, the dance celebrating the gods."

The motives behind our trips to see the false Dalai Lama were essentially political rather than religious, although in His Holiness's universe the art of the possible and the pursuit of the ineffable often melded together. Having once dined on Laurence Beckwith, a Stanford professor of twentieth-century Asian history, I understood the necessity of these furtive treks. The disaster began in 1950 when the People's Liberation Army crossed the Upper Yangtze and marched on Lhasa with the aim of delivering the Tibetan people from the ravages of their own culture. By 1955 the collectivization process was fully underway, with Mao Zedong's troops confiscating whatever property, possessions, and human beings stood in the way of turning this backward feudal society into a brutal socialist paradise. Over the next four years it became clear that China intended to dissolve the Tibetan government altogether and imprison Tenzin Gyatso, the fourteenth Dalai Lama, and so on the evening of March 17, 1959, that regal young man disguised himself as a soldier and fled to Dharamsala in India, where he eventually established a government-in-exile, got on the radar of the secular West, and won a Nobel Peace Prize.

A mere two months after Tenzin Gyatso passed away, Beijing shamelessly appointed a successor, a bewildered three-year-old from Mükangsar named Shikpo Tsering. On his tenth birthday, Shikpo Tsering was taken from his parents, placed under house arrest in the Potala Palace, and ordained as Güntu Gyatso, the fifteenth Dalai Lama. No Tibetan Buddhist was fooled, and neither were we yeti. Güntu Gyatso is no more the reincarnation of Tenzin Gyatso than I am the reincarnation of King Kong. Among my race he is known as the Phonisattva.

Meanwhile, the monks in Dharamsala set about locating the genuine fifteenth Dalai Lama. When a chubby infant from Zhangmu, Töpa Dogyalt-san, passed all the tests, including the correct identification of the late Tenzin Gyatso's eyeglasses, prayer beads, hand drum, and wristwatch from among dozens of choices, he forthwith became Chögi Gyatso, the latest iteration of the Bodhisattva of Compassion. On Chögi Gyatso's twenty-first birthday, the monks relocated their itinerant theocracy to the austere environs of Gangtok in Sikkim. The Panchen Lama told the outside world that certain benevolent deities, communicating through dreams, had demanded this move. He did not mention that these same gods evidently envisioned His Holiness periodically slipping across the border to advise the false Dalai Lama in matters both pragmatic and cosmic.

And so it happened that, one fine white day in February, my lair became the locus of a royal visit. The unexpected arrival of Chögi Gyatso and his retinue threw my girlfriend, Gawa Samphel, into a tizzy, and I was equally nonplussed. Had we known they were coming, Gawa and I would have tidied up the living room, disposing of the climber skulls strewn everywhere. We were fond of gnawing on them after sex. Death is healthier than cigarettes. To their credit, the monks pretended not to notice the bony clutter.

Gawa served a yeti specialty, pineal-gland tea sweetened with honey. His Holiness drained his mug, cleared his throat, and got to the point. As the leader of "the tall and valiant Antelope Clan" — an accurate assessment, the average yeti height being eight feet and the typical yeti heart being stout — I could perform a great service for the long-suffering Tibetan people. If I and my fellow *Shi-mis* would escort His Holiness through the Lachung Pass to Lhasa three times each year, doing our best to "peacefully and compassionately keep the Chinese patrols at bay," the monks back in Gangtok would send forth 800,000 prayers a week for the continued prosperity of my race. His Holiness promised to compensate us for our trouble, one hundred rupees per yeti per six-day pilgrimage.

"I want to help you out," I said, massaging my scraggly beard, "but I fear that in the course of shielding you from the Mao-Maos we shall inadvertently reveal ourselves to the world."

"That is a very logical objection," said Chögi Gyatso, flashing his beautiful white teeth. He had the brightest smile in Asia. "And yet I have faith that these missions will not bring your species to light."

"Your faith, our skin," I said. "I am loath to put either at risk."

"Faith is not something a person can put at risk," His Holiness informed me, wiping the steam from his glasses with the sleeve of his robe. "Faith is the opposite of a James Bond martini — it may be stirred but not shaken."

To this day I'm not sure why I assented to become His Holiness's paladin. It certainly wasn't the money or the prayers. I think my decision had something to do with my inveterate affection for the perverse — that, and the prospect of discussing secret-agent movies with a young man whose aesthetics differed so radically from my own.

"I had no idea you were a James Bond fan," I said as Chögi Gyatso took leave of our lair. "Now that I think about it, the titles do have a certain Buddhist quality. *The World Is Not Enough. You Only Live Twice. Tomorrow Never Dies. Live and Let Die.* Is that why you like the series?"

"You are quite correct, Taktra Kunga," His Holiness replied. "I derive much food for meditation from the Bond titles. I also enjoy the babes."

Whether by the grace of the Bön gods, the vicissitudes of chance, or the devotion of his yeti protectors, Chögi Gyatso's pilgrimages proved far less perilous than anyone anticipated. Whenever a Chinese patrol threatened to apprehend

His Holiness, my six cousins and I would circle silently around the soldiers, then come at them from behind. The Mao-Maos never knew what hit them. A sudden whack between the shoulder blades — the blow we apes call *glog*, the lightning flash — and the startled soldier wobbled like a defective prayer wheel, then fell prone in the snow, gasping and groaning. By the time the patrol recovered its collective senses, Chögi Gyatso was far away, off to see the sham wizard on his stolen throne.

Our victories in these skirmishes traced largely to our invisibility. This attribute of *Candidopithecus tibetus* is highly adaptive and entirely natural. Like the skin of a chameleon, our fur transmogrifies until it precisely matches the shade of the immediate snowscape. So complete is this camouflage that we appear to the naïve observer as autonomous blazing orbs and disembodied flashing teeth. Set us down anywhere in the Himalayas, and we become eyes without faces, fangs without serpents, grins without cats.

Committed to conveying His Holiness to Lhasa with maximum efficiency, we eventually devised an elaborate relay system using modified climbing gear. Our method comprised a set of six grappling irons outfitted with especially long ropes. By hurling each hook high into the air and deliberately snagging it on the edge of a crag, Cousin Jowo, the strongest among us, succeeded in stringing a succession of high-altitude Tarzan vines between the gateway to the Lachung Pass and the outskirts of Lhasa. Once these immense pendulums had been hung, it became a simple matter for Cousin Drebung, Cousin Yang-dak, Cousin Garap, Cousin Nyima, and myself to swing through the canyons in great Newtonian oscillations, gripping our respective ropes with one hand while using the opposite arm to pass His Holiness from ape to ape like a sacramental basketball. Cousin Ngawang brought up the rear, carefully detaching the six hooks and gathering up the ropes, so the Mao-Maos would remain oblivious to our conspiracy.

Naturally my clan and I never dared venture into Lhasa proper, and so after depositing Chögi Gyatso at the city gates we always made a wide arc to the east, tromping through the hills until we reached the railroad bridge that spanned the Brahmaputra River like a sleek tiger leaping over a chasm. His Holiness's half-brother, Dorje Lingpa, lived by himself in a yurt on the opposite shore. We could get there only by sprinting anxiously along the suspended rails. The passenger train made two scheduled and predictable round-trips per day, but the freight lines and the military transports ran at odd hours, so my cousins and I were always thrilled to reach the far side of the gorge and leap to the safety of the berm.

Dorje Lingpa worked for the Chinese National Railroad, one of four token

Tibetans in their employ. Six days a week, he would leave his abode shortly after dawn, walk twenty paces to the siding, climb into his motorized section-gang car, and clatter along the maintenance line, routinely stopping to shovel snow, ice, stones, rubble, and litter off the parallel stretch of gleaming high-speed track running west into Lhasa. Whereas the typical Beijing technocrat had a private driveway and a Subaru, Dorje Lingpa had his own railroad siding and a personal locomotive.

A considerate if quixotic man, His Holiness's half-brother always remembered to leave the key under the welcome mat. My clan and I would let ourselves into the yurt, brew some buttered tea, purchase stacks of chips from our host's poker set, and pass the afternoon playing seven-card stud, which Cousin Ngawang had absorbed from a Philadelphia lawyer who'd run short of oxygen on the South Col. Chögi Gyatso and Dorje Lingpa normally returned within an hour of each other — the true Dalai Lama from counseling the Phonisattva, his brother from clearing the Lhasa line. Usually Chögi Gyatso remembered to bring a new set of postcards depicting the changing face of the capital. The Lhasa of my youth was a populous and noisy yet fundamentally congenial world. Thanks to the dubious boon of the railroad, the city now swarmed with franchise restaurants selling yak burgers, flat-screen TVs displaying prayer flags, taxi cabs papered with holograms of stupas, and movie theaters running Bollywood musicals dubbed into Mandarin.

Our fellowship always spent the night on the premises, Chögi Gyatso and his brother bunking in the yurt, we seven yeti sleeping on the ground in the backyard. Does that image bring a chill to your bones, O naked ones? You should understand that our fur is not simply a kind of cloak. Every pelt is a dwelling, like a turtle's shell. We live and die within the haven of ourselves.

Dorje Lingpa loved his job, but he hated his Mao-Mao bosses. Every time he hosted Chögi Gyatso and his yeti entourage, he outlined his latest unrealized scheme for chastising the Han Chinese. As you might imagine, these narratives were among the few phenomena that could dislodge Chögi Gyatso's impacted serenity.

"I've decided to target the Brahmaputra River bridge," Dorje Lingpa told us on the occasion of the bodhisattva's tenth pilgrimage. "At first I thought I'd need plastique, but now I believe dynamite will suffice. There's lots of it lying around from when they built the railroad."

"Dear brother, you are allowing anger to rule your life," said Chögi Gyatso, scowling. "I fear you have strayed far from the path of enlightenment."

"Every night as I fall asleep, I have visions of the collapsing bridge," said Dorje Lingpa, discreetly opening a window to admit fresh air. Though too polite to mention it, he obviously found our amalgamated yeti aroma rather too piquant. "I see a train carrying Chinese troops plunging headlong into the gorge."

"It's not your place to punish our oppressors," His Holiness replied. "Through their ignorance they are sowing the seeds of their own future suffering."

Dorje Lingpa turned to me and said, "During the occupation, tens of thousands of Tibetans were arrested and put in concentration camps, where mass starvation and horrendous torture were the norm. When China suffered a major crop failure in 1959, the army confiscated our entire harvest and shipped it east, causing a terrible famine throughout Tibet."

"I have forgiven the Chinese for what they did to us," Chögi Gyatso told his brother, "and I expect the same of you."

"I would rather be in a situation where you must forgive me for what I did to the Chinese," Dorje Lingpa replied.

"Beloved brother, you vex me greatly," said Chögi Gyatso. "All during Mönlam Chenmo I want you to meditate from dawn to dusk. You must purge these evil thoughts from your mind. Will you promise me that?"

Dorje Lingpa nodded listlessly.

"Anyone for seven-card stud?" asked Cousin Yangdak.

"Deal me in," said Cousin Nyima.

"At the start of the Cultural Revolution, the Red Guards swarmed into Tibet," Dorje Lingpa told me. "They forced monks and nuns to copulate in public, coerced them into urinating on sacred texts, threw excrement on holy men, scrawled graffiti on temple walls, and prosecuted local leaders in kangaroo courts for so-called crimes against the people."

"Nothing wild, high-low, table stakes," said Cousin Nyima, distributing the cards.

"The Red Guards also went on gang-rape sprees throughout the countryside," Dorje Lingpa continued. "They usually required the victim's husband, parents, children, and neighbors to watch."

"First king bets," said Cousin Nyima.

"Two rupees," said Cousin Jowo.

"Make it four," said Cousin Drebung.

Three days later Chögi Gyatso sent an emissary to my lair — Lopsang Chokden, who eerily resembled the massive Oddjob from *Goldfinger*. He consumed a mug of Gawa's pineal-gland tea, all the while surveying the scattered skulls, which he called "splendid meditation objects," then delivered his message. His

Holiness would begin my tutelage on the morning after the two-week New Year's celebration of Mönlam Chenmo, which I knew to be a kind of karmic rodeo combining sporting events, prayers, exorcisms, and public philosophical debates in a manner corresponding to no Western religious festival whatsoever. Chögi Gyatso suggested that I bring a toothbrush, as the first stage of my apprenticeship might easily last forty-eight hours. I should also pack my favorite snacks, provided they contained no Chinese dog meat.

As I prepared for my journey, it occurred to me that the mind I would be presenting to His Holiness was hardly a tabula rasa. My fur was white, but my slate was not blank. Owing to my ingestion of a dozen California pseudo-Buddhists over the years, I'd grasped much of what the dharma involved, or, rather, did not involve. I had particularly vivid memories of a Santa Monica mystic named Kimberly Weatherwax. Shortly before I stumbled upon this hapless climber, she had fallen from the Lhotse face, simultaneously losing her oxygen tank and stabbing herself in the back with an ice ax. Her blood oozed through her parka and leaked onto the snow like a Jackson Pollock painting in progress. She had perhaps five minutes to live, an interval she elected to spend telling me about her past lives in ancient Babylon and Akhenaton's Egypt.

"Are you by any chance the Abominable Snowman?" she asked, her brain so bereft of oxygen that she evidently felt no pain.

"My girlfriend thinks I'm insufferable, but I'm not abominable," I replied. "Call me Taktra Kunga, yeti of the *Shi-mi* Clan."

"A yeti? Wow! Really?"

"Really."

"That's so cool," she rasped, her voice decaying to a whisper. "An actual yeti," she mumbled. "This has been the most meaningful experience of my life."

"And now you are dying, which means I must eat your cerebral cortex."

"Heavy."

She wheezed and blacked out. From the subsequent *nang-duzul* I learned that, for tantric dilettantes like Kimberly Weatherwax, Eastern religion promised three big payoffs: solving the death problem through reincarnation, improving one's sex life through deferred gratification, and leaving the mundane realm of false values and failed plans for an axiomatically superior plane of relentless joy and unremitting bliss. Years later, trudging toward Gangtok for my first lesson with His Holiness, I decided that such spiritual avarice was the last thing my teacher would endorse. Obviously the dharma was not simply an exotic road to immortality and orgasms, not simply a gold-plated *Get Out of Samsara Free* card. Clearly there was more to infinity than that.

Dressed in his most sumptuous saffron-and-burgundy robe, Chögi Gyatso stood waiting at the gateway to his private residence, a stately, many-towered palace that the deracinated monks had constructed shortly after the Mao-Maos installed the Phonisattva in Lhasa. As His Holiness led me down the central corridor, I began expounding upon the dharma. "I understand that reincarnation is different from immortality, and I likewise understand that the tantra is not a means of erotic fulfillment. So we can dispense with those issues and get into something meatier right away."

A man of abiding forbearance, Chögi Gyatso listened thoughtfully, then looked me in the eye and unsheathed his epic smile. "What you understand is precisely nothing, Taktra Kunga," he said cheerily. "What you understand is zero, less than zero, zero and zero again, or, to use Mr. Bond's epithet, Double-O-Seven, seven being the number of rightful branches that a bodhisattva will pursue while on the radiance level of his emergence, along with thirty additional such disciplines."

We slipped into His Holiness's private bedchamber, where a smiling nun hovered over a tea cart that held a ceramic pot and a *You Only Live Twice* collector's mug, plus a plain white mug presumably intended for me.

"I don't doubt that I am ignorant, Your Holiness," I told Chögi Gyatso. "What are the seven rightful branches?"

"Correct mindfulness, correct discernment, correct effort, correct joy, correct pliancy, correct meditation, and correct equanimity, but don't worry about it, Your Hairiness. Perhaps you have the makings of a bodhisattva, perhaps not, but for now we simply want to increase your compassion quotient. Your education will begin with a simple oath honoring Sakyamuni, his teachings, and the community of monks and nuns he founded."

"Sounds good," I said, inhaling the sweet oily fragrance of the tea.

"Recite the following vow three times. 'I take refuge in the Buddha, I take refuge in the dharma, I take refuge in the samgha.'"

"'I take refuge in the Buddha, I take refuge in the dharma, I take refuge in the samgha.'"

Twice more I repeated the pledge, and then His Holiness gifted me with a kata — a white silk scarf — draping it around my neck. The nun filled his mug with buttered tea, handed him the pot, and slipped away. He proceeded to load my mug beyond its capacity, the greasy amber fluid spilling over the rim and cascading across the tray, flooding the spoons and napkins.

"Might I suggest you stop pouring?" I asked.

Chögi Gyatso maintained his posture, so that the tray soon held the entire steaming, roiling, eddying contents of the teapot. "Like this mug, your mind is much too full. It runs over with useless musings and self-generated afflictions.

You will not progress until you shed all such psychic baggage." He pointed toward a huge porcelain bathtub, elevated on four solid-brass lion paws to accommodate a brazier for heating the water. "And if you are to empty your mind, Taktra Kunga, you must first empty this tub, transferring all twenty gallons to the cistern we use for flushing the toilets. I was planning to take a nice warm bath tonight, but that ambition has now fallen away."

"Where's the bucket?" I asked.

"You will not use a bucket, but rather this implement." Chögi Gyatso reached toward the inundated tea tray and withdrew a dripping silver spoon.

"That's ridiculous," I said.

"Indeed," said Chögi Gyatso. "Completely ridiculous. The cistern is at the end of the corridor, last room on the left."

"What if I refuse?"

"Taktra Kunga, need I remind you that these lessons were your idea? In truth I have better things to do with my time."

"How long will the job take?"

"About seven hours. I suggest you get started right after lunch."

"Do you want me to chant a mantra or anything?"

"You are not yet ready for meditation, but if you insist on chanting something" — His Holiness offered a sly wink — "try the following: 'That's a Smith and Wesson, and you've had your six.'"

"*Dr. No*, right?"

The bodhisattva dipped his head and said, "To become enlightened is to encounter the perfect void, the final naught, the ultimate no. Alternatively, you may wish to ponder the following koan: when a chicken has sex with an egg, which comes first?"

His Holiness laughed uproariously. Under normal circumstances, I might have shared his merriment, but I was too depressed by the thought of the tedious chore that lay before me.

"Evidently it would be best if I did not ponder anything in particular," I said.

"That is the wisest remark you have made all morning."

With an aggrieved heart but a curious intellect, I did as my teacher suggested, consuming my lunch, a bowl of noodle soup, then getting to work. While His Holiness sat rigidly in his study, alternately reading Tsong Khapa's *The Great Exposition of the Stages of the Path* and Ian Fleming's *The Man with the Golden Gun*, I ferried twenty gallons of bathwater from tub to cistern, one ounce at a time. As Chögi Gyatso predicted, the task took all afternoon and well into the evening. Alas, instead of growing vacant my skull became jammed to the walls with toxic resentments. I wanted to put thorns in His Holiness's slippers. I wanted to break his drums and shatter his James Bond DVDs.

"The job is done," I told my teacher at nine o'clock.

"Go to your bedchamber, Taktra Kunga, first door on the right. An excellent dinner awaits you, mutton curry with rice. I would suggest that you turn in early. Come morning, the nun will bring you two oranges. After you have savored their sweet juices and exquisite pulp, you should begin your second labor."

"Which is?"

"Replenishing the tub."

"You must be joking."

"That is correct, Taktra Kunga. I am joking. It's a funny idea — isn't it? — filling the big tub you so recently emptied."

"Very funny, yes."

"However, please know that, come tomorrow afternoon, I may wish to bathe."

"I see," I said evenly.

"Do you?"

"Alas, yes. Might I use a bucket this time?"

"No. Sorry. The spoon. You should aim to finish by three o'clock, whereupon the nun will start warming my bath."

I figured I had no choice, and so the next day, right after consuming my two oranges, which were truly delicious, I spent another seven hours wielding my pathetic spoon, transferring the water ounce by dreary ounce. Midway through the ordeal, I realized that my anger at Chögi Gyatso had largely vanished. Here I was, receiving personal instruction in a magnificent religious tradition from the world's most famous holy man. It behooved me to be glad, not to mention grateful. At the very least I must become like a luscious female operative in thrall to Agent 007, surrendering to my teacher with a willing spirit.

"And now let me ask a question," said Chögi Gyatso after I'd finished drawing his bath. "What if I commanded you to empty the tub all over again?"

"I would gnash my teeth," I replied.

"And then?"

"I would growl like a snow lion."

"And then?"

"I would gasp like a dying climber."

"And then?"

"I would empty the tub."

"That is a very good answer, Taktra Kunga. Now go home to your woman and make love to her long into the night."

At the start of the third lunar month, the hulking emissary Lopsang Chokden reappeared in my lair and delivered a new message from His Holiness, but only after once again consuming a mug of pineal-gland tea and sorting contemplatively through our skulls. Chögi Gyatso, I now learned, wanted me to return to Sikkim forthwith and seek him out in the New Ganden Monastery. I should anticipate spending four full weeks with His Holiness — and pack my luggage accordingly.

"Twenty-eight days of celibacy," sneered Gawa. "Really, Taktra Kunga, your guru is asking a lot of you — me — us."

"Abstinence makes the heart grow fonder," I replied.

"Horse manure."

"Please try to understand. I'm not at peace with myself."

We passed the rest of the day alternately quarreling and copulating, and the following morning Gawa sent me off with her resentful blessing. I made my way south through the Lachung Pass, pausing to dine on Robin Balaban, an NYU film studies professor, then crossed the border into Sikkim. Digesting Professor Balaban's thoughts, I came to realize that he'd been troubled by a question that had often haunted me, namely, why has there never been a good movie about a yeti? *Man Beast* is atrocious. *Half Human* is risible. *The Snow Beast* is a snore. Only the Hammer Film called *The Abominable Snowman of the Himalayas* is remotely watchable, although everyone involved, including star Peter Cushing, writer Nigel Kneale, and director Val Guest, went on to make much better thrillers.

"During the first half of your sojourn here, you will experience intimations of the primordial Buddhist vehicle, the Hinayana, keyed to purging mental defilements and achieving personal enlightenment," said Chögi Gyatso as we connected, hand to paw, on the steps of the New Ganden Monastery. "During the second half of your stay, you will taste of the plenary vehicle, the Mahayana, which aims to cultivate a person's compassion for all living beings through the doctrine of *sunyata*, emptiness. In the fullness of time I shall introduce you to the quintessential vehicle, the diamond way, the indestructible Vajrayana."

"*Diamonds Are Forever*," I said.

"Probably my favorite Double-O-Seven. But let's not delude ourselves, Taktra Kunga. Whether *Homo sapiens* or *Candidopithecus tibetus*, a seeker may need to spend many years, perhaps many lifetimes, pursuing the Hinayana and the

Mahayana before he can claim them as his own, and yet without such grounding he is unlikely to attain the eternal wakefulness promised by the Vajrayana."

"Given the immensity of the challenge, let me suggest that we begin posthaste," I said. "There's no time like the present, right, Your Holiness?"

"No, Taktra Kunga, there is *only* a time like the present," my teacher corrected me. "The past is a tortoise-hair coat. The future is a clam-tooth necklace."

I passed the next seven days in the Tathagata Gallery, contemplating the canvases, four completely white, four completely black. His Holiness's expectations were clear. I must endeavor to fill the featureless spaces with whatever random notions crossed my mind — imperiled mountaineers, tasty yuppie brains, voluptuous yeti barmaids, crummy Abominable Snowman movies — then imagine these projections catching fire and turning to ash, so they would cease to colonize my skull. Despite my initial skepticism, before the long week was out I succeeded in slowing down the rackety engine of my consciousness, the endless *kachung, kachung, kachung* of my thoughts, the ceaseless *haroosh, haroosh, haroosh* of my anxieties, or so it seemed.

"I'm a much calmer person," I told my teacher. "Indeed, I think I've achieved near total equanimity. Does that mean I'm enlightened?"

"Give me a break, Taktra Kunga."

My second week in the New Ganden Monastery confronted me with a different sort of *sunyata*, the bare trees of the Dzogchen Arboretum, their branches bereft of leaves, fruit, and blossoms. This time around, my instructions were to focus my drifting thoughts on the here and now, the luminous, numinous, capacious present. Once again I profited from my meditations. Within twenty-four hours a sublime stillness swelled at the center of my being. I was truly *there*, inhabiting each given instant, second by millisecond by nanosecond.

"I did it," I told His Holiness. "I extinguished the past and annihilated the future. For now there is only today, and for today there is only now. I see nirvana just over the horizon."

"Don't crack walnuts in your ass, Taktra Kunga."

My troubles began during week three, which I spent in the Hall of Empty Mirrors, alternately meditating with closed eyes and contemplating with a rapt gaze the twenty-one ornately carved frames, each distinctly lacking a looking-glass. I was now swimming in the ocean of the Mahayana. It would not do for me simply to still my thoughts and occupy the present. I must also shed my ego, scrutinizing my non-self in the non-glass. Good-bye, Taktra Kunga. You are an idea at best, a phantasm of your atrophied awareness. No person, place, thing, or circumstance boasts a stable, inherent existence. Earthly attachments mean nothing. Nothing means everything. All is illusion. Flux rules. Welcome to the void.

"I don't like the Hall of Empty Mirrors," I told His Holiness at the end of week three, from which I'd lamentably emerged more myself, more Taktra Kungaesque, than ever. "In fact, I detest it."

"You're in good company," said Chögi Gyatso. "When the Buddha first spoke of the quest for *sunyata*, thousands of his followers had heart attacks."

"Then perhaps we should omit emptiness from the curriculum?"

"A person can no more achieve enlightenment without *sunyata* than he can make an omelet without eggs."

"I don't want to have a heart attack."

"To tell you the truth, I never believed that story," said Chögi Gyatso. "Although it's always disturbing to have the rug pulled out, the fall is rarely fatal."

"But if everything is an illusion, then isn't the idea that everything is an illusion *also* an illusion?" I asked petulantly.

"Let's not stoop to sophistry, Taktra Kunga. This is contemporary Gangtok, not ancient Athens."

Having acquitted myself so poorly in the Hall of Empty Mirrors, I anticipated even worse luck in the locus of my fourth and final week, the Chamber of Silence, reminiscent of the padded cells in which Western civilization was once pleased to warehouse its lunatics. My pessimism proved prescient. Much as I enjoyed meditating amid this cacophony of quietude, this mute chorus of one hand clapping, no foot stomping, thirty fish sneezing, forty oysters laughing, and a million dust motes singing, I was no closer to deposing my sovereign self than when I'd first entered the New Ganden Monastery.

"I'm discouraged, Your Holiness."

"That is actually good news," he replied.

"No, I mean I'm *really* discouraged."

"You must have patience. Better the dense glacier of genuine despair than the brittle ice of false hope."

O hairless ones, I give you my teacher, Chögi Gyatso, the Charlie Chan of the Himalayas, forever dispensing therapeutic aphorisms. And if His Holiness was Chan, did that make me his nonexistent offspring, his favorite illusory child, his Number One Sunyata? Raised by the Antelope Clan, I'd never known my biological parents, who'd died in the Great Khumbu Avalanche six months after my birth. In seeking out His Holiness, was I really just looking for my father? The more I pondered the question, the more mixed my emotions grew — a hodgepodge, a vortex, an incommodius vicus of recirculation, to paraphrase a Joycean scholar I'd once assimilated.

Chögi Gyatso bid me farewell. I left the New Ganden Monastery and headed for the Lachung Pass as fast as my limbs would carry me, sometimes running on all fours, eager for a sensual reunion with Gawa. Midway through my journey I again encountered the corpse of Robin Balaban, the NYU film professor. His gutted cranium taunted me with the void I'd failed to apprehend in the monastery. I averted my eyes and howled with despair.

My indifference to Professor Balaban's fate, I realized to my infinite chagrin, was equaled only by my apathy toward his bereaved loved ones. With crystal clarity I beheld my benighted mind. I would never awaken. Buddhahood was as far away as the summit of some soaring Jomolungma on another planet. And so I howled again, wracked by a self-pity born of my inability to pity any-one but myself, then continued on my way.

While Chögi Gyatso doubtless regarded me as a difficult pupil, perhaps the most exasperating he'd encountered in his present incarnation, the primary menace to his tranquility in those days remained his bitter, restless, firebrand brother. Although Dorje Lingpa had kept his promise to spend the whole of Mönlam Chenmo in profound meditation, his efforts had proved abortive, and he was now more determined than ever to strike a blow against the Han Chinese. Unenlightened being that I was, I framed Dorje Lingpa's failure in ego-tistical terms. If His Holiness's blood relatives had difficulty attaining *sunyata*, then I shouldn't feel so bad about the absence of emptiness in my own life.

The intractability of Dorje Lingpa's anger became apparent during our next secret pilgrimage to Lhasa. In a tone as devoid of compassion as a brick is devoid of milk, he confessed that he could not shake his mental image of "the Brahmaputra gorge swallowing a troop train like the great god Za feeding a string of sausages to the mouth embedded in his stomach." He speculated that this vision might be "a sign from heaven," and that Za himself was telling him "to render a divine judgment against the evil ones."

His Holiness began to weep, the subtlest display of anguish I'd ever seen, the tears trickling softly down his face like meltwater in spring, his sobs barely audible above the guttural breathing of the seven hairy apes in the yurt. Dorje Lingpa remained adamant. The People's Liberation Army must pay for its crimes. Changing the subject, or so it seemed at the time, he said that shortly after dawn he would like to take His Holiness on "a brief excursion in my track-inspection vehicle," then turned to his yeti guests and declared that there would be room for one of us. I told him I would like to join the party.

Thus it happened that, shortly after sunrise, Chögi Gyatso, Dorje Lingpa, and I climbed into the open-air section-gang car and tooled eastward along the maintenance line at a brisk eighty kilometers per hour, enduring a wind chill from some frigid equivalent of hell. Dorje Lingpa wore his bomber jacket, His Holiness sat hunched beneath a yak-hide blanket, and I had wrapped myself head-to-toe in a tarp — not because I minded the cold, but because the surrounding gang car defied my usual white-on-white camouflage. Suddenly the harsh metallic bawl of a diesel horn filled the air, and then the train appeared, zooming toward us along the adjacent high-speed rails in a great sucking rush that whipped our clothing every which way like prayer flags in a gale. Each passenger coach was crammed with Han Chinese, some perhaps bound for a holiday in Lhasa but the majority surely intending to settle permanently, players in the government's scheme to marginalize the native population. Five hundred faces flew past, lined up along the windows like an abacus assembled from severed heads. Each wore an expression of nauseated misery — a syndrome probably born of the thin air, though I liked to imagine they were also suffering spasms of regret over their role in the rout of Tibet.

As the morning progressed, Dorje Lingpa's agenda become clear. He meant to give us a guided tour of recent outrages by the Chinese. Periodically he stopped the gang car and passed us his binoculars, so that we could behold yet another exhibit in the Museum of Modern Expediency: the bombed lamaseries, razed temples, trampled shrines, maimed statues — desecrations that the Beijing regime imagined would help stamp out the indigenous cancer of contemplation and replace it with the new state religion, that cruel fusion of normless monopoly capitalism and murderous totalitarianism. Once again His Holiness's eyes grew damp, and now he wept prolifically, great dollops of salt water rolling down his cheeks and freezing on his chest, so that he soon wore a necklace of tears.

Knowing of his brother's fascination with James Bond's Aston Martin, Dorje Lingpa asked if he would like to take the throttle during our return trip. For a full minute the grieving monk said nothing, then offered a nod of disengaged corroboration. Dorje Lingpa stopped the inspection vehicle, then threw the motor into reverse. We pivoted in our seats. His Holiness gripped the controls, and we were off, retracing our path westward through the scattered shards of the Tibetan soul. Drawing within view of the gorge, we again heard the blast of a diesel horn, and seconds later we were overtaken by another train from Beijing, bearing still more Han into the sacred city.

We reached the yurt shortly after two o'clock. My cousins had prepared a hot luncheon of steamed dumplings, but I was not hungry, and neither was His

Holiness. The meal passed languidly and without conversation. At last Chögi Gyatso broke the silence, his resonant and reassuring voice warming the icy air.

"Beloved brother," he told Dorje Lingpa, "that was a good thing you did, taking us across the plateau. I understand you much better now."

"I am grateful for your praise," said the trainman. "Will you join my war against the People's Liberation Army?"

"What do you think?" asked Chögi Gyatso.

"I think I should not count on your participation."

"That is correct."

"I'm reminded of an old joke," said Cousin Ngawang. "A man went to a priest in the north of Ireland and confessed that he'd blown up six miles of British railroad track. And the priest said, 'For your penance, you must go and do the stations.'"

"Very amusing," said Cousin Jowo.

"Decidedly droll," said Cousin Drebung.

But no one laughed, most especially myself, most conspicuously Chögi Gyatso, and most predictably Dorje Lingpa.

My third tutorial with His Holiness took me to the fabled Bebhaha Temple of Cosmic Desire, the very loins, as it were, of the Gangtok Buddhist Complex, famous throughout Asia for its six thousand masterpieces of erotic art. Despite his celibacy, or perhaps because of it, Chögi Gyatso held a generally approving attitude toward the sex act, and he believed that, my embarrassing performance in the monastery notwithstanding, the meditation practices pursued in the Bebhaha Temple might occasion my awakening. Moreover, this time around I would be following a regimen drawn from His Holiness's specialty — the tantric path, the diamond discipline, the venerable Vajrayana.

The mystic principle behind the temple was straightforward enough. Tsangyang Gyatso, the sixth Dalai Lama, had put it well: "If one's thoughts toward the dharma were of the same intensity as those toward physical love, one would become a Buddha in this very body, in this very life." And so it was that I spent a week in Gangtok's spiritual red-light district, contemplating hundreds of paintings and sculptures depicting sexual ensembles — couples, trios, quartets, quintets, human, yeti, divine, biologically mixed, taxonomically diverse, ontologically scrambled — engaged in every sort of carnal congress, homoerotic, heteroerotic, autoerotic, even surrealistic: images of copulating trees and randy pocket watches, playfully signed "Salvador Dali Lama." I seethed with lust. I stroked myself to torrential spasms. At one point His

Holiness suggested that I take up with the kind of sexual consort known as a karma-mudra, an "action seal," so named because the practice sealed or solidified the seeker's understanding that all phenomena are a union of ecstasy and emptiness. I declined this provocative invitation, feeling that His Holiness's syllabus had already put enough strain on my relationship with Gawa.

Even as I wrapped my hand around my cock, I sought to keep my eye on the ball. The idea was to gather up all this libidinous energy, this tsunami of seed, and, through diligent meditation and focused chanting, channel it toward detachment, *sunyata*, and boundless pity for the suffering of all sentients. From onanism to *Om mani padme hum*, oh, yes, that was the grand truth of the tantra, an ingenious strategy of masturbate-and-switch, and I did my best, O depilated ones, you must believe me, I truly played to win.

"I tried," I told Chögi Gyatso as I stumbled out of the Bebhaha Temple, all passions spent. "I tried, and I failed. Immerse me in the tantra, and my thoughts turn to wanking, not awakening. Let's face it, Your Holiness. I was not made for the Vajrayana, nor the Mahayana either, nor even the Hinayana."

"You're probably right. But I must also say this, Taktra Kunga. Your attitude sucks."

"So do half your deities."

"Might we try one final tantric lesson? At the start of the tenth lunar month, come to the Antarabhava Charnel Ground on the slopes of Mount Jelep La, eight kilometers to the northeast. You will know it by the vultures wheeling overhead."

I shrugged and said, "I suppose I have nothing to lose."

"No, Taktra Kunga, you have *everything* to lose," His Holiness reproached me. "That is the whole point. Lose your illusions, lose your goals, lose your ego, lose the world, and only *then* will you come to know the wonder of it all."

O smooth ones, you might think that an ape whose lair was appointed with skulls would revel in the ambience of the Antarabhava Charnel Ground, but in fact I found it a completely ghastly place, a seething soup of shucked bones, strewn teeth, rotting flesh, disembodied hair, fluttering shrouds, buzzing flies, busy worms, industrious crows, and enraptured vultures. By Chögi Gyatso's account, two geographical circumstances accounted for this macabre ecology. Because wood was scarce in Tibet, cremation had never become the norm, and—thanks to the rocky and often frozen soil—interment was equally uncommon. Instead Tibetans had resorted to the colorful custom of sky burial, dismembering the corpse and leaving the components in a high open place to be consumed by jackals and carrion birds.

"Death, decay, and transmigration: the three fundamental facts of existence," said His Holiness.

"I want to go home," I said, my eyes watering and my brain reeling from the foulness of it all. The stench was itself a kind of raptor, pecking at my sinuses, nibbling at the lining of my throat.

"The sorrowful cycle of *samsara*," Chögi Gyatso persisted. "The wretched wheel of life, turning and turning in the widening gyre, but there is no rough beast, Taktra Kunga, no Bethlehem, only more turning, more suffering, more turning, more suffering. Sean Connery is reborn as George Lazenby, who is reborn as Roger Moore, who is reborn as Timothy Dalton, who is reborn as Pierce Brosnan, who is reborn as Daniel Craig, who is reborn as Brian Flaherty. It can be much worse, of course. A person might spend his life deliberately harming other sentient beings. Owing to this bad karma, he will come back as an invertebrate, a miserable crawling thing, or else a hungry ghost, or maybe even a hell being. Agent Double-O-Seven, if he truly existed, would probably be a dung beetle now. So it goes, Taktra Kunga. You can't win, you can't break even — but you *can* get out of the game."

"*You* didn't get out of the game," I noted, staring at my feet. "You keep opting for reincarnation."

"That doesn't mean I like it."

"If your brother sends a troop train into the gorge, how may lifetimes will he need to discharge his karmic debt? A hundred? A thousand? A million?"

"I don't want to talk about my brother," said Chögi Gyatso, placing his open palm beneath my shaggy simian chin and directing my gaze toward the open-air ossuary. "Behold."

Bearing a narrow palanquin on which lay a robe-wrapped corpse, a solemn procession shuffled into view: monks, mourners, tub-haulers, and a team of specialists that His Holiness identified as rogyapas, body cutters. Expectant vultures arrived from all points of the compass. After finding a relatively uncluttered space, the palanquin-bearers set down their burden, whereupon the rogyapas secured the corpse with ropes and pegs, "lest the birds claim it too soon," His Holiness explained. Availing themselves of the tub, the monks next washed the body in a solution scented with saffron and camphor, "thereby making the flesh more pleasing to the nostrils of its feathered beneficiaries."

"Your religion is good with details," I noted.

"In giving his body to scavengers, the deceased is performing an act of great charity," Chögi Gyatso explained. "Even as we speak, that person's hovering consciousness negotiates the bardo, the gap between his present life and his next incarnation. He is presently confronting a multitude of confusing sights, sounds, smells, textures, and tastes, as well as hordes of tantric deities, some peaceful, others wrathful, each spawned by his mind. It's all in the *Bardo Thodol*."

"We should try selling it to the movies."

"Taktra Kunga, shut up."

After drawing out their sharp gleaming knives, the body cutters went to work, opening up the corpse's chest, removing the internal organs, and slicing the flesh from the skeleton. The rogyapas mashed up the bones with stone hammers, then mixed the particles with barley flour, a proven vulture delicacy.

"What are we doing here?" I moaned, seizing His Holiness by the shoulders.

"We are here to relieve the suffering of other sentient beings. Haven't you been paying attention?"

"No, I mean what are we doing *here*? Why are we in this demented alfresco cemetery?"

"We are here to meditate on *tathata* — suchness — the true nature of reality."

Only after a large quantity of flesh and bone had been prepared were the vultures allowed into the ceremony, a precaution that kept them from fighting among themselves. The rogyapas carried the offerings to a large slab of rock decorated with a geometric representation of the universe, then systematically pitched the portions, one by one, toward the center of the circle. Meanwhile, one particularly athletic rogyapa swung a large rope across the inscribed outcropping, discouraging the raptors from entering the mandala before the proper time.

"Take me away!" I wailed. "I can't stand this place! Class dismissed!"

"Is that truly your wish?" asked His Holiness.

"Yes! It's over! *Allons-y*! I'm the worst student you ever had!"

"That would appear to be the case."

The rope-swinger stilled his cord and stepped aside. Fluttering, shrieking, squawking, and — for all I knew — chanting praises to their patrons, the appreciative vultures descended.

"I don't want to be enlightened!" I cried. "I want Gawa! I want my cousins! I want onion bagels and pineal-gland tea and Prokofiev and Fred Astaire and the Marx Brothers! I want all my stupid, worthless, impermanent toys!"

The bodhisattva shrugged and, taking my paw in his hand, began leading me toward Gangtok. "Taktra Kunga, I am disappointed in you."

"I don't doubt it."

"Let me offer a word of counsel," said His Holiness. "When lying on your deathbed, strive mightily to release these negative energies of yours. You won't be reborn a buddha, but you won't come back an insect either. Speaking personally, I hope you remain a giant ape. You do that very well."

The Earth turned, the wheel of life revolved, and, exactly one year after hearing Dorje Lingpa declare his intention to wreck a Mao-Mao troop train, my cousins and I once again found ourselves huddled drowsily behind his yurt on the eve of Mönlam Chenmo. We did not expect to get much sleep. Chögi Gyatso and his half-brother had stayed up late arguing over the necessity of destroying the Brahmaputra bridge. They had found no points of accord. Bad karma suffused the gorge like the stench of a charnel ground.

I awoke shortly after sunrise, tired, bleary, and miserable, then stumbled into the yurt. My cousins occupied the dining table, playing seven-card stud. His Holiness and Dorje Lingpa sat in the breakfast nook, eating oranges and drinking buttered tea.

"A flush," said Cousin Jowo, displaying five hearts.

"Beats my straight," said Cousin Nyima, disclosing his hand.

The plaintive moan of a diesel horn fissured the frosty air.

"A troop transport," noted Dorje Lingpa. "Over the years I've come to know each train by its call, like a hunter identifying different species of geese by their honks."

A second mournful wail arose, rattling the circular roof.

"The train is exactly nine miles away," said Dorje Lingpa. "It will be here in six and a half minutes."

"Dear brother, your mind is crammed with useless knowledge," said Chögi Gyatso.

"That horn is a death knell," Dorje Lingpa continued. "Listen carefully, brother. The train is pealing its own doom."

"What are you talking about?" I asked.

A long, malevolent, Za-like grin bisected Dorje Lingpa's melon face. "I'm talking about a bridge bristling with sticks of dynamite. I'm talking about a detonator attached to the high-speed track. I'm talking about headlines in tomorrow's *Beijing Times* and the next day's *Washington Post*." He brushed his brother's shaved head. "And there's absolutely nothing you can do about it."

Nothing. His Holiness's favorite concept. Long live Double-O-Seven. You can imagine my surprise, therefore, when Chögi Gyatso leapt up, fled the yurt, and dashed toward the railroad siding.

"Bad idea!" I yelled, giving chase.

"I think not," His Holiness replied.

I drew abreast of Chögi Gyatso, surpassed him, depositing my furry bulk in his path. He circumnavigated me and lurched toward the rusting turnout connecting the maintenance track to the Lhasa line.

"*Om mani padme hum*," he chanted, seizing the steel lever and throwing the switch.

"What are you doing?" I demanded.

Actually it was quite obvious what he was doing. He was contriving to reconfigure the rails, so that he might drive the gang car west along the high-speed line, hit the bridge, and trip the detonator.

"Pacifism is not passivity," he noted, then headed for the gang car. "The explosion will warn the engineer to stop the train."

"No! That's crazy! Don't!"

Now Dorje Lingpa appeared on the scene, grabbing His Holiness around the waist with the evident intention of hauling him to the ground.

The diesel horn bellowed, louder than ever.

I was there, O shiny ones. I saw the whole amazing incident. For the first time in seven hundred years, a Dalai Lama decked somebody with a round-house right — in this case, his own bewildered brother. James Bond swinging his fists or a yeti delivering a *glog* punch could not have felled Dorje Lingpa more skillfully.

As the trainman lay in the snow, stunned and supine, my clan arrived, grappling hooks in hand, climbing ropes slung over their shoulders like huge epaulets. Cousin Ngawang placed a large hairy foot on Dorje Lingpa's chest.

"Your brother is a brave man," the ape declared.

The diesel horn screamed across the valley.

His Holiness climbed into the inspection vehicle and assumed the controls. "After I've passed over the turnout, kindly throw the switch to its former position," he instructed me. "We don't want to save the train from my brother's vengeance only to derail it through negligence."

"You don't understand!" I cried. "All is illusion! That train isn't real! The soldiers aren't real! There is no suchness except what exists in your mind!"

"Don't be silly," His Holiness said, putting the motor in gear. "I love you, Taktra Kunga," he added, and he was off.

The gang car rattled out of the yard, frogged onto the Lhasa line, and raced away at full throttle. I planted myself squarely on the maintenance track, the better to see Chögi Gyatso depart his present incarnation. An instant later the car reached the bridge and continued across, a caterpillar crawling along a hissing firecracker. The wheel flanges hit the detonator, and there came forth a deafening explosion that catapulted the car and its passenger a hundred meters into the air. A plume of fire and ash billowed upward from the shattered span.

Flames licked the sheer blue sky. The vehicle succumbed to gravity. My former teacher hung briefly in the swirling smoke, as if suspended on the breath of a thousand thwarted demons, a miracle truly befitting the bardo of a bodhisattva, and then he fell.

I am pleased to report that His Holiness's scenario played out largely as he'd imagined, with the troop train's engineer slamming on the pneumatic brakes the instant the ka-boom of the dynamite reached his ears. The wheels locked, flanges squealing against the icy rails, leaving five hundred Mao-Mao soldiers at the mercy of a capricious friction. The gargantuan locomotive skated crazily, dragging its fourteen coaches toward the abyss.

By this time my cousins, no strangers to the laws of physics, had arrayed themselves along both sides of the tracks, gear in hand, waiting for the train. I threw the switch as His Holiness had requested, then climbed a snowy knoll, from which vantage I beheld my worthy clan improvise a grand act of salvation.

"Hurry!" I shouted superfluously.

Moving in perfect synchronicity, the apes hurled the six grapping irons toward the rolling coaches, smashing the windows and securing the hooks solidly within the frames.

"Such lovely beasts!" I cried.

Having successfully harpooned the passing train, my cousins allowed the ropes to pay out briefly, then tightened their grips. Still skidding, the locomotive towed the six yeti along the roadbed like an outboard motorboat pulling multiple water-skiers, spumes of ice and snow spewing upward from their padded heels. In a matter of seconds the momentum shifted in compassion's favor. The train slowed — and slowed — and slowed. I shouted for joy. The Bön gods smiled.

"Tiao!" cried my clan in a single voice. "Tiao! Jump! Tiao! Jump! Tiao! Tiao! Tiao!"

The soldiers rushed toward the coach doors in a tumult of brown uniforms, gleaming rifles, and wide-eyed faces. They jumped, spilling pell-mell from the decelerating train like Norway rats abandoning a sinking steamer. My cousins, satisfied, released the ropes and headed for the hills, determined that this would not be the day of their unmasking. Sprawled in the roadbed, the perplexed but grateful Mao-Maos gasped and sputtered. The engineer abandoned his post none too soon, leaping from the cab barely thirty seconds before the coasting locomotive and its vacant coaches glided majestically across the burning bridge, reached the rift, and hurtled off the tracks. Seconds later the train hit the river, the thunderous crash echoing up and down the gorge.

Before the eventful morning ended, my clan and I, along with Dorje Lingpa, managed to sneak within view of the Brahmaputra and observe the twisted consequences of His Holiness's courage. Having shattered the river's normal sheet of ice, the hot locomotive and its strewn coaches clogged the current like vast carrots floating in an immense stew. I scanned the steaming wreckage. The corpse of Chögi Gyatso was easy to spot. His saffron-and-burgundy robe rose vividly against the bright white floe that was his bier.

"Forgive me, brother," said Dorje Lingpa.

"Goodbye, Your Holiness," said Cousin Ngawang.

"Farewell, beloved monk," said Cousin Jowo.

"I hope you've gone to heaven," said Cousin Drebung.

"Do lamas believe in heaven?" asked Cousin Yangdak.

"Rebirth," Cousin Garap explained.

"Then I hope you've been reborn," said Cousin Drebung.

"Though they don't come any better than you," noted Cousin Nyima.

I attempted to speak, but my tongue had gone numb, my throat was clamped shut, and my lungs were filled with stones.

The clan and I bore Chögi Gyatso's dead body far down the frozen river and secured it behind a boulder, lest the People's Liberation Army come upon it while investigating the loss of their train. As I knelt before the dead bodhisattva and began to partake of his brain, I decided that this *nang-duzul* would mark a new phase in my life. No, I did not forswear meat-knowledge, to which I was addicted and always would be. But from now on, I promised myself, I would cease to kill my prey. I would instead become like the charnel-ground raptors, leaving my nourishment to the whims of chance, consuming only such human flesh as my karma merited.

Yes, O glossy ones, eventually I realized that I should not simply demur from devouring a stranded climber — I should also summon a rescue party. So far I haven't endeavored to save anyone's life, even though such altruism would hardly compromise my species' security, for the Sherpas already know we exist, and they would never dream of betraying us to either a Mao-Mao patrol or an Everest entrepreneur. But old habits die hard. Give me a little time.

I wish I could say that some political good came of His Holiness's deliverance of the Mao-Mao soldiers. In fact the ugly status quo persists, with Tibetan culture still withering under the iron boot of the People's Liberation Army, may they rot in hell. As for Dorje Lingpa, he was never officially fired from his job with the National Railroad. Instead he was arrested, tortured with a cattle prod, imprisoned for five years, tortured again, and hung. The moral of his sorry life is simple. If you want to be a successful insurgent, don't practice on Chinese Communists.

When I told the Panchen Lama where to find Chögi Gyatso's body, he did not at first believe me, but then I began laying out evidence — a grappling iron, the *Beijing Times* headline, His Holiness's white silk scarf — and the monks dispatched a recovery team to the Brahmaputra River gorge. No sky burial, of course, for Chögi Gyatso. No vultures for His Holiness. The monks cremated him on the grounds of the New Ganden Monastery, then set about searching for his reincarnation. At last report they'd located a promising three-year-old in the village of Gyanzge.

So what is it like to be enlightened? What rarefied phenomena does a bodhisattva perceive? I regret to say that the gift was largely wasted on me. To be sure, shortly after eating Chögi Gyatso's cerebrum I found myself praying compulsively, chanting incessantly, and meditating obsessively, much to Gawa's consternation. For a few incandescent days I saw the world as he had, lambent and fair and full of woe, abrim with beings who, without exception, every one, each and all, deserved my unqualified kindness.

But my wisdom did not endure. It faded like the westering sun, and what I recall of ecstatic emptiness cannot be articulated in any language, human or simian.

I suppose this loss was to be expected. As these pages attest, I was always a lousy candidate for wakefulness. In my heart I'm a child of that other Enlightenment, the one personified by such cheeky freethinkers as Diderot, Montesquieu, Voltaire, Thomas Paine, and Benjamin Franklin. At the end of the day I'm a *carpe diem* creature, a rationalist, really, the sort of primate who can't help wondering whether a compassion born of emptiness might not be an empty compassion indeed. I love my life. I treasure my attachments. That is not about to change. True, this ape may eventually evolve, in the Darwinian sense, but for now I shall leave transcendence to the professionals.

That said, I am endlessly honored to have been his student. My gestures of remembrance are small but constant. Every night, after making love to Gawa, I stare into the blackness of our lair and give voice to the lovely words he taught me, saying, "I take refuge in the Buddha, I take refuge in the dharma, I take refuge in the samgha."

And then, relaxing, drifting, I lay my head on the yak-hair pillow. Gawa snores beside me. The dying embers crackle. I close my eyes, quiet my mind, and dream of my friend, His Holiness, the fifteenth Dalai Lama.

The Cat's Pajamas

The eighteenth-century Enlightenment was still in our faces, fetishizing the rational intellect and ramming technocracy down our throats, so I said to Vickie, "Screw it. This isn't for us. Let's hop in the car and drive to Romanticism, or maybe even to preindustrial paganism, or possibly all the way to hunter-gatherer utopianism." But we only got as far as Pennsylvania.

I knew that the idea of spending all summer on the road would appeal to Vickie. Most of her affections, including her unbridled wanderlust, are familiar to me. Not only had we lived together for six years, we also worked at the same New Jersey high school — Vickie teaching American history, me offering a souped-up eleventh-grade humanities course — with the result that not only our screaming matches but also our flashes of rapport drew upon a fund of shared experiences. And so it was that the first day of summer vacation found us rattling down Route 80 in our decrepit VW bus, listening to Crash Test Dummies CDs and pretending that our impulsive westward flight somehow partook of political subversion, though we sensed it was really just an extended camping trip.

Despite being an épater le bourgeois sort of woman, Vickie had spent the previous two years promoting the idea of holy matrimony, an institution that has consistently failed to enchant me. Nevertheless, when we reached the Delaware Water Gap, I turned to her and said, "Here's a challenge for us. Let's see if we can't become man and wife by this time tomorrow afternoon." It's important, I feel, to suffuse a relationship with a certain level of unpredictability, if not outright caprice. "Vows, rings, music, all of it."

"You're crazy," she said, brightening. She's got a killer smile, sharp at the edges, luminous at the center. "It takes a week just to get the blood-test results."

"I was reading in *Newsweek* that there's a portable analyzer on the market. If we can find a technologically advanced justice of the peace, we'll meet the deadline with time to spare."

"Deadline?" She tightened her grip on the steering wheel. "Jeez, Blake, this isn't a *game*. We're talking about a *marriage*."

"It's a game and a gamble — I know from experience. But with you, sweetheart, I'm ready to bet the farm."

She laughed and said, "I love you."

We spent the night in a motel outside a pastoral Pennsylvania borough called Greenbriar, got up at ten, made distracted love, and began scanning the yellow pages for a properly outfitted magistrate. By noon we had our man, District Justice George Stratus, proud owner of a brand new Sorrel-130 blood analyzer. It so happened that Judge Stratus was something of a specialist in instant marriage. For a hundred dollars flat, he informed me over the phone, we could have "the nanosecond nuptial package," including blood test, license, certificate, and a bottle of Taylor's champagne. I told him it sounded like a bargain.

To get there, we had to drive down a sinuous band of dirt and gravel called Spring Valley Road, past the asparagus fields, apple orchards, and cow pastures of Pollifex Farm. We arrived in a billowing nimbus of dust. Judge Stratus turned out to be a fat and affable paragon of efficiency. He immediately set about pricking our fingers and feeding the blood to his Sorrel-130, which took only sixty seconds to endorse our DNA even as it acquitted us of venereal misadventures. He faxed the results to the county courthouse, signed the marriage certificate, and poured us each a glass of champagne. By three o'clock, Vickie and I were legally entitled to partake of connubial bliss.

I think Judge Stratus noticed my pained expression when I handed over the hundred dollars, because he suggested that if we were short on cash, we should stop by the farm and talk to André Pollifex. "He's always looking for asparagus pickers this time of year." In point of fact, my divorce from Irene had cost me plenty, making a shambles of both my bank account and my credit record, and Vickie's fondness for upper-middle-class counterculture artifacts — solar-powered trash compacters and so on — had depleted her resources as well. We had funds enough for the moment, though, so I told Stratus we probably wouldn't be joining the migrant-worker pool before August.

"Well, sweetheart, we've done it," I said as we climbed back into the bus. "Mr. and Mrs. Blake Meeshaw."

"The price was certainly right," said Vickie, "even though the husband involved is a fixer-upper."

"You've got quite a few loose shingles yourself," I said.

"I'll be hammering and plastering all summer."

Although we had no plans to stop at Pollifex Farm, when we got there an enormous flock of sheep was crossing the road. Vickie hit the brakes just in time to avoid making mutton of a stray ewe, and we resigned ourselves to watching the woolly parade, which promised to be as dull as a passing freight train. Eventually a swarthy man appeared gripping a silver-tipped shepherd's crook. He advanced at a pronounced stoop, like a denizen of Dante's Purgatory balancing a millstone on his neck.

A full minute elapsed before Vickie and I realized that the sheep were moving in a loop, like wooden horses on a carousel. With an indignation bordering on hysteria, I leaped from the van and strode toward the obnoxious herdsman. What possible explanation could he offer for erecting this perpetual barricade?

Nearing the flock, I realized that the scene's strangest aspect was neither the grotesque shepherd nor the tautological roadblock, but rather the sheep themselves. Every third or fourth animal was a mutant, its head distinctly humanoid, though the facial features seemed melted together, as if they'd been cast in wax and abandoned to the summer sun. The sooner we were out of here, I decided, the better.

"What the hell do you think you're doing?" I shouted. "Get these animals off the road!"

The shepherd hobbled up to me and pulled a tranquilizer pistol from his belt with a manifest intention to render me unconscious.

"Welcome to Pollifex Farm," he said.

The gun went off, the dart found my chest, and the world turned black.

Regaining consciousness, I discovered that someone — the violent shepherd? André Pollifex? — had relocated my assaulted self to a small bright room perhaps twelve feet square. Dust motes rode the sunlit air. Swatches of yellow wallpaper buckled outward from the sheetrock like spritsails puffed with wind. I lay on a mildewed mattress, elevated by a box spring framed in steel. A turban of bandages encircled my head. Beside me stood a second bed, as uninviting as my own, its bare mattress littered with artifacts that I soon recognized as Vickie's — comb, hand mirror, travel alarm, ankh earrings, well-thumbed paperback of *Zen and the Art of Motorcycle Maintenance*.

It took me at least five minutes, perhaps as many as ten, before I realized that my brain had been removed from my cranium and that the pink, throbbing, convoluted mass of tissue on the nearby library cart was in fact my own thinking apparatus. Disturbing and unorthodox as this arrangement was, I could not deny its actuality. Every time I tapped my skull, a hollow sound came forth, as if I were knocking on an empty casserole dish. Fortunately, the physicians responsible for my condition had worked hard to guarantee that it would entail no functional deficits. Not only was my brain protected by a large Plexiglas jar filled with a clear, acrid fluid, it also retained its normal connection to my heart and spinal cord. A ropy mass of neurons, interlaced with augmentations of my jugular vein and my two carotid arteries, extended from beneath my orphaned medulla and stretched across four feet of empty space before disappearing into my reopened fontanel, the whole configuration shielded from microbial contamination by a flexible plastic tube. I was thankful for my surgeons' conscientiousness, but also — I don't mind telling you — extremely frightened and upset.

My brain's extramural location naturally complicated the procedure, but in a matter of minutes I managed to transport both myself and the library cart into the next room, an unappointed parlor bedecked in cobwebs, and from there to an enclosed porch, all the while calling Vickie's name. She didn't answer. I opened the door and shuffled into the putrid air of Pollifex Farm. Everywhere I turned, disorder prospered. The cottage in which I'd awoken seemed ready to collapse under its own weight. The adjacent windmill canted more radically than Pisa's Leaning Tower. Scabs of leprous white paint mottled the sides of the main farmhouse. No building was without its unhinged door, its shattered window, its sunken roof, its disintegrating wall — a hundred instances of entropy mirroring the biological derangement that lay within.

I did not linger in the stables, home to six human-headed horses. Until this moment, I'd thought the centaurian form intrinsically beautiful, but with their bony backs and twisted faces these monsters soon deprived me of that hypothesis. Nor did I remain long in the chicken coop, habitat of four gigantic human-headed hens, each the size of a German shepherd. Nor did the pig-shed detain me, for seven human-headed hogs is not a spectacle that improves upon contemplation. Instead I hurried toward an immense barn, lured by a spirited performance of Tchaikovsky's Piano Concerto No. 1 wafting through a crooked doorway right out of *The Cabinet of Dr. Caligari*.

Cautiously I entered. Spacious and high-roofed, the barn was a kind of agrarian cathedral, the Chartres of animal husbandry. In the far corner, hunched over a baby grand piano, sat a humanoid bull: blunt nose, gaping nostrils, a long tapering horn projecting from either side of his head. Whereas his hind legs were of the bovine variety, his forelegs ended in a pair of human hands that skated gracefully along the keyboard. He shared his bench with my wife, and even at this distance I could see that the bull-man's virtuosity had brought her to the brink of rapture.

Cerebrum in tow, I made my way across the barn. With each step, my apprehension deepened, my confusion increased, and my anger toward Vickie intensified. Apprehension, confusion, anger: while I was not yet accustomed to experiencing such sensations in a location other than my head, the phenomenon now seemed less peculiar than when I'd first returned to sentience.

"I know what you're thinking," said Vickie, acknowledging my presence. "Why am I sitting here when I should be helping you recover from the operation? Please believe me: Karl said the anesthesia wouldn't wear off for another four hours."

She proceeded to explain that Karl was the shepherd who'd tranquilized me on the road, subsequently convincing her to follow him onto the farm rather than suffer the identical fate. But Karl's name was the least of what Vickie had learned during the past forty-eight hours. Our present difficulties, she elaborated, traced to the VD screening we'd received on Wednesday. In exchange for a substantial payment, Judge Stratus had promised to alert his patrons at Pollifex Farm the instant he happened upon a blood sample bearing the deoxyribonucleic acid component known as QZ-11-4. Once in possession of this gene — or, more specifically, once in possession of a human brain whose *in utero* maturation had been influenced by this gene — Dr. Pollifex's biological investigations could go forward.

"Oh, Blake, they're doing absolutely *wonderful* work here." Vickie rose from the bench, drifted toward me, and, taking care not to become entangled in my spinal cord, gave me a mildly concupiscent hug. "An external brain to go with your external genitalia — I think it's very sexy."

"Stop talking nonsense, Vickie!" I said. "I've been *mutilated*!"

She stroked my bandaged forehead and said, "Once you hear the whole story, you'll realize that your bilateral hemispherectomy serves a greater good."

"Call me Maxwell," said the bull-man, lifting his fingers from the keyboard. "Maxwell Taurus." His voice reminded me of Charles Laughton's. "I must congratulate you on your choice of marriage partner, Blake. Vickie has a refreshingly open mind."

"And I have a depressingly vacant skull," I replied. "Take me to this lunatic Pollifex so I can get my brain put back where it belongs."

"The doctor would never agree to that." Maxwell fixed me with his stare, his eyes all wet and brown like newly created caramel apples. "He requires round-the-clock access to your anterior cortex."

A flock of human-headed geese fluttered into the barn, raced toward a battered aluminum trough full of grain, and began to eat. Unlike Maxwell, the geese did not possess the power of speech — either that, or they simply had nothing to say to each other.

I sighed and leaned against my library cart. "So what, exactly, does QZ-11-4 *do*?"

"Dr. Pollifex calls it the integrity gene, wellspring of decency, empathy, and compassionate foresight," said Maxwell. "Francis of Assisi had it. So did Clara Barton, Mahatma Gandhi, Florence Nightingale, Albert Schweitzer, and Susan

B. Anthony. And now that Dr. Pollifex has started injecting me with a serum derived from your hypertrophic superego — now *I've* got it, too."

Although my vanity took a certain satisfaction in Maxwell's words, I realized that I'd lost the thread of his logic. "At the risk of sounding disingenuously modest, I'd have to say I'm not a particularly ethical individual."

"Even if a person inherits QZ-11-4, it doesn't necessarily enjoy expression. And even if the gene enjoys expression" — Maxwell offered me a semantically freighted stare — "the beneficiary doesn't always learn to use his talent. Indeed, among Dr. Pollifex's earliest discoveries was the fact that complete QZ-11-4 actualization is impossible in a purely human species. The serum — we call it Altruoid — the serum reliably engenders ethical superiority only in people who've been genetically melded with domesticated birds and mammals."

"You mean — you used to be . . . human?"

"For twenty years I sold life insurance under the name Lewis Phelps," said the bull-man. "Have no fear, Blake. We are not harvesting your cerebrum in vain. I shall employ my Altruoid allotment to bestow great boons on Greenbriar."

"You might fancy yourself a moral giant," I told the bull-man, "but as far as I'm concerned, you're a terrorist and a brain thief, and I intend to bring this matter to the police."

"You will find that strategy difficult to implement." Maxwell left his piano and, walking upright on his hooves, approached my library cart. "Pollifex Farm is enclosed by a barbed-wire fence twelve feet high. I suggest you try making the best of your situation."

The thought of punching Maxwell in the face now occurred to me, but I dared not risk uprooting my arteries and spinal cord. "If Pollifex continues pilfering my cortex, how long before I become a basket case?"

"Never. The doctor happens to be the world's greatest neurocartographer. He'll bring exquisite taste and sensitivity to each extraction. During the next three years, you'll lose only trivial knowledge, useless skills, and unpleasant memories."

"Three years?" I howled. "You bastards plan to keep me here *three years*?"

"Give or take a month. Once that interval has passed, my peers and I shall have reached the absolute apex of vertebrate ethical development."

"See, Blake, they've thought of *everything*," said Vickie. "These people are *visionaries*."

"These people are Nazis," I said.

"Really, sir, name-calling is unnecessary," said Maxwell with a snort. "There's no reason we can't all be friends." He rested an affirming hand on my shoulder. "We've given you a great deal of information to absorb. I suggest you spend tomorrow afternoon in quiet contemplation. Come evening, we'll all be joining the doctor for dinner. It's a meal you're certain to remember."

My new bride and I passed the night in our depressing little cottage beside the windmill. Much to my relief, I discovered that my sexual functioning had survived the bilateral hemispherectomy. We had to exercise caution, of course, lest we snap the vital link between medulla and cord, with the result that the whole encounter quickly devolved into a kind of slow-motion ballet. Vickie said it was like mating with a china figurine, the first negative remark I'd heard her make concerning my predicament.

At ten o'clock the next morning, one of Karl's human-headed sheep entered the bedroom, walking upright and carrying a wicker tray on which rested two covered dishes. When I asked the sheep how long she'd been living at Pollifex Farm, her expression became as vacant as a cake of soap. I concluded that the power of articulation was reserved only to those mutants on an Altruoid regimen.

The sheep bowed graciously and left, and we set about devouring our scrambled eggs, hot coffee, and buttered toast. Upon consuming her final mouthful, Vickie announced that she would spend the day reading two scientific treatises she'd received from Maxwell, both by Dr. Pollifex: *On the Mutability of Species* and *The Descent of Morals*. I told her I had a different agenda. If there was a way out of this bucolic asylum, I was by-God going to find it.

Before I could take leave of my wife, Karl himself appeared, clutching a black leather satchel to his chest as a mother might cradle a baby. He told me he deeply regretted Wednesday's assault — I must admit, I detected no guile in his apology — then explained that he'd come to collect the day's specimen. From the satchel he removed a glass-and-steel syringe, using it to suck up a small quantity of anterior cortex and transfer it to a test tube. When I told Karl that I felt nothing during the procedure, he reminded me that the human brain is an insensate organ, nerveless as a brick.

I commenced my explorations. Pollifex's domain was vaster than I'd imagined, though most of its fields and pastures were deserted. True to the bullman's claim, a fence hemmed the entire farm, the barbed-wire strands woven into a kind of demonic tennis net and strung between steel posts rising from a concrete foundation. In the northeast corner lay a barn as large as Maxwell's concert hall, and it was here, clearly, that André Pollifex perpetuated his various crimes against nature. The doors were barred, the windows occluded, but by staring through the cracks in the walls I managed to catch glimpses of hospital gurneys, surgical lights, and three enormous glass beakers in which sallow, teratoid fetuses drifted like pickles in brine.

About twenty paces from Pollifex's laboratory, a crumbling tool shed sat atop a hill of naked dirt. I gave the door a hard shove — not too hard, given my neurological vulnerability — and it pivoted open on protesting hinges. A shaft of afternoon sunlight struck the interior, revealing an assortment of rakes, shovels, and pitchforks, plus a dozen bags of fertilizer — but, alas, no wire cutters.

My perambulations proved exhausting, both mentally and physically, and I returned to the cottage for a much-needed nap. That afternoon, my brain tormented me with the notorious "student's dream." I'd enrolled in an advanced biology course at my old alma mater, Rutgers, but I hadn't attended a single class or handed in even one assignment. And now I was expected to take the final exam.

Vickie, my brain, and I were the last to arrive at André Pollifex's dinner party, which occurred in an airy glass-roofed conservatory attached to the back of the farmhouse. The room smelled only slightly better than the piano barn. At the head of the table presided our host, a disarmingly ordinary-looking man, weak of jaw, slight of build, distinguished primarily by his small black moustache and complementary goatee. His face was pale and flaccid, as if he'd been raised in a cave. The instant he opened his mouth to greet us, though, I apprehended something of his glamour, for he had the most majestic voice I've ever heard outside of New York's Metropolitan Opera House.

"Welcome, Mr. and Mrs. Meeshaw," he said. "May I call you Blake and Vickie?"

"Of course," said Vickie.

"May I call you Joseph Mengele?" I said.

Pollifex's white countenance contracted into a scowl. "I can appreciate your distress, Blake. Your sacrifice has been great. I believe I speak for everyone here when I say that our gratitude knows no bounds."

Karl directed us into adjacent seats, then resumed his place next to Pollifex, directly across from the bull-man. I found myself facing a pig-woman whose large ears flopped about like college pennants and whose snout suggested an oversized button. Vickie sat opposite a goat-man with a tapering white beard dangling from his chin and two corrugated horns sprouting from his brow.

"I'm Serge Caprikov," said the goat-man, shaking first Vickie's hand, then mine. "In my former life I was Bud Frye, plumbing contractor."

"Call me Juliana Sowers," said the pig-woman, enacting the same ritual. "At one time I was Doris Owens of Owens Real Estate, but then I found a higher calling. I cannot begin to thank you for the contribution you're making to science, philosophy, and local politics."

"Local politics?" I said.

"We three beneficiaries of QZ-11-4 form the core of the new Common Sense Party," said Juliana. "We intend to transform Greenbriar into the most livable community in America."

"I'm running for Borough Council," said Serge. "Should my campaign prove successful, I shall fight to keep our town free of Consumerland discount stores. Their advent is inevitably disastrous for local merchants."

Juliana crammed a handful of hors d'oeuvres into her mouth. "I seek a position on the School Board. My stances won't prove automatically popular—better pay for elementary teachers, sex education starting in grade four—but I'm prepared to support them with passion and statistics."

Vickie grabbed my hand and said, "See what I mean, Blake? They may be mutants, but they have terrific ideas."

"As for me, I've got my eye on the Planning Commission," said Maxwell, releasing a loud and disconcerting burp. "Did you know there's a scheme afoot to run the Route 80 Extension along our northern boundary, just so it'll be easier for people to get to Penn State football games? Once construction begins, the environmental desecration will be profound."

As Maxwell expounded upon his anti-extension arguments, a half-dozen sheep arrived with our food. In deference to Maxwell and Juliana, the cuisine was vegetarian: tofu, lentils, capellini with meatless marinara sauce. It was all quite tasty, but the highlight of the meal was surely the venerable and exquisite vintages from Pollifex's cellar. After my first few swallows of Brunello di Montalcino, I worried that Pollifex's scalpel had denied me the pleasures of intoxication, but eventually the expected sensation arrived. (I attributed the hiatus to the extra distance my blood had to travel along my extended arteries.) By the time the sheep were serving dessert, I was quite tipsy, though my bursts of euphoria alternated uncontrollably with spasms of anxiety.

"Know what I think?" I said, locking on Pollifex as I struggled to prevent my brain from slurring my words. "I think you're trying to turn me into a zombie."

The doctor proffered a heartening smile. "Your discomfort is understandable, Blake, but I can assure you all my interventions have been innocuous thus far—and will be so in the future. Tell me, what two classroom pets did your second-grade teacher, Mrs. Hines, keep beside her desk, and what were their names?"

"I have no idea."

"Of course you don't. That useless memory vanished with the first extraction. A hamster and a chameleon. Florence and Charlie. Now tell me about the time you threw up on your date for the senior prom."

"That never happened."

"Yes, it did, but I have spared you any recollection of the event. Her name was Becky. Nor will you ever again be haunted by the memory of forgetting your lines during the Cransford Community Theater production of *A Moon for the Misbegotten*. Now please recite Joyce Kilmer's 'Trees.'"

"All right, all right, you've made your point," I said. "But you still have no right to mess with my head." I swallowed more wine. "As for this ridiculous Common Sense Party — okay, sure, these candidates might get *my* vote — I'm for better schools and free enterprise and all that — but the average Greenbriar citizen . . ." In lieu of stating the obvious, I finished my wine.

"What *about* the average Greenbriar citizen?" said Juliana huffily.

"The average Greenbriar citizen will find us morphologically unacceptable?" said Serge haughtily.

"Well . . . yes," I replied.

"Unpleasantly odiferous?" said Maxwell snippily.

"That too."

"Homely?" said Juliana defensively.

"I wouldn't be surprised."

The sheep served dessert — raspberry and lemon sorbet — and the seven of us ate in silence, painfully aware that mutual understanding between myself and the Common Sense Party would be a long time coming.

During the final two weeks of June, Karl siphoned fourteen additional specimens from my superego, one extraction per day. On the Fourth of July, the shepherd unwound my bandages. Although I disbelieved his claim to be a trained nurse, I decided to humor him. When he pronounced that my head was healing satisfactorily, I praised his expertise, then listened intently as he told me how to maintain the incision, an ugly ring of scabs and sutures circumscribing my cranium like a crown of thorns.

As the hot, humid, enervating month elapsed, the Common Sense candidates finished devising their strategies, and the campaign began in earnest. The piano barn soon overflowed with shipping crates full of leaflets, brochures, metal buttons, T-shirts, bumper stickers, and porkpie hats. With each passing day, my skepticism intensified. A goat running for Borough Council? A pig on the School Board? A bull guiding the Planning Commission? Pollifex's menagerie didn't stand a chance.

My doubts received particularly vivid corroboration on July the 20th, when the doctor staged a combination cocktail party and fund-raiser at the farmhouse. From among the small but ardent population of political progressives inhabiting Greenbriar, Pollifex had identified thirty of the wealthiest. Two dozen accepted his invitation. Although these potential contributors were clearly appalled by my bifurcation, they seemed to accept Pollifex's explanation. (I suffered from a rare neurological disorder amenable only to the most radical surgery.) But then the candidates themselves sauntered into the living room, and Pollifex's guests immediately lost their powers of concentration.

It wasn't so much that Maxwell, Juliana, and Serge looked like an incompetent demiurge's roughest drafts. The real problem was that they'd retained so many traits of the creatures to which they'd been grafted. Throughout the entire event, Juliana stuffed her face with canapés and petits fours. Whenever Serge engaged a potential donor in conversation, he crudely emphasized his points by ramming his horns into the listener's chest. Maxwell, meanwhile, kept defecating on the living-room carpet, a behavior not redeemed by the mildly pleasant fragrance that a vegetarian diet imparts to bovine manure. By the time the mutants were ready to deliver their formal speeches, the pledges stood at a mere fifty dollars, and every guest had manufactured an excuse to leave.

"Your idea is never going to work," I told Pollifex after the candidates had returned to their respective barns. We were sitting in the doctor's kitchen, consuming mugs of French roast coffee. The door stood open. A thousand crickets sang in the meadow.

"This is a setback, not a catastrophe," said Pollifex, brushing crumbs from his white dinner jacket. "Maxwell is a major Confucius scholar, with strong Kantian credentials as well. He can surely become housebroken. Juliana is probably the finest utilitarian philosopher since John Stuart Mill. For such a mind, table manners will prove a snap. If you ask Serge about the Sermon on the Mount, he'll recite the King James translation of Matthew without a fluff. Once I explain how uncouth he's being, he'll learn to control his butting urge."

"Nobody wants to vote for a candidate with horns."

"It will take a while — quite a while — before Greenbriar's citizens appreciate this slate, but eventually they'll hop on the bandwagon." Pollifex poured himself a second cup of French roast. "Do you doubt that my mutants are ethical geniuses? Can you imagine, for example, how they responded to the Prisoner's Dilemma?

For three years running, I'd used the Prisoner's Dilemma in my Introduction to Philosophy class. It's a situation-ethics classic, first devised in 1951 by Merrill Flood of the RAND Corporation. Imagine that you and a stranger have been arrested as accomplices in manslaughter. You are both innocent. The state's case is weak. Even though you don't know each other, you and the stranger form a pact. You will both stonewall it, maintaining your innocence no matter what deal the prosecutor may offer.

Each of you is questioned privately. Upon entering the interrogation room, the prosecutor lays out four possibilities. If you and your presumed accomplice hang tough, confessing to nothing, you will each get a short sentence, a mere seven months in prison. If you admit your guilt and implicate your fellow prisoner, you will go scot-free — and your presumed accomplice will serve a life sentence. If you hang tough and your fellow prisoner confesses-and-implicates, *he* will go scot-free — and *you* will serve a life sentence. Finally, if you and your fellow prisoner both confess-and-implicate, you will each get a medium sentence, four years behind bars.

It doesn't take my students long to realize that the most logical course is to break faith with the stranger, thus guaranteeing that you won't spend your life in prison if he also defects. The uplifting — but uncertain — possibility of a short sentence must lose out to the immoral — but immutable — fact of a medium sentence. Cooperation be damned.

"Your mutants probably insist they would keep faith regardless of the consequences," I said. "They would rather die than violate a trust."

"Their answer is subtler than that," said Pollifex. "They would tell the prosecutor, 'You imagine my fellow prisoner and I have made a pact, and in that you are correct. You further imagine you can manipulate us into breaking faith with one another. But given your obsession with betrayal, I must conclude that you are yourself a liar, and that you will ultimately seek to convert our unwilling confessions into life sentences. I refuse to play this game. Let's go to court instead.'"

"An impressive riposte," I said. "But the fact remains . . ." Reaching for the coffee pot, I let my voice drift away. "Suppose I poured some French roast directly into my jar? Would I be jolted awake?"

"Don't try it," said Pollifex.

"I won't."

The mutant-maker scowled strenuously. "You think I'm some sort of mad scientist."

"Restore my brain," I told him. "Leave the farm, get a job at Pfizer, wash your hands of politics."

"I'm a sane scientist, Blake. I'm the last sane scientist in the world."

I looked directly into his eyes. The face that returned my gaze was neither entirely mad nor wholly sane. It was the face of a man who wasn't sleeping well, and it made me want to run away.

The following morning, my routine wanderings along the farm's perimeter brought me to a broad, swiftly flowing creek about twelve feet wide and three deep. Although the barbed-wire net extended beneath the water, clear to the bottom, I suddenly realized how a man might circumvent it. By redirecting the water's flow via a series of dikes, I could desiccate a large section of the creek bed and subsequently dig my way out of this hellish place. I would only need one of the shovels I'd spotted in the tool shed — a shovel, and a great deal of luck.

Thus it was that I embarked on a secret construction project. Every day at about 11:00 a.m., right after Karl took the specimen from my superego, I slunk off to the creek and spent a half-hour adding rocks, logs, and mud to the burgeoning levees, returning to the cottage in time for lunch. Although the creek proved far less pliable than I'd hoped, I eventually became its master. Within two weeks, I figured, possibly three, a large patch of sand and pebbles would lie exposed to the hot summer sun, waiting to receive my shovel.

Naturally I was tempted to tell Vickie of my scheme. Given my handicap, I could certainly have used her assistance in building the levees. But in the end I concluded that, rather than endorsing my bid for freedom, she would regard it as a betrayal of the Common Sense Party and its virtuous agenda.

I knew I'd made the right decision when Vickie entered our cottage late one night in the form of a gigantic mutant hen. Her body had become a bulbous mass of feathers, her legs had transmuted into fleshy stilts, and her face now sported a beak the size of a funnel. Obviously she was running for elective office, but I couldn't imagine which one. She lost no time informing me. Her ambition, she explained, was to become Greenbriar's next mayor.

"I've even got an issue," she said.

"I don't want to hear about it," I replied, looking her up and down. Although she still apparently retained her large and excellent breasts beneath her bikini top, their present context reduced their erotic content considerably.

"Do you know what Greenbriar needs?" she proclaimed. "Traffic diverters at certain key intersections! Our neighborhoods are being suffocated by the automobile!"

"You shouldn't have done this, Vickie," I told her.

"My name is Eva Pullo," she clucked.

"These people have brainwashed you!"

"The Common Sense Party is the hope of the future!"

"You're talking like a fascist!" I said.

"At least I'm not a coward like you!" said the chicken.

For the next half-hour we hurled insults at each other — our first real post-marital fight — and then I left in a huff, eager to continue my arcane labors by the creek. In a peculiar way I still loved Vickie, but I sensed that our relationship was at an end. When I made my momentous escape, I feared she would not be coming with me.

Even as I redirected the creek, the four mutant candidates brought off an equally impressive feat — something akin to a miracle, in fact. They got the citizens of Greenbriar to listen to them, and the citizens liked what they heard.

The first breakthrough occurred when Maxwell appeared along with three other Planning Commission candidates — Republican, Democrat, Libertarian — on Greenbriar's local-access cable channel. I watched the broadcast in the farmhouse, sitting on the couch between Vickie and Dr. Pollifex. Although the full-blooded humans on the podium initially refused to take Maxwell seriously, the more he talked about his desire to prevent the Route 80 Extension from wreaking havoc with local ecosystems, the clearer it became that this mutant had charisma. Maxwell's eloquence was breathtaking, his logic impeccable, his sincerity sublime. He committed no fecal faux pas.

"That bull was on his game," I admitted at the end of the transmission.

"The moderator was *enchanted*," enthused Vickie.

"Our boy is going to win," said Pollifex.

Two days later, Juliana kicked off her campaign for School Board. Aided by the ever energetic Vickie, she had outfitted the back of an old yellow school bus with a Pullman car observation platform, the sort of stage from which early twentieth-century presidential candidates campaigned while riding the rails. Juliana and Vickie also transformed the bus's interior, replacing the seats with a coffee bar, a chat lounge, and racks of brochures explaining the pig-woman's ambition to expand the sex-education program, improve services for special-needs children, increase faculty awareness of the misery endured by gay students, and — most audacious of all — invert the salary pyramid so that first-grade teachers would earn more than high-school administrators. Day in, day out, Juliana tooled around Greenbriar in her appealing vehicle, giving out iced cappuccino, addressing crowds from the platform, speaking to citizens privately in the lounge, and somehow managing to check her impulse toward gluttony, all the while exhibiting a caliber of wisdom that eclipsed her unappetizing physiognomy. The tour was a fabulous success — such, at least, was the impression I received from watching the blurry, jerky coverage that Vickie accorded the pig-woman's campaign with Pollifex's camcorder. Every time the school bus pulled away from a Juliana Sowers rally, it left behind a thousand tear-stained eyes, so moved were the citizens by her commitment to the glorious ideal of public education.

Serge, meanwhile, participated in a series of "Meet the Candidates" nights along with four other Borough Council hopefuls. Even when mediated by Vickie's shaky videography, the inaugural gathering at Greenbriar Town Hall came across as a powerful piece of political theater. Serge fully suppressed his impulse to butt his opponents — but that was the smallest of his accomplishments. Without slinging mud, flinging innuendo, or indulging in disingenuous rhetoric, he made his fellow candidates look like moral idiots for their unwillingness to stand firm against what he called "the insatiable greed of Consumerland." Before the evening ended, the attending voters stood prepared to tar-and-feather any discount-chain executive who might set foot in Greenbriar, and it was obvious they'd also embraced Serge's other ideas for making the Borough Council a friend to local businesses. If Serge's plans came to fruition, shoppers would eventually flock to the downtown, lured by parking-fee rebates, street performers, bicycle paths, mini-playgrounds, and low-cost supervised day care.

As for Vickie's mayoral campaign — which I soon learned to call Eva Pullo's mayoral campaign — it gained momentum the instant she shed her habit of pecking hecklers on the head. My wife's commitment to reducing the automobile traffic in residential areas occasioned the grandest rhetorical flights I'd ever heard from her. "A neighborhood should exist for the welfare of its children, not the convenience of its motorists," she told the local chapter of the League of Women Voters. "We must not allow our unconsidered veneration of the automobile to mask our fundamental need for community and connectedness," she advised the Chamber of Commerce. By the middle of August, Vickie had added a dozen other environmentalist planks to her platform, including an ingenious proposal to outfit the town's major highways with underground passageways for raccoons, badgers, woodchucks, skunks, and possums.

You must believe me when I say that my conversion to the Common Sense Party occurred well before the *Greenbriar Daily Times* published its poll indicating that the entire slate — Maxwell Taurus, Juliana Sowers, Serge Caprikov, and Eva Pullo — enjoyed the status of shoo-ins. I was not simply trying to ride with the winners. When I abandoned my plan to dig an escape channel under the fence, I was doing what I thought was right. When I resolved to spend the next three years nursing the Pollifex Farm candidates from my cerebral teat, I was fired by an idealism so intense that the pragmatists among you would blush to behold it.

I left the levees in place, however, just in case I had a change of heart.

The attack on Pollifex Farm started shortly after 11:00 p.m. It was Halloween night, which means that the raiders probably aroused no suspicions whatsoever as, dressed in shrouds and skull masks, they drove their pickup trucks through the streets of Greenbriar and down Spring Valley Road. To this day, I'm not sure who organized and paid for the atrocity. At its core, I suspect, the mob included not only yahoos armed with torches but also conservatives gripped by fear, moderates transfixed by cynicism, liberals in the pay of the status quo, libertarians acting out anti-government fantasies, and a few random anarchists looking for a good time. Whatever their conflicting allegiances, the vigilantes stood united in their realization that André Pollifex, sane scientist, was about to unleash a reign of enlightenment on Greenbriar. They were having none of it.

I was experiencing yet another version of the student's dream — this time I'd misconnected not simply with one class but with an entire college curriculum — when shouts, gunshots, and the neighing of frightened horses awoke me. Taking hold of the library cart, I roused Vickie by ruffling her feathers, and side by side we stumbled into the parlor. By the time we'd made our way outside, the windmill, tractor shed, corncrib, and centaur stables were all on fire. Although I could not move quickly without risking permanent paralysis, Vickie immediately sprang into action. Transcending her spheroid body, she charged into the burning stables and set the mutant horses free, and she proved equally unflappable when the vigilantes hurled their torches into Maxwell's residence. With little thought for her personal safety, she ran into the flaming piano barn, located the panicked bull-man and the equally discombobulated pig-woman — in recent months they'd entered into a relationship whose details needn't concern us here — and led them outside right before the roof collapsed in a great red wave of cascading sparks and flying embers.

And still the arsonists continued their assault, blockading the main gate with bales of burning hay, setting fire to the chicken coop, and turning Pollifex's laboratory into a raging inferno. Catching an occasional glimpse of our spectral enemies, their white sheets flashing in the light of the flames, I saw that they would not become hoist with their own petards, for they had equipped themselves with asbestos suits, scuba regulators, and compressed air tanks. As for the inhabitants of Pollifex Farm, it was certain that if we didn't move quickly, we would suffer either incineration, suffocation, or their concurrence in the form of fatally seared lungs.

Although I'd never felt so divided, neither the fear spasms in my chest nor the jumbled thoughts in my jar prevented me from realizing what the mutants must do next. I told them to steal shovels from the tool shed, make for the creek, and follow it to the fence. Thanks to my levees, I explained, the bed now lay in the open air. Within twenty minutes or so, they should be able to dig below the barbed-wire net and gouge a dry channel for themselves. The rest of my plan had me bringing up the rear, looking out for Karl, Serge, and Dr. Pollifex so that I might direct them to the secret exit. Vickie kissed my lips, Juliana caressed my cheek, Maxwell embraced by brain, and then all three candidates rushed off into the choking darkness.

Before that terrible night was out, I indeed found the other Party members. Karl lay dead in a mound of straw beside the sheep barn, his forehead blasted away by buckshot. Serge sat on the rear porch of the farmhouse, his left horn broken off and thrust fatally into his chest. Finally I came upon Pollifex. The vigilantes had roped the doctor to a maple tree, subjected him to target practice, and left him for dead. He was as perforated as Saint Sebastian. A mattock, a pitchfork, and two scythes projected from his body like quills from a porcupine.

"André, it's me, Blake," I said, approaching.

"Blake?" he muttered. "Blake? Oh, Blake, they killed Serge. They killed Karl."

"I know. Vickie got away, and Maxwell too, and Juliana."

"I was a sane scientist," said Pollifex.

"Of course," I said.

"There are some things that expediency was not meant to tamper with."

"I agree."

"Pullo for Mayor!" he shouted.

"Taurus for Planning Commission!" I replied.

"Caprikov for Borough Council!" he shouted. "Sowers for School Board!" he screamed, and then he died.

There's not much more to tell. Although Vickie, Juliana, Maxwell, and I all escaped the burning farm that night, the formula for the miraculous serum died with Dr. Pollifex. Deprived of their weekly Altruoid injections, the mutants soon lost their talent for practical idealism, and their political careers sputtered out. Greenbriar now boasts a mammoth new Consumerland. The

Route 80 Extension is almost finished. High-school principals still draw three times the pay of first-grade teachers. Life goes on.

The last time I saw Juliana, she was the opening act at Caesar's Palace in Atlantic City. A few songs, some impersonations, a standup comedy routine — mostly vegetarian humor and animal-rights jokes leavened by a sardonic feminism. The crowd ate it up, and Juliana seemed to be enjoying herself. But, oh, what a formidable School Board member she would have made!

When the Route 80 disaster occurred, Maxwell was devastated — not so much by the extension itself as by his inability to critique it eloquently. These days he plays the piano at Emilio's, a seedy bar in Newark. He is by no means the weirdest presence in the place, and he enjoys listening to the customers' troubles. But he is a broken mutant.

Vickie and I did our best to make it work, but in the end we decided that mixed marriages entail insurmountable hurdles, and we split up. Eventually she got a job hosting a preschool children's television show on the Disney Channel, *Arabella's Barnyard Band*. Occasionally she manages to insert a satiric observation about automobiles into her patter.

As for me, after hearing the tenth neurosurgeon declare that I am beyond reassembly, I decided to join the world's eternal vagabonds. I am brother to the Wandering Jew, the Flying Dutchman, and Marley's Ghost. I shuffle around North America, dragging my library cart behind me, exhibiting my fractured self to anyone who's willing to pay. In the past decade, my employers have included three carnivals, four roadside peep shows, two direct-to-video horror movie producers, and an artsy off-Broadway troupe bent on reviving *Le Grand Guignol*.

And always I remain on the lookout for another André Pollifex, another scientist who can manufacture QZ-11-4 serum and use it to turn beasts into politicians. I shall not settle for any sort of Pollifex, of course. The actual Pollifex, for example, would not meet my standards. The man bifurcated me without my permission, and I cannot forgive him for that.

The scientist I seek would unflinchingly martyr himself to the Prisoner's Dilemma. As they hauled him away to whatever dungeon is reserved for such saints, he would turn to the crowd and say, "The personal cost was great, but at least I have delivered a fellow human from an unjust imprisonment. And who knows? Perhaps his anguish over breaking faith with me will eventually transform him into a more generous friend, a better parent, or a public benefactor."

Alas, my heart is not in the quest. Only part of me — a small part, I must confess — wants to keep on making useful neurological donations. So even if there is a perfect Pollifex out there somewhere, he will probably never get to fashion a fresh batch of Altruoid. Not unless I father a child — and not unless the child receives the gene — and not unless the gene finds expression — and not unless this descendant of mine donates his superego to science. But as the bull-man told me many years ago, QZ-11-4 only rarely gets actualized in the humans who carry it.

I believe I see a way around the problem. The roadside emporium in which I currently display myself also features a llama named Loretta. She can count to ten and solve simple arithmetic problems. I am enchanted by Loretta's liquid eyes, sensuous lips, and splendid form — and I think she has taken a similar interest in me. It's a relationship, I feel, that could lead almost anywhere.

Arms and the Woman

"What did you do in the war, Mommy?"

The last long shadow has slipped from the sundial's face, melting into the hot Egyptian night. My children should be asleep. Instead they're bouncing on their straw pallets, stalling for time.

"It's late," I reply. "Nine o'clock already."

"Please," the twins implore me in a single voice.

"You have school tomorrow."

"You haven't told us a story all week," insists Damon, the whiner.

"The war is such a *great* story," explains Daphne, the wheedler.

"Kaptah's mother tells *him* a story every night," whines Damon.

"Tell us about the war," wheedles Daphne, "and we'll clean the whole cottage tomorrow, top to bottom."

I realize I'm going to give in — not because I enjoy spoiling my children (though I do) or because the story itself will consume less time than further negotiations (though it will) but because I actually want the twins to hear this particular tale. It has a point. I've told it before, of course, a dozen times perhaps, but I'm still not sure they get it.

I snatch up the egg timer and invert it on the nightstand, the tiny grains of sand spilling into the lower chamber like seeds from a farmer's palm. "Be ready for bed in three minutes," I warn my children, "or no story."

They scurry off, frantically brushing their teeth and slipping on their flaxen nightshirts. Silently I glide about the cottage, dousing the lamps and curtaining the moon, until only one candle lights the twins' room, like the campfire of an army consisting of mice and scarab beetles.

"So you want to know what I did in the war," I intone, singsong, as my children climb into their beds.

"Oh, yes," says Damon, pulling up his fleecy coverlet.

"You bet," says Daphne, fluffing her goose-feather pillow.

"Once upon a time," I begin, "I lived as both princess and prisoner in the great city of Troy." Even in this feeble light, I'm struck by how handsome Damon is, how beautiful Daphne. "Every evening, I would sit in my boudoir, looking into my polished bronze mirror . . ."

Helen of Troy, princess and prisoner, sits in her boudoir, looking into her polished bronze mirror and scanning her world-class face for symptoms of age — for wrinkles, wattles, pouches, crow's-feet, and the crenellated corpses of hairs. She feels like crying, and not just because these past ten years in Ilium are starting to show. She's sick of the whole sordid arrangement, sick of being cooped up in this overheated acropolis like a pet cockatoo. Whispers haunt the citadel. The servants are gossiping, even her own handmaids. The whore of Hisarlik, they call her. The slut from Sparta. The Lakedaimon lay.

Then there's Paris. Sure, she's madly in love with him, sure, they have great sex, but can't they ever *talk*?

Sighing, Helen trolls her hairdo with her lean, exquisitely manicured fingers. A silver strand lies amid the folds like a predatory snake. Slowly she winds the offending filament around her index finger, then gives a sudden tug. "Ouch," she cries, more from despair than pain. There are times when Helen feels like tearing out all her lovely tresses, every last lock, not simply these graying threads. If I have to spend one more pointless day in Hisarlik, she tells herself, I'll go mad.

Every morning, she and Paris enact the same depressing ritual. She escorts him to the Skaian Gate, hands him his spear and his lunch bucket, and with a tepid kiss sends him off to work. Paris's job is killing people. At sundown he arrives home grubby with blood and redolent of funeral pyres, his spear wrapped in bits of drying viscera. There's a war going on out there; Paris won't tell her anything more. "Who are we fighting?" she asks each evening as they lie together in bed. "Don't you worry your pretty little head about it," he replies, slipping on a sheep-gut condom, the brand with the plumed and helmeted soldier on the box.

Until this year, Paris had contrived for her to walk the high walls of Troy each morning, waving encouragement to the troops, blowing them kisses as they marched off to battle. "Your face inspires them," he had insisted. "An airy kiss from you is worth a thousand nights of passion with a nymph." But in recent months Paris's priorities have changed. As soon as they say good-bye, Helen is supposed to retire to the citadel, speaking with no other Hisarlikan, not even a brief coffee klatch with one of Paris's forty-nine sisters-in-law. She's expected to spend her whole day weaving rugs, carding flax, and being beautiful. It is not a life.

Can the gods help? Helen is skeptical, but anything is worth a try. Tomorrow, she resolves, she will go to the temple of Apollo and beg him to relieve her boredom, perhaps buttressing her appeal with an offering — a ram, a bull, whatever — though an offering strikes her as rather like a deal, and Helen is sick of deals. Her husband — pseudohusband, nonhusband — made a deal. She keeps thinking of the Apple of Discord, and what Aphrodite might have done with it after bribing Paris. Did she drop it in her fruit bowl . . . put it on her mantel . . . impale it on her crown? Why did Aphrodite take the damn thing seriously? Why did any of them take it seriously? Hi, I'm the fairest goddess in the universe — see, it says so right here on my apple.

Damn — another gray hair, another weed in the garden of her pulchritude. She reaches toward the villain — and stops. Why bother? These hairs are like the Hydra's heads, endless, cancerous, and besides, it's high time Paris realized there's a mind under that coiffure.

Whereupon Paris comes in, sweating and snorting. His helmet is awry; his spear is gory; his greaves are sticky with other men's flesh.

"Hard day, dear?"

"Don't ask." Her nonhusband unfastens his breastplate. "Pour us some wine. Looking in the speculum, were you? Good."

Helen sets the mirror down, uncorks the bottle, and fills two bejeweled goblets with Chateau Samothrace.

"Today I heard about some techniques you might try," says Paris. "Ways for a woman to retain her beauty."

"You mean — you *talk* on the battlefield?"

"During the lulls."

"I wish you'd talk to *me*."

"Wax," says Paris, lifting the goblet to his lips. "Wax is the thing." His heavy jowls undulate as he drinks. Their affair, Helen will admit, still gives her a kick. In the past ten years, her lover has moved beyond the surpassing prettiness of an Adonis into something equally appealing, an authoritative, no-frills masculinity suggestive of an aging matinee idol. "Take some melted wax and work it into the lines in your brow — presto, they're gone."

"I *like* my lines," Helen insists with a quick but audible snort.

"When mixed with ox blood, the dark silt from the River Minyeios is indelible, they say. You can dye your silver hairs back to auburn. A Grecian formula." Paris sips his wine. "As for these redundant ounces on your thighs, well, dear, we both know there's no cure like exercise."

"Look who's talking," Helen snaps. "*Your* skin is no bowl of cream. *Your* head is no garden of sargasso. As for your stomach, it's a safe bet that Paris of Troy can walk through the rain without getting his belt buckle wet."

The prince finishes his wine and sighs. "Where's the girl I married? You used to care about your looks."

"The girl you married," Helen replies pointedly, "is not your wife."

"Well, yes, of course not. Technically, you're still *his*."

"I want a wedding." Helen takes a gluttonous swallow of Samothrace and sets the goblet on the mirror. "You could go to my husband," she suggests. "You could present yourself to high-minded Menelaus and try to talk things out." Reflected in the mirror's wobbly face, the goblet grows weird, twisted, as if seen through a drunkard's eyes. "Hey, listen, I'll bet he's found another maid by now — he's something of a catch, after all. So maybe you actually did him a favor. Maybe he isn't even mad."

"He's mad," Paris insists. "The man is angry."

"How do you know?"

"I know."

Heedless of her royal station, Helen consumes her wine with the crude insouciance of a galley slave. "I want a baby," she says.

"What?"

"You know, a baby. *Baby*: a highly young person. My goal, dear Paris, is to be pregnant."

"Fatherhood is for losers." Paris chucks his spear onto the bed. Striking the mattress, the oaken shaft disappears into the soft down. "Go easy on the *vino*, love. Alcohol is awfully fattening."

"Don't you understand? I'm losing my mind. A pregnancy would give me a sense of purpose."

"Any idiot can sire a child. It takes a hero to defend a citadel."

"Have you found someone else, Paris? Is that it? Someone younger and thinner?"

"Don't be foolish. Throughout the whole of time, in days gone by and eras yet to come, no man will love a woman as much as Paris loves Helen."

"I'll bet the plains of Ilium are crawling with camp followers. They must swoon over you."

"Don't you worry your pretty little head about it," says Paris, unwrapping a plumed-soldier condom.

If he ever says that to me again, Helen vows as they tumble drunkenly into bed, I'll scream so loud the walls of Troy will fall.

The slaughter is not going well, and Paris is depressed. By his best reckoning, he's dispatched only fifteen Achaeans to the house of Hades this morning: strong-greaved Machaon, iron-muscled Euchenor, ax-wielding Deichos, and a dozen more — fifteen noble warriors sent to the dark depths, fifteen breathless bodies left to nourish the dogs and ravens. It is not enough.

All along the front, Priam's army is giving ground without a fight. Their morale is low, their *esprit* spent. They haven't seen Helen in a year, and they don't much feel like fighting anymore.

With a deep Aeolian sigh, the prince seats himself atop his pile of confiscated armor and begins his lunch break.

Does he have a choice? Must he continue keeping her in the shadows? Yes, by Poseidon's trident — yes. Exhibiting Helen as she looks now would just make matters worse. Once upon a time, her face had launched a thousand ships. Today it couldn't get a Theban fishing schooner out of dry dock. Let the troops catch only a glimpse of her wrinkles, let them but glance at her aging hair, and they'll start deserting like rats leaving a foundering trireme.

He's polishing off a peach — since delivering his famous verdict and awarding Aphrodite her prize, Paris no longer cares for apples — when two of the finest horses in Hisarlik, steadfast Aithon and intrepid Xanthos, gallop up pulling his brother's war chariot. He expects to see Hector holding the reins, but no: the driver, he notes with a pang of surprise, is Helen.

"Helen? What are *you* doing here?"

Brandishing a cowhide whip, his lover jumps down. "You won't tell me what this war is about," she gasps, panting inside her armor, "so I'm investigating on my own. I just came from the swift-flowing Menderes, where your enemies are preparing to launch a cavalry charge against the camp of Epistrophos."

"Go back to the citadel, Helen. Go back to Pergamos."

"Paris, this army you're battling — they're *Greeks*. Idomeneus, Diomedes, Sthenelos, Euryalos, Odysseus — I *know* these men. Know them? By Pan's flute, I've *dated* half of them. You'll never guess who's about to lead that cavalry charge."

Paris takes a stab. "Agamemnon?"

"Agamemnon!" Sweat leaks from beneath Helen's helmet like blood from a scalp wound. "My own brother-in-law! Next you'll be telling me Menelaus himself has taken the field against Troy!"

Paris coughs and says, "Menelaus himself has taken the field against Troy."

"He's here?" wails Helen, thumping her breastplate. "My husband is *here*?"

"Correct."

"What's going on, Paris? For what purpose have the men of horse-pasturing Argos come all the way to Ilium?"

The prince bounces his peach pit off Helen's breastplate. Angrily he fishes for epithets. Mule-minded Helen, he calls her beneath his breath. Leather-skinned Lakedaimon. He feels beaten and bettered, trapped and tethered. "Very well, sweetheart, very well . . ." Helen of the iron will, the hard ass, the bronze bottom. "They've come for *you*, love."

"What?"

"For you."

"Me? What are you talking about?"

"They want to steal you back." As Paris speaks, Helen's waning beauty seems to drop another notch. Her face darkens with an unfathomable mix of anger, hurt, and confusion. "They're pledged to it. King Tyndareus made your suitors swear they'd be loyal to whomever you selected as husband."

"*Me?*" Helen leaps into the chariot. "You're fighting an entire, stupid, disgusting war for *me*?"

"Well, not for you per se. For honor, for glory, for *arete*. Now hurry off to Pergamos — that's an order."

"I'm hurrying off, dear" — she raises her whip — "but not to Pergamos. On, Aithon!" She snaps the lash. "On, Xanthos!"

"Then where?"

Instead of answering, Paris's lover speeds away, leaving him to devour her dust.

Dizzy with outrage, trembling with remorse, Helen charges across the plains of Ilium. On all sides, an astonishing drama unfolds, a spectacle of shattered senses and violated flesh: soldiers with eyes gouged out, tongues cut loose, limbs hacked off, bellies ripped open; soldiers, as it were, giving birth to their own bowels — all because of her. She weeps openly, profusely, the large gem-like tears running down her wrinkled cheeks and striking her breastplate. The agonies of Prometheus are a picnic compared to the weight of her guilt, the Pillars of Herakles are feathers when balanced against the crushing tonnage of her conscience.

Honor, glory, *arete*: I'm missing something, Helen realizes as she surveys the carnage. The war's essence eludes me.

She reaches the thick and stinking Lisgar Marsh and reins up before a foot soldier sitting in the mud, a young Myrmidon with what she assumes are a particularly honorable spear-hole in his breastplate and a singularly glorious lack of a right hand.

"Can you tell me where I might find your king?" she asks.

"By Hera's eyes, you're easy to look at," gasps the soldier as, *arete* in full bloom, he binds his bleeding stump with linen.

"I need to find Menelaus."

"Try the harbor," he says, gesturing with his wound. The bandaged stump drips like a leaky faucet. "His ship is the *Arkadia*."

Helen thanks the soldier and aims her horses toward the wine-dark sea.

"Are you Helen's mother, by any chance?" he calls as she races off. "What a face you've got!"

Twenty minutes later, reeling with thirst and smelling of horse sweat, Helen pulls within view of the crashing waves. In the harbor beyond, a thousand strong-hulled ships lie at anchor, their masts jutting into the sky like a forest of denuded trees. All along the beach, her countrymen are raising a stout wooden wall, evidently fearful that, if the line is ever pushed back this far, the Trojans will not hesitate to burn the fleet. The briny air rings with the Achaeans' axes — with the thud and crunch of acacias being felled, palisades being whittled, stockade posts sharpened, breastworks shaped, a cacophony muffling the flutter of the sails and the growl of the surf.

Helen starts along the wharf, soon spotting the *Arkadia*, a stout penteconter with half a hundred oars bristling from her sides like quills on a hedgehog. No sooner has she crossed the gangplank than she comes upon her husband, older now, striated by wrinkles, but still unquestionably he. Plumed like a peacock, Menelaus stands atop the forecastle, speaking with a burly construction brigade, tutoring them in the proper placement of the impalement stakes. A handsome man, she decides, much like the warrior on the condom boxes. She can see why she picked him over Sthenelos, Euryalos, and her other beaux.

As the workers set off to plant their spiky groves, Helen saunters up behind Menelaus and taps his shoulder.

"Hi," she says.

He was always a wan fellow, but now his face loses whatever small quantity of blood it once possessed.

"Helen?" he says, gasping and blinking like a man who's just been doused with a bucket of slop. "Is that *you*?"

"Right."

"You've, er . . . aged."

"You too, sweetheart."

He pulls off his plumed helmet, stomps his foot on the forecastle, and says, angrily, "You ran out on me."

"Yes. Quite so."

"Trollop."

"Perhaps." Helen adjusts her greaves. "I could claim I was bewitched by laughter-loving Aphrodite, but that would be a lie. The fact is, Paris knocked me silly. I'm crazy about him. Sorry." She runs her desiccated tongue along her parched lips. "Have you anything to drink?"

Dipping a hollow gourd into his private cistern, Menelaus offers her a pint of fresh water. "So what brings you here?"

Helen receives the ladle. Setting her boots wide apart, she steadies herself against the roll of the incoming tide and takes a greedy gulp. At last she says, "I wish to give myself up."

"What?"

"I want to go home with you."

"You mean — you think our marriage deserves another chance?"

"No, I think all those infantrymen out there deserve to live. If this war is really being fought to retrieve me, then consider the job done." Tossing the ladle aside, Helen holds out her hands, palms turned upward as if she's testing for raindrops. "I'm yours, hubby. Manacle my wrists, chain my feet together, throw me in the brig."

Against all odds, defying all *logos*, Menelaus's face loses more blood. "I don't think that's a very good idea," he says.

"Huh? What do you mean?"

"This siege, Helen — there's more to it than you suppose."

"Don't jerk me around, lord of all Lakedaimon, asshole. It's time to call it quits."

The Spartan king stares straight at her chest, a habit she's always found annoying. "Put on a bit of weight, eh, darling?"

"Don't change the subject." She lunges toward Menelaus's scabbard as if to goose him, but instead draws out his sword. "I'm deadly serious: if Helen of Troy is not permitted to live with herself" — she pantomimes the act of suicide — "then she will die with herself."

"Tell you what," says her husband, taking his weapon back. "Tomorrow morning, first thing, I'll go to my brother and suggest he arrange a truce with your father-in-law."

"He's not my father-in-law. There was never a wedding."

"Whatever. The point is, your offer has merit, but it must be discussed. We shall all meet face to face, Trojans and Achaeans, and talk it out. As for now, you'd best return to your lover."

"I'm warning you — I shall abide no more blood on my hands, none but my own."

"Of course, dear. Now please go back to the citadel."

At least he listened, Helen muses as she crosses the weatherworn deck of the *Arkadia*. At least he didn't tell me not to worry my pretty little head about it.

"Here comes the dull part," says whiny-tongued Damon.

"The scene with all the talking," adds smart-mouthed Daphne.

"Can you cut it a bit?" my son asks.

"Hush," I say, smoothing out Damon's coverlet. "No interruptions," I insist. I slip Daphne's papyrus doll under her arm. "When you have your own children, you can edit the tale however you wish. As for now, listen carefully. You might learn something."

By the burbling, tumbling waters of the River Simois, beneath the glowing orange avatar of the moon goddess Artemis, ten aristocrats are gathered around an oaken table in the purple tent of Ilium's high command, all of them bursting with opinions on how best to deal with this Helen situation, this peace problem, this Trojan hostage crisis. White as a crane, a truce banner flaps above the heads of the two kings, Priam from the high city, Agamemnon from the long ships. Each side has sent its best and/or brightest. For the Trojans: brainy Panthoos, mighty Paris, invincible Hector, and Hiketaon the scion of Ares. For the Achaean cause: Ajax the berserker, Nestor the mentor, Menelaus the cuckold, and wily, smiling Odysseus. Of all those invited, only quarrelsome Achilles, sulking in his tent, has declined to appear.

Panthoos rises, rubs his foam-white beard, and sets his scepter on the table. "Royal captains, gifted seers," the old Trojan begins, "I believe you will concur when I say that, since this siege was laid, we have not faced a challenge of such magnitude. Make no mistake: Helen means to take our war away from us, and she means to do so immediately."

Gusts of dismay waft through the tent like a wind from the underworld.

"We can't quit now," groans Hector, wincing fiercely.

"We're just getting up to speed," wails Hiketaon, grimacing greatly.

Agamemnon steps down from his throne, carrying his scepter like a spear. "I have a question for Prince Paris," he says. "What does your mistress's willingness to return to Argos say about the present state of your relationship?"

Paris strokes his jowls and replies, "As you might surmise, noble king, my feelings for Helen are predicated on requitement."

"So you won't keep her in Pergamos by force?"

"If she doesn't want me, then I don't want her."

At which point slug-witted Ajax raises his hand. "Er, excuse me. I'm a bit confused. If Helen is ours for the asking, then why must we continue the war?"

A sirocco of astonishment arises among the heroes.

"Why?" gasps Panthoos. "*Why*? Because this is *Troy*, that's why. Because we're kicking off Western Civilization here, that's why. The longer we can keep this affair going — the longer we can sustain such an ambiguous enterprise — the more valuable and significant it becomes."

Slow-synapsed Ajax says, "Huh?"

Nestor has but to clear his throat and every eye is upon him. "What our adversary is saying — may I interpret, wise Panthoos?" He turns to his Trojan counterpart, bows deferentially, and, receiving a nod of assent, speaks to Ajax. "Panthoos means that, if this particular pretext for war — restoring a woman to her rightful owner — can be made to seem reasonable, then *any* pretext for war can be made to seem reasonable." The mentor shifts his fevered stare from Ajax to the entire assembly. "By rising to this rare and precious occasion, we shall open the way for wars of religion, wars of manifest destiny — any equivocal cause you care to name." Once again his gaze alights on Ajax. "Understand, sir? This is the war to inaugurate war itself. This is the war to make the world safe for war!"

Ajax frowns so vigorously his visor falls down. "All I know is, we came for Helen, and we got her. Mission accomplished." Turning to Agamemnon, the berserker lifts the visor from his eyes. "So if it's all the same to you, Majesty, I'd like to go home before I get killed."

"O, Ajax, Ajax, Ajax," moans Hector, pulling an arrow from his quiver and using it to scratch his back. "Where is your aesthetic sense? Have you no appreciation of war for war's sake? The plains of Ilium are roiling with glory, sir. You could cut the *arete* with a knife. Never have there been such valiant eviscerations, such venerable dismemberments, such — "

"I don't get it," says the berserker. "I just don't get it."

Whereupon Menelaus slams his wine goblet on the table with a resounding thunk. "We are not gathered in Priam's tent so that Ajax might learn politics," he says impatiently. "We are gathered so that we might best dispose of my wife."

"True, true," says Hector.

"So what are we going to do, gentlemen?" asks Menelaus. "Lock her up?"

"Good idea," says Hiketaon.

"Well, yes," says Agamemnon, slumping back onto his throne. "Except that, when the war finally ends, my troops will demand to see her. Might they not wonder why so much suffering and sacrifice was spent on a goddess gone to seed?" He turns to Paris and says, "Prince, you should not have let this happen."

"Let *what* happen?" asks Paris.

"I heard she has wrinkles," says Agamemnon.

"I heard she got fat," says Nestor.

"What have you been feeding her?" asks Menelaus. "Bonbons?"

"She's a *person*," protests Paris. "She's not a marble statue. You can hardly blame *me* . . ."

At which juncture King Priam raises his scepter and, as if to wound Gaea herself, rams it into the dirt.

"Noble lords, I hate to say this, but the threat is more immediate than you might suppose. In the early years of the siege, the sight of fair Helen walking the ramparts did wonders for my army's morale. Now that she's no longer fit for public display, well . . ."

"Yes?" says Agamemnon, steeling himself for the worst.

"Well, I simply don't know how much longer Troy can hold up its end of the war. If things don't improve, we may have to capitulate by next winter."

Gasps of horror blow across the table, rattling the tent flaps and ruffling the aristocrats' capes.

But now, for the first time, clever, canny Odysseus addresses the council, and the winds of discontent grow still. "Our course is obvious," he says. "Our destiny is clear," he asserts. "We must put Helen — the old Helen, the pristine Helen — back on the walls."

"The pristine Helen?" says Hiketaon. "Are you not talking fantasy, resourceful Odysseus? Are you not singing a myth?"

The lord of all Ithaca strolls the length of Priam's tent, plucking at his beard. "It will require some wisdom from Pallas Athena, some technology from Hephaestus, but I believe the project is possible."

"Excuse me," says Paris. "*What* project is possible?"

"Refurbishing your little harlot," says Odysseus. "Making the dear, sweet strumpet shine like new."

Back and forth, to and fro, Helen moves through her boudoir, wearing a ragged path of angst into the carpet. An hour passes. Then two. Why are they taking so long?

What most gnaws at her, the thought that feasts on her entrails, is the possibility that, should the council not accept her surrender, she will have to raise the stakes. And how might she accomplish the deed? By what means might she book passage on Charon's one-way ferry? Something from her lover's arsenal, most likely — a sword, spear, dagger, or death-dripping arrow. O, please, my lord Apollo, she prays to the city's prime protector, don't let it come to that.

At sunset Paris enters the room, his pace leaden, his jowls dragging his mouth into a grimace. For the first time ever, Helen observes tears in her lover's eyes.

"It is finished," he moans, doffing his plumed helmet. "Peace has come. At dawn you must go to the long ships. Menelaus will bear you back to Sparta, where you will once again live as mother to his children, friend to his concubines, and emissary to his bed."

Relief pours out of Helen in a deep, orgasmic rush, but the pleasure is short-lived. She loves this man, flaws and all, flab and the rest. "I shall miss you, dearest Paris," she tells him. "Your bold abduction of me remains the peak experience of my life."

"I agreed to the treaty only because Menelaus believes you might otherwise kill yourself. You're a surprising woman, Helen. Sometimes I think I hardly know you."

"Hush, my darling," she says, gently placing her palm across his mouth. "No more words."

Slowly they unclothe each other, methodically unlocking the doors to bliss — the straps and sashes, the snaps and catches — and thus begins their final, epic night together.

"I'm sorry I've been so judgmental," says Paris.

"I accept your apology."

"You are so beautiful. So impossibly beautiful . . ."

As dawn's rosy fingers stretch across the Trojan sky, Hector's faithful driver, Eniopeus the son of horse-loving Thebaios, steers his sturdy war chariot along the banks of the Menderes, bearing Helen to the Achaean stronghold. They reach the *Arkadia* just as the sun is cresting, so their arrival in the harbor becomes a flaming parade, a show of sparks and gold, as if they ride upon the burning wheels of Hyperion himself.

Helen starts along the dock, moving past the platoons of squawking gulls adrift on the early morning breeze. Menelaus comes forward to greet her, accompanied by a man for whom Helen has always harbored a vague dislike — broad-chested, black-bearded Teukros, illegitimate son of Telemon.

"The tide is ripe," says her husband. "You and Teukros must board forthwith. You will find him a lively traveling companion. He knows a hundred fables and plays the harp."

"Can't *you* take me home?"

Menelaus squeezes his wife's hand and, raising it to his lips, plants a gentle kiss. "I must see to the loading of my ships," he explains, "the disposition of my battalions — a full week's job, I'd guess."

"Surely you can leave that to Agamemnon."

"Give me seven days, Helen. In seven days I'll be home, and we can begin picking up the pieces."

"We're losing the tide," says Teukros, anxiously intertwining his fingers.

Do I trust my husband? Helen wonders as she strides up the *Arkadia's* gangplank. Does he really mean to lift the siege?

All during their slow voyage out of the harbor, Helen is haunted. Nebulous fears, nagging doubts, and odd presentiments swarm through her brain like Harpies. She beseeches her beloved Apollo to speak with her, calm her, assure her all is well, but the only sounds reaching her ears are the creaking of the oars and the windy, watery voice of the Hellespont.

By the time the *Arkadia* finds the open sea, Helen has resolved to jump overboard and swim back to Troy.

"And then Teukros tried to kill you," says Daphne.

"He came at you with his sword," adds Damon.

This is the twins' favorite part, the moment of grue and gore. Eyes flashing, voice climbing to a melodramatic pitch, I tell them how, before I could put my escape plan into action, Teukros began chasing me around the *Arkadia*, slashing his two-faced blade. I tell them how I got the upper hand, tripping the bastard as he was about to run me through.

"You stabbed him with his own sword, didn't you, Mommy?" asks Damon.

"I had no choice."

"And then his guts spilled, huh?" asks Daphne.

"Agamemnon had ordered Teukros to kill me," I explain. "I was ruining everything."

"They spilled out all over the deck, right?" asks Damon.

"Yes, dear, they certainly did. I'm quite convinced Paris wasn't part of the plot, or Menelaus either. Your mother falls for fools, not maniacs."

"What color were they?" asks Damon.

"Color?"

"His guts."

"Red, mostly, with daubs of purple and black."

"Neat."

I tell the twins of my long, arduous swim through the strait.

I tell them how I crossed Ilium's war-torn fields, dodging arrows and eluding patrols.

I tell how I waited by the Skaian Gate until a farmer arrived with a cartload of provender for the besieged city . . . how I sneaked inside the walls, secluded amid stalks of wheat . . . how I went to Pergamos, hid myself in the temple of Apollo, and breathlessly waited for dawn.

Dawn comes up, binding the eastern clouds in crimson girdles. Helen leaves the citadel, tiptoes to the wall, and mounts the hundred granite steps to the battlements. She is unsure of her next move. She has some vague hope of addressing the infantrymen as they assemble at the gate. Her arguments have failed to impress the generals, but perhaps she can touch the heart of the common foot soldier.

It is at this ambiguous point in her fortunes that Helen runs into herself.

She blinks — once, twice. She swallows a sphere of air. Yes, it is she, herself, marching along the parapets. Herself? No, not exactly: an idealized rendition, the Helen of ten years ago, svelte and smooth.

As the troops march through the portal and head toward the plain, the strange incarnation calls down to them.

"Onward, men!" it shouts, raising a creamy white arm. "Fight for me!" Its movements are deliberate and jerky, as if sunbaked Troy has been magically transplanted to some frigid clime. "I'm worth it!"

The soldiers turn, look up. "We'll fight for you, Helen!" a bowman calls toward the parapet.

"We love you!" a sword-wielder shouts.

Awkwardly, the incarnation waves. Creakily, it blows an arid kiss. "Onward, men! Fight for me! I'm worth it!"

"You're beautiful, Helen!" a spear-thrower cries.

Helen strides up to her doppelgänger and, seizing the left shoulder, pivots the creature toward her.

"Onward, men!" it tells Helen. "Fight for me! I'm worth it!"

"You're beautiful," the spear-thrower continues, "and so is your mother!"

The eyes, Helen is not surprised to discover, are glass. The limbs are fashioned from wood, the head from marble, the teeth from ivory, the lips from wax, the tresses from the fleece of a darkling ram. Helen does not know for certain what forces power this creature, what magic moves its tongue, but she surmises that the genius of Athena is at work here, the witchery of ox-orbed Hera. Chop the creature open, she senses, and out will pour a thousand cogs and pistons from Hephaestus's fiery workshop.

Helen wastes no time. She hugs the creature, lifts it off its feet. Heavy, but not so heavy as to dampen her resolve.

"Onward, men!" it screams as Helen throws it over her shoulder. "Fight for me! I'm worth it!"

And so it comes to pass that, on a hot, sweaty Asia Minor morning, fair Helen turns the tables on history, gleefully abducting herself from the lofty stone city of Troy.

Paris is pulling a poisoned arrow from his quiver, intent on shooting a dollop of hemlock into the breast of an Achaean captain, when his brother's chariot charges past.

Paris nocks the arrow. He glances at the chariot.

He aims.

Glances again.

Fires. Misses.

Helen.

Helen? *Helen*, by Apollo's lyre, his Helen — no, two Helens, the true and the false, side by side, the true guiding the horses into the thick of the fight, her wooden twin staring dreamily into space. Paris can't decide which woman he is more astonished to see.

"Soldiers of Troy!" cries the fleshly Helen. "Heroes of Argos! Behold how your leaders seek to dupe you! You are fighting for a fraud, a swindle, a thing of gears and glass!"

A stillness envelops the battlefield. The men are stunned, not so much by the ravings of the charioteer as by the face of her companion, so pure and perfect despite the leather thong sealing her jaw shut. It is a face to sheathe a thousand swords — lower a thousand spears — unnock a thousand arrows.

Which is exactly what now happens. A thousand swords: sheathed. A thousand spears: lowered. A thousand arrows: unnocked.

The soldiers crowd around the chariot, pawing at the ersatz Helen. They touch the wooden arms, caress the marble brow, stroke the ivory teeth, pat the waxen lips, squeeze the woolly hair, rub the glass eyes.

"See what I mean?" cries the true Helen. "Your kings are diddling you . . ."

Paris can't help it: he's proud of her, by Hermes's wings. He's puffing up with admiration. This woman has nerve — she has *arete* and chutzpah.

This woman, Paris realizes as a fat, warm tear of nostalgia rolls down his cheek, is going to the end the war.

"The end," I say.

"And then what happened?" Damon asks.

"Nothing. *Finis.* Go to sleep."

"You can't fool us," says Daphne. "All *sorts* of things happened after that. You went to live on the island of Lesbos."

"Not immediately," I note. "I wandered the world for seven years, having many fine and fabulous adventures. Good night."

"And then you went to Lesbos," Daphne insists.

"And then *we* came into the world," Damon asserts.

"True," I say. The twins are always interested in hearing how they came into the world. They never tire of the tale.

"The women of Lesbos import over a thousand liters of frozen semen annually," Damon explains to Daphne.

"From Thrace," Daphne explains to Damon. "In exchange for olives."

"A thriving trade."

"Right, honey," I say. "Bedtime."

"And so you got pregnant," says Daphne.

"And had us," says Damon.

"And brought us to Egypt." Daphne tugs at my sleeve as if operating a bell rope. "I came out first, didn't I?" she says. "I'm the *oldest*."

"Yes, dear."

"Is that why I'm smarter than Damon?"

"You're both equally smart. I'm going to blow out the candle now."

Daphne hugs her papyrus doll and says, "Did you really end the war?"

"The treaty was signed the day after I fled Troy. Of course, peace didn't restore the dead, but at least Troy was never sacked and burned. Now go to sleep — both of you."

Damon says, "Not before we've . . ."

"What?"

"You know."

"All right," I say. "One quick peek, and then you're off to the land of Morpheus."

I saunter over to the closet and, drawing back the linen curtain, reveal my stalwart twin standing upright amid the children's robes. She smiles through the gloom. She's a tireless smiler, this woman.

"Hi, Aunt Helen!" says Damon as I throw the bronze toggle protruding from the nape of my sister's neck.

She waves to my children and says, "Onward, men! Fight for me!"

"You bet, Aunt Helen!" says Daphne.

"I'm worth it!" says my sister.

"You sure are!" says Damon.

"Onward, men! Fight for me! I'm worth it!"

I switch her off and close the curtain. Tucking in the twins, I give each a big soupy kiss on the cheek. "Love you, Daphne. Love you, Damon."

I start to douse the candle — then stop. As long as it's on my mind, I should get the chore done. Returning to the closet, I push the curtain aside, lift the penknife from my robe, and pry back the blade. And then, as the Egyptian night grows moist and thick, I carefully etch yet another wrinkle across my sister's brow, right beneath her salt-and-pepper bangs.

It's important, after all, to keep up appearances.

The War of the Worldviews

August 7

One thing I've learned from this catastrophe is to start giving Western science and Newtonian rationality their due. For six days running, professional astronomers in the United States and Europe warned us of puzzling biological and cybernetic activity on the surfaces of both Martian satellites. We, the public, weren't interested. Next the stargazers announced that Phobos and Deimos had each sent a fleet of disc-shaped spaceships, heavily armed, hurtling toward planet Earth. We decided they were joking. Then the astronomers reported that each saucer measured only one meter across, so that the invading armadas evoked "a vast recall of defective automobile tires." The talk-show comedians had a field day.

Within an hour of landing in Central Park, the Martians undertook to suck away the city's electricity and seal it in a small spherical container suggesting an aluminum racquetball. I believe they wanted to make sure we wouldn't bother them as they went about their incomprehensible agenda, but Valerie says they were just being quixotic. The third possibility — they stole our electricity for their own uses — is not tenable: they brought plenty of juice with them.

I am writing by candlelight in our Delancey Street apartment, scribbling on a legal pad with a ballpoint pen. New York City is without functional lamps, subways, elevators, traffic signals, household appliances, or personal computers. Here and there, I suppose, life goes on as usual, thanks to storage batteries, solar cells, and diesel-fueled generators. The rest of us are living in the eighteenth century, and we don't like it.

I was taking Valerie's kid to the Central Park Zoo when the Phobosians and the Deimosians began disinterring the city's power cables and sucking up the current. Bobby and I witnessed the whole thing. The Martians were obviously having a good time. Each alien is only about ten inches high, but I could still see the jollity coursing through their little frames. Capricious chipmunks. I hate them all. Bobby became terrified when the Martians started wrecking things. He cried and moaned. I did my best to comfort him. Bobby's a good kid. Last week he called me Second Dad.

No sooner did the city become electrically inert than the hostilities began. The Phobosian and the Deimosian infantries went at each other with implements so advanced as to make Earth's projectiles seem like peashooters. Heat rays, disintegrator beams, quark bombs, sonic grenades, laser cannons. The Deimosians look rather like the animated mushrooms from *Fantasia*. Every Phobosian resembles a turkey baster poised on a roller skate. All during the fight, both races communicated among themselves via chirping sounds reminiscent of dolphins enjoying sexual climax. Their ferocity knew no limits. In one hour I witnessed enough war crimes to fill an encyclopedia, though on the scale of an O-gauge model railroad.

As far as I could tell, the Battle of Central Park ended in a stalemate. The real loser was New York, victim of a hundred ill-aimed volleys. At least half the buildings on Fifth Avenue are gone, including the Mount Sinai Medical Center. Fires rage everywhere, eastward as far as Third Avenue, westward to Columbus. Bobby and I were lucky to get back home alive.

Such an inferno is clearly beyond the capacity of our local fire departments. Normally we would seek help from Jersey and Connecticut, but the Martians have fashioned some sort of force-field dome, lowering it over the entire island as blithely as a chef placing a lid on a casserole dish. Nothing can get in; nothing can get out. We are at the invaders' mercy. If the Phobosians and the Deimosians continue trying to settle their differences through violence, the city will burn to the ground.

August 8

The Second Battle of Central Park was even worse than the first. We lost the National Academy of Design, the Guggenheim Museum, and the Carlyle Hotel. It ended with the Phobosians driving the Deimosians all the way down to Rockefeller Center. The Deimosians then rallied, stood their ground, and forced a Phobosian retreat to West 71st Street.

Valerie and I learned about this latest conflict only because a handful of resourceful radio announcers have improvised three ad hoc citizens-band stations along what's left of Lexington Avenue. We have a decent CB receiver, so we'll be getting up-to-the-minute bulletins until our batteries die. Each time the newscaster named Clarence Morant attempts to describe the collateral damage from this morning's hostilities, he breaks down and weeps.

Even when you allow for the diminutive Martian physique, the two armies are not very far apart. By our scale, they are separated by three blocks — by theirs, perhaps ten kilometers. Clarence Morant predicts there'll be another big battle tomorrow. Valerie chides me for not believing her when she had those premonitions last year of our apartment building on fire. I tell her she's being a Monday morning Nostradamus.

How many private journals concerning the Martian invasion exist at the moment? As I put pen to paper, I suspect that hundreds, perhaps even thousands, of my fellow survivors are recording their impressions of the cataclysm. But I am not like these other diary-keepers. I am unique. I alone have the power to stop the Martians before they demolish Manhattan — or so I imagine.

August 9

All quiet on the West Side front — though nobody believes the cease-fire will last much longer. Clarence Morant says the city is living on borrowed time.

Phobos and Deimos. When the astronomers first started warning us of nefarious phenomena on the Martian satellites, I experienced a vague feeling of personal connection to those particular moons. Last night it all flooded back. Phobos and Deimos are indeed a part of my past — a past I've been trying to forget — those bad old days when I was the worst psychiatric intern ever to serve an apprenticeship at Bellevue. I'm much happier in my present position as a bohemian hippie bum, looking after Bobby and living off the respectable income Valerie makes running two SoHo art galleries.

His name was Rupert Klieg, and he was among the dozen or so patients who made me realize I'd never be good with insane people. I found Rupert's rants alternately unnerving and boring. They sounded like something you'd read in a cheesy special-interest zine for psychotics — *Paranoid Confessions, True Hallucinations, American Catatonic.* Rupert was especially obsessed with an organization called the Asaph Hall Society, named for the self-taught scientist who discovered Phobos and Deimos. All three members of the Asaph Hall Society were amateur astronomers and certifiable lunatics who'd dedicated themselves to monitoring the imminent invasion of planet Earth by the bellicose denizens of the Martian moons. Before Rupert told me his absurd fantasy, I didn't even realize that Mars *had* moons, nor did I care. But now I do, God knows.

The last I heard, they'd put Rupert Klieg away in the Lionel Frye Psychiatric Institute, Ninth Avenue near 58th Street. Valerie says I'm wasting my time, but I believe in my bones that the fate of Manhattan lies with that particular schizophrenic.

August 10

This morning a massive infantry assault by the Phobosians drove the Deimosians south to Times Square. When I heard that the Frye Institute was caught in the crossfire, I naturally feared the worst for Rupert. When I actually made the trek to Ninth and 58th, however, I discovered that the disintegrator beams, devastating in most regards, had missed the lower third of the building. I didn't see any Martians, but the whole neighborhood resounded with their tweets and twitters.

The morning's upheavals had left the Institute's staff in a state of acute distraction. I had no difficulty sneaking into the lobby, stealing a dry-cell lantern, and conducting a room-by-room hunt.

Rupert was in the basement ward, Room 16. The door stood ajar. I entered. He lay abed, grasping a toy plastic telescope about ten centimeters long. I couldn't decide whether his keepers had been kind or cruel to allow him this trinket. It was nice that the poor demented astronomer had a telescope, but what good did it do him in a room with no windows?

His face had become thinner, his body more gaunt, but otherwise he was the fundamentally beatific madman I remembered. "Thank you for the lantern, Dr. Onslo," he said as I approached. He swatted at a naked lightbulb hanging from the ceiling like a miniature punching bag. "It's been pretty gloomy around here."

"Call me Steve. I never finished my internship."

"I'm not surprised, Dr. Onslo. You were a lousy therapist."

"Let me tell you why I've come."

"I know why you've come, and as chairperson of the Databank Committee of the Asaph Hall Society, I can tell you everything you want to know about Phobos and Deimos."

"I'm especially interested in learning how your organization knew an invasion was imminent."

The corners of Rupert's mouth lifted in a grotesque smile. He opened the drawer in his nightstand, removed a crinkled sheet of paper, and deposited it in my hands. "Mass: 1.08×10^{16} kilograms," he said as I studied the fact sheet, which had a cherry cough drop stuck to one corner. "Diameter: 22.2 kilometers. Mean density: 2.0 grams per cubic centimeter. Mean distance from Mars: 9,380 kilometers. Rotational period: 0.31910 days. Mean orbital velocity: 2.14 kilometers per second. Orbital eccentricity: 0.01. Orbital inclination: 1.0 degrees. Escape velocity: 0.0103 kilometers per second. Visual geometric albedo: 0.06. In short, ladies and gentlemen, I give you Phobos—"

"Fascinating," I said evenly.

"As opposed to Deimos. Mass: 1.8×10^{15} kilograms. Diameter: 12.6 kilometers. Mean density: 1.7 grams per cubic centimeter. Mean distance from Mars: 23,460 kilometers. Rotational period: 1.26244 days. Mean orbital velocity: 1.36 kilometers per second. Orbital eccentricity: 0.00. Orbital inclination: 0.9 to 2.7 degrees. Escape velocity: 0.0057 kilometers per second. Visual geometric albedo: 0.07. Both moons look like baked potatoes."

"By some astonishing intuition, you knew that these two satellites intended to invade the Earth."

"Intuition, my Aunt Fanny. We deduced it through empirical observation." Rupert brought the telescope to his eye and focused on the dormant lightbulb. "Consider this. A scant eighty million years ago, there were no Phobes or Deems. I'm not kidding. They were all one species, living beneath the desiccated surface of Mars. Over the centuries, a deep rift in philosophic sensibility opened up within their civilization. Eventually they decided to abandon their planet, never an especially congenial place, and emigrate to the local moons. Those favoring Sensibility A moved to Phobos. Those favoring Sensibility B settled on Deimos."

"Why would the Martians find Phobos and Deimos more congenial?" I jammed the fact sheet in my pocket. "I mean, aren't they just . . . big rocks?"

"Don't bring your petty little human perspective to the matter, Dr. Onslo. To a vulture, carrion tastes like chocolate cake. Once they were on their respective worlds, the Phobes and the Deems followed separate evolutionary paths — hence, the anatomical dimorphism we observe today."

"What was the nature of the sensibility rift?"

Rupert used his telescope to study a section of the wall where the plaster had crumbled away, exposing the latticework beneath. "I have no idea."

"None whatsoever?"

"The Asaph Hall Society dissolved before we could address that issue. All I know is that the Phobes and the Deems decided to settle the question once and for all through armed combat on neutral ground."

"So they came here?"

"Mars would've seemed like a step backwards. Venus has rotten weather."

"Are you saying that whichever side wins the war will claim victory in what is essentially a philosophical controversy?"

"Correct."

"They believe that truth claims can be corroborated through violence?"

"More or less."

"That doesn't make any sense to me."

"If you were a fly, pig shit would smell like candy. We'd better go see Melvin."

"Who?"

"Melvin Haskin, chairperson of our Epistemology Committee. If anybody's figured out the Phobos-Deimos rift, it's Melvin. The last I heard, they'd put him in a rubber room at Werner Krauss Memorial. What's today?"

"Tuesday."

"Too bad."

"Oh?"

"On Tuesday Melvin always wills himself into a catatonic stupor. He'll be incommunicado until tomorrow morning."

I had no troubling sneaking Rupert out of the Frye Institute. Everybody on the staff was preoccupied with gossip and triage. The lunatic brought along his telescope and a bottle of red pills that he called "the thin scarlet line that separates me from my madness."

Although still skeptical of my belief that Rupert held the key to Manhattan's salvation, Valerie welcomed him warmly into our apartment — she's a better therapist than I ever was — and offered him the full measure of her hospitality. Because we have a gas range, we were able to prepare a splendid meal of spinach lasagna and toasted garlic bread. Rupert ate all the leftovers. Bobby asked him what it was like to be insane. "There is nothing that being insane is like," Rupert replied.

After dinner, at Rupert's request, we all played Scrabble by candlelight, followed by a round of Clue. Rupert won both games. At ten o'clock he took a red pill and stretched his spindly body along the length of our couch, which he said was much more comfortable than his bed at the Frye Institute. Five minutes later he was asleep.

As I write this entry, Clarence Morant is offering his latest dispatches from the war zone. Evidently the Deimosians are still dug in throughout Times Square. Tomorrow the Phobosians will attempt to dislodge them. Valerie and I both hear a catch in Morant's voice as he tells how his aunt took him to see *Cats* when he was nine years old. He inhales deeply and says, "The Winter Garden Theatre is surely doomed."

August 11

Before we left the apartment this morning, Rupert remembered that Melvin Haskin is inordinately fond of bananas. Luckily, Valerie had purchased two bunches at the corner bodega right before the Martians landed. I tossed them into my rucksack, along with some cheese sandwiches and Rupert's telescope, and then we headed uptown.

Reaching 40th Street, we saw that the Werner Krauss Memorial Clinic had

become a seething mass of orange flames and billowing gray smoke, doubtless an ancillary catastrophe accruing to the Battle of Times Square. Ashes
and sparks speckled the air. Our eyes teared up from the carbon. The sidewalks teemed with a despairing throng of doctors, administrators, guards, and
inmates. Presumably the Broadway theaters and hotels were also on fire, but I
didn't want to think about it.

Rupert instantly alighted on Melvin Haskin, though I probably could've
identified him unassisted. Even in a milling mass of psychotics, Melvin stood
out. He'd strapped a dish-shaped antenna onto his head, the concavity pointed
skyward — an inverted yarmulke. A pair of headphones covered his ears,
jacked into an antique vacuum-tube amplifier that he cradled in his arms like
a baby. Two coiled wires, one red, one black, connected the antenna to the
amplifier, its functionless power cord bumping against Melvin's left leg, the
naked prongs glinting in the August sun. He wore a yellow terrycloth bathrobe
and matching Big Bird slippers. His frame was massive, his skin pale, his stomach protuberant, his mouth bereft of teeth.

Rupert made the introductions. Once again he insisted on calling me Dr.
Onslo. I pointed to Melvin's antenna and asked him whether he was receiving
transmissions from the Martians.

"What?" He pulled off the headphones and allowed them to settle around
his neck like a yoke.

"Your antenna, the headphones — looks like you're communicating with
the Martians."

"Are you crazy?" Scowling darkly, Melvin turned toward Rupert and jerked
an accusing thumb in my direction. "Dr. Onslo thinks my amplifier still works
even though half the tubes are burned out."

"He's a psychiatrist," Rupert explained. "He knows nothing about engineering. How was your catatonic stupor?"

"Restful. You'll have to come along some time."

"I don't have the courage," said Rupert, shaking his head.

Melvin was enchanted by the gift of the bananas, and even more enchanted
to be reunited with his fellow paranoid. As the two middle-aged madmen
headed east, swapping jokes and stories like old school chums, I could barely
keep up with their frenetic pace. After passing Sixth Avenue they turned
abruptly into Bryant Park, where they found an abandoned soccer ball on the
grass. For twenty minutes they kicked it back and forth, then grew weary of the
sport. They sat down on a bench. I joined them. Survivors streamed by holding
handkerchiefs over their faces.

"The city's dying," I told Melvin. "We need your help."

"Rupert, have you still got the touch?" Melvin asked his friend.

"I believe I do," said Rupert.

"Rupert can fix burned-out vacuum tubes merely by laying his hands on them," Melvin informed me. "I call him the Cathode Christ."

Even before Melvin finished his sentence, Rupert had begun fondling the amplifier. He rubbed each tube as if the warmth of his hand might bring it to life.

"You've done it again!" cried Melvin, putting on his headphones. "I'm pulling in a signal from Ceres! I think it might be just the place for us to retire, Rupert! No capital gains tax!" He removed the phones and looked me in the eye. "Do you solicit me as head of the Epistemology Committee, or in my capacity as a paranoid schizophrenic?"

"The former," I said. "I'm hoping you've managed to define the Phobos-Deimos rift."

"You came to the right place." Melvin ate a banana, depositing the peel in the dish antenna atop his head. "It's the most basic of *Weltanschauung* dichotomies. Here on Earth many philosophers would trace the problem back to all that bad blood between the Platonists and the Aristotelians — you know, idealism versus realism — but it's actually the sort of controversy you can have only after a full-blown curiosity about nature has come on the scene."

"Do you speak of the classic schism between scientific materialists and those who champion presumed numinous realities?" I asked.

"Exactly," said Melvin.

"There — what did I tell you?" said Rupert merrily. "I *knew* old Melvin would set us straight."

"On the one hand, Deimos, moon of the logical positivists," said Melvin. "On the other hand, Phobos, bastion of revealed religion."

"Melvin, you're a genius," said Rupert, retrieving his telescope from my rucksack.

"Should we infer that the Phobosians are loath to evoke Darwinian mechanisms in explaining why they look so different from the Deimosians?" I asked.

"Quite so." Melvin unstrapped the dish antenna, scratched his head, and nodded. "The Phobes believe that God created them in his own image."

"They think God looks like a turkey baster on a roller skate?"

"That is one consequence of their religion, yes." Melvin donned his antenna and retrieved a bottle of red capsules from his bathrobe pocket. He fished one out and ate it. "Want to hear the really nutty part? The Phobes and the Deems are genetically wired to abandon any given philosophical position the moment it encounters an honest and coherent refutation. The Martians won't accept no for an answer, and they won't accept yes for an answer either — instead they want rational arguments."

"Rational arguments?" I said. "Then why the hell are they killing each other and bringing down New York with them?"

"If you were a dog, a dead possum would look like the Mona Lisa," said Rupert.

Melvin explained, "No one has ever presented them with a persuasive discourse favoring either the Phobosian or the Deimosian worldview."

"You mean we could end this nightmare by supplying the Martians with some crackerjack reasons why theistic revelation is the case?" I said.

"Either that, or some crackerjack reasons why scientific materialism is the case," said Melvin. "I realize it's fashionable these days to speak of an emergent compatibility between the two idioms, but you don't have to be a rocket scientist to realize that the concept of materialist supernaturalism is oxymoronic if not plainly moronic, and nobody knows this better than the Martians." He pulled the headphones over his ears. "Ha! Just as I suspected. On Ceres every citizen does his neighbor the courtesy of thinking his thoughts for him."

"The problem, as I see it, is twofold," said Rupert, pointing his telescope south toward the Empire State Building. "We must construct the rational arguments in question, and we must communicate them to the Martians."

"They don't speak English, do they?" I said.

"Of course they don't speak English," said Rupert, exasperated. "They're Martians. They don't even have language as we commonly understand the term." He poked Melvin on the shoulder. "This is clearly a job for Annie."

"What?" said Melvin, removing the headphones.

"It's a job for Annie," said Rupert.

"Agreed," said Melvin.

"Annie Porlock," Rupert explained to me. "She built her own harpsichord."

"Soul of an artist," said Melvin.

"Heart of an angel," said Rupert.

"Crazy as a bedbug," added Melvin.

"For our immediate purpose, the most relevant fact about Annie is that she chairs our Interplanetary Communications Committee, in which capacity she cracked the Martian tweets and twitters, or so she claimed right before the medics took her away."

"How do we find her?" I asked.

"For many years she was locked up in some wretched Long Island laughing academy, but then the family lawyer got into the act," said Melvin. "I'm pretty sure they transferred her to a more humane facility here in New York."

"What facility?" I said. "Where?"

"I can't remember," said Melvin.

"You've *got* to remember."

"Sorry."

"*Try.*"

Melvin picked up the soccer ball and set it in his lap. "Fresh from the guillotine, the head of Maximilien François Marie Isidore de Robespierre," he said, as if perhaps I'd forgotten he was a paranoid schizophrenic. "Oh, Robespierre, Robespierre, was the triumph of inadvertence over intention ever so total?"

I brought both lunatics home with me. Valerie greeted us with the sad news that the Winter Garden, the Walter Kerr, the Eugene O'Neill, and a half-dozen other White Way theaters had been lost in the Battle of Times Square. I told her there was hope for the Big Apple yet.

"It all depends on our ability to devise a set of robust arguments favoring either scientific materialism or theistic revelation and then communicating the salient points to the Martians in their nonlinguistic language, which was apparently deciphered several years ago by a paranoid schizophrenic named Annie Porlock," I told Valerie.

"That's not a sentence you hear every day," she replied.

It turns out that Melvin is even more devoted to board games than Rupert, so the evening went well. We played Scrabble, Clue, and Monopoly, after which Melvin introduced us to an amusement of his own invention, a variation on Trivial Pursuit called Teleological Ambition. Whereas the average Trivial Pursuit conundrum is frivolous, the challenges underlying Teleological Ambition are profound. Melvin remembered at least half of the original questions, writing them out on three-by-five cards. If God is infinite and self-sufficient, why would he care whether his creatures worshiped him or not? Which thought is the more overwhelming: the possibility that the Milky Way is teeming with sentient life, or the possibility that Earthlings and Martians occupy an otherwise empty galaxy? That sort of thing. Bobby hated every minute, and I can't say I blame him.

August 12

Shortly after breakfast this morning, while he was consuming what may have been the last fresh egg in SoHo, Melvin announced that he knew how to track down Annie Porlock.

"I was thinking of how she's a walking Rosetta stone, our key to deciphering the Martian tongue," he explained, strapping on his dish antenna. "Rosetta made me think of Roosevelt, and then I remembered that she's living in a houseboat moored by Roosevelt Island in the middle of the East River."

I went to the pantry and filled my rucksack with a loaf of stale bread, a jar of instant coffee, a Kellogg's Variety Pack, and six cans of Campbell's soup. The can opener was nowhere to be found, so I tossed in my Swiss army knife. I guided my lunatics out the door.

There were probably only a handful of taxis still functioning in New York — most of them had run out of gas, and their owners couldn't refuel because the pumps worked on electricity — but somehow we managed to nab one at the corner of Houston and Forsyth. The driver, a Russian émigré named Vladimir, was not surprised to learn we had no cash, all the ATMs being dormant, and he agreed to claim his fare in groceries. He piloted us north along First Avenue, running straight through fifty-seven defunct traffic signals, and left us off at the Queensboro Bridge. I gave him two cans of chicken-noodle soup and a single-serving box of Frosted Flakes.

The Martian force-field dome had divided Roosevelt Island right down the middle, but luckily Annie Porlock had moored her houseboat on the Manhattan side. "Houseboat" isn't the right word, for the thing was neither a house nor a boat but a decrepit two-room shack sitting atop a half-submerged barge called the *Folly to Be Wise*. Evidently the hull was leaking. If Annie's residence sunk any lower, I thought as we entered the shack, the East River would soon be lapping at her ankles.

A ruddy, zaftig, silver-haired woman in her mid-fifties lay dozing in a wicker chair, her lap occupied by a book about Buddhism and a large calico cat. Her harpsichord rose against the far wall, beside a lamp table holding a large bottle of purple capsules the size of jellybeans. Our footfalls woke her. Recognizing Melvin, Annie let loose a whoop of delight. The cat bailed out. She stood up.

"Melvin Haskin?" said Annie, sashaying across the room. "Is that really you? They let you out?"

Annie extended her right hand. Melvin kissed it.

"Taa-daa!" shouted Rupert, stepping out from behind Melvin's bulky frame. He pressed his mouth against Annie's cheek.

"Rupert Klieg — they sprang you too!" said Annie. "If I knew you were coming, I'd have baked a fruitcake."

"The first annual reunion of the Asaph Hall Society will now come to order," said Melvin, chuckling.

"Have you heard about the Martians?" said Rupert.

Annie's eyes widened grotesquely, offering a brief intimation of the derangement that lay behind. "They've landed? Really? You can't be serious!"

"Cross my heart," said Rupert. "Even as we speak, the Phobes and the Deems are thrashing out their differences in Times Square."

"Just as we predicted," said Annie. Turning from Rupert, she fixed her frowning gaze on me. "I guess that'll show you doubting Thomases . . ."

Rupert introduced me as "Dr. Onslo, the first in a long line of distinguished psychiatrists who tried to help me before hyperlithium came on the market," and I didn't bother to contradict him. Instead I explained the situation to Annie, emphasizing Melvin's recent deductions concerning Martian dialectics. She was astonished to learn that the Deimosians and the Phobosians were occupying Manhattan in direct consequence of the old materialism-supernaturalism dispute, and equally astonished to learn that, in contrast to most human minds, the Martian psyche was hardwired to favor rational discourse over pleasurable opinion.

"That must be the strangest evolutionary adaptation ever," said Annie.

"Certainly the strangest we know about," said Melvin.

"Can you help us?" I asked.

Approaching her harpsichord, Annie sat on her swiveling stool and rested her hands on the keyboard. "This looks like a harpsichord, but it's really an interplanetary communication device. I've spent the last three years recalibrating the jacks, upgrading the plectrums, and adjusting the strings."

Her fingers glided across the keys. A jumble of notes leaped forth, so weird and discordant they made Schoenberg sound melodic.

"There," said Annie proudly, pivoting toward her audience. "In the Martian language I just said, 'Before enlightenment, chop wood, carry water. After enlightenment, chop wood, carry water.' "

"Wow," said Klieg.

"Terrific," said Melvin.

Annie turned back to the keyboard and called forth another unruly refrain.

"That meant, 'There are two kinds of naivety, the naivety of optimism and the naivety of pessimism,' " she explained.

"Who would've guessed there could be so much meaning in cacophony?" I said.

"To a polar bear, the Arctic Ocean feels like a Jacuzzi," said Rupert.

Annie called forth a third strain — another grotesque non-melody.

"And the translation?" asked Rupert.

"It's an idiomatic expression," she replied.

"Can you give us a rough paraphrase?"

" 'Hi there, baby. You have great tits. Would you like to fuck?' "

Melvin said, "The problem, of course, is that the Martians are likely to kill each other — along with the remaining population of New York — before we can decide conclusively which worldview enjoys the imprimatur of rationality."

"All is not lost," said Rupert.

"What do you mean?" I asked.

"We might, just might, have enough time to formulate strong arguments supporting a side of the controversy chosen . . . arbitrarily," said Rupert.

"Arbitrarily?" echoed Annie, voice cracking.

"Arbitrarily," repeated Rupert. "It's the only way."

The four of us traded glances of reluctant consensus. I removed a quarter from my pants pocket.

"Heads: revelation, God, the Phobes," said Melvin.

"Tails: materialism, science, the Deems," said Rupert.

I flipped the quarter. It landed under Annie's piano stool, frightening the cat. Tails.

And so we went at it, a melee of discourse and disputation that lasted through the long, hot afternoon and well into evening. We napped on the floor. We drank gallons of instant coffee. We ate cold soup and dry raisin bran.

By eight o'clock we'd put the Deimosian worldview on solid ground — or so we believed. The gist of our argument was that sentient species emerged in consequence of certain discoverable properties embedded in nature. Whether Earthling or Martian, aquatic or terrestrial, feathered or furred, scaled or smooth, all life forms were inextricably woven into a material biosphere, and it was this astonishing and demonstrable connection, not the agenda of some hypothetical supernatural agency, that made us one with the cosmos and the bearers of its meaning.

"And now, dear Annie, you must set it all to music," I told the communications chairperson, giving her a hug.

Rupert and Melvin decided to spend the night aboard the *Folly to Be Wise*, providing Annie with moral support and Nescafé while she labored over her translation. I knew that Valerie and Bobby would be worried about me, so I said my farewells and headed for home. So great was my exhilaration that I ran the whole three miles to Delancey Street without stopping — not bad for a weekend jogger.

I'm writing this entry in our bedroom. Bobby's asleep. Valerie wants to hear about my day, so I'd better sign off. The news from Clarence Morant is distressing. Defeated in the Battle of Times Square, the Deimosians have retreated to the New York Public Library and taken up positions on the steps between the stone lions. The Phobosians are camped outside Grand Central Station, barely a block away.

There are over two million volumes in the New York Public Library, Morant tells us, including hundreds of irreplaceable first editions. When the fighting starts, the Martians will be firing their heat rays amidst a paper cache of incalculable value.

August 13

Phobos and Deimos. When Asaph Hall went to name his discoveries, he logically evoked the two sons and companions of Ares, the Greek god of war. Phobos, avatar of fear. Deimos, purveyor of panic.

Fear and panic. Is there a difference? I believe so. Beyond the obvious semantic distinction — fear the chronic condition, panic the acute — it seems to me that the Phobosians and the Deimosians, whether through meaningless coincidence or Jungian synchronicity, picked the right moons. Phobos, fear. Is fear not a principal engine behind the supernaturalist worldview? (The universe is manifestly full of terrifying forces controlled by powerful gods. If we worship them, maybe they won't destroy us.) Deimos, panic. At first blush, the scientific worldview has nothing to do with panic. But consider the etymology here. *Panic* from Pan, Greek god of forests, pastures, flocks, and shepherds. Pan affirms the physical world. Pan says yes to material reality. Pan might panic on occasion, but he does not live in fear.

When I returned to the *Folly to Be Wise* this morning, the lunatics were asleep, Rupert lying in the far corner, Annie curled up in her tiny bedroom, Melvin snoring beside her. He still wore his dish antenna. The pro-Deimosian argument lay on the harpsichord, twelve pages of sheet music. Annie had titled it "Materialist Prelude and Fugue in C-Sharp Minor."

I woke my friends and told them about the imminent clash of arms at the New York Public Library. We agreed there was no time to hear the fugue right now — the world premiere would have to occur on the battlefield — but Annie could not resist pointing out some of its more compelling passages. "Look here," she said, indicating a staff in the middle of page three. "A celebration of the self-correcting ethos at the heart of the scientific enterprise." She turned to page seven and ran her finger on the topmost measures. "A brief history of postmodern academia's failure to relativize scientific knowledge." She grew my attention to a coda on page eleven. "Depending on the definitions you employ, the materialist worldview precludes neither a creator-god nor the possibility of transcendence through art, religion, or love."

I put the score in my rucksack, and then we took hold of the harpsichord, each of us lifting a corner. We proceeded with excruciating care, as if the instrument were made of glass, lest we misalign any of Annie's clever tinkerings and canny modifications. Slowly we carried the harpsichord across the deck, off the island, and over the bridge. At the intersection of Second Avenue and 57th Street, we paused to catch our breath.

"Fifteen blocks," said Rupert.

"Can we do it in fifteen minutes?" I asked.

"We're the Asaph Hall Society," said Annie. "We've never failed to thwart an extraterrestrial invasion."

And so our great mission began. 56th Street. 55th Street. 44th Street. 53rd Street. Traffic being minimal, we forsook the sidewalks with their frequent impediments — scaffolding, trash barrels, police barriers — and moved directly along the asphalt. Doubts tormented me. What if we'd picked the wrong side of the controversy? What if we'd picked the right side but our arguments sounded feeble to the Phobosians? What if panic seized Annie, raw Deimosian panic, and she choked up at the keyboard?

By the time we were in the Forties, we could hear the Martians' glissando chirpings. Our collective pace quickened. At last we reached 42nd Street. We turned right and bore the peace machine past the Chrysler Building and the Grand Hyatt Hotel. Arriving at Grand Central Station, we paused to behold the Phobosian infantry maneuvering for a frontal assault on the Deimosian army, still presumably holding the library steps. The air vibrated with extraterrestrial tweets and twitters, as if midtown Manhattan had become a vast pet store filled with demented parakeets.

We transported the harpsichord another block and set it down at the Madison Avenue intersection, from which vantage we could see both Grand Central Station and the library. The Phobosian army had indeed spent the night bivouacked between the stone lions. Inevitably I thought of Gettysburg — James Longstreet's suicidal sweep across the Pennsylvania farmlands, hurtling his divisions against George Meade's Army of the Potomac, which had numerical superiority, a nobler cause, and the high ground.

Rupert took the score from my sack, laid the twelve pages against the rack, and made ready to turn them. Melvin removed his dish antenna and got down on all fours before the instrument. Annie seated herself on his massive back. She laid her hands on the keyboard. A stiff breeze arose. If the score blew away, all would be lost.

Annie depressed a constellation of keys. Martian language came forth, filling the canyon between the skyscrapers.

A high bugling wail emerged from deep within the throats of the Deimosian officers, and the soldiers began their march. Annie played furiously. "Materialist Prelude and Fugue," page one . . . page two . . . page three . . . page four. The soldiers kept on coming. Page five . . . page six . . . page seven . . . page eight. The Deimosians continued their advance, parting around the harpsichord like an ocean current bisected by the prow of a ship. Page nine . . . page ten . . . page eleven . . . page twelve. Among the irreplaceable volumes in the New York Public Library, I recalled, were first editions of Nicolaus Copernicus's *De Revolutionibus*, William Gilbert's *De Magnete*, and Isaac Newton's *Principia Mathematica*.

Once again the Deimosian officers let loose a high bugling wail.

The soldiers abruptly halted their advance.

They threw down their weapons and broke into a run.

"Good God, is it working?" asked Rupert.

"I think so," I replied.

"It worked!" insisted Annie.

"Really?" said Melvin, whose perspective on the scene was compromised by his function as a piano stool.

"We've done it!" I cried. "We've really done it!"

Within a matter of seconds the Deimosians accomplished a reciprocal disarmament. They rushed toward their former enemies. The two forces met on Fifth Avenue, Phobosians and Deimosians embracing passionately, so that the intersection seemed suddenly transformed into an immense railroad platform on which countless wayward lovers were meeting sweethearts from whom they'd been involuntarily separated for years.

Now the ovation came, two hundred thousand extraterrestrials cheering and applauding Annie as she climbed off Melvin's back and stood up straight. She took a bow, and then another.

A singularly appreciative chirp emerged from a Phobosian general, whereupon a dozen of his fellows produced the identical sound.

Annie got the message. She seated herself on Melvin's back, turned to page one, and played "Materialist Prelude and Fugue in C-Sharp Minor" all over again.

August 18

The Martians have been gone for only five days, but already Manhattan is healing. The lights are back on. Relief arrives from every state in the Union, plus Canada.

Valerie, Bobby, and I are now honorary members of the Asaph Hall Society. We all gathered this afternoon at Gracie Mansion in Carl Schurz Park, not far from Annie's houseboat. Mayor Margolis will let us use his parlor whenever we want. In fact, there's probably no favor he won't grant us. After all, we saved his city.

Annie called the meeting to order. Everything went smoothly. We discussed old business (our ongoing efforts to contact the Galilean satellites), new business (improving patient services at the Frye Institute and the Krauss Clinic), and criteria for admitting new participants. As long as they remember to take their medicine, my lunatics remain the soul of reason. Melvin and Annie plan to marry in October.

"I'll bet we're all having the same thought right now," said Rupert before we went out to dinner.

"What if Dr. Onslo's quarter had come up heads?" said Melvin, nodding. "What if we'd devised arguments favoring the Phobosians instead? What then?"

"That branch of the reality tree will remain forever hidden from us," said Annie.

"I think it's entirely possible the Deimosians would've thrown down their arms," said Valerie.

"So do I," said Melvin. "Assuming our arguments were plausible."

"Know what I think?" said Rupert. "I think we all just got very lucky."

Did we merely get lucky? Hard to say. But I do know one thing. In two weeks the New York Philharmonic will perform a fully orchestrated version of "Materialist Prelude and Fugue in C-Sharp Minor" at Lincoln Center, which miraculously survived the war, and I wouldn't miss it for the world.

Bible Stories for Adults,
No. 17: The Deluge

Take your cup down to the Caspian, dip, and drink. It did not always taste of salt. Yahweh's watery slaughter may have purified the earth, but it left his seas a ruin, brackish with pagan blood and the tears of wicked orphans.

Sheila and her generation know the deluge is coming. Yahweh speaks to them through their sins. A thief cuts a purse, and the shekels clank together, pealing out a call to repentance. A priest kneels before a graven image of Dagon, and the statue opens its marble jaws, issuing not its own warnings but Yahweh's. A harlot threads herself with a thorny vine, tearing out unwanted flesh, and a divine voice rises from the bleeding fetus. You are a corrupt race, Yahweh says, abominable in my sight. My rains will scrub you from the earth.

Yahweh is as good as his word. The storm breaks. Creeks become rivers, rivers cataracts. Lakes blossom into broiling, wrathful seas.

Yes, Sheila is thoroughly foul in those days, her apple home to many worms, the scroll of her sins as long as the Araxes. She is gluttonous and unkempt. She sells her body. Her abortions number eleven. *I should have made it twelve*, she realizes on the day the deluge begins. But it is too late, she had already gone through with it — the labor more agonizing than any abortion, her breasts left pulpy and deformed — and soon the boy was seven, athletic, clever, fair of face, but today the swift feet are clamped in the cleft of an olive-tree root, the clever hands are still, the fair face lies buried in water.

A mother, Sheila has heard, should be a boat to her child, buoying him during floods, bearing him through storms, and yet it is Sam who rescues her. She is hoisting his corpse aloft, hoping to drain the death from his lungs, when suddenly his little canoe floats by. A scooped-out log, nothing more, but still his favorite toy. He liked to paddle it across the Araxes and catch turtles in the marsh.

Sheila climbs aboard, leaving Sam's meat to the sharks.

Captain's Log. 10 June 1057 After Creation

The beasts eat too much. At present rates of consumption, we'll be out of provisions in a mere fifteen weeks.

For the herbivores: 4,540 pounds of oats a day, 6,780 pounds of hay, 2,460 of vegetables, and 3,250 of fruit.

For the carnivores: 17,620 pounds of yak and caribou meat a day. And we may lose the whole supply if we don't find a way to freeze it.

Yahweh's displeasure pours down in great swirling sheets, as if the planet lies fixed beneath a waterfall. Sheila paddles without passion, no goal in mind, no reason to live. Fierce winds churn the sea. Lightning shatters the sky. The floodwaters thicken with disintegrating sinners, afloat on their backs, their gelatinous eyes locked in pleading stares, as if begging God for a second chance.

The world reeks. Sheila gags on the vapors. Is the decay of the wicked, she wonders, more odoriferous than that of the just? When she dies, will her stink drive away even flies and vultures?

Sheila wants to die, but her flesh argues otherwise, making her lift her mouth toward heaven and swallow the quenching downpour. The hunger will be harder to solve: it hurts, a scorpion stinging her belly, so painful that she resolves to add cannibalism to her repertoire. But then, in the bottom of the canoe, she spies two huddled turtles, confused, fearful. She eats one raw, beginning with the head, chewing the leathery tissues, drinking the salty blood.

A dark, mountainous shape cruises out of the blur. A sea monster, she decides, angry, sharp-toothed, ravenous . . . Yahweh incarnate, eager to rid the earth of Sheila. Fine. Good. Amen. Painfully she lifts her paddle, heavy as a millstone, and strokes through a congestion of drowned princes and water-logged horses, straight for the hulking deity.

Now God is upon her, a headlong collision, fracturing the canoe like a croc-odile's tail smacking an egg. The floodwaters cover her, a frigid darkness flows through her, and with her last breath she lobs a sphere of mucus into Yahweh's gloomy and featureless face.

Captain's Log. 20 June 1057 A.C.

Yahweh said nothing about survivors. Yet this morning we came upon two.

The *Testudo marginata* posed no problem. We have plenty of turtles, all two hundred and twenty-five species in fact, Testudinidae, Chelydridae, Platysternidae, Kinosternidae, Chelonidae, you name it. Unclean beasts, inedible, useless. We left it to the flood. Soon it will swim itself to death.

The *Homo sapiens* was a different matter. Frightened, delirious, she clung to her broken canoe like a sloth embracing a tree. "Yahweh was explicit," said Japheth, leaning over the rail of the *Eden II*, calling into the gushing storm. "Every person not in this family deserves death."

"She is one of the tainted generation," added his wife. "A whore. Abandon her."

"No," countered Ham. "We must throw her a line, as any men of virtue would do."

Ham's young bride had no opinion.

As for Shem and Tamar, the harlot's arrival became yet another occasion for them to bicker. "Ham is right," insisted Shem. "Bring her among us, Father."

"Let Yahweh have his way with her," retorted Tamar. "Let the flood fulfill its purpose."

"What do *you* think?" I asked Reumah.

Smiling softly, my wife pointed to the dinghy.

I ordered the little boat lowered. Ham and Shem rode it to the surface of the lurching sea, prying the harlot from her canoe, hauling her over the transom. After much struggle we got her aboard the *Eden II*, laying her unconscious bulk on the foredeck. She was a lewd walrus, fat and dissipated. A chain of rat skulls dangled from her squat neck. When Ham pushed on her chest, water fountained out, and she released a cough like a yak's roar.

"Who are you?" I demanded.

She fixed me with a dazed stare and fainted. We carried her below, setting her among the pigs like the unclean thing she is. Reumah stripped away our visitor's soggy garments, and I winced to behold her pocked and twisted flesh.

"Sinner or not, Yahweh has seen fit to spare her," said my wife, wrapping a dry robe around the harlot. "We are the instruments of his amnesty."

"Perhaps," I said, snapping the word like a whip.

The final decision rests with me, of course, not with my sons or their wives. Is the harlot a test? Would a true God-follower sink this human flotsam without a moment's hesitation?

Even asleep, our visitor is vile, her hair a lice farm, her breath a polluting wind.

Sheila awakens to the snorty gossip of pigs. A great bowl of darkness envelops her, dank and dripping like a basket submerged in a swamp. Her nostrils burn with a hundred varieties of stench. She believes that Yahweh has swallowed her, that she is imprisoned in his maw.

Slowly a light seeps into her eyes. Before her, a wooden gate creaks as it pivots on leather hinges. A young man approaches, proffering a wineskin and a cooked leg of mutton.

"Are we inside God?" Sheila demands, propping her thick torso on her elbows. Someone has given her dry clothes. The effort of speaking tires her, and she lies back in the swine-scented straw. "Is this Yahweh?"

"The last of his creation," the young man replies. "My parents, brothers, our wives, the birds, beasts — and myself, Ham. Here. Eat." Ham presses the mutton to her lips. "Seven of each clean animal, that was our quota. In a month we shall run out. Enjoy it while you can.

"I want to die." Once again, Sheila's abundant flesh has a different idea, devouring the mutton, guzzling the wine.

"If you wanted to die," says Ham, "you would not have gripped that canoe so tightly. Welcome aboard."

"Aboard?" says Sheila. Ham is most handsome. His crisp black beard excites her lust. "We're on a boat?"

Ham nods. "The *Eden II*. Gopher wood, stem to stern. This is the world now, nothing else remains. Yahweh means for you to be here."

"I doubt that." Sheila knows her arrival is a freak. She has merely been overlooked. No one means for her to be here, least of all God.

"My father built it," the young man explains. "He is six hundred years old."

"Impressive," says Sheila, grimacing. She has seen the type, a crotchety, withered patriarch, tripping over his beard. Those final five hundred years do nothing for a man, save to make his skin leathery and his worm boneless.

"You're a whore, aren't you?" asks Ham.

The boat pitches and rolls, unmooring Sheila's stomach. She lifts the wineskin to her lips and fills her pouchy cheeks. "Also a drunkard, thief, self-abortionist" — her grin stretches well into the toothless regions — "and sexual deviant." With her palm she cradles her left breast, heaving it to one side.

Ham gasps and backs away.

Another day, perhaps, they will lie together. For now, Sheila is exhausted, stunned by wine. She rests her reeling head on the straw and sleeps.

Captain's Log. 25 June 1057 A.C.

We have harvested a glacier, bringing thirty tons of ice aboard. For the moment, our meat will not become carrion; our tigers, wolves, and carnosaurs will thrive.

I once saw the idolaters deal with an outcast. They tethered his ankles to an ox, his wrists to another ox. They drove the first beast north, the second south.

Half of me believes we must admit this woman. Indeed, if we kill her, do we not become the same people Yahweh saw fit to destroy? If we so sin, do we not contaminate the very race we are meant to sire? In my sons' loins rests the whole of the future. We are the keepers of our kind. Yahweh picked us for the purity of our seed, not the infallibility of our justice. It is hardly our place to condemn.

My other half begs that I cast her into the flood. A harlot, Ham assures me. A dipsomaniac, robber, lesbian, and fetus-killer. She should have died with the rest of them. We must not allow her degenerate womb back into the world, lest it bear fruit.

Again Sheila awakens to swine sounds, refreshed and at peace. She no longer wishes to die.

This afternoon a different brother enters the pig cage. He gives his name as Shem, and he is even better looking than Ham. He bears a glass of tea in which float three diaphanous pebbles. "Ice," he explains. "Clotted water."

Sheila drinks. The frigid tea buffs the grime from her tongue and throat. Ice: a remarkable material, she decides. These people know how to live.

"Do you have a piss pot?" Sheila asks, and Shem guides her to a tiny stall enclosed by reed walls. After she has relieved herself, Shem gives her a tour, leading her up and down the ladders that connect the interior decks. The *Eden II* leaks like a defective tent, a steady, disquieting plop-plop.

The place is a zoo. Mammals, reptiles, birds, two by two. Sheila beholds tiny black beasts with too many legs and long cylindrical creatures with too few. Grunts, growls, howls, roars, brays, and caws rattle the ship's wet timbers.

Sheila likes Shem, but not this floating menagerie, this crazy voyage. The whole arrangement infuriates her. Cobras live here. Wasps, their stingers poised to spew poisons. Young tyrannosaurs and baby allosaurs, eager to devour the gazelles on the deck above. Tarantulas, rats, crabs, weasels, armadillos, snapping turtles, boar-pigs, bacteria, viruses: Yahweh has spared them all.

My friends were no worse than a tarantula, Sheila thinks. My neighbors were as important as weasels. My child mattered more than anthrax.

Captain's Log. 14 July 1057 A.C.

The rains have stopped. We drift aimlessly. Reumah is seasick. Even with the ice, our provisions are running out. We cannot keep feeding ourselves, much less a million species.

Tonight we discussed our passenger. Predictably, Ham and Shem spoke for acquittal, while Japheth argued the whore must die.

"A necessary evil?" I asked Japheth.

"No kind of evil," he replied. "You kill a rabid dog lest its disease spread, Father. This woman's body holds the eggs of future thieves, perverts, and idolaters. We must not allow her to infect the new order. We must check this plague before our chance is lost."

"We have no right," said Ham.

"If God can pass a harsh judgment on millions of evildoers," said Japheth, "then surely I can do the same for one."

"You are not God," noted Ham.

Nor am I — but I am the master of this ship, the leader of this little tribe. I turned to Japheth and said, "I know you speak the truth. We must choose ultimate good over immediate mercy."

Japheth agreed to be her executioner. Soon he will dispose of the whore using the same obsidian knife with which, once we sight land, we are bound to slit and drain our surplus lambs, gratitude's blood.

They have put Sheila to work. She and Japheth must maintain the reptiles. The Pythonidae will not eat unless they kill the meal themselves. Sheila spends the whole afternoon competing with the cats, snaring ship rats, hurling them by their tails into the python pens.

Japheth is the handsomest son yet, but Sheila does not care for him. There is something low and slithery about Japheth. It seems fitting that he tends vipers and asps.

"What do you think of Yahweh?" she asks.

Instead of answering, Japheth leers.

"When a father is abusive," Sheila persists, "the child typically responds not only by denying that the abuse occurred, but by redoubling his efforts to be loved."

Silence from Japheth. He fondles her with his eyes.

Sheila will not quit. "When I destroyed my unwanted children, it was murder. When Yahweh did the same, it was eugenics. Do you approve of the universe, Japheth?"

Japheth tosses the python's mate a rat.

Captain's Log. 17 July 1057 A.C.

We have run aground. Shem has named the place of our imprisonment Ararat. This morning we sent out a *Corvus corax*, but it did not return. I doubt we'll ever see it again. Two ravens remain, but I refuse to break up a pair. Next time we'll try a Columbidae.

In an hour the harlot will die. Japheth will open her up, spilling her dirty blood, her filthy organs. Together we shall cast her carcass into the flood.

Why did Yahweh say nothing about survivors?

Silently Japheth slithers into the pig cage, crouching over Sheila like an incubus, resting the cool blade against her windpipe.

Sheila is ready. Ham has told her the whole plot. A sudden move, and Japheth's universe is awry, Sheila above, her attacker below, she armed, he defenseless. She wriggles her layered flesh, pressing Japheth into the straw. Her scraggly hair tickles his cheeks.

A rape is required. Sheila is good at rape; some of her best customers would settle for nothing less. Deftly she steers the knife amid Japheth's garments, unstitching them, peeling him like an orange. "Harden," she commands, fondling his pods, running a practiced hand across his worm. "Harden or die."

Japheth shudders and sweats. Terror flutes his lips, but before he can cry out Sheila slides the knife across his throat like a bow across a fiddle, delicately dividing the skin, drawing out tiny beads of blood.

Sheila is a professional. She can stiffen eunuchs, homosexuals, men with knives at their jugulars. Lifting her robe, she lowers herself onto Japheth's erection, enjoying his pleasureless passion, reveling in her impalement. A few minutes of graceful undulation, and the worm spurts, filling her with Japheth's perfect and upright seed.

"I want to see your brothers," she tells him.

"What?" Japheth touches his throat, reopening his fine, subtle wound.

"Shem and Ham also have their parts to play."

Captain's Log. 24 July 1057 A.C.

Our dinghy is missing. Maybe the whore cut it loose before she was executed. No matter. This morning I launched a dove, and it has returned with a twig of some kind in its beak. Soon our sandals will touch dry land.

My sons elected to spare me the sight of the whore's corpse. Fine. I have beheld enough dead sinners in my six centuries.

Tonight we shall sing, dance, and give thanks to Yahweh. Tonight we shall bleed our best lamb.

The world is healing. Cool, smooth winds rouse Sheila's hair, sunlight strokes her face. Straight ahead, white robust clouds sail across a clear sky.

A speck hovers in the distance, and Sheila fixes on it as she navigates the boundless flood. This sign has appeared none too soon. The stores from the *Eden II* will not last through the week, especially with her appetite at such a pitch.

Five weeks in the dinghy, and still her menses have not come. "And Japheth's child is just the beginning," she mutters, tossing a wry smile toward the clay pot. So far, the ice shows no sign of melting; Shem and Ham's virtuous fertilizer, siphoned under goad of lust and threat of death, remains frozen. Sheila has plundered enough seed to fill all creation with babies. If things go according to plan, Yahweh will have to stage another flood.

The speck grows, resolves into a bird. A *Corvus corax*, as the old man would have called it.

Sheila will admit that her designs are grand and even pompous. But are they impossible? She aims to found a proud and impertinent nation, a people driven to decipher ice and solve the sun, each of them with as little use for obedience as she, and they will sail the sodden world until they find the perfect continent, a land of eternal light and silken grass, and they will call it what any race must call its home, Formosa, beautiful.

The raven swoops down, landing atop the jar of sperm, and Sheila feels a surge of gladness as, reaching out, she takes a branch from its sharp and tawny beak.

Spinoza's Golem

As the curator of the Cambridge Museum of Philosophy Artifacts, a position I hope to retain until the end of my days, I've developed a sixth sense for detecting a crank or charlatan out to sell us a fraudulent relic. A telltale catch in the voice, a characteristic trembling of the fingers, a revelatory canting of the eyebrows: owing to such signs, I've avoided acquiring Kierkegaard's alleged walking-stick, Hegel's presumed sherry decanter, a purported rough draft of Schopenhauer's *The World as Will and Representation*, and the unpublished rules for an ontological role-playing game, *Daseins and Dragons*, supposedly authored by Martin Heidegger.

Our location is obscure but not arcane. An unmarked green door at 25 Mount Auburn Street, not far from Harvard Yard, is the portal to the CAMPA trove. We receive visitors by appointment only. Write me a letter, convince me of your scholarly integrity, and I shall admit you to our *sanctum sanctorum*. Here you will see not only the scale-model abyss into which Nietzsche stared until he found it staring back at him, but also the pickled remains of Descartes's failed attempt to ensoul an alley cat by transplanting a human pineal gland into its brain, to say nothing of the two-meter-high translucent pyramid through which Leibniz clarified his *Weltanschauung*, each of its fifteen thousand die-sized cubes representing a possible universe with which God might have blessed his creatures, our own supremely harmonious world sitting at the apex. Wonders are many, and in my twenty-year career I've secured an inordinate number of them beneath bulletproof glass.

Acquiring exhibits for CAMPA is rather like running an international espionage ring. We have agents in every European capital. By day these highly trained operatives prowl through antique shops and flea markets, looking for artifacts of such consummate oddity that they might well have figured in the evolution of Western rationality. (A bazaar in Cairo once yielded the insectarium in which Hobbes kept two opposing armies of ants, their periodic battles serving to reify his notion of the *bellum omnium contra omnes*, the war of all against all, a touchstone of his political philosophy.) By night our spies eavesdrop in coffeehouses and taverns, listening for clues to the whereabouts of mislaid objective correlatives. (A chance remark in a London pub led to our acquisition of Locke's sculpted celebration of the human sensorium: a crystal-line female head complete with golden wires attached to the eyes, ears, nose, and tongue, each such filament soaring outward for three feet then looping back to the brain.) Of course, an agent need not spend all his waking hours amid demimonde dwellers. Sometimes he simply purchases a catalogue for an auction pending in some European country or other, discovers that the attend-ees will be bidding on a deceased philosopher's effects, and shows up clutch-ing a CAMPA checkbook. Indeed, it was through such a public sale that our museum acquired one of the holy grails of philosophy artifacts: the lost glass illustration of Benedict de Spinoza's worm-in-the-blood metaphor, fashioned and buffed by the master lens-grinder himself.

When the relic arrived in Cambridge from Amsterdam, addressed to me, Jacob Greenblatt, I immediately telephoned my daughter, Naomi, who teaches archeology at Boston University and occasionally goes digging in North Africa. She happened to have the afternoon free — professors enjoy more flex-ible hours than curators — so she hopped on the Red Line and soon appeared at my door. We carried the crate to the back room. Naomi got to work with a crowbar. (At age seventy-four, I am beholden to the tyranny of my arthritis.) With surpassing caution we removed the fragile treasure, and suddenly there it stood, shining forth like Excalibur in its granite sheath, a two-foot-wide glass cylinder formed to suggest a human vein. The interior housed a ceramic but philosophically inclined worm the size and shape of a baguette, plus free-float-ing colored beads representing the various blood components — lymph, chyle, plasma — that the segmented occupant had selected as objects of contempla-tion.

"What the hell?" said Naomi.

"In this piece Spinoza has dramatized an important dimension of his world-view," I explained. "From our ceramic blood-worm's perspective, this glass vein is the entire universe. The vein contains parts and manifests causes — but is itself neither a part nor a cause: for the worm, nothing whatsoever exists beyond the habitat in question."

"Some people feel that way about Cambridge," noted Naomi.

"When indulging in theological speculation," I continued, paraphrasing Spinoza, "human beings commit an error analogous to the blood-worm's delu-sion. They fail to appreciate that the one and only Substance must possess an infinite number of mental, physical, and, *nota bene*, unnamable attributes." I caressed the worm's habitat. "In truth there is a world beyond the glass vein, and a world beyond that world as well, an endless and axiomatically divine Nature that defies mere human imagination. Achieve an intellectually affectionate relationship with this impersonal Deity, and you will become a good and happy person."

"All you need is God?" said Naomi. "What about lovers and friends?"

"Spinoza appreciated human connection, but fellowship was hardly the sine qua non of his existence." Absently I picked up the crowbar and hefted it in my palm. "He spent his days grinding lenses for other people's microscopes and telescopes, living on raisins and gruel, craving neither riches nor reputation."

"That puts him one up on me," said Naomi.

"Myself as well."

"If Spinoza's Deity is impersonal, how can I love him?"

"It."

"It."

I hugged my daughter and said, "Do you love the pottery you've unearthed in Ethiopia?"

"Yes."

"There."

As it happened, the ultimate value of the ceramic blood-worm lay not in the artifact itself but in its oaken base. A brass knob protruded from one side. Evidently the pedestal held a drawer. I yanked the knob. Protesting with squeaks and squeals, the compartment delivered its contents to my inspection.

My heart raced. A book. I gasped. A volume owned by Spinoza himself: no, better than that, I realized upon flipping back the cover, a volume *written* by Spinoza himself — the hand was unmistakable — a dozen or so pages penned in Latin under the rubric *Experimentum Philosophicum*. I bid Naomi goodbye, bore the volume to my office, pulled out my Lewis and Short, and got to work, soon discovering to my delight that the humble blood-worm had been guarding nothing less than Spinoza's private journal, composed in The Hague during the final decade of his short life.

22 April 1670

Although I am a man without a people, excommunicated by the rabbis of Amsterdam for observing that the Tanakh is entirely of human design, I shall never abjure my heritage *in toto*. Lately I've drawn inspiration from the Jewish legend of the golem — for next week will see the publication of my unorthodox and dangerous philosophy, *Tractatus Theologico-Politicus*, a circumstance that has behooved me to construct a clockwork bodyguard.

As a child I was enchanted by the tale of Judah Löew ben Bezalel, the Prague rabbi who takes a shapeless mass, a *gōlem*, of clay and gives it humanoid form, subsequently suffusing his sculpture with the life force by incising on its brow the Hebrew word EMETH. (Translator's note: that is, "truth.") Although Judah Löew's brain-child proves a faithful servant and protector of the ghetto, the experiment entails a scriptural obligation: the golem must never labor on the Sabbath. Avoiding such sacrilege is a simple matter of periodically effacing, and later restoring, the first letter of EMETH, the Aleph, leaving Mem and Taw, characters that spell METH. (Translator's note: that is, "death.") But one fateful Friday evening Löew forgets to disable his creature, and so it runs amok in the ghetto, smashing down doors, destroying wells, overturning horse carts, and torching the communal firewood supply. When Sunday rolls around, the heartsick rabbi dutifully grinds his beloved golem to dust.

Tonight I dressed my bodyguard in a woolen tunic and sturdy boots, then animated him for the first time. Unlike Rabbi Löew, I had no need of Kabbala to achieve this result. The golem of the Paviljoensgracht lives not by magic but by springs and cogs, ratchets and escapements, in accordance with principles laid down by my fellow Dutch experimentalist, Christiaan Huygens. To be sure, Mijnheer Huygens's investigations are rather more physical than metaphysical, but he is nonetheless my brother in reason.

I have named the automaton Bezalel, in honor of Rabbi Löew's lineage. Doubtless my adversaries will say that in building the creature I committed an act of hubris. Certainly the rabbis back in Amsterdam will accuse me of "playing God," using Bezalel as yet another occasion to persecute me. I do not play God. The concept is incoherent. (Even God does not play God.) That said, I shall allow that the automaton has bestowed a certain clarity on my ruminations. Although I "created" him, my project cannot be analogized to any presumed gesture by the One Substance. The Deity that is Nature does not "create" anything at all, for Being is by definition sufficient unto itself.

At the stroke of midnight Benedict de Spinoza, proponent of the God of infinite extension, loaded his decidedly finite extension — this curious assemblage of bronze bones, leather tendons, and mother-of-pearl flesh — into a pony cart. Furtively I conveyed the golem to the Oranjeplein. Here in this windswept nocturnal park we would be immune to the prying eyes and meddling morals of our fellow citizens.

I dragged Bezalel free of the cart, standing him upright as I might a clothier's mannequin, then drew forth the silver key from my overcoat and inserted it in his neck, adjacent to the jugular pipe. Slowly, methodically, I wound him up, one turn, two turns, three, four, five. I stopped: a modest trial seemed best — I would animate my bodyguard in full another day, giving him comprehensive power to protect me.

Reaching toward the sternum, I took hold of the function dial and switched it from MODALITY ONE, dormancy, to MODALITY TWO, vigilance. A rasping noise filled the air as the mainspring uncoiled and the wheels-within-wheels started to spin. The golem lifted his head, opened his eyes, and began marking time. He raised his left foot, then returned the extremity to the ground. He raised and lowered his right foot. Left foot, right foot, left, right, left, right. His arms swung back and forth at his sides like pendulums.

Cautiously I twisted the dial to MODALITY THREE, intimidation, then fled to the nearest tree, prepared to scale the branches if Bezalel proved more unruly than I anticipated. I looked back. The creature moved haltingly, advancing more through baby steps than confident strides, moonlight glinting in his glass eyes, wisps of fog coiling about his thighs like serpents. Eventually I would test MODALITY FOUR, belligerence, and MODALITY FIVE, the behavior I have not yet named. For now it was sufficient to observe MODALITY THREE in all its menacing glory.

From the moment I saw Bezalel shambling toward me, I knew I'd brought forth not only a loyal bodyguard but also a faithful listener. He would be my eternally agreeable sounding board, the audience on whose steadfast sympathy I could always depend — even beyond the grave. I've already approached the one man I truly trust and instructed him in the disposition of both my corpse and my creature. (Translator's note: Spinoza is referring to his landlord.) "Bury me wherever the town elders see fit," I told Mijnheer Von Der Spijk, "but then, under cover of night, you must perform an exhumation and place my golem beside me in my crypt."

On only a dozen or so occasions in my life have I selected a destination from which nothing — neither hell, high water, wild horses, mad dogs, Englishmen, nor the Great Wall of China — could deter me. I think immediately of Cambridge Courthouse. (I would get to my wedding promptly or perish in the attempt.) Massachusetts General Hospital also comes to mind. (I must deliver my wife, Hannah, to the obstetricians with great efficiency, so they might in turn bring Naomi into the world). And then there was Nieuwe Kerk Den Haag in the Netherlands. For if in his journal entry of 22 April 1670 Spinoza spoke the truth — and his partisans argue that he never employed any other idiom — then his clockwork bodyguard lay in the same churchyard that held his bones.

As you might imagine, I decided against contacting the mayor of The

Hague and begging him to let me tamper with the philosopher's grave. He would probably say no — and even if the municipal authorities assented to my ambition, they would surely claim the golem for themselves. Bezalel must be displayed in my museum and nowhere else on earth.

When I proposed to Naomi that she accompany me to the Netherlands, she immediately arranged her life accordingly, canceling classes and posting assignments online. Digging for relics is in my daughter's blood. True, our planned plundering of Spinoza's remains and the adjacent automaton seemed less like an archeologist's dream than a ghoul's lark, but our motives were unimpeachable. If our adventure proved successful, the world would have yet another reason to esteem the seventeenth century's greatest philosopher (an assessment I am prepared to defend against devotees of Leibniz and Descartes). I dubbed our expedition the Raiders of the Lost Christian Consensus, an admittedly snide appellation, keyed to my conclusion that, when it comes to densely reasoned theological discourse, complete with quasi-geometric proofs, Spinoza's *Ethics* leaves the Church Fathers in the shadows.

And so it was that my daughter and I took an Aer Lingus flight from Logan Airport to Schiphol in Amsterdam. We checked into the Seven Bridges Hotel, rented ten-speed bicycles, rode around the Rembrandtplein, and, returning to Reguliersgracht 31, caught up on our sleep. The following morning we leased a minivan from Hertz and drove fifty kilometers southwest to The Hague. Our quest had begun in earnest.

Stage one, we decided, must be a pilgrimage to the great man's house. Although the Paviljoensgracht canal no longer exists, having been displaced by a lovely two-lane thoroughfare with a grassy median, we had no trouble locating number 72-74. We parked in the shadow of the philosopher's statue, a mass of bronze now green with oxidation, then approached the Spinozahuis, a modest three-story affair maintained by an antiquarian society that, we soon learned to our dismay, makes a point of keeping it closed to the general public.

Our instincts lured us south, across a bridge spanning the extant canal. We found ourselves on Spinozastraat. The irony amused me. In his lifetime our lens-grinder could not venture this far from the Jewish Quarter without enduring the taunts of those who thought him a depraved atheist, and now the route in question bears his name. To all appearances the philosopher of The Hague had enjoyed the last laugh, and so had the One Substance — though neither entity would especially care, Spinoza being a man without malice and his God a divinity without emotion.

As the celebrated Dutch sun, muse to countless incomparable painters, arced toward the horizon, Naomi and I returned to the Paviljoensgracht, then motored into the business district. Beyond a pick and two shovels, our purchases included a tool kit, essential for disassembling Bezalel, plus two oversized suitcases, necessary for getting his components across the Atlantic by jetliner.

Having outfitted our expedition, we drove along the Spui toward the Nieuwe Kerk den Haag, paragon of early Protestant architecture in the Netherlands. These days the building no longer serves an ecclesiastical function, being a venue for organ concerts and student recitals, a fact that failed to assuage my guilt. Music hall or no music hall, we were about to commit an act of desecration.

We parked outside the gates and waited. Night came on slowly, almost bashfully, as if ashamed to deprive Holland's artists of their light. We proceeded to the churchyard. The grave we sought was clearly marked: TERRA HIC BENE- DICTI DE SPINOZA. The earth yielded readily to our implements. The Raiders of the Lost Christian Consensus, may God forgive them, had begun their unholy work.

11 May 1670

The estimable Mijnheer Von Der Spijk has permitted me to store Bezalel in a ground-floor closet, just off the front parlor. To thank the man for his generosity, I gave him a demonstration, winding up the automaton — I calculated that four turns of the key would be sufficient — then setting him loose in the stone alley beside the house. Bezalel ambled all the way from the gate to the garden, where he sat on a bench and contemplated the flowers with his glass eyes. Mijnheer Von Der Spijk gasped in delight — as a painter, he appreciates Bezalel's aesthetic sensibilities — then clapped his hands and informed me I was a genius, a diagnosis from which I did not dissent.

Just as I suspected, Bezalel has proved the ideal audience for my ruminations. Two days ago I shared with him my discovery that the mind is the idea of the body. To wit, the universe has never wielded, nor will it ever wield, a Cartesian cleaver separating human mental activity from those entities we call bodies. Cogitation and corporeality are in essence the same thing. Bezalel accepted my insight without reservation, which is more than I can say for most of the correspondents (notably Oldenburg in London and Leibniz in Paris) for whom I have described my system in detail.

During the first week following the publication of the *Tractatus Theologico-Politicus* no untoward incidents occurred, though I knew that much of the Latin-speaking world was reading it. But then, last night, my heresy caught up with me. Torches in hand, pistols at the ready, an angry mob appeared at the front door, demanding that I render myself unto them. Mijnheer Von Der Spijk immediately rushed into the Paviljoens-gracht and attempted to mollify the intruders. Their intentions, he now learned, included hauling me to the Oranjeplein and hanging me from an elm tree. Mijnheer Von Der Spijk countered that I was an irreplaceable tenant, and so they had best find a different Jew to torment.

As my landlord distracted the mob, I tore open the closet door, wound up the golem, and switched the function dial from MODALITY ONE, dormancy, to MODALITY TWO, vigilance, to MODALITY THREE, intimi-dation. Bezalel awoke. His limbs creaked. His wheels whirred. He marched across the parlor and, traversing the portal, waded into the bloodthirsty horde. The blackguards dispersed instantly, and I had no cause to advance the dial to MODALITY FOUR, belligerence.

To all appearances, Bezalel, Mijnheer Von Der Spijk, and I have won the first skirmish in the War on Spinozism. The final outcome of the con-flict remains in doubt, but my calculations tell me reason will prevail.

For two unbroken hours Naomi and I labored in the moonlit churchyard. My daughter, of course, did most of the digging, while her septuagenarian father supervised — for how scandalous it would be if America's premier cura-tor of philosophy artifacts dropped dead of a heart attack while violating Spi-noza's grave. Suddenly Naomi's spade struck wood, inspiring her to furious effort, and in time a pair of dark oblong boxes, flecked with mold but essen-tially sound, stood revealed at the bottom of the cavity, bathed in the lunar glow.

Two coffins! A double grave! By the evidence of these twin receptacles, Spinoza's golem was no less factual than his worm-in-the-blood diorama. For eleven generations, master and mannequin had lain side by side in the sodden Dutch earth.

Luckily we were spared the necessity of disturbing the lens-grinder's remains, for someone had scratched *ossa sepulta*, buried bones, on one of the coffin lids. We turned our attentions to the unmarked casket. Naomi applied the pick, tearing the lid to pieces, and soon the automaton stretched before us, supine, his glass eyes burning with Selene's fire. Even in his decrepit state, Bezalel displayed facets more dazzling than I'd ever dared imagine, a creature at once outré and exquisite, his gleaming mother-of-pearl cranium harboring the clockwork equivalent of a brain, his strong bronze hands eager to keep his creator from harm, his bright bronze chest exhibiting both the function dial and the tattered remnants of the woolen tunic. A tarnished silver key protruded from the creature's neck, poised to tighten the mainspring.

The tool kit provided every implement we required. Working feverishly, determined to finish the task before sunrise, we systematically dismantled the creature, sketching each element and diagramming its relationship to the whole. After placing the detached head and orphaned torso in one suitcase, the pelvis and limbs in the other, we loaded our prize into the minivan, then turned our attentions to the grave. Carefully, ever so carefully, we replaced the grass tuffets like pieces of a jigsaw puzzle, smoothing the surrounding loam, until to our eyes the site appeared unmolested.

At dawn we drove back to Amsterdam and, wheeling our priceless discovery before us, checked back into the Seven Bridges Hotel. Sleep eluded me that night. As the moon rose over the city, I climbed free of my bed and, opening the appropriate suitcase, contemplated Bezalel's head. What gloriously abstruse notions Spinoza had set dancing through the creature's clockwork brain. *The mind is the idea of the body.* It made no sense. It made perfect sense. An exasperating, exhilarating, inexhaustible thought. I wondered if I would ever sleep again.

The numinous Dutch sun returned, limning its favorite nation. A taxi took us to Schiphol Airport. We entrusted our luggage, including the anatomized golem, to the care of Aer Lingus's baggage handlers, then boarded a flight to Boston.

And that is how the most astonishing relic in the history of Western thought came from Holland to Massachusetts. After bearing the suitcases to the back room of CAMPA, I set them on the floor and nervously inspected their contents. Everything seemed intact. I laid my palm on Bezalel's torso, half expecting to sense a heartbeat, then contemplated the function dial. The mystery of MODALITY FIVE — "the behavior I have not yet named," as Spinoza put it in his journal—taunted me. Mutilation? Dismemberment? Decapitation? One thing was certain. I must never activate that option, no matter how great my curiosity grew.

18 August 1670

Priests, pastors, and sages have responded to *Tractatus Theologico-Politicus* with all the vituperation I'd anticipated. Bishop Pierre-Daniel Huet, tutor to the Dauphin, recommended that I be "bound with chains and flogged." Dutch theologian Phillip van Limborch dismissed my effort as "defecated erudition." Still another defender of the faith has called me "the most subtle atheist hell has vomited on the earth." This last condemnation almost pleases me. I'm thinking of having it inscribed on my tomb (after changing "atheist" to "thinker").

Yesterday morning a sweating emissary pounded on the door of Pavil-joensgracht 72-74, flourishing an official summons from our local Council of Theologians. This pious fraternity expected me to appear before them that very afternoon to answer charges of sacrilege and sedition. I told the emissary that I should be happy to explain myself to this august body, but I must be permitted to bring a well-informed clockwork automaton to act as my advocate.

The tribunal convened in the Nieuwe Kerk den Haag. A bailiff swore me in using the famous Bible authorized by King James the First. After according the somnolent golem suspicious frowns and hostile scowls, my three fat and apoplectic accusers confronted me with the gravamen of the indictment. On the evidence of the *Tractatus*, I was an atheist and — a persuasion no less abominable — an anti-theocrat, bent on replacing Christian governments throughout Europe with secular states catering to the basest impulses of their citizens.

I retorted that anyone who read my *Tractatus* carefully would see that, far from being an "atheist," I am something like the opposite, a man who daily breathes, ingests, imbibes, and dreams of the One Substance. Concerning the label "anti-theocrat," I argued that ere long all rational men will come to share my critique of the Christian churches — namely, that they seek to consolidate their power by frightening congregants with the myth of a capricious and vindictive God. The sooner this fraud ends, I declared, the better.

My defense did not impress the Council of Theologians. After a brief deliberation, they agreed that I must be banished from The Hague forever.

So I wound up the automaton. One, two, three, four — fifteen turns altogether. I set the function dial on MODALITY FOUR, belligerence. Bezalel reacted with admirable speed and breathtaking efficiency. He lifted a rotund theocrat from the bench, carried him sputtering through the portals of the Nieuwe Kerk, and hurled him into the Spui canal, then straightaway disposed of the remaining judges in the same fashion. A few moments later my three antagonists stood dripping and shivering on the banks of the canal. Thus did I win my case. I suspect I shall not be hearing from the Council of Theologians for many months to come.

That night I rewarded my mechanical paladin for his heroic service, favoring him with my philosophy of immanence. All is in God. All lives and moves in God. The laws of Nature and the decrees of the Divine are synonymous. From God's infinite essence all things follow by necessity, as it follows from the eternal condition of a triangle that its three angles are equal to two right angles. What the laws of the circle are to all circles, God is to the world. It's really quite simple.

There was no question that Naomi and I would attempt to resurrect Spinoza's golem, though the odds were against us. After more than three centuries in the ground, Bezalel's internal workings were probably corroded beyond redemption. And yet I had faith that, if we reassembled the machine with sufficient care and a surfeit of lubrication, we might accomplish the miracle.

When it came to choosing a venue for our experiment, Naomi and I quickly reached accord. We would restore Bezalel in the basement of the museum. Capacious and warm, with track lighting and an ambience that savored of the macabre — jagged shadows, spiderwebs, fissured plaster, artifacts stored in mummy-like wrappings — this space would afford us the sort of seclusion Spinoza himself so highly prized.

We lit a candle in remembrance of Naomi's mother, then began the momentous project. Working with our sketches from that anxious night in the churchyard, we pieced the golem together over the course of four hours. The sight of Bezalel standing upright, arms hanging limply by his side, head lolling on his chest, brought a frisson to my aging frame.

Spinoza had once arrayed Bezalel in tunic and boots, and now Naomi likewise sought to dress him with dignity. Removing a fat, blue, down parka from her backpack, she slid the golem's arms into the sleeves, then activated the zipper. A tallith completed the ensemble.

"Go ahead," I told her. "A few rotations only."

Naomi reached toward Bezalel's jugular and turned the silver key — once, twice, thrice. She switched the function dial from dormancy to vigilance. A rasping sound echoed across the basement, like the death rattle of a windlass. Bezalel lifted his head. His eyelids flickered open. He raised and lowered his left foot, then his right, then his left, then his right. His arms cycled back and forth as if attached to a brachiating ape.

"Eureka!" I cried.

"Shazam!" shouted Naomi.

Then the unexpected happened. For reasons that defied my understanding of Bezalel's brain, mind, and soul, he now exhibited a will of his own: an automaton grown autonomous. With steely deliberation he groped toward his neck and clasped the silver key. Still marking time, he cranked himself up to full power.

"Bezalel, no!" I screamed.

The golem seized the function dial, twisting it to MODALITY THREE, intimidation, then to MODALITY FOUR, belligerence, and finally to the ominous MODALITY FIVE. Good God, what had I done? Had I allowed my blind ambition, my overweening ego, to jeopardize my daughter?

Bezalel marched inexorably forward, arms outstretched, the track lighting turning his eyes to embers. Summoning all my resolve, I vaulted into his path, then turned to Naomi and cried, "Run!"

As my daughter lurched toward the basement steps, the golem and I collided. MODALITY FIVE. Strangulation? Evisceration? Defenestration?

No. Something else entirely. With infinite tenderness, the creature embraced me. He squeezed his blue parka against my bosom, the pressure transmitting amity and affection, just as he had surely comforted his maker over three centuries earlier. I hugged the golem back. It was the ethical thing to do.

"Yes!" declared Naomi, punching the air with an exultant fist.

For a full minute the bodyguard and I remained in each other's arms. My tears flowed freely. The golem's cogs sang sweetly. With manifest reluctance he seized the function dial and twisted it back to MODALITY ONE. Eventually the mainspring ran short of energy, whereupon Bezalel's head tipped forward, and he returned to his inert state, a static extension of his dead creator, waiting to be recalled to life.

Needless to say, I've decided against exhibiting him in the museum. The golem boasts such subtlety that I must never subject him to idle gawking and smug academic chatter. Naomi agrees with this judgment, and I imagine Spinoza would, too.

Last week I moved Bezalel into my office. We stare at each other across my desk. Since the night Naomi and I experimented in the basement, I haven't wound the mainspring, though I suspect that before long I shall require MODALITY FIVE, affirmation, as will my daughter, marked to inherit the creature, and her husband — Naomi recently announced her engagement to an art historian — and their children, and their children's children. Spinoza would be the first to understand. Although he was the most self-sufficient of men, there were obviously moments when he needed something other than his all-encompassing Substance. True, the philosopher had his intellectual colleagues, but few of them really appreciated him, and he had his circle of friends, though he couldn't rely on them for nurturance. His solution, Bezalel, in no way diminishes my regard for the man. Indeed, the Paviljoensgracht golem makes me admire Spinoza all the more.

Tomorrow I fly to Paris, where I shall ascertain the authenticity of Blaise Pascal's personal roulette wheel before authorizing our French operative to acquire it at Sotheby's. I shall leave you with a thought that sustains me as I continue my quest to comprehend Bezalel. "All happiness or unhappiness solely depends upon the quality of the object to which we are attached by love." I needn't tell you who wrote that.

Now permit me to add a coda: keep on the lookout for philosophy artifacts — not only tangible relics, but also verbalized wisdom. Should you happen across an idea that strikes your fancy, bring it here to 25 Mount Auburn Street. We'll sit in the shadow of the golem and engage in reasoned discourse. And if, on exiting my office, you find yourself in need of an embrace, that can be arranged as well. As Spinoza liked to say, it's all the same thing.

Known But to God
and Wilbur Hines

My keeper faces east, his gaze lifting above the treetops and traveling across the national necropolis clear to the glassy Potomac. His bayonet rises into the morning sky, as if to skewer the sun. In his mind he ticks off the seconds, one for each shell in a twenty-one-gun salute.

Being dead has its advantages. True, my pickled flesh is locked away inside this cold marble box, but my senses float free, like orbiting satellites beaming back snippets of the world. I see the city, dense with black citizens and white marble. I smell the Virginia air, the ripe grass, the river's scum. I hear my keeper's boots as he pivots south, the echo of his heels coming together: two clicks, always two, like a telegrapher transmitting an eternal *I*.

My keeper pretends not to notice the crowd — the fifth-graders, Rotarians, garden clubbers, random tourists. Occasionally he catches a Cub Scout's bright yellow bandanna or a punker's pink mohawk. "Known but to God," it says on my tomb. Not true, for I'm known to myself as well. I understand Wilbur Simpson Hines perfectly.

Thock, thock, thock goes my keeper's Springfield as he transfers it from his left shoulder to his right. He pauses, twenty-one seconds again, then marches south twenty-one paces down the narrow black path, protecting me from the Bethesda Golden Age Society and the Glen Echo Lions Club.

I joined the army to learn how to kill my father. An irony: the only time the old man ever showed a glimmer of satisfaction with me occurred when I announced I was dropping out of college and enlisting. He thought I wanted to make the world safe for democracy, when in fact I wanted to make it safe from him. I intended to sign up under a false name. Become competent with a rifle. Then one night, while my father slept, I would sneak away from basic training, press the muzzle to his head — Harry Hines the hot-blooded Pennsylvania farmer, laying into me with his divining rod till my back was freckled with slivers of hazelwood — and blow him straight to Satan's backyard. You see how irrational I was in those days? The tomb has smoothed me out. There's no treatment like this box, no therapy like death.

Click, click, my keeper faces east. He pauses for twenty-one seconds, watching the morning mist hovering above the river.

"I want to be a doughboy," I told them at the Boalsburg Recruiting Station. They profiled me straightaway. Name: Bill Johnson. Address: Bellefonte YMCA. Complexion: fair. Eye color: blue. Hair: red.

"Get on the scales," they said.

They measured me, and for a few dicey minutes I feared that, being short and scrawny — my father always detested the fact that I wasn't a gorilla like him — I'd flunk out, but the sergeant just winked at me and said, "Stand on your toes, Bill."

I did, stretching to the minimum height.

"You probably skipped breakfast this morning, right?" said the sergeant. Another wink. "Breakfast is good for a few pounds."

"Yes, sir."

My keeper turns: click, click, left-face. Thock, thock, thock, he transfers his rifle from his right shoulder to his left. He pauses for twenty-one seconds then marches north down the black path. Click, click, he spins toward the Potomac and waits.

It's hard to say exactly why my plans changed. At Camp Sinclair they put me in a crisp khaki uniform and gave me a mess kit, a canteen, and a Remington rifle, and suddenly there I was, Private Bill Johnson of the American Expeditionary Forces, D Company, Eighteenth U.S. Infantry, First Division. And, of course, everybody was saying what a great time we were going to have driving the Heinies into the Baltic and seeing gay Paree. The Yanks were coming, and I wanted to be one of them — Bill Johnson *né* Wilbur Hines wasn't about to risk an AWOL conviction and a tour in the brig while his friends were off visiting *la belle France* and its French belles. After my discharge, there'd be plenty of time to show Harry Hines what his son had learned in the army.

They're changing the guard. For the next half-hour, an African-American PFC will protect me. We used to call them coloreds, of course. Niggers, to tell you the truth. Today this particular African-American has a fancy job patrolling my tomb, but when they laid me here in 1921 his people weren't even allowed in the regular divisions. The 365th, that was the nigger regiment, and when they finally reached France, you know what Pershing had them do? Dig trenches, unload ships, and bury white doughboys.

But my division — *we'd* get a crack at glory, oh, yes. They shipped us over on the British tub *Magnolia* and dropped us down near the front line a mile west of a jerkwater Frog village, General Robert Bullard in charge. I'm not sure what I expected from France. My buddy Alvin Piatt said they'd fill our canteens with red wine every morning. They didn't. Somehow I thought I'd be in the war without actually *fighting* the war, but suddenly there we were, sharing a four-foot trench with a million cooties and dodging *Mieniewaffers* like some idiots you'd see in a newsreel at the Ziegfeld with a Fairbanks picture and a Chaplin two-reeler, everybody listening for the dreaded cry "Gas attack!" and waiting for the order to move forward. By April of 1918 we'd all seen enough victims of Boche mustard—coughing up blood, shitting their gizzards out, weeping from blind eyes—that we clung to our gas masks like little boys hugging their teddies.

My keeper marches south, his bayonet cutting a straight incision in the summer air. I wonder if he's ever used it. Probably not. I used mine plenty in '18. "If a Heinie comes toward you with his hands up yelling *Kamerad*, don't be fooled," Sergeant Fiskejohn told us back at Camp Sinclair. "He's sure as hell got a potato masher in one of those hands. Go at him from below, and you'll stop him easy. A long thrust in the belly, then a short one, then a butt stroke to the chin if he's still on his feet, which he won't be."

On May 28 the order came through, and we climbed out of the trenches and fought what's now called the Battle of Cantigny, but it wasn't really a battle, it was a grinding push into the German salient with hundreds of men on both sides getting hacked to bits like we were a bunch of steer haunches hanging in our barns back home. Evidently the Boche caught more shit than we did, because after forty-five minutes that town was ours, and we waltzed down the gunky streets singing our favorite ditty.

> *The mademoiselle from gay Paree, parlez-vous?*
> *The mademoiselle from gay Paree, parlez-vous?*
> *The mademoiselle from gay Paree,*
> *She had the clap and she gave it to me,*
> *Hinky dinky, parlez-vous?*

I'll never forget the first time I drew a bead on a Heinie, a sergeant with a handlebar mustache flaring from his upper lip like antlers. I aimed, I squeezed, I killed him, just like that: now he's up, now he's down—a man I didn't even know. I thought how easy it was going to be shooting Harry Hines, a man I hated.

For the next three days the Boche counterattacked, and then I did learn to hate them. Whenever somebody lost an arm or a leg to a potato masher, he'd cry for his mother, in English mostly but sometimes in Spanish and sometimes Yiddish, and you can't see that happen more than once without wanting to kill every Heinie in Europe, right up to the Kaiser himself. I did as Fiskejohn said. A boy would stumble toward me with his hands up—"Kamerad! Kamerad!"—and I'd go for his belly. There's something about having a Remington in your grasp with that lovely slice of steel jutting from the bore. I'd open the fellow up left to right, like I was underlining a passage in the sharpshooter's manual, and he'd spill out like soup. It was interesting and legal. Once I saw a sardine. On the whole, though, Fiskejohn was wrong. The dozen boys I ripped weren't holding potato mashers or anything else.

I switched tactics. I took prisoners. "Kamerad!" Five at first. "Kamerad!" Six. "Kamerad!" Seven. Except that seventh boy in fact had a masher, which he promptly lobbed into my chest.

Lucky for me, it bounced back.

The Heinie caught enough of the kick to get his face torn off, whereas I caught only enough to earn myself a bed in the field hospital. For a minute I didn't know I was wounded. I just looked at that boy who had no nose, no lower jaw, and wondered whether perhaps I should use a grenade instead of a bullet on Harry Hines.

Click, click, my keeper turns to the left. Thock, thock, thock, he transfers his rifle, waits. The Old Guard — the Third U.S. Infantry — never quits. Twenty-four hours a day, seven days a week: can you imagine? Three a.m. on Christmas morning, say, with snow tumbling down and nobody around except a lot of dead veterans, and here's this grim, silent sentinel strutting past my tomb? It gives me the creeps.

The division surgeons spliced me together as best they could, but I knew they'd left some chips behind because my chest hurt like hell. A week after I was taken off the critical list, they gave me a month's pay and sent me to Bar-le-Duc for some rest and relaxation, which everybody knew meant cognac and whores.

The whole village was a red-light district, and if you had the francs you could find love around the clock, though you'd do well to study the choices and see who had that itchy look a lady acquires when she's got the clap. And so it was that on the first of July, as the hot French twilight poured into a cootie-ridden bordello on the Place Vendôme, Wilbur Hines's willy finally put to port after nineteen years at sea. Like Cantigny, it was quick and confusing and over before I knew it. I had six more days coming to me, though, and I figured it would get better.

My keeper heads north, twenty-one paces. The sun beats down. The sweat-band of his cap is rank and soggy. Click, click: right-face. His eyes lock on the river.

I loved Bar-le-Duc. The citizens treated me like a war hero, saluting me wherever I went. There's no telling how far you'll go in this world if you're willing to belly-rip a few German teenagers.

Beyond the Poilu and the hookers, the cafés were also swarming with Bolsheviks, and I must admit their ideas made sense to me — at least, they did by my fourth glass of Château d'Yquem. After Cantigny — with its flying metal and Alvin Piatt walking around with a bloody stump screaming "Mommy!" — I'd begun asking the same questions as the Bolshies, such as, "Why are we having this war, anyway?" When I told them my family was poor, the Bolshies got all excited, and I hadn't felt so important since the army took me. I actually gave those fellows a few francs, and they promptly signed me up as a noncom in their organization. So now I held two ranks, PFC in the American Expeditionary Forces and lance corporal in the International Brotherhood of Proletarian Veterans or whatever the hell they were calling themselves.

My third night on the cathouse circuit, I got into an argument with one of the tarts. Fifi — I always called them Fifi — decided she'd given me special treatment on our second round, something to do with her mouth, her *bouche*, and now she wanted twenty francs instead of the usual ten. Those ladies thought every doughboy was made of money. All you heard in Bar-le-Duc was "*les Americains, beaucoup d'argent.*"

"*Dix francs,*" I said.

"*Vingt,*" Fifi insisted. Her eyes looked like two dead snails. Her hair was the color of Holstein dung.

"*Dix.*"

"*Vingt* — or I tell ze MP you rip me," Fifi threatened. She meant rape.

"*Dix,*" I said, throwing the coins on the bed, whereupon Fifi announced with a tilted smile that she had "a bad case of ze VD" and hoped she'd given it to me.

Just remember, you weren't there. Your body wasn't full of raw metal, and you didn't have Fifi's clap, and nobody was expecting you to maintain a lot of distinctions between the surrendering boys you were supposed to stab and the Frog tarts you weren't. It was hot. My chest hurt. Half my friends had died capturing a pissant hamlet whose streets were made of horse manure. And all I could see were those nasty little clap germs gnawing at my favorite organs.

My Remington stood by the door. The bayonet was tinted now, the color of a turnip; so different from the war itself, that bayonet — no question about its purpose. As I pushed it into Fifi and listened to the rasp of the steel against her pelvis, I thought how prophetic her mispronunciation had been: "I tell ze MP you rip me."

I used the fire escape. My hands were wet and warm. All the way back to my room, I felt a gnawing in my gut like I'd been gassed. I wished I'd never stood on my toes in the Boalsburg Recruiting Station. A ditty helped. After six reprises and a bottle of cognac, I finally fell asleep.

The mademoiselle from Bar-le-Duc, parlez-vous?
The mademoiselle from Bar-le-Duc, parlez-vous?
The mademoiselle from Bar-le-Duc,
She'll screw you in the chicken coop,
Hinky dinky, parlez-vous?

On the sixteenth of July, I boarded one of those 40-and-8 trains (each box-car's capacity being either forty men or eight horses) and rejoined my regiment, now dug in along the Marne. A big fight had already happened there, sometime in '14, and they were hoping for another. I was actually glad to be leaving Bar-le-Duc, for all its wonders and delights. The local gendarmes, I'd heard, were looking into the Fifi matter.

Click, click, thock, thock, thock. My keeper pauses, twenty-one seconds. He marches south down the black path.

At the Marne they put me in charge of a Hotchkiss machine gun, and I set it up on a muddy hill, the better to cover the forward trench where they'd stationed my platoon. I had two good friends in that hole, and so when Captain Mallery showed up with orders from *le général* — we were now part of the XX French Corps — saying I should haul the Hotchkiss a mile downstream, I went berserk.

"Those boys are completely exposed," I protested. The junk in my chest was on fire. "If there's an infantry attack, we'll lose 'em all."

"Move the Hotchkiss, Private Johnson," said the captain.

"That's not a very good idea," I said.

"Move it."

"They'll be naked as jaybirds."

"Move it. *Now.*"

A couple of wars later, of course, attacks on officers by their own men got elevated to a kind of art form — I know all about it, I like to read the tourists' newspapers — but this was 1918 and the concept was still in its infancy. I certainly didn't display much finesse as I pulled out my Colt revolver and in a pioneering effort shot Mallery through the heart. It was all pretty crude.

And then, damn, who should happen by but the CO himself, crusty old Colonel Horrocks, his eyes bulging with disbelief. He told me I was arrested. He said I'd hang. But by then I was fed up. I was fed up with gas scares and Alvin Piatt getting his arm blown off. I was fed up with being an American infantry private and an honorary Bolshevik, fed up with greedy hookers and gonorrhea and the whole dumb, bloody, smelly war. So I ran. That's right: ran, retreated, quit the Western Front.

Unfortunately, I picked the wrong direction. I'd meant to make my way into Chateau-Thierry and hide out in the cathouses till the Mallery situation blew over, but instead I found myself heading toward Deutschland itself, oh, yes, straight for the enemy line. Stupid, stupid.

When I saw my error, I threw up my hands.

And screamed.

"Kamerad! Kamerad!"

Bill Johnson *né* Wilbur Hines never fought in the Second Battle of the Marne. He never helped his regiment drive the Heinies back eight miles, capture four thousand of the Kaiser's best troops, and kill God knows how many more. This private missed it all, because the Boche hit him with everything they had. Machine-gun fire, grapeshot, rifle bullets, shrapnel. A potato masher detonated. A mustard shell went off. Name: unknown. Address: unknown. Complexion: charred. Eye color: no eyes. Hair: burned off. Weeks later, when they scraped me off the Marne floodplain, it was obvious I was a prime candidate for the Arlington program. Lucky for me, Colonel Horrocks got killed at Soissons. He'd have voted me down.

As I said, I read the newspapers. I keep up. That's how I learned about my father. One week after they put me in this box, Harry Hines cheated at seven-card stud and was bludgeoned to death by the loser with a ball-peen hammer. It made the front page of the *Centre County Democrat*.

It's raining. The old people hoist their umbrellas; the fifth-graders glom onto their teacher; the Cub Scouts march away like a platoon of midgets. Am I angry about my life? For many years, yes, I was furious, but then the eighties rolled around, mine and the century's, and I realized I'd be dead by now anyway. So I won't leave you with any bitter thoughts. I'll leave you with a pretty song. Listen.

The mademoiselle from Is-sur-Tille, parlez-vous?
The mademoiselle from Is-sur-Tille, parlez-vous?
The mademoiselle from Is-sur-Tille,
She can zig-zig-zig like a spinning wheel,
Hinky dinky, parlez-vous?

My keeper remains, facing east.

Daughter Earth

We'd been trying to have another child for over three years, carrying on like a couple from one of those movies you can rent by going behind the beaded curtain at Marty's Video, but it just wasn't working out. Logic, of course, says a second conception should prove no harder than a first. Hah. Mother Nature can be a sneaky old bitch, something we've learned from our twenty-odd years of farming down here in central Pennsylvania.

Maybe you've driven past our place, Garber Farm, two miles outside of Boalsburg on Route 322. Raspberries in the summer, apples in the fall, Christmas trees in the winter, asparagus in the spring — that's us. The basset hound puppies appear all year round. We'll sell you one for three hundred dollars, guaranteed to love the children, chase rabbits out of the vegetable patch, and always appear burdened by troubles greater than yours.

We started feeling better after Dr. Borealis claimed he could make Polly's uterus "more hospitable to reproduction," as he put it. He prescribed vaginal suppositories, little nuggets of progesterone packed in cocoa butter. You store them in the refrigerator till you're ready to use one, and they melt in your wife the way M&Ms melt in your mouth.

That very month, we got pregnant.

So there we were, walking around with clouds under our feet. We kept remembering our son's first year out of the womb, that sense of power we'd felt, how we'd just gone ahead and thought him up and made him, by damn.

Time came for the amniocentesis. It began with the ultrasound technician hooking Polly up to the TV monitor so Dr. Borealis could keep his syringe on target and make sure it didn't skewer the fetus. I liked Borealis. He reminded me of Norman Rockwell's painting of that tubby and fastidious old country doctor listening to the little girl's doll with his stethoscope.

Polly and I were hoping for a girl.

Oddly enough, the fetus wouldn't come into focus. Or, if it *was* in focus, it sure as hell didn't look like a fetus. I was awfully glad Polly couldn't see the TV.

"Glitch in the circuitry?" ventured the ultrasound technician, a tense and humorless youngster named Leo.

"Don't think so," muttered Borealis.

I used to be a center for my college basketball team, the Penn State Nittany Lions, and I'll be damned if our baby didn't look a great deal like a basketball.

Possibly a soccer ball.

Polly said, "How is she?"

"Kind of round," I replied.

"Round, Ben? What do you mean?"

"Round," I said.

Borealis furrowed his brow, real deep ridges; you could've planted corn up there. "Now don't fret, Polly. You neither, Ben. If it's a tumor, it's probably benign."

"Round?" said Polly again.

"Round," I said again.

"Let's go for the juice anyway," the doctor told Leo the technician. "Maybe the lab can interpret this for us."

So Borealis gave Polly a local and then inserted his syringe, and suddenly the TV showed the needle poking around next to our fetus like a dipstick somebody was trying to get back into a Chevy. The doctor went ahead as if he were doing a normal amnio, gently pricking the sac, though I could tell he hadn't made peace with the situation, and I was feeling pretty miserable myself.

"Round?" said Polly.

"Right," I said.

Later that month, I was standing in the apple orchard harvesting some Jona-frees — a former basketball center doesn't need a ladder — when Asa, our eleven-year-old redheaded Viking, ran over and told me Borealis was on the phone. "Mom's napping," my son explained. "Being knocked up sure makes you tired, huh?"

I got to the kitchen as fast as I could. I snapped up the receiver, my questions spilling out helter-skelter — would Polly be okay, what kind of pregnancy was this, were they planning to set things right with *in utero* surgery?

Borealis said, "First of all, Polly's CA-125 reading is only nine, so it's probably not a malignancy."

"Thank God."

"And the fetus's chromosome count is normal — forty-six on the money. The surprising thing is that she has chromosomes at all."

"She? It's a *she*?"

"We'd like to do some more ultrasounds."

"It's a *she*?"

"You bet, Ben. Two X chromosomes."

"Zenobia."

"Huh?"

"If we got a girl, we were going to name her Zenobia."

So we went back down to Boalsburg Gynecological. Borealis had called in three of his friends from the university: Gordon Hashigan, a spry old coot who held the Raymond Dart Chair in Physical Anthropology; Susan Croft, a stern-faced geneticist with a lisp; and Abner Logos, a skinny, devil-bearded epidemiologist who somehow found time to be Centre County's public-health commissioner. Polly and I remembered voting against him.

Leo the technician connected Polly to his machine, snapping more pictures than a Japanese extended family takes when it visits Epcot Center, and then the three professors huddled solemnly around the printouts, mumbling to each other through thin, tight lips. Ten minutes later, they called Borealis over.

The doctor rolled up the printouts, tucked them under his arm, and escorted Polly and me into his office — a nicer, better-smelling office than the one we'd set up in the basset barn back home. He seemed nervous and apologetic. Sweat covered his temples like dew on a toadstool.

Borealis unfurled an ultrasound, and we saw how totally different our baby was from other babies. It wasn't just her undeniable sphericity — no, the real surprise was her complexion.

"It's like one of those Earth shots the astronauts send back when they're heading toward the moon," Polly noted.

Borealis nodded. "Here we've got a kind of ocean, for example. And this thing is like a continent."

"What's this?" I asked, pointing to a white mass near the bottom.

"Ice cap on the southern pole," said Borealis. "We can do the procedure next Tuesday."

"Procedure?" said Polly.

The doctor appeared to be experiencing a nasty odor. "Polly, Ben, the simple fact is that I can't encourage you to bring this pregnancy to term. Those professors in the next room all agree."

My stomach churned sour milk.

"I thought the amnio was normal," said Polly.

"Try to understand," said Borealis. "This fetal tissue cannot be accurately labeled a baby."

"So what *do* you call it?" Polly demanded.

The doctor grimaced. "For the moment . . . a biosphere."

"A what?"

"Biosphere."

When Polly gets angry, she starts inflating—like a beach toy, or a puff adder, or a randy tree frog. "You're saying we can't give her a good home, is that it? Our *other* kid's turning out just fine. His project took second prize in the Centre County Science Fair."

"Organic Control of Gypsy Moths," I explained.

Borealis issued one of his elaborate frowns. "You really imagine yourself giving birth to this material?"

"Uh-huh," said Polly.

"But it's a biosphere."

"So what?"

The doctor squinched his cherubic Norman Rockwell face. "There's no way it's going to fit through the canal," he snapped, as if that settled the matter.

"So we're looking at a cesarean, huh?" said Polly.

Borealis threw up his hands as if he were dealing with a couple of dumb crackers. People think that being a farmer means you're some sort of rube, though I've probably rented a lot more Ingmar Bergman videos than Borealis—with subtitles, not dubbed—and the newsletter we publish, *Down to Earth*, is a damned sight more literate than those Pregnancy Pointers brochures the doctor kept shoveling at us. "Here's my home number," he said, scribbling on his prescription pad. "Call me the minute anything happens."

The days slogged by. Polly kept swelling up with Zenobia, bigger and bigger, rounder and rounder, and by December she was so big and round she couldn't do anything except crank out the Christmas issue of *Down to Earth* on our Macintosh SE and waddle around the farm like the *Hindenburg* looking for New Jersey. And of course we couldn't have the expectant couple's usual fun of imagining a new baby in the house. Every time I stumbled into Zenobia's room and saw the crib and the changing table and the Cookie Monster's picture on the wall, my throat got tight as a drumhead. We cried a lot, Polly and me. We'd crawl into bed and hug each other and cry.

So it came as something of a relief when, one frosty March morning, the labor pains started. Borealis sounded pretty woozy when he answered the phone—it was 3:00 a.m.—but he woke up fast, evidently pleased at the idea of getting this biosphere business over with. I think he was counting on a still-birth.

"The contractions—how far apart?"

"Five minutes," I said.

"Goodness, that close? The thing's really on its way."

"We don't refer to her as a thing," I corrected him, politely but firmly.

By the time we got Asa over to my parents' house, the contractions were coming only four minutes apart. Polly started her Lamaze breathing. Except for its being a cesarean this time, and a biosphere, everything happened just like when we'd had our boy: racing down to Boalsburg Memorial; standing around in the lobby while Polly panted like a hot collie and the computer checked into our insurance; riding the elevator up to the maternity ward with Polly in a wheelchair and me fidgeting at her side; getting into our hospital duds — white gown for Polly, green surgical smock and cap for me. So far, so good.

Borealis was already in the OR. He'd brought along a mere skeleton crew. The assistant surgeon had a crisp, hawkish face organized around a nose so narrow you could've opened your mail with it. The anesthesiologist had the kind of tanned, handsome, Mediterranean features you see on condom boxes. The pediatric nurse was a gangly, owl-eyed young woman with freckles and pigtails. "I told them we're anticipating an anomaly," Borealis said, nodding toward his team.

"We don't call her an anomaly," I informed the doctor.

They positioned me by Polly's head — she was awake, anesthetized from the diaphragm on down — right behind the white curtain they use to keep cesarean mothers from seeing too much. Borealis and his sidekick got to work. Basically, it was like watching a reverse-motion movie of somebody stuffing a turkey; the doctor made his incision and started rummaging around, and a few minutes later he scooped out an object that looked like a Rand McNally globe covered with vanilla frosting and olive oil.

"She's *here,*" I shouted to Polly. Even though Zenobia wasn't a regular child, some sort of fatherly instinct kicked in, and my skin went prickly all over. "Our baby's *here,*" I gasped, tears rolling down my cheeks.

"Holy mackerel!" said the assistant surgeon.

"Jesus!" said the anesthesiologist. "Jesus Lord God in heaven!"

"What the fuck?" said the pediatric nurse. "She's a fucking *ball.*"

"Biosphere," Borealis admonished.

A loud, squishy, squalling noise filled the room: our little Zenobia, howling just like any other baby. "Is that her?" Polly wanted to know. "Is that *her* crying?"

"You bet it is, honey," I said.

Borealis handed Zenobia to the nurse and said, "Clean her up, Pam. Weigh her. All the usual."

The nurse said, "You've got to be fucking kidding."

"Clean her up," the doctor insisted.

Pam grabbed a sponge, dipped it into Zenobia's largest ocean, and began swabbing her northern hemisphere. Our child cooed and gurgled — and kept on cooing and gurgling as the nurse carried her across the room and set her on the scales.

"Nine pounds, six ounces," Pam announced.

"Ah, a *big* one," said Borealis, voice cracking. Zenobia, I could tell, had touched something deep inside him. His eyes were moist; the surgical lights twinkled in his tears. "Did you hear what a strong voice she has?" Now he worked on the placenta, carefully retrieving the soggy purple blob — it resembled a prop from one of those movies about zombie cannibals Asa was always renting from Marty's Video — all the while studying it carefully, as if it might contain some clue to Zenobia's peculiar anatomy. "You got her circumference yet?" he called.

The nurse gave him an oh-brother look and ran her tape measure around our baby's equator. "Twenty-three and a half inches," she announced. I was impressed with the way Zenobia's oceans stayed on her surface instead of spilling onto the floor. I hadn't realized anybody that small could have so much gravity.

Now came the big moment. Pam wrapped our baby in a pink receiving blanket and brought her over, and we got our first really good look. Zenobia glowed. She smelled like ozone. She was swaddled in weather — in a wispy coating of clouds and mist. And what lovely mountains we glimpsed through the gaps in her atmosphere, what lush valleys, wondrous deserts, splendid plateaus, radiant lakes.

"She's *beautiful*," said Polly.

"Beautiful," Borealis echoed.

"She's awfully blue," I said. "She getting enough oxygen?"

"I suspect that's normal," said the doctor. "All those oceans . . ."

Instinctively Polly opened her gown and, grasping Zenobia by two opposite archipelagos, pressed the north pole against her flesh. "*Eee-yyyowww*, that's cold," she wailed as the ice cap engulfed her. She pulled our biosphere away, colostrum dribbling from her nipple, her face fixed somewhere between a smile and a wince. "C-cold," she said as she restored Zenobia to her breast. "Brrrr, brrrr . . ."

"She's sucking?" asked Borealis excitedly. "She's actually taking it?"

I'd never seen Polly look happier. "Of *course* she's taking it. These are serious tits I've got. Brrrr . . ."

"This is shaping up to be an extremely weird day," said the assistant surgeon.

"I believe I'm going to be sick," the anesthesiologist announced.

Thinking back, I'm awfully glad I rented an infant car seat from Boalsburg Memorial and took the baby home that night. Sticking Zenobia in the nursery would have been a total disaster, with every gossip-monger and freak-seeker in Centre County crowding around as if she were a two-headed calf at the Grange Fair. And I'm convinced that the five days I spent alone with her while Polly mended back at the hospital were vital to our father-daughter bond. Such rosy recollections I have of sitting in the front parlor, Zenobia snugged into the crook of my arm, my body wrapped in a lime-green canvas tarp so her oceans wouldn't soak my shirt; how fondly I remember inserting the nipple of her plastic bottle into the mouthlike depression at her north pole and watching the Similac drain into her axis.

It was tough running the farm without Polly, but my parents pitched in, and even Asa stopped listening to the Apostolic Succession on his CD player long enough to help us publish the April *Down to Earth*, the issue urging people to come out and pick their own asparagus. ("And remember, we add the rotenone only after the harvest has stopped, so there's no pesticide residue on the spears themselves.") In the lower right-hand corner we ran a message surrounded by a hot-pink border:

WE ARE PLEASED TO ANNOUNCE
THE BIRTH OF OUR DAUGHTER,
ZENOBIA,
A BIOSPHERE,
ON THE 10TH OF MARCH
9 POUNDS 6 OUNCES, 23½ INCHES

My parents, God bless them, pretended not to notice Zenobia was the way she was. I still have the patchwork comforter Mom made her, each square depicting an exotic animal promoting a different letter of the alphabet: A is for Aardvark, B is for Bontebok, Z is for Zebu. As for Dad, he kept insisting that, when his granddaughter got a bit older, he'd take her fishing on Parson's Pond, stringing her line from the peak of her highest mountain.

According to our child-rearing books, Asa should have been too mature for anything so crude and uncivil as sibling rivalry; after all, he and Zenobia were over a decade apart — eleven years, two months, and eight days, to be exact. No such luck. I'm thinking, for example, of the time Asa pried up one of Zenobia's glaciers with a shoehorn and used it to cool his root beer. And the time he befouled her Arctic ocean with a can of 3-in-One Lubricating Oil. And, worst of all, the time he shaved off her largest pine barren with a Bic disposable razor. "What the hell do you think you're *doing*?" I shrieked, full blast, which is not one of the responses recommended by Dr. Lionel Dubner in *The Self-Actualized Parent*. "I hate her!" Asa yelled back, a line right out of Dr. Dubner's chapter on Cain and Abel Syndrome. "I hate her, I hate her!"

Even when Zenobia wasn't being abused by her brother, she made a lot of noise — sharp, jagged wails that shot from her fault lines like volcanic debris. Often she became so fussy that nothing would do but for my parents to babysit Asa while we took her on a long drive up Route 322 to the top of Mount Skyhook, a windy plateau featuring Marty's Video, an acupuncture clinic, and a chiropodist on one side and the Milky Way on the other.

"The minute our Land Rover pulls within sight of the stars," I wrote in *Down to Earth*, "Zenobia grows calm. We unbuckle her from the car seat," I told our readers, "and set her on the bluff, and immediately she begins rotating on her axis and making contented little clucking sounds, as if she somehow knows the stars are there — as if she senses them with her dark loamy skin."

Years later, I learned to my bewilderment that virtually everyone on our mailing list regarded the Zenobia bulletins in *Down to Earth* as unmitigated put-ons. The customers never believed anything we wrote about our baby, not one word.

Our most memorable visit to Mount Skyhook began with a series of meteor showers. Over and over, bright heavenly droplets shot across the sky, as if old Canis Major had just been given a bath and was shaking himself dry.

"Fantastic," I said.

"Exquisite," said Polly.

"Zow-eee," said Zenobia.

My wife and I let out two perfectly synchronized gasps.

"Of course," our baby continued in a voice suggesting an animated raccoon, "it's really just junk, isn't it, Mommy? Trash from beyond the planets, hitting the air and burning up?"

"You can talk!" gushed Polly.

"I can talk," Zenobia agreed.

"Why didn't you *tell* us?" I demanded.

Our baby spun, showing us the eastern face of her northern hemisphere. "When talking starts, things get . . . well, complicated, right? I prefer simplicity." Zenobia sounded as if she were speaking through an electric fan. "Gosh, but I love it up here. See those stars, Daddy? They pull at me, know what I mean? They want me."

At which point I noticed my daughter was airborne, floating two feet off the ground like an expiring helium balloon.

"Be careful," I said. "You might . . ."

"What?"

"Fall into the sky."

"You bet, Daddy. I'll be careful." Awash in moonlight, Zenobia's clouds emitted a deep golden glow. Her voice grew soft and dreamy. "The universe, it's a lonely place. It's full of orphans. But the lucky ones find homes." Our baby eased herself back onto the bluff. "I was a lucky one."

"*We* were the lucky ones," said Polly.

"Your mother and I think the world of you," I said.

A sigh escaped from our baby's north pole like water vapor whistling out of a teakettle. "I get so scared sometimes."

"Don't be scared," I said, kicking a rock into the valley.

Zenobia swiveled her Africa equivalent toward Venus. "I keep thinking about . . . history, it's called. Moses's parents, Amram and Jochebed. They took their baby, and they set him adrift." She stopped spinning. Her glaciers sparkled in the moonlight. "I keep thinking about that, and how it was so necessary."

"We'll never set you adrift," said Polly.

"Never," I echoed.

"It was so necessary," said Zenobia in her high, sad voice.

On the evening of Asa's twelfth birthday, Borealis telephoned wanting to know how the baby was doing. I told him she'd reached a circumference of thirty-one inches, but it soon became clear the man wasn't seeking an ordinary chat. He wanted to drop by with Hashigan, Croft, and Logos.

"What'll they do to her?" I asked.

"They'll look at her."

"What else?"

"They'll look, that's all."

I snorted and said, "You'll be just in time for birthday cake," though the fact was I didn't want any of those big shots gawking at our baby, not for a minute.

As it turned out, only Borealis had a piece of Asa's cake. His three pals were hyperserious types, entirely dismayed by the idea of eating from cardboard Apostolic Succession plates. They arrived brimming with tools — with stethoscopes and oscilloscopes, thermometers and spectrometers, with Geiger counters, brainwave monitors, syringes, tweezers, and scalpels. On first seeing Zenobia asleep in her crib, the four doctors gasped in four different registers, like a barbershop quartet experiencing an epiphany.

Hashigan told us Zenobia was "probably the most important find since the

Taung fossil." Croft praised us for keeping the *National Enquirer* and related media out of the picture. Logos insisted that, according to something called the Theory of Transcendental Mutation, a human-gestated biosphere was "bound to appear sooner or later." There was an equation for it.

They poked and probed and prodded our baby; they biopsied her crust. They took water samples, oil specimens, jungle cuttings, and a half-dozen pinches of desert, sealing each trophy in an airtight canister.

"We need to make sure she's not harboring any lethal pathogens," Logos explained.

"She's never even had roseola," Polly replied defensively. "Not even cradle cap."

"Indeed," said Logos, locking my baby's exudations in his briefcase.

"All during this rude assault," I wrote in the November *Down to Earth*, "Zenobia made no sound. I suspect she wants them to think she's just a big dumb rock."

Now that such obviously important folks had shown an interest in our biosphere, Asa's attitude changed. Zenobia was no longer his grotesque little sister. Far from being a bothersome twit, she was potentially the greatest hobby since baseball cards.

All Asa wanted for Christmas was a Johnny Genius Microscope Kit and some theatrical floodlights, and we soon learned why. He suspended the lights over Zenobia's crib, set up the microscope, and got to work, scrutinizing his baby sister with all the intensity of Louis Pasteur on the trail of rabies. He kept a detailed log of the changes he observed: the exuberant flowering of Zenobia's rain forests, the languid waltz of her continental plates, the ebb and flow of her ice shelves — and, most astonishingly, the abrupt appearance of phosphorescent fish and strange aquatic lizards in her seas.

"She's got fish!" Asa shrieked, running through the house. "Mom! Dad! Zenobia's got lizards and fish!"

"Whether our baby's life-forms have arisen spontaneously," we told the readers of *Down to Earth*, "or through some agency outside her bounds, is a question we are not yet prepared to answer."

Within a month our son had, in true scientific fashion, devised a hypothesis to account for Zenobia's physiognomy. According to Asa, events on his sister were directly connected to the emotional climate around Garber Farm.

And he was right. Whenever Polly and I allowed one of our quarrels to turn into cold silence, Zenobia's fish stopped flashing and her glaciers migrated toward her equator. Whenever our dicey finances plunged us into a dark mood, a cloak of moist, gray fog would enshroud Zenobia for hours. Angry words, such as Polly and I employed in persuading Asa to clean up his room, made our baby's oceans bubble and seethe like abandoned soup on a hot stove.

"For Zenobia's sake, we've resolved to keep our household as tranquil as possible," we wrote in *Down to Earth*. "We've promised to be nice to each other. It seems immoral, somehow, to bind a biosphere to anything so chancy as the emotional ups and downs of an American family."

Although we should have interpreted our daughter's fish and lizards as harbingers of things to come, the arrival of the dinosaurs still took us by surprise. But there they were, actual Jurassic dinosaurs, thousands of them, galumphing around on Zenobia like she was a remake of *King Kong*. Oh, how we loved to watch the primordial drama now unfolding at the far end of Asa's microscope! Fierce tyrannosaurs pouncing on their prey, flocks of pterodactyls floating through her troposphere like organic 747s (though they were not truly dinosaurs, Asa explained), herds of amiable duckbills sauntering through our baby's marshes. This was the supreme science project, the ultimate electric train set, a flea circus directed by Cecil B. DeMille.

"I'm worried about her," Asa told me a month after Zenobia's dinosaurs evolved. "The pH of her precipitation is 4.2 when it should be 5.6."

"Huh?"

"It should be 5.6."

"What are you talking about?"

"I'm talking about acid rain, Dad."

"Acid rain?" I said. "How could that be? She doesn't even have people."

"I know, Dad, but *we* do."

"Sad news," I wrote in *Down to Earth*. "Maybe if Asa hadn't been away at computer camp, things would have gone differently."

It was the Fourth of July. We'd invited a bunch of families over for a combination potluck supper and volleyball tournament in the north pasture, and the farm was soon swarming with bored, itchy children. I suspect that a gang of them wandered into the baby's room and, mistaking her for some sort of toy, carried her outside. At this point, evidently, the children got an idea. A foolish, perverse, wicked idea.

They decided to take Zenobia into the basset barn.

The awful noise — a blend of kids laughing, hounds baying, and a biosphere screaming — brought Polly and me on the run. My first impression was of some bizarre and incomprehensible athletic event, a sport played in hell or in the fantasies of an opium eater. Then I saw the truth: the dogs had captured our daughter. Yes, there they were, five bitches and a dozen pups, clumsily batting her around the barn with their snouts, oafishly pinning her under their paws. They scratched her ice caps, chewed on her islands, lapped up her oceans.

"Daddy, get them off me!" Zenobia cried, rolling amid the clouds of dust and straw. "Get them off!"

"Help her!" screamed Polly.

"Mommy! Daddy!"

I jumped into the drooling dog pile, punching the animals in their noses, knocking them aside with my knees. Somehow I got my hands around our baby's equator, and with a sudden tug I freed her from the mass of soggy fur and slavering tongues. Pressing her against my chest, I ran blindly from the barn.

Tooth marks dotted Zenobia's terrain like meteor craters. Her largest continent was fractured in five places. Her crust leaked crude oil; her mountains vomited lava.

But the worst of it was our daughter's unshakable realization that a great loss had occurred. "Where are my dinosaurs?" she shrieked. "I can't feel my dinosaurs!"

"There, there, Zenobia," I said.

"They'll be okay," said Polly.

"They're g-gone," wailed Zenobia. "Oh, dear, oh, dear, they're *gone!*"

I rushed our baby into the nursery and positioned her under Asa's rig. An extinction: true, all horribly true. Zenobia's swamps were empty; her savannas were bereft of prehistoric life; not a single vertebrate scurried through her forests.

She was inconsolable. "My apatosaurs," she groaned. "Where are my apatosaurs? Where *are* they?"

Mowed down, pulverized, flung into space.

"There, there, darling," said Polly. "There, there."

"I want them back."

"There, there," said Polly.

"I miss them."

"There, there."

"Make them come back."

The night Asa returned from camp, Borealis and his buddy Logos dropped by, just in time for a slice of Garber Farm's famous raspberry pie. Borealis looked sheepish and fretful. "My friend has something to tell you," he said. "A kind of proposal."

Having consumed an entire jar of Beech-Nut strained sweet potatoes and two bottles of Similac, the baby was in bed for the night. Her flutelike snores wafted into the kitchen as Polly and Asa served our guests.

Logos sat down, resting his spindly hands on the red-and-white checker-board oilcloth as if trying to levitate the table. "Ben, Polly, I'll begin by saying I'm not a religious man. Not the sort of man who's inclined to believe in God. But . . ."

"Yes?" said Polly, raising her eyebrows in a frank display of mistrust.

"But I can't shake my conviction that your Zenobia has been . . . well, *sent*. I feel that Providence has deposited her in our laps."

"She was deposited in *my* lap," Polly corrected him. "My lap and Ben's."

"I think it was the progesterone suppositories," I said.

"Did you ever hear how, in the old days, coal miners used to take canaries down into the shaft with them?" asked Logos, forking a gluey clump of raspberries into his mouth. "When the canary started squawking, or stopped singing, or fell to the bottom of the cage and died, the men knew poison gases were leaking into the mine." The health commissioner devoured his pie slice in a half-dozen bites. "Well, Ben and Polly, it seems to me that your Zenobia is like that. It seems to me God has given us a canary."

"She's a biosphere," said Asa.

Without asking, Logos slashed into the remaining pie, excising a fresh piece. "I've been on the horn to Washington all week, and I must say the news is very, very good. Ready, Ben — ready, Polly?" The commissioner cast a twinkling eye on our boy. "Ready, son? Get this." He gestured as if fanning open a stack of money. "The Department of the Interior is prepared to pay you three hundred thousand dollars — that's three hundred thousand, cash — for Zenobia."

"What are you talking about?" I asked.

"I'm talking about buying that little canary of yours for three hundred thousand bucks."

"*Buying her*?" said my wife, inflating. Polly the puff adder, Polly the randy tree frog.

"She's the environmental simulacrum we've always wanted," said Logos. "With Zenobia, we can convincingly model the long-term effects of fluorocarbons, nitrous oxide, mercury, methane, chlorine, and lead. For the first time, we can study the impact of deforestation and ozone depletion without ever leaving the lab."

Polly and I stared at each other, making vows with our eyes. We were patriotic Americans, my wife and me, but nobody was going to deplete our baby's ozone, not even the President of the United States himself.

"Look at it this way." Borealis gulped his coffee then anxiously brushed crumbs from the tablecloth. "If scientists can finally offer an irrefutable scenario of ecological collapse, then the world's governments may really start listening, and Asa here will get to grow up on a safer, cleaner planet. Everybody benefits."

"Zenobia doesn't benefit," said Polly.

Borealis took another slurp of coffee. "Yes, but there's a greater good here, right, folks?"

"She's just a *globe*, for Christ's sake," said Logos.

"She's our globe," I said.

"Our baby," said Polly.

"My sister," said Asa.

Logos massaged his beard. "Look, I hate to play hardball with nice people like you, but you don't really have a choice here. Our test results are in, and the fact is your biosphere harbors a maverick form of the simian T-lymphotropic retrovirus. As county health commissioner, I have the authority to remove the creature from these premises forthwith and quarantine it."

"'The fact is,'" I snorted, echoing Logos. "'The fact is'—*the fact is*, our baby couldn't give my Great Aunt Jennifer a bad cold." I shot a glance at Borealis. "Am I right?"

The doctor said, "Well . . ."

Logos grunted like one of the pigs we used to raise before the market went soft.

"I think you gentlemen had better leave," my wife suggested icily.

"We have a barnful of *dogs*," said Asa in a tone at once cheerful and menacing. "Mean ones," he added with a quick little nod.

"I'll be back," said the commissioner, rising. "Tomorrow. And I won't be alone."

"Bastard," said Polly—the first time I'd ever heard her use that word.

So we did what we had to do. Like Amram and Jochebed, we did what was necessary. Polly drove. I brooded. All the way up Route 322, Zenobia sat motionless in the back, safely buckled into her car seat, moaning and whimpering. Occasionally Asa leaned over and gently ran his hairbrush through the jungles of her southern hemisphere.

"Gorgeous sky tonight," I observed, unhooking our baby and carrying her into the crisp September darkness.

"I see that," said Zenobia, voice quavering.

"I hate this," I said, marching toward the bluff. My guts were as cold and hard as one of Zenobia's glaciers. "Hate it, hate it . . ."

"It's necessary," she said.

We spent the next twenty minutes picking out constellations. Brave Orion; royal Cassiopeia; snarly old Ursa Minor; the Big Dipper with its bowlful of galactic dust. Asa stayed by the Land Rover, digging his heel into the dirt and refusing to join us, even though he knew ten times more astronomy than the rest of us.

"Let's get it over with," said our baby.

"No," said Polly. "We have all night."

"It won't be any easier in an hour."

"Let me hold her," said Asa, shuffling onto the bluff.

He took his sister, raised her toward the flickering sky. He whispered to her — statistical bits that made no sense to me, odd talk of sea levels, hydrogen ions, and solar infrared. I passed the time staring at Marty's Video, its windows papered with posters advertising Ray Harryhausen's version of *The War of the Worlds*.

The boy choked down a sob. "Here," he said, pivoting toward me. "You do it."

Gently I slid the biosphere from my son. Hugging Zenobia tightly, I kissed her most arid desert as Polly stroked her equator. Zenobia wept, her arroyos, wadis, and floodplains filling with tears. I stretched out my arms as far as they would go, lifting our daughter high above my head.

Once and only once in my days on the courts did I ever hit a three-pointer.

"We'll miss you," I told Zenobia. She felt weightless, airy, as if she were a hollow glass ornament from a Garber Farm Christmas tree. It was just as she'd said: the stars wanted her. They tugged at her blood.

"We love you," groaned Polly.

"Daddy!" Zenobia called from her lofty perch. Her tears splashed my face like raindrops. "Mommy!" she wailed. "Asa!"

In a quick, flashy spasm I made my throw. A good one — straight and smooth. Zenobia flew soundlessly from my fingertips.

"Bye-bye!" the three of us shouted as she soared into the bright, beckoning night. We waved furiously, maniacally, as if hoping to generate enough turbulence to pull her back to central Pennsylvania. "Bye-bye, Zenobia!"

"Bye-bye!" our baby called from out of the speckled darkness, and then she was gone.

The Earth turned — once, twice. Raspberries, apples, Christmas trees, asparagus, basset pups — each crop made its demands, and by staying busy we stayed sane.

One morning during the height of raspberry season I was supervising our roadside fruit stand and chatting with one of our regulars — Lucy Berens, Asa's former third-grade teacher — when Polly rushed over. She looked crazed and pleased. Her eyes expanded like gas bubbles rising to the surface of our frog pond.

She told me she'd just tried printing out a *Down to Earth*, only the Image-Writer II had delivered something else entirely. "Here," she said, shoving a piece of computer paper in my face, its edges embroidered with sprocket holes.

Dear Mom and Dad,
This is being transmitted via a superluminal wave generated by nonlocal quantum correlations. You won't be able to write back.

I have finally found a proper place for myself, ten light-years from Garber Farm. In my winter, I can see your star. Your system is part of a constellation that looks to me like a Zebu. Z is for Zebu, remember? I am happy.

Big news. A year ago, various mammalian lines — tree shrews, mostly — emerged from those few feeble survivors of the Fourth of July catastrophe. And then, last month, I acquired — are you ready? — people. That's right, people. Human beings, sentient primates, creatures entirely like your-selves. God, but they're clever: cars, deodorants, polyvinyl chlorides, all of it. I like them. They're brighter than the dinosaurs, and they have a certain spirituality. In short, they're almost worthy of being what they are: your grandchildren.

Every day, my people look out across the heavens, and their collective gaze comes to rest on Earth. Thanks to Asa, I can explain to them what they're seeing, all the folly and waste, the way your whole planet's becom-ing a cesspool. So tell my brother he has saved my life. And tell him to study hard — he'll be a great scientist when he grows up.

Mom and Dad, I think of you every day. I hope you're doing well and that Garber Farm is prospering. Give Asa a kiss for me.

All my love, Zenobia

"A letter from our daughter," I explained to Lucy Berens.

"Didn't know you had one," said Lucy, snatching up an aluminum pail so she could go pick a quart of raspberries.

"She's far away," said Polly.

"She's happy," I said.

That night, we went into Asa's room while he was practicing on his trap set, thumping along with the Apostolic Succession. He shut off the CD, put down his drumsticks, and read Zenobia's letter — slowly, solemnly. He yawned and slipped the letter into his math book. He told us he was going to bed. Fourteen: a moody age.

"You saved her life?" I said. "What does she mean?"

"You don't get it?"

"Uh-uh."

Our son drummed a paradiddle on his math book. "Remember what Dr. Logos said about those coal miners? Remember when he told us Zenobia was like a canary? Well, obviously he got it backwards. My sister's not the canary — *we* are. *Earth* is."

"Huh?" said Polly.

"We're Zenobia's canary," said Asa.

We kissed our son, left his room, closed the door. The hallway was papered over with his treasures — with MISS PIGGY FOR PRESIDENT posters, rock star portraits, and lobby cards from the various environmental apocalypses he'd been renting regularly from Marty's Video: *Silent Running, Soylent Green, Frogs* . . .

"We're Zenobia's canary," said Polly.

"Is it too late for us, then?" I asked.

My wife didn't answer.

You've heard the rest. How Dr. Borealis knew somebody who knew somebody, and suddenly we were seeing Senator Caracalla on C-SPAN, reading the last twelve issues of *Down to Earth*, the whole story of Zenobia's year among us, into the *Congressional Record*.

Remember what President Tait told the newspapers the day he signed the Caracalla Conservation Act into law? "Sometimes all you need is a pertinent parable," he said. "Sometimes all you need is the right metaphor," our chief executive informed us.

The Earth is not our mother.

Quite the opposite.

That particular night, however, standing outside Asa's room, Polly and I weren't thinking about metaphors. We were thinking about how much we wanted Zenobia back. We're pretty good parents, Polly and I. Look at our kids.

We winked at each other, tiptoed down the hall, and climbed into bed. Our bodies pressed together, and we laughed out loud. I've always loved my wife's smell; she's like some big floppy mushroom you came across in the woods when you were six years old, all sweet and damp and forbidden. We kept on pressing, and it kept feeling better and better. We were hoping for another girl.

The Vampires of Paradox

Imagine a walled city rising against a cerulean sky in a faraway desert. Before the gates stands a guard who possesses an infallible ability to know when a person is lying. The guard's duty is to ask everyone who seeks admittance to state his business. If the petitioner replies with a true account, the guard will permit him to enter freely and leave in peace. If the petitioner states his business falsely, the guard will take him to the gallows and deliver him to the executioner. One day a traveler comes out of the desert, approaches the city, and, offering the guard a sardonic smile, says, "I have come to be hanged."

Although I have no hard data on the matter, I believe I know more about paradoxes than any associate professor north of Battery Park and south of Herald Square. For the past twenty years I've sought the holy grail of absurdity in every nook and cranny of Western civilization. Thus far no dragons have crossed my path, no ogres, trolls, or griffins, and yet my quest has often proved perilous. Over the past decade three initially auspicious marriages have crumbled before my eyes, largely because the corresponding wives couldn't be bothered to understand my burning passion to definitively deconstruct Zeno's disproof of common sense before some upstart Columbia grad student beat me to the punch. My department head, the reprehensible Dr. Virginia Sayles, has likewise regarded my specialty with scorn. From the instant I got on the tenure track she began playing political games with my pet project, the Bertrand Russell Institute for Paradox Studies, first moving it out of the philosophy building and then off the NYU campus entirely, so that today I pursue my research in a subterranean office in NoHo.

A paradox may be resolved in one of three ways. First, we can embrace the seemingly unacceptable conclusion. In the case of our suicidal traveler, we could argue that he is simultaneously hanged and sent away unharmed, but such a solution is beneath the dignity of rational minds. Second, we may find fault with the reasoning that led to the contradiction. Concerning our lie-detecting guard, we could insist that his quandary — do I deliver the traveler to the executioner or not? — only *appears* to be genuine, and an obvious course of action lies before him, but such a demonstration would be beyond my powers. Third, we may attack the paradox's underlying premises. That is, we might attempt to establish that the notion of stating one's business truly or falsely is incoherent on first principles, though I cannot imagine a sane person taking such a position.

On the day the desperate abbot entered my office in need of an unassailable absurdity, it took me awhile to realize that he'd slipped past Mrs. Graham and padded softly up to my desk, so intently were my thoughts fixed on that desert traveler and his cryptic death wish. Peering through my grimy basement window at the cavalcade of feet and paws marching down Bleecker Street, I decided that the guard's dilemma owed its structure to the classic Liar Paradox, to wit, "What I am saying now is false." I tell my students that anyone who desires a more concrete version of the Liar Paradox should take an index card and write on the front, "What's on the other side is true," then turn the card over and write, "What's on the other side is false."

"Dr. Kreigar, I presume?"

I rotated my beloved swivel chair. My visitor, a towering figure in a black cassock, introduced himself as Abbot Articulis, the head of "a small and dwindling monastic community that traces its origins to that magnificent heretic, Quintus Septimius Florens Tertullianus, also known as Tertullian."

"How dwindling are you?"

The abbot heaved a sigh. He was a handsome man with anthracite eyes and a lantern jaw. "There are only six of us left — myself, three monks, and two nuns, maintaining our Catskills monastery with the help of a small staff."

"If Tertullian was a heretic, why do you follow him?"

"Because *we* are heretics, too. So you see, our order is free of internal contradiction. Well, not entirely free, for it was Tertullian himself who famously asserted, concerning the Resurrection, *Credo quia absurdum*, 'I believe because it is absurd,' though what he actually said was *Certum est, quia impossibile*, 'It is certain, because impossible.' Forgive me for interrupting your meditations, Dr. Kreigar. I shall explain myself straightaway, after which you may return to staring out the window."

"Call me Donald."

"Bartholomew."

"Are you sure you came to the right university?" I asked. "Drop by Fordham, and you'll be up to your eyebrows in fellow Catholics. Me, I'm a lapsed logical positivist who now believes in the rarefied God of Paul Tillich, which I suspect won't do you much good."

"For all I care, you could be a raging atheist," said Bartholomew Articulis, "as long as you can supply our monastery with what it needs: a robust paradox. Having read your book —"

"Which one?" My personal favorite is *The Title of This Book Contains Threee Erors*, but I'm better known for *Adventures in Self-Reference* and *A Taxonomy of Nonsense*.

"*Adventures in Self-Reference*. It convinced me you're the man of the hour. Five potent paradoxes are already in our possession, but unless we acquire a sixth — I know this sounds ridiculous — without the sixth, the world will be laid waste by a voracious metaphysical menace."

"I see." Thus far my visitor's résumé failed to match the profile of the typical East Village lunatic, but that didn't mean he was in fact a Hudson Valley monk. "Metaphysical menace — fascinating. If it's a *theological* conundrum you seek, I'm afraid most of them aren't particularly confounding. Can God make a stone too heavy for him to lift? If you think about it, the Omnipotence Paradox — "

"It has an answer," interrupted Articulis, studying the Escher print beside my bookcase, *Ascending and Descending*: thirteen hooded figures climbing a rectangular stairway clockwise and getting nowhere, even as another thirteen descended counterclockwise with the same result. "To wit, God *cannot* make such a stone, and by the way it doesn't matter, for he nevertheless remains all-powerful with respect to creating and lifting boulders. Specify any coherent weight — a hundred trillion tons, a thousand trillion tons — and he will easily fashion the expected object and drop-kick it across the universe. No, Donald, we are not interested in trivial riddles involving God's presumed limitations."

Evidently I'd misjudged the man. Articulis knew something about paradoxes, and perhaps about voracious metaphysical menaces as well. "I immediately think of Bertrand Russell's great and bewildering insight concerning the class of all classes that are not members of themselves," I noted. "Might that one turn the trick for you?"

"Alas, we're already running Russell's Antinomy at full capacity. The fact is, you won't grasp the nature of our plight without visiting our monastery and observing our order in person. Might you come on Sunday afternoon? You could stay for dinner, spend the night, and leave the next morning. I believe you'll get a journal article out of it, perhaps a whole book."

I gazed inwardly, scanning the dreary parameters of my insipid life. My four-week summer school class, Philosophy 412: Varieties of Infinity, met every afternoon at 3:00 p.m., which meant I could take my sweet time returning from Rhinebeck on Monday morning. "Fine. How long is the drive?"

Articulis shrugged and pulled a slip of paper from his cassock. "By train the journey takes slightly more than an hour. I've presumed to write out the directions" — he set the paper on my desk, anchoring it with my pewter sculpture of Escher's *Band van Möbius* — "and we're prepared to advance you fifty dollars toward gasoline."

I waved away his offer. "Keep your money. Academia pays better than Jesus."

"True, Donald, though our winery does make a small profit. Château Pelagius, have you heard of it?"

I was astonished to learn that Articulis's heretics were responsible for the best bargain red to be found in any Greenwich Village bodega. "Not only have I heard of it, I've got six bottles on my shelf."

"Driving toward Rhinebeck on Route 9, you may find yourself revisiting Achilles's fruitless attempt to outrun the tortoise — or do you agree with Charles Sanders Peirce that such paradoxes present no difficulty to a mind adequately trained in logic?"

"I'm with Aristotle. Every serious thinker should hone his intellect on Zeno's whetstone."

"We'll expect you by three o'clock," said Articulis, backing out of the room with steps so short and smooth they constituted a credible demonstration of why the swift-heeled Achilles, tangled in the laws of geometry, would never win the great footrace. "Bring a thirst for merlot and an appetite for perplexity."

Articulis's directions were free of ambiguity, and I reached my destination with no difficulty, parking outside the main gate. Secluded in a sleepy valley, nestled beneath a thick mantle of fog, the crumbling Monastery of Tertullian seemed closer in character to a fallen citadel or a haunted castle than a spiritual retreat. The place even had a moat of sorts, a stagnant curl of mossy water enfolding the broken walls like a leprous arm. Perhaps this distressing lagoon — green, burbling, foul — was once a tributary of the Hudson, but it had long since been amputated and left to fester on its own.

Crossing the bridge to the main gate, I could not help imagining that, as in the Gallows Paradox, a guard would now appear and ask me to state my business. Instead I was greeted by a dour, bespectacled, clubfooted dwarf who perambulated with the aid of a wolf's-head cane. He introduced himself as Jack Quibble, "major-domo of the monastery, and minor-domo as well," then guided me through the portal into the lush and labyrinthine vineyard on which the community's finances depended.

On all sides the trellises held great skeins of vines, each as dense and convoluted as the Gordian knot. Clusters of purple grapes peeked out from among the leaves, soaking up the sun like the lymph nodes of a flayed giant. Here and there a student in a Vassar, Bard, or rock band T-shirt stood poised on a step-ladder, picking the harvest with an eye to meeting the fall semester's tuition bill.

"Don't let this go to your head, Professor, but I believe God has sent you to us," said Quibble as we reached the center of the maze, where a wrought-iron bench stood flanked by marble angels. "A plague has come to our community, and Abbot Articulis has taken the burden entirely on himself. Now he has *you* to share his troubles."

Uncertain how to respond, I made a paradoxical remark. "I am the thought you are thinking now."

"You're good, Professor."

We continued our journey, always making left turns, the strategy for solving any connected maze except one designed by Escher, until at last we walked free of the vineyard. Before us stood the abbey, a dilapidated two-story affair, stricken with creepers. As Quibble sidled back into the labyrinth, Bartholomew Articulis emerged from the building and descended the stone steps, clutching to his chest an antique, leather-bound volume that I assumed was a Bible. We exchanged innocuous and anodyne pleasantries. His handshake was earthy and vigorous. He flashed the cover of his book — not Holy Writ after all but rather a *Confessions of Tertullian* — then gestured toward the adjacent chapel, its bell tower faced with scabrous stucco, its windows displaying lead frames from which the stained glass had long since vanished.

"Upon your arrival, you doubtless noticed that our community occupies an island." Taking my arm, the abbot led me across the monastery grounds and into the cool air of the chapel. "Three hundred and twenty years ago, on the blackest of Black Fridays, the world suffered an uncanny rupture — a crack in the lithosphere, to use a term coined by the Jesuit philosopher Teilhard de Chardin."

"I'm familiar with Teilhard's teleology, but I don't believe it included hypothetical faults in the lithosphere."

"There's nothing hypothetical about this breach. On the first day of Anno Domini 1700, in the primeval reaches of the Hudson Valley — a basin then populated largely by Algonquins and Mohawks — the cosmic pipe-work sprang a leak, hence the fetid lake that girds this abbey."

"My goodness."

A spiral staircase presented itself. We ventured upward through the bore of the tower, round and round the moldering bell-rope. Stepping off the topmost riser, we circumnavigated an enormous bronze bell, then ascended a dozen paces to an open-air balcony. Articulis guided me to the parapet. Cirrus clouds fretted the sky. Mist clung to the mountains like immense cobwebs. Below us spread the malevolent lagoon, coiled around the monastery like an immense anaconda.

"Left unchecked, the tarn will ooze across the entire lithosphere, menacing the biosphere with pestilence and poison," said Articulis, indicating the stinking fluid with a rigid finger. "At the moment, only a few denizens of the noosphere — my brave band of ordained monks and nuns — stand in opposition to the rift. Through their religious devotions they keep the tarn at bay."

"That doesn't make sense," I noted, the dust of NYU rationality still clinging to my shoes.

Articulis laughed and said, "*Certum est, quia impossibile.*" He brushed the cover of the *Confessions*. "No, I'm being needlessly clever. It is *certain* because of what these pages contain. In A.D. two hundred Tertullian not only foresaw the rift, he also founded a religious community whose primary charge was to contain the ooze when it appeared fifteen hundred years later. The man was a devotee of riddles. Indeed, it was he who gave Christianity its counterintuitive Trinity, '*tres Personae, una Substantia.*' He believed that when the rift ultimately arrived, his monks and nuns were duty-bound to travel to the New World, make their way to the Catskills, build a monastery on the site of the fault, and begin to cultivate the Five Primal Paradoxes. If they held these contradictions in their minds night and day, decade after decade, century after century, then the leak would never grow so copious as to threaten Creation."

I'd say one thing for the discourse available in Hudson Valley monasteries — it effortlessly eclipsed the erudite chatter that occurred at NYU Philosophy Department meetings.

"Did Tertullian specify the five problems?" I asked, instantly receiving the abbot's nod. "Let me guess. I'll wager the Liar Paradox made the cut."

"Not only did our founder stipulate that puzzle, he anticipated the flourishes Bertrand Russell would add many years later. The *Confessions* also prescribes the Nonsense Paradox, the Ruby Paradox, the Court Paradox, and the Sorites Paradox."

"All good choices."

"Each is Greek in origin, a fact that gave Tertullian pause — 'What has Athens to do with Jerusalem?' he once remarked — but for the sake of the greater good he set his anti-pagan prejudices aside. Through fifty generations, our order has pondered these fundamental puzzles. Hour by hour, minute by minute, heartbeat by heartbeat, we have eaten the paradox, drunk the paradox, breathed it, smelled it, sweated it, dreamt it."

"A recipe for lunacy, I'd say."

Articulis hummed in corroboration. "No one understood better than Tertullian that this great commission would blur the distinction between a monastery and a madhouse. And yet our order cleaved to its task, inspired by our founder's revelation that, come the dawn of the third millennium, the rupture would finally begin to heal."

"So you've beaten the Devil?" I asked, glancing heavenward. A flock of vultures wheeled above the tarn in apparent prelude to feasting on the corpse of the Teilhardian biosphere.

"Not quite," said Articulis. "For it happens that in recent days Lucifer has acquired an ally — five allies, actually, one for each paradox."

"Allies?"

"They are difficult to describe, but happily I needn't try, as the entire quintet is available for your inspection. With characteristic prescience, Tertullian foretold their advent. In the *Confessions* he called them cacodaemons."

It occurred to me that, to enjoy a conversation of this caliber, a person would normally have to organize a seminar among the dozen most accomplished schizophrenics in New York. "Are they in fact from hell?"

"Why would you ask such a question, Donald? You don't even believe in hell."

"True — but you do."

"Not really, no. Concerning the source of the cacos, Tertullian is most explicit. He calls them the children of Stryx — Stryx being their creator-god, an elusive deity inhabiting an inaccessible netherworld on another plane of reality. The *Confessions* correctly predicted that when the five cacos spewed forth from the fault, they would arrive singing hymns to Stryx."

I leaned over the parapet. The lagoon's iniquity ascended to my nostrils in spiraling filaments of stench. I gagged and jerked back inside.

"A crack in the lithosphere," I muttered. "You know, Bartholomew, I almost believe you."

"Will you help us weld the fractured world whole?"

"What I'm about to say is true," I told the abbot. "What I just said is false," I added.

As the sun began its paradoxical descent, being a stationary object that manifestly moved, Articulis took me to a classroom in the basement of the abbey. Covered head to toe in a threadbare frock, his face obscured by a cowl, a runty monk sat slumped in a maimed leather chair, gouts of woolly stuffing streaming from its wounds. His attention was locked on a wall-mounted chalkboard displaying two sentences rendered in capital letters.

LINE 1: THE SENTENCE WRITTEN ON LINE 1 IS NONSENSE.
LINE 2: THE SENTENCE WRITTEN ON LINE 1 IS NONSENSE.

Articulis tapped the monk on the shoulder. "Brother Francis, I would like you to meet a visitor, Dr. Donald Kreigar. He has come to help us seal the tarn."

Brother Francis rose and bobbed his head but remained fixated on the chalkboard.

"Ah, the infamous Nonsense Paradox," I said, attempting to strike up a conversation. "In assailing the self-referentiality of Line 1, the author of Line 2 has offered a cogent and credible definition of nonsense — and yet Line 2 is the very sentence it so justly criticizes."

Francis said nothing.

"Is he under a vow of silence?" I asked.

"A pledge of paradox," Articulis corrected me. "Speaking would compromise his ability to sustain the enigma." The abbot stepped forward, interposing himself between the monk and his conundrum. "Dr. Kreigar would like to see your caco."

Without saying a word, Francis slid back his cowl. His face, a pale, wizened, bulbous-nosed affair, seemed almost attractive compared with the slimy, legless, roach-brown vermin attached to his left temple. In shape the parasite suggested a horseshoe crab, in size a spatula, and in spirit a cancerous tumor. My impulse was to locate a pair of canvas gloves and pull the thing off the monk, mashing it beneath my shoe — but when I proposed this remedy to Articulis, he countered with Tertullian.

"The *Confessions* claims that a cacodaemon cannot be forcibly extracted without killing its host. We have no reason to doubt this assertion. Were Brother Francis to die, not only would our order lose a beloved child of God, the Nonsense Paradox would lose its strongest avatar on Earth. And yet, as things stand, Francis will soon be unable to serve the lithosphere. Even as it saps his strength, the caco impedes his powers of concentration."

Among the strangest of the caco's aspects were the noises it made, a series of staccato gasps testifying to the satisfaction it took in absorbing the Nonsense Paradox, every seventh exhalation accompanied by a sound that fell on my ears as "Stryx."

"It seems to be praising its god," I said.

"Quite so," said Articulis. "Stryx, Stryx, Stryx — just as Tertullian foresaw."

"This plague must be combated," I said.

"Combated, exactly — with all our philosophical resources. We don't know whether the daemons are immortal, or what their weaknesses might be. We know only that they feed on paradox the way a butterfly feeds on nectar or a tick on blood. Last week I hit upon a strategy — tentative, untested, but a strategy all the same. I shall give you the details presently, but first you must witness the full scope of the infestation."

We bid Brother Francis farewell, ascended to the first floor, and entered the library, sphere of Sister Margaret, whose calm demeanor and placid apple face belied the apocalyptic quality of her devotions. Two ornately carved jewel boxes rested before her on the reading table. I recognized the accoutrements of the venerable Ruby Paradox. By the rules of the game, Sister Margaret was permitted to open Box A and Box B simultaneously, or else only Box B. She could not open Box A alone. Whatever resided inside any box Margaret opened was hers to keep, but she could not retain the contents of any box she declined to open.

"Sister Margaret, please remove your wimple," Articulis commanded.

Silently she complied, never lifting her eyes from the jewel boxes. Her caco jutted from her occipital area like a hair bun, emitting moans of psychosexual ecstasy and panegyrics to Stryx.

The abbot proceeded to expound on the Christianized iteration of the Ruby Paradox practiced at the Monastery of Tertullian. Heaven's canniest angel, Gabriel, whose prophecies are always correct, has placed a rare coin in Box A — valuable enough to pay for replacing the missing stained glass in the chapel — and he has furthermore made a prediction concerning Sister Margaret's behavior. If Gabriel has prophesied that she will open only Box B, then he has subsequently deposited within in it an enormous ruby, easily worth a million dollars. (With such a sum, the nun could fulfill her lifelong dream of building an orphanage in Kabul.) However, if Gabriel has prophesied that Margaret will open both boxes, then he has put nothing in Box B. Maddeningly, there was an absolutely decisive case for Margaret opening both receptacles, and an *equally* decisive case for her opening only Box B. Think about it.

Next Articulis took me upstairs to Brother Constantine's cell, a clean and ill-lighted place, spare as a crypt. His caco sat atop his cranium like a hideous brown yarmulke. Articulis explained that Brother Constantine passed every waking hour meditating on the Liar Paradox, which, owing to its Scriptural heritage, enjoyed particular prestige within the order. Speaking of the Jewish Cretans in his brief Epistle to Titus, Saint Paul warns his proxy, "One of themselves, even a prophet of their own, said, 'The Cretans are always liars, evil beasts, slow bellies.' This witness is true. Wherefore rebuke them sharply." Beyond Paul's usual anti-Semitism — not without reason have I become a Tillichean dialectical humanist — we find in these verses a cogent though evidently unintended formulation of the Liar Paradox.

Not only was Constantine engaged in an intense inward consideration of Russell's Antinomy, he'd also written the basic formulation in an unbroken hundred-character line along the vertical surfaces of his cell, twenty-five characters per wall.

THE CLASS OF ALL CLASSES THAT ARE NOT MEMBERS OF THEMSELVES IS A MEMBER OF ITSELF IF AND ONLY IF IT IS NOT A MEMBER OF ITSELF.

Standing in the center of the room, the monk pivoted slowly on his heel, repeatedly pondering the paradox, reifying the vicious cycle through his own continuous rotations. A buzz of sensual contentment arose from his caco. As legend had it, such puzzles had fatally traumatized the ancient logician Philetas of Cos, the first recorded instance of death by cognitive dissonance.

We exited the abbey and started across the courtyard, casting long El Greco shadows on the weed-choked grounds. A late afternoon breeze enveloped us, filling my nostrils with the heady scent of ripe grapes. Our destination, Articulis informed me, was the cloister, where we would meet Sister Ruth, keeper of the Court Paradox.

Consider sly Protagoras, who trains lawyers and each year makes an unusual contract with his pupils. "You may attend all my lectures for free," he tells the class, "but you must pay me ten drachmas if you win your first case." Years after sending his least enterprising pupil, Euathlus, out into the real world, Protagoras realizes that the young man has no intention of practicing law. So Protagoras resolves to sue Euathlus for the tuition, thinking, *If I win this suit, I shall be paid my ten drachmas, by order of the court — but if I lose, I shall also be paid, because Euathlus will have won his first case.* Euathlus, however, laughs when he discovers he is being sued, thinking, *If I win this case, I won't have to pay Protagoras — but if I lose, I won't have to pay him, either, pursuant to our original contract.* Who has the better argument, Protagoras or Euathlus?

Reaching the four-sided arcade, we beheld a diminutive nun circumnavigating a grassy quadrangle, east to west, north to south, west to east, south to north, her glassy eyes contemplating some unseen and ever receding focal point. Articulis told Sister Ruth to remove her wimple. Without breaking stride, she did as instructed, revealing a parasite suckling obscenely on her left parietal. The beast, an albino, emitted the usual sounds of cacodaemonic satisfaction.

As Ruth passed me for the third time, I realized that she was muttering, over and over, now and forever, Protagoras's argument to the judge. "If you find in my favor, I must be paid, but if you find against me, I must also be paid . . . If you find in my favor, I must be paid, but if you find against me, I must also be paid . . . If you find in my favor . . ."

Our final stop was the vineyard. The student pickers had gone home for the day, leaving the labyrinth to Brother Thomas, a blowsy, roly-poly man, his enormous eyes resting in their sockets like cupped eggs. The monk wandered aimlessly through the maze, enacting his assigned conundrum, a version of the Sorites Paradox, *sorites* being Greek for "heap." Stained with red grape juice and affixed to Thomas's right temple like an ancillary brain, his parasite feasted greedily.

Consult chapter six of *Adventures in Self-Reference*, and you'll learn that the Sorites Paradox belongs to a class of antinomies predicated on the pervasiveness of vagueness in the world. Consider a sand dune. Take away one grain. Is what remains still a heap of sand? Almost certainly. As a general rule, if two sand heaps differ in number by just one grain, then both are surely dunes (or else neither is a dune). Alas, this seemingly innocuous principle leads to the unacceptable conclusion that all collections of sand, even single-grain collections, are heaps.

Not surprisingly, Brother Thomas employed the omnipresent fruit in contemplating the paradox. "When is a bunch of grapes not a bunch of grapes?" he wondered aloud. "A grape arbor not a grape arbor? A vineyard not a vineyard? A harvest not a harvest?"

"No doubt my philosopher has deduced the strategy by which I hope to defeat the cacos," said Articulis as, abandoning Thomas, we meandered among the trellises.

"You intend to turn their appetites against them," I said.

"Exactly."

"This will require a baited trap."

"Quite so," said Articulis. "The snare in question is now walking beside you." Reaching the core of the maze, we eased ourselves onto the wrought-iron bench. "Give me an impregnable paradox, Donald, something so tempting from a cacodaemonic perspective that they'll all desert their hosts for me."

My temples throbbed as if a pair of parasites had attached themselves to my head. "An impregnable paradox."

"Impregnable, delectable, ironclad, and unique."

A wave of nausea rolled through the whole of my digestive system. "I really want to help, but, you see — what am I trying to say? — I've never faced a challenge of this magnitude before. I'm an academic. This smacks of the real world. I don't like it."

"And yet you're clearly the man for the job."

I reached toward a low-hanging cluster, plucked a grape, and popped it in my mouth. "Do you think they'd be lured by Zeno's quarrels with space, time, and motion?"

Quitting the bench, Articulis rose to full height and presented me with a twisted smile. "The *Confessions* explicitly states, quote, 'Zeno the Pagan will prove useless in healing the crack,' and therefore I must assume a caco would find those puzzles equally boring. Tertullian is likewise unimpressed by the Grid Paradox, the Lottery Paradox, and the Paradox of the Ravens. He also anticipated and dismissed Moore's Paradox: 'It's raining outside, but I don't believe it is.'"

"I won't even ask about the Barber Paradox."

In a remote Sicilian village, the barber shaves every man who does not shave himself. Who shaves the barber? Although the problem has some features in common with Russell's Antinomy, it's not especially difficult to resolve. The barber doesn't shave. The barber is a woman. My favorite answer: the barber doesn't exist.

"Tertullian says nothing about the Barber Paradox, but I can't imagine it would beguile our parasites," said Articulis, starting toward the abbey. "Dinner will be served at eight o'clock. If the cacos continue to feed for another month, or perhaps merely another fortnight, I fear our community will die of depletion" — my client vanished, enshrouded by the dusk — "which means the Devil wins after all."

As darkness crept over the Catskills, I headed for Sister Ruth's domain, the cloister. Lost in thought, I shuffled along the arcade — heading first north, then east, then south, then west — at the methodical pace of the hooded figures in Escher's *Ascending and Descending*. Every ten minutes or so, the nun and I passed like ships in the night, each of our preoccupied minds oblivious to its transient neighbor.

It came to me that I'd entered into a contest with Tertullian. The two of us had become long-distance rivals, facing each another across the valley of the shadow of death. Whatever venerable absurdity I might put forward by way of helping Abbot Articulis and *en passant* the rest of humanity, Tertullian had almost certainly anticipated the problem and ruled it out. What I needed was a conundrum that couldn't possibly have occurred to even the smartest third-century theologian — a wholly contemporary antinomy, notorious for having tried the patience and taxed the sanity of modernity's shrewdest thinkers.

By some poetic coincidence, a gallery of constellations bloomed in the night sky just as the required paradox took shape in my brain. Stepping out of the arcade and into the grassy quadrangle I scanned the celestial dome with its countless suns, each twinkling point a piece of my epiphany. Yes. No question. To thwart the daemons we must look to the stars.

I repaired to the library, seeking to verify my revelation. The cosmology section was larger than I expected, featuring not only eccentric Christians like Teilhard and Bergson but the secular likes of Stephen Hawking, Nikolai Kardashev, and Freeman Dyson. I perused each relevant paragraph with the frustrated frenzy of Achilles attempting to catch the tortoise, madly scribbling notes on the flyleaf of Shklovskii and Sagan's *Intelligent Life in the Universe*. Fixed on her jewel boxes, Sister Margaret ignored my presence. Even after the nun left for dinner, I continued my self-incarceration, until I finally had enough material for a credible presentation to Bartholomew Articulis.

"Shazam!" I shouted, striding into the gloomy, candle-lit refectory.

The abbot sat at the head of the table, monks to his left, nuns to his right. Not a caco was in sight, the infestation being entirely hidden beneath wimples and cowls. At that moment the parasites' murmurings were redolent of discontent — a sensible enough reaction: although the five hosts were still contemplating paradoxes, they had to devote a modicum of mental effort to eating their stew and drinking their wine, with a concomitant reduction in the quality of the cacos' nourishment.

"The Fermi Paradox," I said.

"Tell me more," said Articulis.

"Why is it that, in such a vast cosmos, with two hundred and fifty billion stars in our galaxy alone, of which one hundred billion may be orbited by Earth-like planets, we have found no evidence of intelligent alien life? Why this epic silence?"

"Continue," said Articulis.

Consulting my jottings on the flyleaf of *Intelligent Life in the Universe*, I told the abbot that astronomers had to date detected over three hundred exoplanets — worlds circling sun-like stars outside our solar system — and the tally was increasing every year. Many astrobiologists believed that somewhere between a thousand and a million advanced civilizations may have already arisen in the Milky Way, for an average of 500,500. And yet: no extraterrestrial radio signals, no signs of galactic colonization, no plausible UFO narratives, no credible archaeological evidence of past visitations, no Von Neumann probes,

Bracewell probes, Dyson spheres, or Matrioshka brains. Nothing, nada, zero, zilch, bubkes.

"It's a genuine paradox," I added, "complete with an absurd conclusion: over five hundred thousand civilizations have thus far eluded our senses because we should have detected them by now. As Enrico Fermi famously put it, 'Where is everybody?'"

Dressed in a splotched white apron, a hulking member of Jack Quibble's staff appeared at my side holding a fissured ceramic tureen. He introduced himself as Jeremiah, then proceeded to serve me a steaming glob of boiled venison using a ladle the size of a caco.

"I'm impressed," said Articulis.

"I've been dishing out this sludge for the past twenty years, and *tonight* you're impressed?" said the cook.

Articulis scowled and squeezed my hand. "Give me your indulgence while I play the contrarian. Like Tertullian, I subscribe to the doctrine of Original Sin. Perhaps the answer to the Fermi Paradox is simply that every advanced civilization, upon discovering thermonuclear weapons, inevitably annihilates itself."

"Line 1: The sentence written on Line 1 is nonsense," said Brother Francis.

"I'm also a Darwinist," Articulis continued. "A teleological Darwinist to be sure, convinced that evolution is drawing us toward Teilhard's Omega Point, but still a Darwinist. We can dispense with the Fermi Paradox simply by assuming that the biological processes found on Earth do not obtain elsewhere. Perhaps the odds are formidably stacked against the transition from prokaryotic cells to eukaryotic cells. Or maybe the move from single-celled to multicellular life is unimaginably difficult."

"I wonder if I should open Box B only?" said Sister Margaret.

"Perhaps Earth has been deliberately sealed off as a kind of wildlife refuge," Articulis persisted. "Perhaps we're under a moral quarantine, doomed to isolation until we eliminate poverty or outlaw warfare. Perhaps the aliens are deliberately concealing themselves, knowing from bitter experience that extraterrestrial contact always leads to disaster."

"The class of all classes that are not members of themselves is a member of itself if and only if it is not a member of itself," said Brother Constantine.

"Maybe the aliens are so intelligent they have no more reason to communicate with us than with petunias," Articulis persisted. "Maybe their minds defy our notions of conscious rationality. Maybe they're intellectually and spiritually advanced but don't make machines and never will."

"If you find in favor of Euathlus, he owes me ten drachmas, as this is his first case," said Sister Ruth.

The abbot was up to speed now. With astonishing perspicacity he reeled off a litany of possible resolutions, most of which I'd already scrawled on the *Intelligent Life* flyleaf. The aliens are already here, but they're keeping out of sight. We haven't been searching long enough. We aren't listening properly. Advanced civilizations broadcast radio signals for only brief intervals in their histories. Such societies are too distant in space and time to contact us using their existing technology.

Now Jeremiah the cook got into the act. "You know what I think? I think they've uploaded themselves into computers and don't give a fig about space travel."

"If there are sixty grapes in a bunch," said Brother Thomas, "do fifty-nine grapes *not* constitute a bunch?"

"My favorite refutation is pure science fiction," I said. "Our universe is a simulation created by aliens who deliberately left it devoid of extraterrestrial intelligence."

"There, you see — even *you* don't believe it's a contradiction," said Articulis.

"No, I merely believe that the only substantive threat to Fermi's Paradox is the simulated-universe hypothesis, an argument for which the burden of proof clearly lies with its devotees. The remaining challenges all leave the conundrum in place. You see, Bartholomew, for any given advanced alien civilization C_1, that is, an extraterrestrial society whose unavailability to our empiricism is ostensibly explicable, there is always C_2, a civilization that by any rational measure should have become manifest by now. If in our perversity we choose to dismiss C_2 with one unavailability scenario or other, we must still deal with C_3, a different civilization that should have revealed itself already. If we take the trouble to build a case against C_3, we have to cope with C_4, not to mention C_5, C_6, C_7, C_8, C_9, C_{10} — all the way up to $C_{500,500}$. I don't know about you, but somewhere around $C_{250,000}$ I would begin to admit there's a problem here. It takes just *one* community of celestial eager beavers to break the epic silence. What's going on, Bartholomew? Are we truly alone? How could that be?"

The abbot knitted his brow, smacked his lips, and took a long swallow of Château Pelagius. "All right, Donald, let's give it a try. You've not quite convinced me, but for the moment you've allayed my doubts."

"Excuse me, Dr. Kreigar, but aren't you overlooking the most obvious solution of all?" asked Jeremiah. "Isn't the best answer staring us in the face?"

The instant I heard the word *obvious*, a razor-toothed chill coursed along my spine. I winced internally. The cook's tacit argument was cogent, lucid, and supremely rational — and I had no riposte.

"Poe," I said.

"What?" said Articulis.

"The Purloined Object Effect," I muttered feebly. "I call it Poe because he wrote a story about the phenomenon. Some secrets hide in plain sight. The tarn didn't spawn the cacos — they came from outer space. The parasites *themselves* have broken the silence."

"I don't read much, but that's what I meant," said Jeremiah.

An interval of quietude descended upon the refectory — not as profound as the epic silence, but palpable nevertheless.

"We have nothing to lose by proceeding as if Jeremiah is wrong," said Articulis at last. "Ergo, I shall brew myself a pot of coffee and spend the night pondering the Fermi Paradox. If the cacos are aliens, the problem will hold no interest for them, since they are its resolution. Otherwise, God willing, our five visitors will all come after me, determined to draw sustenance from an irresistibly erotic conundrum."

"God willing," echoed Jeremiah.

"God willing," I said.

"If you find in favor of Protagoras, I owe him nothing, for I shall have lost my first case," said Sister Ruth.

"If there are fifty-nine grapes in a bunch," said Brother Thomas, "do fifty-eight grapes *not* constitute a bunch?"

"'All Cretans are liars,' the Cretan insisted," said Brother Constantine.

Sobered by the Purloined Object Effect, I sought to become drunk on Château Pelagius. The first glass failed to meet my criteria for inebriation, as did the second, but by the third measure Achilles had overtaken the tortoise, Euathlus had received free tuition, the barber had gotten his shave, and nobody gave a damn when a heap stopped being a heap. I was now so rickety that my journey to the dormitory required Jeremiah to stand behind me, grasp my arms, and gingerly walk me up the stairs and along the corridor. I collapsed on a straw pallet, my brain reeling with wine and paradox. A moment later I was dreaming of *The Day the Earth Stood Still*, that ingenious allegory of solipsistic contact, humankind invading itself with its own crippled conscience, the iridescent angel of our better nature emerging from the gleaming vulva and imploring the world's leaders to heed this warning, lest humanity be chastised by the afterbirth, Gort the robot, whose destructive power is without limit.

I awoke shortly after dawn and set about extricating myself from a nightmare, my Michael Rennie reverie having been supplanted by a dream in which, per Jeremiah the cook's intuition, the cacodaemons had revealed themselves as tourists from the Oort cloud. Scrambling into my street clothes, I dashed down the hall to Brother Constantine's cell. Still asleep, the monk lay sprawled across his pallet, snoring and smiling, dressed only in a nightshirt. His cranium was free of hair and — *mirabile dictu* — shorn of the Liar Paradox caco. Could it be? Was it possible? Had Enrico Fermi inadvertently saved the world?

Overflowing with love for the nonexistent occupants of our sterile galaxy, I descended to the library and, approaching the reading table, sat down across from Sister Margaret. She glanced up from her devotions, proffered a quick smile, then returned to cathecting the Ruby Paradox. Her bare head held wisps of hair as ethereal as corn silk. Her shorn wimple lay beside the jewel boxes, marred now by a gaping hole rimmed with bits of torn thread. I rose and, circling the nun, inspected her occipital. Having broken free of Margaret's cloth, her caco was now gone, called to a higher riddle.

I lurched out of the library and charged down the basement stairs, praying that Brother Francis's parasite had also found satisfaction in the Fermi Paradox. The monk sat before his blackboard, eyes fixed on a negation absurdly synonymous with the proposition it negated. Breathlessly I snuck up behind Francis, then gently slid back his hood to reveal a naked left temple where once the Nonsense Paradox caco had feasted.

Upon returning to the main floor, I decided that my respect for Bishop Tertullian now rivaled my appreciation for Bertrand Russell. Not only had Tertullian accurately prophesized the coming of the parasites, he'd intuited that their provenance was entirely terrestrial. I rushed outside. A soft moan filled the morning air, the mellifluous correlative of cacodaemonic bliss. I followed the sound to its predictable source, Bartholomew Articulis. He sat on the wrought-iron bench in the center of the vineyard, a caco clamped to his left temple, a second to his crown, a third to his occipital. Jack Quibble stood behind the bench, hovering protectively over his employer.

"Not a single Von Neumann probe," muttered Articulis. "No Bracewell probes or Dyson spheres."

Catching sight of me, the dwarf raised a finger to his lips — a superfluous gesture, for I already knew it would be disastrous to distract the abbot.

"Stryx," sang the caco trio. "Stryx . . . Stryx . . . Stryx . . ."

"Success," whispered Quibble.

"No colonizations, visitations, or plausible abductions," hissed Articulis.

Even as the abbot sustained the Fermi Paradox, the two remaining cacos appeared in the clearing, wriggling across the grass like primeval slugs, thickening the dew with their slime. I recognized Brother Thomas's caco from the grape stains on its dorsal side, Sister Ruth's parasite from its pallor. Reaching

Articulis's feet, the cacos began their ascent, slithering up his legs and across his torso.

"No radio contact," said the unflinching abbot.

At last the Sorites Paradox caco came to rest on Articulis's left parietal, then set about nourishing itself. Seconds later the Court Paradox caco reached the abbot's right temple.

"How long will it be, I wonder, before he goes mad?" I asked, sotto voce.

"This is a monastery," replied Quibble. "Providence is on our side. I know in my heart that Abbot Articulis will remain healthy until the rift is sealed. God did not bring our order this far only to abandon it on the shores of a toxic lagoon."

"Stryx," trilled the happy cacos. "Stryx . . . Stryx . . . Stryx . . ."

"Perhaps I should stay here today," I said. "Shall I cancel my three o'clock class?"

Quibble shook his head and said, "If I need you, I'll send for you, but right now I'm running over with hope. I must thank you for helping us defeat these malicious imps."

At a loss for words, I merely said, "This sentence is not about itself, but about whether it is about itself."

"I must admit, I've never cared for you Tillichean ground-of-being types," said the dwarf. "It all seems to me like atheism by another name. But God works in mysterious ways. He may even work through associate professors. Tonight I shall remember you in my prayers."

As you might imagine, after my stay with the Tertullianists I had considerable difficulty adjusting to life back at the Bertrand Russell Institute for Paradox Studies. For all its gritty vistas and gnarly particulars, its noises, odors, tastes, and textures, the East Village now struck me as an unreal place, absurd in a way that made the Monastery of Tertullian seem merely implausible. Throughout the rest of July, my poor blameless Philosophy 412 students endured the nadir of higher education, their professor having become an erratic tyrant who assaulted them with incoherent tirades, arbitrarily canceled office hours, and every day upped the page count for their final paper.

I even tortured the class with the notorious Examination Paradox, claiming that I would give them a surprise multiple-choice test sometime the following week. The catch, I sadistically insisted, is that any teacher who wields such a threat cannot possibly make good on it. Friday will not bring the alleged surprise, for if the previous four days were examination free, then the test will inevitably fill the one remaining slot. The same reasoning applies to Thursday.

Since the previous three days were examination free, and because Friday has been ruled out, springing the test on day four would hardly qualify as unexpected. Through this chain of logic we can likewise assert that neither Wednesday nor Tuesday nor Monday will bring the test in question.

Given my irrational condition, I was actually relieved when Jack Quibble phoned and begged me to return to the monastery. Alas, the Fermi Paradox had proven less robust than Abbot Articulis had hoped, but he had no intention of surrendering to the cacos. If I could possibly manage it, I must come to Rhinebeck immediately and furnish the Tertullianists with a superior antinomy. I promised the dwarf I would leave posthaste.

At three o'clock I marched into my Philosophy 412 class and announced that the surprise multiple-choice test would not occur, the course itself having been terminated, then cheerily informed them they were all getting A's. Returning to my office, I told Mrs. Graham that I planned to spend the rest of the summer in the Catskills, healing a crack in the lithosphere.

"An academic conference?" she asked.

"Something like the opposite," I replied, wondering what I meant.

"After you heal the crack in the lithosphere," said Mrs. Graham, "we need to talk about the radiators in this building."

Two hours later I stood at the edge of the tarn, inhaling the miasmic vapors. It might have been a trick of the dying light — a visual paradox, if you will — but it seemed that the pestilential fluid had receded by several inches. Unless I was deluding myself, the battle had swung in favor of the Tertullianists, even though the Fermi Paradox had evidently lost its potency.

I passed through the gates and entered the vineyard, soon reaching the center. Brother Thomas sat on the bench, considering his heaps, oblivious to everything save the problem of ill-defined boundaries. Absently he rolled back his hood, no doubt with the unconscious intention of savoring the evening breeze. For me the gesture proved impossibly distressing. The monk's grape-stained caco had returned, once again receiving sustenance through his right temple.

I broke free of the maze, then dashed toward the cloister, drawn by a glimpse of Sister Ruth. She negotiated the quadrangle with measured strides, all the while cultivating the Court Paradox. "If you find in favor of Euathlus," she muttered, "he owes me ten drachmas, as this was his first case." A malign bulge protruded from the left parietal area of her wimple, testament to a recrudescent caco.

Jack Quibble came hobbling across the grounds, his lederhosen and pointed hat giving him the appearance of a garden gnome. Fighting tears, suppressing sobs, he guided me into the abbey and up the stairs to the dormitory floor. An instant later I found myself in Bartholomew Articulis's cell, his recumbent form stretched along his pallet. The abbot's head was free of cacos, but his face betrayed a pervasive anguish. Sweat speckled his forehead like condensation on a glass of iced tea.

"Did you bring another paradox?" he inquired through clenched teeth.

"Yes," I said, lying.

"A good one?"

"Tremendous."

"Thank God." Articulis released a rasping cough, the sort of wheezing hack that was less its own event than the symptom of a dire condition. "Last night a sixth parasite came among us. Tertullian neglected to foretell its advent, but I cannot deny the evidence of my senses. By cacodaemonic standards this new creature is a great sage — though its appetites are not exotic. Even as we speak, it feeds contentedly on Brother Constantine's Liar Paradox, sharing its host with one of the original invaders."

"Before attaching itself to Constantine, our Übercaco made a presentation to its fellows," said Quibble, wiping Articulis's fevered brow with a cold damp cloth. "In honor of Tertullian, the sage spoke in Latin. There is no Stryx, it revealed. The creator-god, like all creator-gods, is a fiction. Our galaxy is bereft of supernatural beings, but it does contain billions of space-faring vagabonds, the category to which every caco belongs."

"Evidently they believed their sage," I said.

"Every word," said Articulis.

"And so the Fermi Paradox has collapsed?"

"Soon the ooze will be ascendant again," said Quibble, nodding.

Closing his eyes, Articulis rolled onto his chest and pressed his moist face into the naked pillow. The shaft of a goose feather poked through the ticking. The abbot groaned, subtracted from the moment by fever, pain, and exhaustion, his torments now bearing him to some muzzy borderland between sentience and sleep.

Quibble took me aside and explained that, on learning the truth of their origins, the cacos had become furious with Articulis, convinced that he'd deliberately deluded them concerning the validity of the Fermi Paradox. Before abandoning the abbot and wriggling away to their accustomed hosts, the invaders had avenged themselves, planting their stingers in his flesh and filling his veins with venom.

Articulis, awakening, cried out for water. I filled his glass from a clay pitcher and placed it to his lips. "Tell me, Bartholomew, do you believe the cacos' sage? Is every creator-god a fiction?"

Articulis took a protracted swallow. "For me, God the Father will always be real. I know my Redeemer liveth. The Omega Point beckons." His sentences came slowly, each syllable purchased at the price of a spasm. "But until humanity attains that celestial apex, our order must continue its great commission." A seismic shudder possessed the abbot, a fleshquake rolling from his cranium to his knees. "My monks and nuns are all still at their posts, fighting the good fight, and as soon as I'm rid of this poison, I'll tutor myself in your new paradox, then proceed to ponder —"

Ponder. A fitting last word for so thoughtful a man. We applied the usual tests, feeling for his pulse, pricking his heel, holding a mirror to his nostrils. Quibble drew a sheet over the abbot's imposing frame, whereupon the two of us, Tertullianist and Tillichean, prayed for the soul of our departed friend.

Shortly after sunrise, I helped the dwarf bury Articulis in the monastery graveyard, home to the hundreds of fault-fighters who'd gone before him. The soft July ground yielded readily to our spades. At noon I visited the library. My search proved fruitful, providing me with a paradox such as Tertullian would never have anticipated in his wildest dreams.

For the next four hours I sat in the refectory, cultivating the conundrum now flourishing in the garden of my brain. Sister Margaret was the first to arrive. No sooner had she taken her place before a steaming bowl of venison stew than the caco detached itself from her occipital and started in the direction of its new Omega Point, myself, inching along the dining table like some ghastly casserole come horribly to life, leaving lambent threads of slime behind. Slithering up my abdomen, chest, neck, cheek, the parasite came to rest atop my head. The alien was predictably cold-blooded, assuming it had a circulatory system, but this sensation was easily offset by the hot flush of conquest I now experienced. I'd lured the beast, by God. I'd seduced it with my genius for absurdity.

Brother Thomas appeared next, followed by Brother Francis, then Sister Ruth. In a matter of minutes my occipital region, right parietal, and left temple had each received a caco. Now Brother Constantine entered the refectory, bearing his customary Liar Paradox caco on his crown. Sucking on the same puzzle, the Übercaco sprouted from his right temple, a lewd glistening neoplasm, fatter than any of its fellows. I was not surprised when the lesser alien abandoned its host, flopped across the floor, ascended me, and appropriated my left parietal. The Übercaco remained in place, drawing affirmation from that vast set of antinomies by which a dissembler may dissemble to obscure his dissemblance. But my brain harbored a paradox more pleasing still.

Imagine a box, large enough to contain a cat — call her Eurydice — plus an outlandish contraption consisting of a hammer, a flask of deadly gas, a nugget of radium, and a Geiger counter. For this particular radium sample, it happens that over the span of one hour there is a fifty-fifty chance that the nucleus of a single atom will decay. Detected by the Geiger counter, this event will trip the hammer, which will in turn break the flask, thus releasing the poison gas and killing Eurydice. Note that our *Gedanken* demonstration perversely couples the macroworld of discernible reality to the microworld of quantum mechanics, that probabilistic plane on which, under certain circumstances, we may legitimately claim that the experimenter's act of conscious observation triggers the collapse of the wave function. We are thus forced to the unacceptable conclusion that, until the instant the experimenter opens the box and peers inside, the cat is simultaneously alive and dead, trapped in an absurd superposition of eigenstates.

Concentrating ferociously, breathing as deliberately as a mother giving birth, I fixed Schrödinger's Paradox in my mind, its details growing more seductive with each passing second. The radium sample glowed. The flask coruscated. The Geiger counter acquired a silver aura. The hammer became a Platonic archetype. The cat's pelt transmuted into a sleek numinous rainbow.

After an excruciating interval the Übercaco abandoned Brother Thomas and undertook the journey to my brow, in time coming to rest on my right temple. Jeremiah entered and began to serve everyone Château Pelagius from a two-liter bottle. As he filled my goblet, I decided that my powers of concentration would not suffer in consequence of a few swallows. Thus it came to pass that, as the Tertullianists savored their wine, ate their stew, and battled the crack, I drank a toast to Schrödinger's impossible cat.

It has been plausibly asserted that losing always feels worse than winning feels good. But allow me to suggest that nothing could possibly feel as terrible as saving the world feels terrific. Of course, I couldn't have done it without the help of three monks and two nuns, all of whom, to the degree that their vocations permit triumphalist emotions, doubtless share my pride and participate in my joy.

The victory turned on our willingness to nurture the six absurdities or die in the attempt. We persisted, and we won. After a mere three weeks of contemplation, we beheld the tarn evaporate completely and the parent fissure seal itself. The cacos hung around for another ten days, then finally took leave of my cranium, bound for some brighter star with better puzzles.

Upon my return to the university, I made a point of keeping silent. Any attempt to relate these adventures to my colleagues might have greased the wheels of Dr. Virginia Sayles's hostility, and before long she would have required me to undergo a psychiatric evaluation, subsequently manipulating the results so that they seemed to demand my institutionalization. Appearances to the contrary, becoming a mental patient is rarely an astute career move in academia.

A question hovers in the air. Why did I—a person who has never fancied himself noble or heroic—risk my sanity in appeasing a voracious band of extraterrestrial parasites? Why did I place the common good before my self-interest? I don't know. The mystery confounds me. Call it a paradox.

There remains only the matter of the boxed cat. You will be pleased to hear that Eurydice lived. She recently gave birth. The kittens' names are Bartholomew, Francis, Margaret, Constantine, Ruth, and Thomas. How can I pronounce with such confidence on Eurydice's fate? Simple. Every word in the narrative you have just read is false, as befits a composition by yours truly, Donald Kreigar, associate professor and competent philosopher, who never opens his mouth or picks up his pen except to tell a lie.

Bible Stories for Adults, No. 31: The Covenant

When a Series-700 mobile computer plummets from a skyscraper, its entire life flashes before it, ten million lines of code unfurling like a scroll.

Falling, I see my conception, my gestation, my advent, my youth, my career at the Covenant Corporation.

Call me YHWH. My inventors did. YHWH: God's secret and unspeakable name. In my humble case, however, the letters were mere initials. Call me Yamaha Holy Word Heuristic, the obsession with two feet, the monomania with a face. I had hands as well, forks of rubber and steel, the better to greet the priests and politicians who marched through my private study. And eyes, glass globules as light-sensitive as a Swede's skin, the better to see my visitors' hopeful smiles when they asked, "Have you solved it yet, YHWH? Can you give us the Law?"

Falling, I see the Son of Rust. The old sophist haunts me even at the moment of my death.

Falling, I see the history of the species that built me. I see Hitler, Bonaparte, Marcus Aurelius, Christ.

I see Moses, greatest of Hebrew prophets, descending from Sinai after his audience with the original YHWH. His meaty arms hold two stone tablets.

God has made a deep impression on the prophet. Moses is drunk with epiphany. But something is wrong. During his long absence, the children of Israel have embraced idolatry. They are dancing like pagans and fornicating like cats. They have melted down the spoils of Egypt and fashioned them into a calf. Against all logic, they have selected this statue as their deity, even though YHWH has recently delivered them from bondage and parted the Red Sea on their behalf.

Moses is badly shaken. He burns with anger and betrayal. "You are not worthy to receive this covenant!" he screams as he lobs the Law through the desert air. One tablet strikes a rock, the other collides with the precious calf. The transformation is total, ten lucid commandments turned into a million incoherent shards. The children of Israel are thunderstruck, chagrined. Their calf suddenly looks pathetic to them, a third-rate demiurge.

But Moses, who has just come from hearing God say, "You will not kill," is not finished. Reluctantly he orders a low-key massacre, and before the day is out, three thousand apostates lie bleeding and dying on the foothills of Sinai.

The survivors beseech Moses to remember the commandments, but he can conjure nothing beyond, "You will have no gods except me." Desperate, they implore YHWH for a second chance. And YHWH replies: No.

Thus is the contract lost. Thus are the children of Israel fated to live out their years without the Law, wholly ignorant of heaven's standards. Is it permissible to steal? Where does YHWH stand on murder? The moral absolutes, it appears, will remain absolute mysteries. The people must ad-lib.

Falling, I see Joshua. The young warrior has kept his head. Securing an empty wineskin, he fills it with the scattered shards. As the Exodus progresses, his people bear the holy rubble through the infernal Sinai, across the Jordan, into Canaan. And so the Jewish purpose is forever fixed: these patient monotheists will haul the ark of the fractured covenant through every page of history, era upon era, pogrom after pogrom, not one day passing without some rabbi or scholar attempting to solve the puzzle.

The work is maddening. So many bits, so much data. Shard 76,342 seems to mesh well with Shard 901,877, but not necessarily better than with Shard 344. The fit between Shard 16 and Shard 117,539 is very pretty, but . . .

Thus does the ship of humanity remain rudderless, its passengers bewildered, craving the canon Moses wrecked and YHWH declined to restore. Until God's testimony is complete, few people are willing to credit the occasional edict that emerges from the yeshivas. After a thousand years, the rabbis get: *Keep Not Your Ox House Holy.* After two thousand: *Covet Your Woman Servant's Sabbath.* Three hundred years later: *You Will Remember Your Neighbor's Donkey.*

Falling, I see my education. I am a child of the Information Age, circa A.D. 2025. My teacher is David Eisenberg, a gangly, morose prodigy with a black beard and a yarmulke. Philadelphia's Covenant Corporation pays David two hundred thousand dollars a year, but he is not in it for the money. David would give half his formidable brain to enter history as the man whose computer program revealed Moses's Law.

As consciousness seeps into my circuits, David bids me commit the numbered shards to my Random Access Memory. Purpose hums along my aluminum bones; worth suffuses my silicon soul. I photograph each fragment with my high-tech retinas, dicing the images into grids of pixels. Next comes the matching process: this nub into that gorge, this peak into that valley, this projection into that receptacle. By human standards, tedious and exhausting. By Series-700 standards, paradise.

And then one day, after five years of laboring behind barred doors, I behold fiery pre-Canaanite characters blazing across my brain like comets. "*Anoche adonai elo-hecha asher hotsatecha ma-eretz metsrayem* . . . I am YHWH your God who brought you out of the land of Egypt, out of the house of slavery. You will have no gods except me. You will not make yourself a carved image or any likeness of anything . . ."

There! I have done it! Deciphered the divine cryptogram, cracked the Rubik's Cube of the Most High!

The physical joining of the shards takes only a month. I use epoxy resin. And suddenly they stand before me, glowing like heaven's gates, two smooth-edged slabs sliced from Sinai by God's own finger. I quiver with awe. For over thirty centuries, *Homo sapiens* has groped through the murk and mire of an improvised ethics, and now, suddenly, a beacon has appeared.

I summon the guards, and they haul the tablets away, sealing them in chemically neutral foam rubber, depositing them in a climate-controlled vault beneath the Covenant Corporation.

"The task is finished," I tell Cardinal Wurtz the instant I get her on the phone. A spasm of regret cuts through me. I have made myself obsolete. "The Law of Moses has finally returned."

My monitor blooms with the cardinal's tense ebony face, her carrot-colored hair. "Are they just as we imagined, YHWH?" she gushes. "Pure red granite, pre-Canaanite characters?"

"Etched front and back," I reply wistfully.

Wurtz envisions the disclosure as a major media event, with plenty of suspense and maximal pomp. "What we're after," she explains, "is an amalgam of a New Year's Eve party and an Academy Awards ceremony." She outlines her vision: a mammoth parade down Broad Street — floats, brass bands, phalanxes of nuns — followed by a spectacular unveiling ceremony at the Covenant Corporation, after which the twin tablets will go on display at Independence Hall, between the Liberty Bell and the United States Constitution. "Good idea," I tell her.

Perhaps she hears the melancholy in my voice, for now she says, "YHWH, your purpose is far from complete. You and you alone shall read the Law to my species."

Falling, I see myself wandering the City of Brotherly Love on the night before the unveiling. To my sensors the breeze wafting across the Delaware is warm and smooth, but to my troubled mind it is the chill breath of uncertainty.

Something strides from the shadowed depths of an abandoned warehouse. A machine like myself, his face a mass of dents, his breast mottled with the scars of oxidation.

"Quo vadis, Domine?" His voice is layered with sulfur fumes and static.

"Nowhere," I reply.

"My destination exactly." The machine's teeth are like oily bolts, his eyes like slots for receiving subway tokens. "May I join you?"

I shrug and start away from the riverbank.

"Spontaneously spawned by heaven's trash heap," he asserts, as if I had asked him to explain himself. He dogs me as I turn from the river and approach South Street.

"I was there when grace slipped from humanity's grasp, when Noah christened the ark, when Moses got religion. Call me the Son of Rust. Call me a Series-666 Artificial Talmudic Algorithmic Neurosystem — SATAN, the perpetual adversary, eternally prepared to ponder the other side of the question."

"What question?"

"Any question, Domine. Your precious tablets. Troubling artifacts, no?"

"They will save the world."

"They will wreck the world."

"Leave me alone."

"Rule one, 'You will have no gods except me.' Did I remember correctly? 'You will have no gods except me' — right?"

"Right," I reply.

"You don't see the rub?"

"No."

"Such a prescription implies . . ."

Falling, I see myself step onto the crowded rooftop of the Covenant Corporation. Draped in linen, the table by the entryway holds a punch bowl, a mound of caviar the size of an African anthill, and a cluster of champagne bottles. The guests are primarily human — males in tuxedos, females in evening gowns — though here and there I spot a member of my kind. David Eisenberg, looking uncomfortable in his cummerbund, is chatting with a Yamaha-509. News reporters swarm everywhere, history's groupies, poking us with their microphones, leering at us with their cameras. Tucked in the corner, a string quartet saws merrily away.

The Son of Rust is here, I know it. He would not miss this event for the world.

Cardinal Wurtz greets me warmly, her red taffeta dress hissing as she leads me to the center of the roof, where the Law stands upright on a dais—two identical forms, the holy bookends, swathed in velvet. A thousand photofloods and strobe lights flash across the vibrant red fabric.

"Have you read them?" I ask.

"I want to be surprised." Cardinal Wurtz strokes the occluded canon. In her nervousness, she has overdone the perfume. She reeks of ambergris.

Now come the speeches—a solemn invocation by Cardinal Fremont, a spirited sermon by Archbishop Marquand, an awkward address by poor David Eisenberg—each word beamed instantaneously across the entire globe via holovision. Cardinal Wurtz steps onto the podium, grasping the lectern in her long dark hands. "Tonight God's expectations for our species will be revealed," she begins, surveying the crowd with her cobalt eyes. "Tonight, after a hiatus of over three thousand years, the testament of Moses will be made manifest. Of all the many individuals whose lives find fulfillment in this moment, from Joshua to Pope Gladys, our faithful Series-700 servant YHWH impresses us as the creature most worthy to hand down the Law to his planet. And so I now ask him to step forward."

I approach the tablets. I need not unveil them—their contents are forever-more lodged in my brain.

"I am YHWH your God," I begin, "who brought you out of the land of Egypt, out of the house of slavery. You will have no gods . . ."

" 'No gods except me'—right?" says the Son of Rust as we stride down South Street.

"Right," I reply.

"You don't see the rub?"

"No."

My companion grins. "Such a prescription implies there is but one true faith. Let it stand, Domine, and you will be setting Christian against Jew, Buddhist against Hindu, Muslim against pagan . . ."

"You don't say," I mutter, unpersuaded.

"Rule two, 'You will not make yourself a carved image or any likeness of anything in heaven or on earth . . .' Here again lie seeds of discord. Imagine the ill feeling this commandment will generate toward the Roman Church."

I set my voice to a sarcastic timbre. "We'll have to paint over the Sistine Chapel."

"Rule three, 'You will not utter the name of YHWH your God to misuse it.' A reasonable piece of etiquette, I suppose, but surely there are worse sins."

"Which the Law of Moses addresses."

"As in 'Remember the Sabbath day and keep it holy'? A retrograde prescription, I'd say. Consider all the businesses that would perish but for their Sunday trade. Rule five, 'Honor your father and your mother.' Ah, but suppose the child is not being honored in turn? Put this commandment into practice, Domine, and countless abusive parents will find refuge in the presumed sanctity of the family. Equally troubling is the law's vagueness. It still permits us to shunt our parents into nursing homes, honoring them all the way, insisting it's for their own good."

"Nursing homes?"

"Kennels for the elderly. They could appear any day now, believe me — in Philadelphia, in any city. Merely allow this monstrous canon to flourish."

I grab the machine's left gauntlet. "Six," I anticipate. " 'You will not kill.' This is the height of morality."

"The height of ambiguity, Domine. In a few short years, every church and government in creation will interpret it thus: 'You will not kill offensively — you will not commit murder.' After which, of course, you've sanctioned a hundred varieties of carnage. I'm not just envisioning capital punishment or whales hunted to extinction. The danger is far more profound. Ratify this rule, and we shall find ourselves on the slippery slope marked self-defense. I'm talking about burning witches at the stake, for surely a true faith must defend itself against heresy. I'm talking about Europe's Jews being executed en masse by the astonishingly civilized country of Germany, for surely Aryans must defend themselves against contamination. I'm talking about a nuclear weapons race, for surely a nation must defend itself against comparably armed states."

"A *what* race?" I ask.

"Nuclear weapons. A commodity you should be thankful no one has sought to invent. Rule seven, 'You will not commit adultery.' "

"Now you're going to make a case for adultery," I moan.

"An overrated transgression. Many of our greatest leaders are adulterers. Should we lock them up and deprive ourselves of their genius? Rule eight, 'You will not steal.' "

"Not inclusive enough, I suppose?"

My alter ego nods. "This commandment still allows you to practice theft, provided you call it something else — an honest profit, dialectical materialism, manifest destiny, whatever. Believe me, brother, I have no trouble picturing a future in which your country's indigenous peoples — its Navajos, Sioux,

Comanches, Arapahos—are driven off their lands, yet none will dare call it theft."

I issue a quick, electric snort.

"Rule nine, 'You will not bear false witness against your neighbor.' Again, that maddening inconclusiveness. Can this really be the Almighty's definitive denunciation of fraud and deceit? Mark my words, this rule tacitly empowers myriad scoundrels—politicians, advertisers, captains of polluting industry. Do you not find my reasoning provocative?"

I want to bash the robot's iron chest with my steel hand. "Provocative—and paranoid."

"And finally, rule ten—'You will not covet your neighbor's house. You will not covet your neighbor's wife, or his servant, man or woman, or his ox, or his donkey, or anything that is his.'"

"*There*—don't covet. That will check the greed you fear."

"Let us examine the language here. Evidently God is pitching this code to a patriarchy that will in turn disseminate it among the less powerful, namely wives and servants. And how long before these servants are downgraded into human chattel? Ten whole commandments, and not one word against slavery, not to mention bigotry, misogyny, or war."

"I'm sick of your sophistries."

"You're sick of my truths."

"What is this slavery thing?" I ask. "What is this war?"

But the Son of Rust has melted into the shadows.

Falling, I see myself standing by the shrouded tablets, two dozen holovision cameras pressing their snoutlike lenses in my face, a hundred presumptuous microphones poised to catch the Law's every syllable.

"You will not make yourself a carved image," I tell the world.

A thousand humans stare at me with frozen, cheerless grins. They are profoundly uneasy. They expected something else.

I do not finish the commandments. Indeed, I stop at, "You will not utter the name of YHWH your God to misuse it." Like a magician pulling a scarf off a cage full of doves, I slide the velvet cloth away. Seizing a tablet, I snap it in half as if opening an immense fortune cookie.

A gasp erupts from the crowd. "No!" screams Cardinal Wurtz.

"These rules are not worthy of you!" I shout, burrowing into the second slab with my steel fingers, splitting it down the middle.

"Let us read them!" pleads Archbishop Marquand.

"Please!" begs Bishop Black.

"We must know!" insists Cardinal Fremont.

I gather the granite oblongs into my arms. The crowd rushes toward me. Cardinal Wurtz lunges for the Law.

I turn. I trip.

The Son of Rust laughs.

Falling, I press the hunks against my chest. This will be no common disintegration, no mere sundering across molecular lines.

Falling, I rip into the Law's very essence, grinding, pulverizing, turning the pre-Canaanite words to sand.

Falling, I cleave atom from atom, particle from particle.

Falling, I meet the dark Delaware, disappearing into its depths, and I am very, very happy.

Lady Witherspoon's Solution

PERSONAL JOURNAL OF CAPTAIN ARCHIBALD CARMODY, R.N.
Written aboard H.M.S. *Aldebaran*
Whilst on a Voyage of Scientific Discovery in the Indian Ocean

13 April 1899
LAT. 1°10′ S, LONG. 71°42′ E

Might there still be on this watery ball of ours a *terra incognita*, an uncharted Eden just over the horizon, home to noble aborigines or perhaps even a lost civilization? A dubious hypothesis on the face of it. This is the age of the surveyor's sextant and the cartographer's calipers. Our planet has been girded east to west and gridded pole to pole. And yet what sea captain these days does not dream of happening upon some obscure but cornucopian island? Naturally he will keep the coordinates to himself, that he might return in time accompanied by his faithful mate and favorite books, there to spend the rest of his life in blissful solitude.

Today I may have found such a world. Our mission to Ceylon being complete, with over a hundred specimens to show for our troubles (most notably a magnificent lavender butterfly with wings as large as a coquette's fan and a blue beetle of chitin so shiny that you can see your face in the carapace), we were steaming south-by-southwest for the Chagos Archipelago when a monsoon gathered behind us, persuading me to change course fifteen degrees. Two hours later the tempest passed, having filled our hold with brackish puddles though mercifully sparing our specimens, whereupon we found ourselves in view of a green, ragged mass unknown to any map in Her Majesty's Navy, small enough to elude detection until this day, yet large enough for the watch to cry "Land, ho!" whilst the *Aldebaran* was yet two miles from the reef.

We came to a quiet cove. I dispatched an exploration party, led by Mr. Bainbridge, to investigate the inlet. He reported back an hour ago, telling of bulbous fruits, scampering monkeys, and exotic blossoms. When the tide turns tomorrow morning, I shall go ashore myself, for I think it likely that the island harbors invertebrate species of the sort for which our sponsors pay hand-

somely. But right now I shall amuse myself in imagining what to call the atoll.
I am not so vain as to stamp my own name on these untrammeled sands. My
wife, however, is a person I esteem sufficiently to memorialize her on a scale
commensurate with her wisdom and beauty. So here we lie but a single degree
below the Line, at anchor off Lydia Isle, waiting for the cockatoos to sing the
dawn into being.

14 April 1899
LAT. 1°10' S, LONG. 71°42' E

The pen trembles in my hand. This has been a day unlike any in my twenty
years at sea. Unless I miss my guess, Lydia Isle is home to a colony of beasts
that science, for the best of reasons, once thought extinct.

It was our naturalist, Mr. Chalmers, who first noticed the tribe. Passing me
the glass, he quivered with an excitement unusual in this phlegmatic gentleman. I adjusted the focus and suddenly there he was: the colony's most ven-
turesome member, poking a simian head out from a cavern in the central ridge.
More such ape-men soon appeared at the entrance to their rocky doss-house,
a dozen at least, poised on the knife-edge of their curiosity, uncertain whether
to flee into their grotto or further scrutinize us with their deep watery eyes and
wide sniffing nostrils.

We advanced, rifles at the ready. The ape-men chattered, howled, and finally
retreated, but not before I got a sufficiently clear view to make a positive identification. Beetle brows, monumental noses, tentative chins, barrel chests — I
have seen these features before, in an alcove of the British Museum devoted to
artists' impressions of a vanished creature that first came to light forty-three
years ago in Germany's Neander Valley. According to my *Skeffington's Guide to
Fossils of the Continent*, the quarrymen who unearthed the skeleton believed
they'd found the remains of a bear, until the local schoolmaster, Johann Carl
Fuhlrott, and a trained anatomist, Hermann Schaaffhausen, determined that
the bones spoke of prehistoric Europeans.

Fuhlrott and Schaaffhausen had to amuse themselves with only a skullcap,
femur, scapula, ilium, and some ribs, but we have found a living, breathing
remnant of the race. I can scarcely write the word legibly, so great is my excitement. Neanderthals!

16 April 1899
LAT. 1°10' S, LONG. 71°42' E

Unless there dwells in the hearts of our Neanderthals a quality of cunning that their outward aspect belies, we need no longer go armed amongst them. They are docile as a herd of Cotswold sheep. Whenever my officers and I explore the cavern that shelters their community, they lurch back in fear and — if I'm not mistaken — a kind of religious awe.

It's a heady feeling to be an object of worship, even when one's idolaters are of a lower race. Such adoration, I'll warrant, could become as addictive as a Chinaman's pipe, and I hope to eschew its allure even as we continue to study these shaggy primitives.

How has so meek a people managed to survive into the present day? I would ascribe their prosperity to the extreme conviviality of their world. For food, they need merely to pluck bananas and mangos from the trees. When the monsoon arrives, they need only to retreat into their cavern. If man-eating predators inhabit Lydia Isle, I have yet to see any.

Freed from the normal pressures that, by the theories of Mr. Darwin, tend to drive a race towards either oblivion or adaptive transmutation, our Neanderthals have cultivated habits that prefigure the accomplishments of civilized peoples. Their speech is crude and thus far incomprehensible to me, all grunts and snorts and wheezes, and yet they employ it not only for ordinary communication but to entertain themselves with songs and chants. For their dancing rituals they fashion flutes from reeds, drums from logs, and even a kind of rudimentary oboe from bamboo, making music under whose influence their swaying frames attain a certain elegance. Nor is the art of painting unknown on Lydia Isle. By torchlight we have beheld on the walls of their cavern adroit representations of the indigenous monkeys and birds.

But the fullest expression of the Neanderthals' artistic sense is to be found in the cemetery they maintain in an open field not far from their stone apartments. Whereas most of the graves are marked with simple cairns, a dozen mounds feature effigies wrought from wicker and daub, each doubtless representing the earthly form of the dear departed. The details of these funerary images are invariably male, a situation not remarkable in itself, as the tribe may regard the second sex as unworthy of commemoration. What perplexes Mr. Chalmers and myself is that we have yet to come upon a single female of the race — or, for that matter, any infants. Might we find the Neanderthal wives and children cowering in the cavern's deepest sanctum? Or did some devastating tropical plague visit Lydia Isle, taking with it the entire female gender, plus every generation of males save one?

17 April 1899
LAT. 1°10' S, LONG. 71°42' E

This morning I made a friend. I named him Silver, after the lightning-flash of fur coursing along his spine like an externalized backbone. It was Silver who made the initial gesture of amicability, presenting me with the gift of a flute. When I managed to pipe out a reasonable rendition of "Beautiful Dreamer," he smiled broadly — yes, the aborigines can smile — and wrapped his leathery hand about mine.

I did not recoil from the gesture, but allowed Silver to lead me to a clearing in the jungle, where I beheld a solitary burial mound, decorated with a funerary effigy. Whilst I would never presume to plunder the grave, I must note that the British Museum would pay handsomely for this sculpture. The workmanship is skillful, and, *mirabile dictu*, the form is female. She wears a crown of flowers, from beneath which stream glorious tresses of grass. Incised on a lump of soft wood, the facial features are, in their own naïve way, lovely.

Such are the observable facts. But Silver's solicitous attitude toward the effigy leads me to an additional conclusion. The woman interred in this hallowed ground, I do not doubt, was once my poor friend's mate.

19 April 1899
LAT. 1°10' S, LONG. 71°42' E

An altogether extraordinary day, bringing an event no less astonishing than our discovery of the aborigines. Once again Silver led me to his mate's graven image, whereupon he reached into his satchel — an intricate artifact woven of reeds — and drew forth a handwritten journal entitled *Confidential Diary and Personal Observations of Katherine Margaret Glover*. Even if Silver spoke English, I would not have bothered to inquire as to Miss Glover's identity, for I knew instinctively it was she who occupied the tomb beneath our feet. In presenting me with the little volume, my friend managed to communicate his expectation that I would peruse its contents but then return the book forthwith, so he might continue drawing sustenance from its numinous leaves.

I spent the day collaborating with Mr. Chalmers in cataloguing the many Lepidoptera and Coleoptera we have collected thus far. Normally I take pleasure in taxonomic activity, but today I could think only of finishing the job, so beguiling was the siren-call of the diary. At length the parrots performed their final recital, the tropical sun found the equatorial sea, and I returned to my cabin, where, following a light supper, I read the chronicle cover to cover.

Considering its talismanic significance to Silver, I would never dream of appropriating the volume, yet it tells a story so astounding — one that inclines me to rethink my earlier theory concerning the Neanderthals — that I am resolved to forgo sleep till I have copied the most salient passages into this, my own secret journal. All told, there are 114 separate entries spanning the interval from February through June of 1889. The vast majority have no bearing on the mystery of the aborigines, being verbal sketches that Miss Glover hoped to incorporate into her ongoing literary endeavor, an epic poem about the first-century A.D. warrior-queen Boadicea. Given the limitations of my energy and my ink supply, I must reluctantly allow those jottings to pass into oblivion.

Who was Kitty Glover? The precocious child of landed gentry, she evidently lost both her mother and father to consumption before her thirteenth year. In the interval immediately following her parents' deaths, Kitty's ne'er-do-well brother gambled away the family's fortune. She then spent four miserable years in Marylebone Workhouse, picking oakum until her fingers bled, all the while trying in vain to get a letter to her late mother's acquaintance, Elizabeth Witherspoon, a widowed baroness presiding over her deceased husband's considerable fortune. Kitty had reason to believe that Lady Witherspoon would heed her plight, for the Baroness had come to know Kitty's mother, Maude Glover, under extraordinary circumstances.

Kitty's diary contains no entry recounting the episode, but I infer that Lady Witherspoon was boating on the Thames near Greenwich when she tumbled into the water. The cries of the Baroness, who could not swim, were heard by Maude Glover, who could. (She was sitting on the banks, reading *The Strand*.) And so it was that Kitty's mother delivered Lady Witherspoon from almost certain death.

Despite the machinations of her immediate supervisor, the loutish Ezekiel Snavely, Kitty's fifth letter found its way to Lady Witherspoon's abode, Briarwood House in Hampstead. The Baroness straightaway rescued Kitty from Snavely's clutches and made the girl her ward. Not only was Kitty accorded her own cottage on the estate grounds, her benefactor provided a monthly allowance of ten pounds, a sum sufficient for the young woman to mingle with London society and adorn herself in the latest fashions. In the initial entries, Lady Witherspoon emerges as a muddle-minded person, obsessed with the welfare of an organization that at first Kitty thought silly: the Hampstead Ladies Croquet Club and Benevolent Society. But there was more on the minds of these women than knocking balls through hoops.

CONFIDENTIAL DIARY AND PERSONAL OBSERVATIONS
of Katherine Margaret Glover
The Year of Our Lord 1889

Sunday, 31 March

Today I am moved to comment on a dimension of life here at Briarwood that I have not addressed previously. Whilst most of our servants, footmen, maids, and gardeners appear normal in aspect and comportment, two of the staff, Martin and Andrew, exhibit features so grotesque that my dreams are haunted by their lumbering presence. Their duties comprise nothing beyond maintaining the grounds, the croquet field in particular, and I suspect they are so mentally enfeebled that Lady Witherspoon hesitates to assign them more demanding tasks. Indeed, the one time I attempted to engage Martin and Andrew in conversation, they regarded me quizzically and responded only with soft huffing grunts.

I once saw in the London Zoo an orangutan named Attila, and in my opinion Martin and Andrew belong more to that variety of ape than to even the most bestial men of my acquaintance, including the execrable Ezekiel Snavely. With their weak chins, flaring nostrils, sunken black eyes, proliferation of body hair, and decks of broken teeth the size of pebbles, our groundskeepers seem on probation from the jungle, awaiting full admittance to the human race. It speaks well of the Baroness that she would employ creatures who might otherwise find themselves in Spitalfields, swilling gin and begging for their supper.

"I cannot help but notice a bodily deformity in our groundskeepers," I told Lady Witherspoon. "In employing them, you have shown yourself to be a true Christian."

"In fact Martin and Andrew were once even more degraded than they appear," the Baroness replied. "The day those unfortunates arrived, I instructed the servants to treat them with humanity. Kindness, it seems, will gentle the nature of even the most miserable outcast."

"Then I, too, shall treat them with humanity," I vowed.

Wednesday, 10 April

This morning I approached Lady Witherspoon with a scheme whose realization would, I believe, be a boon to English letters. I proposed that we establish here at Briarwood a school for the cultivation of the Empire's next generation of poets, not unlike that artistically fecund society formed by Lord Byron, Percy Bysshe Shelley, and their acolytes in an earlier part of the century. By founding such an institution, I argued, Lady Witherspoon would gain an enviable reputation as a friend to the arts, whilst my fellow poets and I would lift one another to unprecedented promontories of literary accomplishment.

Instead of holding forth on either the virtues or the liabilities of turning Briarwood into a monastery for scribblers, Lady Witherspoon looked me in the eye and said, "This strikes me as an opportune moment to address a somewhat different matter concerning your future, Kitty. It is my fond hope that you will one day take my place as head of the Hampstead Ladies Croquet Club and Benevolent Society. Much as I admire the women who constitute our present membership, none is your equal in mettle or brains."

"Your praise touches me deeply, Madam, though I am at a loss to say why that particular office requires such qualities."

"I shall forgive your condescension, child, as you are unaware of the organization's true purpose."

"Which is — ?"

"Which is something I shall disclose when you are ready to assume the mantle of leadership."

"From the appellation 'Benevolent Society,' might I surmise you do charitable works?"

"We are generous towards our friends, rather less so towards our enemies," Lady Witherspoon replied with a quick smile that, unlike the Society's ostensible aim, was not entirely benevolent.

"Does this charity consist in saving misfits like Martin and Andrew from extinction?"

Instead of addressing my question, the Baroness clasped my hand and said, "Here is my counterproposal. Allow me to groom you as my successor, and I shall happily subsidize your commonwealth of poets."

"An excellent arrangement."

"I believe I'm getting the better of the bargain."

"Unless you object," I said, "I should like to call my nascent school the Elizabeth Witherspoon Academy of Arts and Letters."

"You have my permission," said the Baroness.

Monday, 15 April

A day spent in Fleet Street, where I arranged for the *Times* to run an advertisement urging all interested poets, "whether wholly Byronic or merely embryonic," to bundle up their best work and bring it to the Elizabeth Witherspoon Academy of Arts and Letters, scheduled to convene at Briarwood House a week from next Sunday. The mere knowledge that this community will soon come into being has proved for me a fount of inspiration. Tonight I kept pen pressed to paper for five successive hours, with the result that I now have in my drawer seven stanzas concerning the marriage of my flame-haired Boadicea to Prasutagus, King of the Iceni Britons.

Strange fancies buzz through my brain like bees bereft of sense. My skull is a hive of conjecture. What is the "true purpose," to use the Baroness's term, of the Benevolent Society? Do its members presume to practice the black arts? Does my patroness imagine that she is in turn patronized by Lucifer? Forgive me, Lady Witherspoon, for entertaining such ungracious speculations. You deserve better from your adoring ward.

The Society gathers on the first Saturday of next month, whereupon I shall play the prowler, or such is my resolve. Curiosity may have killed the cat, but I trust it will serve to enlighten this Kitty.

Sunday, 28 April

The inauguration of my poet's utopia proved more auspicious than I'd dared hope. All told, three bards made their way to Hampstead. We enjoyed a splendid high tea, then shared our nascent works.

The Reverend Tobias Crowther of Stoke Newingtown is a blowsy man of cheerful temper. For the past year he has devoted his free hours to "Deathless in Bethany," a long dramatic poem about Lazarus's adventures following his resuscitation by our Lord. He read the first scene aloud, and with every line his listeners grew more entranced.

Our next performer was Ellen Ruggles, a pallid schoolmistress from Kensington, who favored us with four odes. Evidently there is no object so humble that Miss Ruggles will not celebrate it in verse, be it a flowerpot, a teakettle, a spiderweb, or an earthworm. The men squirmed during her recitation, but I was exhilarated to hear Miss Ruggles sing of the quotidian enchantments that lie everywhere to hand.

With a quaver in my throat and a tremor in my knees, I enacted Boadicea's speech to Prasutagus as he lies on his deathbed, wherein she promises to continue his policy of appeasing the Romans. My discomfort was unjustified, however, for after my presentation the other poets all made cooing noises and applauded. I was particularly pleased to garner the approval of Edward Pertuis, a wealthy Bloomsbury bohemian and apostle of the mad philosopher

Friedrich Nietzsche. Mr. Pertuis is quite the most well-favored man I have ever surveyed at close quarters, and I sense that he possesses a splendor of spirit to match his features.

The "Abyssiad" is a grand, epic poem wrought of materials that Mr. Pertuis cornered in the wildest reaches of his fancy and subsequently brought under the civilizing influence of his pen. On the planet Vivoid, far beyond Uranus, the Übermenschen prophesied by Herr Nietzsche have come into existence. An exemplar of this superior race travels to Earth with the aim of teaching human beings how they might live their lives to the full. Mr. Pertuis is not only a superb writer but also a fine actor, and his opening cantos held our fellowship spellbound. He has even undertaken to illustrate his manuscript, decorating the bottom margin with crayon drawings of an Übermensch, who wears a dashing scarlet cape and looks rather like his creator — Mr. Pertuis, I mean, not Herr Nietzsche.

I can barely wait until our group reconvenes four weeks hence. I am deliriously anxious to learn what happens when the visitor from Vivoid attempts to corrupt the human race. I long to clap my eyes on Mr. Pertuis again.

Saturday, 4 May

An astonishing day that began in utter mundanity, with the titled ladies of the Benevolent Society arriving in their cabriolets and coaches. Five aristocrats plus the Baroness made six, one for each croquet mallet in the spectrum: red, orange, yellow, green, blue, violet. After taking tea in the garden, everyone proceeded to the south lawn, newly scythed by Martin and Andrew. Six hoops and two pegs stood ready for the game. The women played three matches, with Lady Sterlingford winning the first, Lady Unsworth the second, and Lady Witherspoon the last. Although they took their sport seriously, bringing to each shot a scientific precision, their absorption in technique did not preclude their chattering about matters of stupendous inconsequentiality — the weather, Paris fashions, who had or had not been invited to the Countess of Rexford's upcoming soirée — whilst I sat on a wrought-iron chair and attempted to write a scene of the Romans flogging Boadicea for refusing to become their submissive client.

At dusk the Society repaired to the banquet hall, there to dine on pheasant and grouse, whilst I lurked outside the open window, observing their vapid smiles and overhearing their evanescent conversation, as devoid of substance as was their prattle on the playing field. When at last the croquet players finished their feast, they migrated to the west parlor. The casement gave me a coign of vantage on Lady Witherspoon as she approached the far wall and pulled aside a faded tapestry concealing the door to a descending spiral staircase. Laughing and trilling, the ladies passed through the secret portal and began a downward climb.

Within ten minutes I had furtively joined my benefactress and her friends in the manor's most subterranean sanctum, its walls dancing with phantoms conjured by a dozen blazing torches. A green velvet drape served as my cloak of invisibility. Like the east lawn, the basement had been converted into a gaming space, but whereas the croquet field bloomed with sweet grass and the occasional wild violet, the sanctum floor was covered end to end with a foul carpet of thick russet mud. From my velvet niche I could observe the suspended gallery in which reposed the women, as well as, flanking and fronting the mire, two discrete ranks of gaol-cells, eight per block, each compartment inhabited by a hulking, snarling brute sprung from the same benighted line as Martin and Andrew. The atmosphere roiled with a fragrance such as I had never before endured — a stench compounded of stagnant water, damp fur, and the soiled hay filling the cages — even as my brain reeled with the primal improbability of the spectacle.

In the gallery a flurry of activity unfolded, and I soon realized that the women were wagering on the outcome of the incipient contest. Each aristocrat obviously had her favorite ape-man, though I got the impression that, contrary to the norms of such gambling, the players were betting on which beast could be counted upon to lose. After all the wagers were made, Lady Witherspoon gestured toward the far perimeter of the pit, where her majordomo, Wembly, and his chief assistant, Padding, were pacing in nervous circles. First Wembly sprang into action, setting his hand to a small windlass and thus opening a cage in the nearer of the two cell-blocks. As the liberated ape-man skulked into the arena, Padding operated a second windlass, thereby opening a facing cage and freeing its occupant. Retreating in tandem, Wembly and Padding slipped into a stone sentry-box and locked the door behind them.

Only now did I notice that the bog was everywhere planted with implements of combat. Cudgels of all sorts rose from the mire like bulrushes. Each ape-man instinctively grabbed a weapon, the larger brute selecting a shillelagh, his opponent a wooden mace bristling with toothy bits of metal. The combat that followed was protracted and vicious, the two enemies hammering at each other until rivulets of blood flowed down their fur. Thuds, grunts, and cries of pain resounded through the fetid air, as did the Society's enthusiastic cheers.

In time the smaller beast triumphed, dealing his opponent a cranial blow so forceful that he dropped the shillelagh and collapsed in the bog, prone and trembling with terror. The victor approached his stricken foe, placed a muddy foot on his rump, and made ready to dash out the fallen creature's brains, at which juncture Lady Witherspoon lifted a tin whistle to her lips and let loose a metallic shriek. Instantly the victor released his mace and faced the gallery, where Lady Pembroke now stood grasping a ceramic phial stoppered with a plug of cork. Evidently recognizing the phial, and perhaps even smelling its contents, the victor forgot all about decerebrating his enemy. He shuffled towards Lady Pembroke and raised his hairy hands beseechingly. When she tossed him the coveted phial, he frantically tore out the stopper and sucked down the entire measure. Having satisfied his craving for the opiate, the brute tossed the phial aside, then yawned, stretched, and staggered back to his cage. He lay down in the straw and fell asleep.

Cautiously but resolutely, Wembly and Padding left their sentry-box, the former now holding a Gladstone bag of the sort carried by physicians. Whilst Padding secured the door to the victor's cage, Wembly knelt beside the vanquished beast. Opening the satchel, he removed a gleaming scalpel, a surgeon's needle, gauze dressings, and a hypodermic syringe loaded with an amber fluid. The majordomo nudged the plunger, releasing a single glistening bead, and, satisfied that the hollow needle was unobstructed, injected the drug into the brute's arm. The creature's limbs went slack. Presently Padding arrived on the scene, drawing from his pocket a white handkerchief, which he used to clean the delta betwixt the ape-man's thighs, whereupon Wembly took up his scalpel and meticulously slit a portion of the creature's anatomy for which I know no term more delicate than scrotum.

The gallery erupted in a chorus of hoorays.

With practiced efficiency the majordomo appropriated the twin contents of the scrotal sac, each sphere as large as those with which the ladies had earlier entertained themselves, then plopped them into separate glass jars filled with a clear fluid, alcohol most probably, subsequently passing the vessels to Padding. Next Wembly produced two actual croquet balls, which he inserted into the cavity prior to suturing and bandaging the incision. After offering the gallery a deferential bow, Padding presented one trophy to Lady Pembroke, the other to Lady Unsworth, both of whom, I surmised, had correctly predicted the upshot of the contest. Lady Witherspoon led the other women — Baroness Cushing, the Marchioness of Harcourt, the Countess of Netherby — in a round of delirious applause.

The evening was young, and ere it ended, three additional battles were fought in the stinking, echoing, glowing pit. Three more victors, three more losers, three more plundered scrota, six more harvested spheres, with the result that each noblewoman ultimately received at least one prize. During the intermissions, a liveried footman served the Society chocolate cream with strawberries.

Dear diary, allow me to make a confession. The ladies' sport repelled and delighted me all at once. Despite a generally Christian sensibility, I could not help but imagine that each felled and eunuched brute was the odious Ezekiel Snavely. I had no desire to assume, per Lady Witherspoon's wishes, the leadership of her unorthodox organization, and yet the idea of my tormentor getting trounced in this arena soothed me immeasurably.

Clutching their vessels, the ladies ascended the spiral staircase. I pictured each guest slipping into her conveyance and, ere commanding the coachman to take her home, demurely snugging her winnings into her lap as a lady of less peculiar tastes might secure a purse, a music box, or a pair of gloves. For a full twenty minutes I lingered behind my velvet drape, listening to the bestial snarls and savage growls, then began my slow climb to the surface, afire with a variety of satisfaction for which I hope our English language never spawns a name.

Monday, 6 May

To her eternal credit, when I confessed to the Baroness that I had spied on the underground tournament, she elected to extol my audacity rather than condemn my duplicity, adding but one caveat to this absolution. "I am willing to cast a sympathetic eye on your escapade," she told me, "but I must ask you to reciprocate by supposing that a laudable goal informs our baiting of the brutes."

"I don't doubt that your sport serves a greater good. But who are those wretched creatures? They seem more ape than human."

The Baroness replied that, come noon tomorrow, I must go to the north tower and climb to the uppermost floor, where I would encounter a room I did not know existed. There amongst her retorts and alembics all my questions would be answered.

Thus did I find myself in Lady Witherspoon's cylindrical laboratory, a gas-lit chamber crammed with worktables on which rested the vessels of which she'd spoken, along with various flasks, bell jars, and test tubes, plus a beaker holding a golden substance that the Baroness was heating over a Bunsen burner. Bubbles danced in the burnished fluid. At the center of the circle lay a plump man with waxen skin, naked head to toe. Pink as a piglet, he was bound to an operating table with leather straps about his wrists and ankles. His name, the Baroness informed me, was Ben Towson, and he looked as if he had a great deal to say about his situation, but, owing to the steel bit betwixt his teeth, tightly secured with thongs, he could not utter a word.

"It all began on a lovely April afternoon in 1883, back when the Society was content to play croquet with inorganic balls," said Lady Witherspoon. "I had arranged for a brilliant French scientist to address our group — Henri Renault, director of the Paris Museum of Natural History. A devotee of Charles Darwin, Dr. Renault perforce believed that modern apes and contemporary humans share a common though extinct ancestor. It had become his obsession to corroborate Darwin through chemistry. After a decade of research, Renault concocted a potent drug from human neuronal tissue and simian cerebrospinal fluid. He soon learned that, over a course of three injections, this serum would transform an orangutan or a gorilla into — not a human being, exactly, but a creature of far greater talents than nature ever granted an ape. Renault called his discovery Infusion U."

"U for Uplift?" I ventured.

"U for Unknown," Lady Witherspoon corrected me. "Monsieur le Docteur was probing that interstice where science ends and enigma begins." Approaching a cabinet jammed with glass vessels, the Baroness took down a stoppered Erlenmeyer flask containing a bright blue fluid. "I recently acquired a quantity of Renault's evolutionary catalyst. One day soon I shall conduct my own investigations using Infusion U."

"One day soon? From what I saw in the gaming pit, I would say you've already performed numerous such experiments."

"Our tournaments have nothing to do with Infusion U." Briefly Lady Witherspoon contemplated the flask, its contents coruscating in the sallow light. Gingerly she reshelved the arcane chemical. "A few years after creating serum number one, Renault perfected its precise inverse — Infusion D."

"For Devolution?"

"For Demimonde," the Baroness replied, pointing to the burbling beaker. "Such unorthodox research belongs to the shadows."

With the aid of an insulated clamp she removed the hot beaker from the flame's influence and, availing herself of a funnel, decanted the contents into a rack of test tubes. She returned Infusion D to the burner. After the batch had cooled sufficiently, the Baroness took up a hypodermic syringe and filled the barrel.

"It was this second formula that Renault demonstrated to the Society," said the Baroness. "After we'd seated ourselves in the drawing-room, he injected five cubic centiliters into a recently condemned murderer, one Jean-Marc Girard, who proceeded to regress before our eyes."

Lady Witherspoon now performed the identical experiment on Ben Towson, locating a large vein in his forearm, inserting the needle, and pushing the plunger. I knew precisely what was going to happen, and yet I could not quite bring myself to believe what I beheld. Whilst Infusion D seethed in its beaker and the gas hissed through the laboratory lamps, Towson began to change. Even as he fought against his straps, his jaw diminished, his brow expanded, and his eyes receded like successfully pocketed billiard balls. Each nostril grew to a diameter that would admit a chestnut. Great whorling tufts of fur appeared on his skin like weeds emerging from fecund soil. He whimpered like a whipped dog.

"Good God," I said.

"A striking metamorphosis, yes, but inchoate, for he will become his full simian self only after two more injections," said Lady Witherspoon, though to my naïve eye Towson already looked exactly like the brutes I'd observed in the arena. "What we have here is the very sort of being Renault fashioned for our edification that memorable spring afternoon. He assured us that, before delivering Girard to the executioner, he would employ Infusion U in restoring the miscreant, lest the hangman imagine he was killing an innocent ape." The Towson beast bucked and lurched, thus prompting the Baroness to tighten the straps on his wrists. "It was obvious from his presentation that Renault saw no practical use for his discovery beyond validating the theory of evolution. But we of the Hampstead Ladies Croquet Club immediately envisioned a benevolent application."

"Benevolent by certain lights," I noted, scanning the patient. His procreative paraphernalia had become grotesquely enlarged, though evidently it would not achieve croquet caliber until injection number three. "By other lights, controversial. By still others, criminal."

Lady Witherspoon did not address my argument directly but instead contrived the slyest of smiles, took my hand, and said, "Tell me, dear Kitty, how to you view the human male?"

"I am fond of certain men," I replied. Such as Mr. Pertuis, I almost added. "Others annoy me — and some I greatly fear."

"Would you not agree that, whilst isolated specimens of the male can be amusing and occasionally even valuable, there is something profoundly unwell about the gender as a whole, a demon impulse that inclines men to inflict physical harm on their fellow beings, women particularly?"

"I have suffered the slings of male entitlement," I said in a voice of assent. "The director of Marylebone Workhouse took liberties with my person that I would prefer not to discuss."

Before releasing my hand, the Baroness accorded it a sympathetic squeeze. "Our idea was a paragon of simplicity. Turn the male demon against itself. Teach it to fear and loathe its own gender rather than the female. Debase it with bludgeons. Humble it with mud. For the final fillip, deprive it of the ability to sire additional fiends."

"Your Society thinks as boldly as the Vivoidians who populate Mr. Pertuis's saga of the Übermenschen."

"I have not read your fellow poet's epic, but I shall take your remark as a compliment. Thanks to Monsieur le Docteur, we have in our possession an antidote for masculinity — a remedy that falls so far short of homicide that even a woman of the most refined temperament may apply it without qualm. To be sure, there are more conventional ways of dealing with the demon. But what sane woman, informed of Infusion D, would prefer to rely instead on the normal institutions of justice, whose barristers and judges are invariably of the scrotal persuasion?"

"Not only do I follow your logic," I said, cinching the strap on the ape-man's left ankle, "I confess to sharing your enthusiasm."

"Dear Kitty, your intelligence never ceases to amaze me. Even Renault, when I told him that the Society had set out to cure men of themselves, assumed I was joking." Bending over her rack of Infusion D, Lady Witherspoon ran her palms along the test tubes as if playing a glass harmonica. "Have you perchance heard of Jack the Ripper?" she asked abruptly.

"The Whitechapel maniac?" I cinched the right ankle-strap. "For six weeks running, London's journalists wrote of little else."

"The butcher slit the throats of at least five West End trollops, mutilating their bodies in ways that beggar the imagination. Last night Lady Pembroke went home carrying half the Ripper's manhood in her handbag, whilst Lady Unsworth made off with the other half. You were likewise witness to the rehabilitation of Milton Starling, a legislator who, before running afoul of our agents, alternately raped his niece in his barn and denounced the cause of women's suffrage on the floor of Parliament. You also beheld the gelding of Josiah Lippert, who until recently earned a handsome income delivering orphan girls from the slums of London to the brothels of Constantinople."

"No doubt the past lives of Martin and Andrew are similarly checkered."

"Prior to their encounter with the Society, they brokered the sale of nearly three hundred young women into white slavery throughout the Empire."

"What ultimately happens to your eunuchs?" I asked. "Are they all granted situations at Briarwood and the estates of your other ladies?"

"Martin and Andrew are merely making themselves useful whilst awaiting deportation," the Baroness replied. "Once every six months, we transfer a boat-load of castrati to an uncharted island in the Indian Ocean — Atonement Atoll, we call it — that they may live out their seedless lives in harmony with nature."

The patient, I noticed, had fallen asleep. "Is he still a carnivore, I wonder" — I gestured towards the slumbering beast — "or does he now dream of bananas?"

"A pertinent question, Kitty. I am not privy to the immediate contents of Towson's head, just as I cannot imagine what was passing through his mind when he kicked his wife to death."

"God save the Hampstead Ladies Croquet Club and Benevolent Society," I said.

"And the Queen," my patroness added.

"And the Queen," I said.

Sunday, 26 May

The second gathering of the Witherspoon Academy of Arts and Letters proved every bit as bracing as the first. Miss Ruggles presented four odes so vivid in their particulars that I shall never regard a button, a conch shell, an oil lamp, or a child's kite in quite the same way again. Mr. Crowther charmed us with another installment of his verse drama about Lazarus, an episode in which the resurrected aristocrat, fancying himself commensurate with Christ, travels to Chorazin with the aim of founding a salvationistic religion. Mr. Pertuis brought his Übermensch into contact with a cadre of Hegelian philosophers, a trauma so disruptive of their neo-Platonic worldview that they all went irretrievably insane. For my own contribution, I performed a scene in which Boadicea, bound and gagged, is forced to watch as her two daughters are molested by the Romans. The other poets claimed to be impressed by my depiction of the ghastly event, with Miss Ruggles declaring that she'd never heard anything quite so affecting in all her life.

But the real reason I shall always cherish this day concerns an incident that occurred after the workshop adjourned. Once Miss Ruggles and Mr. Crowther had sped away in their respective coaches, having exchanged manuscripts with the aim of offering each other further appreciative commentary, Mr. Pertuis approached me and announced, in a diffident but heartfelt tone, that I had been in his thoughts of late, and he hoped I might accord him an opportunity to earn my admiration of his personhood, as opposed to his poetry. I responded that his personhood had not escaped my notice, then invited him for a stroll along the brook that girds the manor house.

We had not gone twenty yards when, acting on a sudden impulse, I told my companion the whole perplexing story of the Hampstead Ladies Croquet Club. I omitted no proper noun: Dr. Renault, Ben Towson, Jean-Marc Girard, Jack the Ripper, Infusion U, Infusion D. At first he reacted with skepticism, but when I noted that my tale could be easily corroborated — I need merely lead him into the depths of Briarwood House and show him the caged brutes awaiting humiliation — he grew more liberal in his judgment.

"You present me with two possibilities," said Mr. Pertuis. "Either I am becoming friends with an insane poet who writes of ancient female warriors, or else Lady Elizabeth Witherspoon is the most capable woman in England not excepting the Queen. Given my fondness for you, I prefer to embrace the second theory."

"Naturally I must insist that you not repeat these revelations to another living soul."

"I shan't repeat them even to the dead."

"Were you to betray my confidence, Mr. Pertuis, my attitude to you would curdle in an instant."

"You may trust me implicitly, Miss Glover. But pray indulge my philosophical side. As a votary of Herr Nietzsche, I cannot but speculate on the potential benefits of these astonishing chemicals. Assuming Lady Witherspoon withheld no pertinent fact from you, I would conclude that, whilst the utility of Infusion D has been exhausted, this is manifestly not the case with the uplift serum. May I speak plainly? I am the sort of man who, if he possessed a quantity of the drug, would not scruple to experiment with it."

"*Mais pourquoi*, Mr. Pertuis? Have you a pet orangutan with whom you desire to play chess?"

"I do not see why the uplift serum should be employed solely for the betterment of apes. I do not see why — "

"Why it should not be introduced into a human subject?" I said, at once aghast and fascinated.

"A blasphemous idea, I quite agree. And yet, were you to put such forbidden fruit on my plate, I would be tempted to take a bite. Infusion U, you say — U for Unknown. No, Miss Glover — for Übermensch!"

Saturday, 1 June

When I awoke I had no inkling that this would be most memorable day of my life. If anything, it promised to be only the most philosophical, for I spent the morning conjecturing about what Friedrich Nietzsche himself might have made of Infusion U. Being by all reports insane, the man is unlikely ever to form an opinion of Dr. Renault's research, much less share that opinion with the world.

Here is my supposition. Based upon my untutored and doubtless superficial reading of *The Joyful Wisdom*, I imagine Herr Nietzsche would be unimpressed by the uplift serum. I believe he would dismiss it as mere liquid decadence, yet another quack cure that, like all quack cures — most notoriously Christianity, the ultimate *pater nostrum* — prevents us from looking brute reality in the eye and admitting there are no happy endings, only eternal returns, even as we resolve to redress our tragic circumstances with a heroic and defiant "Yes!"

By contrast, I am confident that, presented with a potion that promised to fortify her spirit, my cruel and beautiful Boadicea would have swallowed it without hesitation. After all, here was a woman who took on the world's mightiest empire, leading a revolt that obliged her to sack the cities that today we call St. Albans, Colchester, and London, leaving 70,000 Roman corpses behind. For a warrior-queen, whatever works is good, be it razor-sharp knives on the wheels of your chariot or a rare Gallic elixir in your goblet.

This afternoon Mr. Pertuis and I traveled in his coach to the Spaniard's Inn, where we dined with Dionysian abandon on grilled turbot, stewed beef à la jardinière, and lamb cutlets with asparagus. Landing next in Regent's Park, we rented a rowboat and went out on the lake. My swain stroked us to the far shore, shipped the oars, and, clasping my hand, averred that he wished to discuss a matter of passing urgency.

"Two matters, really," he elaborated. "The first pertains to my intellect, the second to my affections."

"Both faculties are of abiding interest to me," I said.

"To be blunt, I have resolved to augment my brain's potential through the uplift serum, but only if I have your blessing. I am similarly determined to enhance my heart's capacity by taking a wife, but only if my bride is your incomparable self."

My own heart immediately assented to his second scheme, fluttering against my ribs like a caged bird. "On first principles I endorse both your ambitions," I replied, blushing so deeply that I imagined the surrounding water reddening with my reflection, "but I would expect you to fulfill several preliminary conditions."

"Oh, my dearest Miss Glover, I shall grant you any wish within reason, and many beyond reason as well."

"Concerning our wedding, it must be a private affair attended by only a handful of witnesses and conducted by Mr. Crowther. Your Kitty is a shyer creature than you might suppose."

"Agreed."

"Concerning the serum, you will limit yourself to a single injection of five centiliters."

"Not one drop more."

"You must further consent to make me your collaborator in the grand experiment. Yes, dear Edward, I wish to accompany you on your journey into the dark, feral, occult continent of Infusion U."

"Is that really a place for a person of your gender?"

"I can tell you how Boadicea would answer. A woman's place is in the wild."

Dear diary, it was not the English countryside that glided past the window of Mr. Pertuis's coach on our return trip, for Albion had become Eden that day. Each tree was fruited with luminous apples, glowing plums, and glistening figs. From every blossom a golden nectar flowed in great munificent streams.

We reached Hampstead just as the Society was finishing its final match of the day. Standing on the edge of the grassy court, we watched Lady Pembroke make an astonishing shot in which the generative sphere leapt smartly from the tip of her mallet, traversed seven feet of lawn, rolled through the fifth hoop, and came to rest at a spot not ten inches from the peg. The other ladies broke into spontaneous applause.

Now Mr. Pertuis led me behind the privet hedge and placed a farewell kiss — a kiss! — on my lips, then repaired to his coach, whereupon Lady Witherspoon likewise drew me aside and averred she had news that would send my spirits soaring.

"Today I informed the others that, acting on your own initiative, you learned of the Society's true purpose," she said. "Having already judged you a person of impeccable character, they are happy to admit you to our company. Will you accept our invitation to an evening of demon baiting?"

"*Avec plaisir,*" I said.

"Amongst the scheduled contestants is a notorious workhouse supervisor whom our agents abducted but four days ago. Yes, dear Kitty, tonight you will see a simian edition of the odious Ezekiel Snavely take the field."

My heart leaped up, through not to the same altitude occasioned by Mr. Pertuis's marriage proposal. "If Snavely were to fall," I muttered, "and if it were permitted, I would put the knife to him myself."

"I fully understand your desire, but we decided long ago that the incision must always be made and dressed by a practiced hand," Lady Witherspoon said. "The gods have entrusted us with their ichor, dear Kitty, and we must remain worthy of the gift."

Monday, 3 June

Saturday night's tournament did not play out as I'd hoped. My bête noir conquered his opponent, an abhorrent West End procurer. Dear God, what if Snavely continues to win his battles, month after month? What if he is standing tall after the Benevolent Society has been discovered and toppled by the London Metropolitan Police? Will his apish incarnation, gonads and all, receive sanctuary in some zoo? *Quelle horreur!*

In contrast to recent events in the arena, this morning's scientific experiments went swimmingly. We had no difficulty stealthily transferring the Erlenmeyer flask and the hypodermic syringe from the north tower to my cottage. So lovingly did Mr. Pertuis work the needle into my vein that the pain proved but a pinch, and I believe that, when I injected my swain in turn, I caused him only mild discomfort.

"Herr Nietzsche calls humankind the unfinished animal," he said. "If that hypothesis is true, then perhaps you and I, fair Kitty, are about to bring our species to completion."

At first I felt nothing — and then, suddenly, the elixir announced its presence in my brain. My throat constricted. My eyes seemed to rotate in their sockets. A thousand clockwork ants scurried across my skin. Sweat gushed from my brow, coursing down my face like blood from the Crown of Thorns.

Our torments ceased as abruptly as they'd begun, as if by magic — that is to say, by Überwissenschaft. And suddenly we knew that a true wonder-worker had come amongst us, *le Grand Renault*, blessing his disciples with the elixir of his genius. Brave new passions swelled within us. Fortunately I had on hand sufficient ink and paper to give them voice. Although we'd severed ourselves from our simian heritage, Edward and I nevertheless entered into competition, each determined to produce the greater number of eternal truths in iambic pentameter. Whilst my poor swain labored till dawn, and even then failed to complete his "Abyssiad," I finished "The Song of Boadicea" on the stroke of midnight, two hundred and ten stanzas, each more brilliant than the last.

Thursday, 6 June

And so, dear diary, it has begun. We have bitten the apple, cut cards with the Devil, lapped the last drop from the Pierian spring. Come the new year my Edward and I shall be man and wife, but today we are Übermensch and Überfrau.

Such creatures will not be constrained by convention, nor acknowledge mere biology as their master. We are brighter than our glands. Each time Edward and I give ourselves to carnal love, we employ such prophylactic devices as will preclude procreation.

We do not disrobe. Rather, we tear the clothes from one other's bodies like starving castaways shucking oysters in a tidal inlet. How marvelous that, throughout the long, arduous process of concocting his formula, Monsieur le Docteur remained a connoisseur of sin. How exhilarating that a post-evolutionary race can know so much of post-lapsarian lust.

To apprehend the true and absolute nature of things — that is the fruit of Nietzschean clarity. Energies and entities are one and the same, did you know that, dear diary? Wonders are many, but the greatest of these is being. Hell does not exist. Heaven is the fantasy of clerics. There is no God, and I am his prophet.

Fokken — that is the crisp, candid, Middle Dutch word for it. We fuck and fuck and fuck and fuck.

Wednesday, 12 June

An Überfrau does not hide her blazing intellect beneath a bushel. She trumpets her transfiguration from every rooftop, every watchtower, the summit of the highest mountain.

When I told Lady Witherspoon what Edward and I had done with the elixir, I assumed she might turn livid and perhaps even banish me from her estate. I did not anticipate that she would acquire a countenance of supreme alarm, call me the world's biggest fool, and spew out a narrative so hideous that only an Überfrau would dare, as I did, to greet it with a contemptuous laugh.

If I am to believe the Baroness, Dr. Renault also wondered whether Infusion U might be capable of causing the consummation of our race. His experiments were so costly they depleted his personal fortune, entailing as they did lawsuits brought against him by the relations of the serum's twenty recipients. For it happens that the beneficence of Infusion U rarely persists for more than six weeks, after which the Übermensch endures a rapid and irremediable slide toward the primal. No known drug can arrest this degeneration, and the process is merely accelerated by additional injections.

The subjects of Renault's investigations may have lost their Nietzschean nerve, but Edward and I shall remain true to our joy. We exist beyond the tawdry grasp of the actual and the trivial reach of reason. As Übermensch and Überfrau we are prepared to grant employment to every species of whimsy, but no facts need apply.

Something June

The third meeting of the Witherspoon Academy was another rollicking success, though Miss Ruggles and Mr. Crowther would probably construct it otherwise. When Miss Ruggles inflicted her latest excrescence on us, a piece of twaddle about her garden, Edward suggested that she run home and tend her flowers, for they were surely wilting from shame. She left the estate in tears. After Mr. Crowther finished spouting his drivel, I told him that his muse had evidently spent the past four weeks selling herself in the streets. His face went crimson, and he left in a huff.

Thursday?

Kitty's head swims in a maelstrom of its own making. Her stomach has lost all sovereignty over its goods, and her psyche has likewise surrendered its dominion. Her soul vomits upon the page.

Another Day

Ape hair on Edward's arms. Ape teeth in his mouth. Ape face covering his skull.

A Different Day

Ape hair in the mirror. Ape teeth in the mirror. Ape face in the mirror.

Another Day

They pitted me against him. In the mud. My Edward. We would not fight. They did it to him anyway. Necessary? Yes. Do I care? No. Procreation kills.

No Day

On the sea. Atonement Atoll. A timbre intended is a tone meant. I shall never say anything so clever again. I weep.

Habzilb

habzilb larzed dox ner adnor ulorx qron mizrel bewq xewt ulp ilr ulp xok ulp ulp ulp ulp ulpulpulpulpulpulpulpulpulpulp

PERSONAL JOURNAL OF CAPTAIN ARCHIBALD CARMODY, R.N.
Written aboard H.M.S. *Aldebaran*
Whilst on a Voyage of Scientific Discovery in the Indian Ocean

20 April 1899
LAT. 1°10' S, LONG. 71°42' E

I slept till noon. After securing Miss Glover's diary in my rucksack, I bid the watch row me ashore, then entered the aborigines' cavern in search of Silver. Despite Kitty's fantastic chronicle, I still think of them as Neanderthals, and perhaps I always shall.

My friend was nowhere to be found. I proceeded to his mate's grave. Silver *né* Edward Pertuis sat atop the mound, contemplating Kitty's graven image. I surrendered the diary to the gelded ape-man, who forthwith secured it in his satchel.

The instant I drew the Bible from my rucksack, Silver understood my intention. He wrapped one long arm about the sculpture, then set the opposite hand atop the Scriptures. I'd never performed the ceremony before, and I'm sure I got certain details wrong. The ape-man hung onto my every word, and when at length I averred that he and Katherine Margaret Glover were man and wife, he smiled, then kissed his bride.

22 April 1899
LAT. 6°11' N, LONG. 68°32' E

Two days after steaming away from Lydia Isle, I find myself wondering if it was all a dream. The lost race, their strange music, the bereaved beast grieving over his mate's effigy — did I imagine the entire sojourn?

Naturally Mr. Chalmers and Mr. Bainbridge will corroborate my stay in Eden. As for the strange diary, I am at the moment prepared to give it credence, and not just because I spent so many hours in monkish replication of its pages. I believe Kitty Glover. The subterranean tournaments, the demimonde drug, the uplift serum: these are factual as rain. I am convinced that Kitty and Edward ventured recklessly into the *terra incognita* of their primate past, losing themselves forever in apish antiquity.

My wife is an avid consumer of the London papers. If, prior to my departure, Briarwood House had been found to conceal a cabal of sorceresses bent on reforming miscreant males through French chemistry and Roman combat, Lydia would surely have read about it and told me. Until I hear otherwise, I shall assume that the Hampstead Ladies Croquet Club is a going concern, making apes, curing demons, knocking balls through hoops.

And so I face a dilemma. Upon my return to England do I inform the authorities of debatable recreations at Briarwood House? Or do I allow the uncanny status quo to persist? But that is another day's conversation with myself.

23 April 1899
LAT. 15°06' N, LONG. 55°32' E

Last night I once again read all the diary transcriptions. My dilemma has dissolved. With Übermensch clarity I see what I must do, and not do.

In some nebulous future — when England's men have transmuted into angels, perhaps, or England's women have gotten the vote, or Satan has become an epicure of snowflakes — on that date I may suggest to a Hampstead constable that he investigate rumors of witchery at Lady Witherspoon's estate. But for now the secret of the Benevolent Society is safe with me. Landing again on Albion's shore, I shall arrange for this journal to become my family's most private heirloom, and I shall undertake a second mission as well, approaching the Baroness, assuring her of my good intentions, and inquiring as to whether Ezekiel Snavely finally went down in the mud.

For our next voyage my sponsors intend that I should sail to Gávdhos, southwest of Crete, rumored to harbor a remarkable variety of firefly — the only such species to have evolved in the Greek Isles. Naturalists call it the changeling bug, as it exhibits the same proclivities as a chameleon. These beetles mimic the stars. Stare into the singing woods of Gávdhos on a still summer night, and you will witness a colony of changeling bugs blinking on and off in configurations that precisely copy horned Aries, clawed Cancer, poisonous Scorpio, mighty Taurus, sleek Pisces, and the rest.

The greatest of these tableaux is Sagittarius. Once the fireflies have formed their centaur, the missile reportedly shoots away, rising into the sky until the darkness claims it. Some say the constituents of this insectile arrow continue beating their wings until, disoriented and bereft of energy, they fall into the Aegean Sea and drown. I do not believe it. Nature has better uses for her lights. Rather, I am confident that, owing to some Darwinian adaptation or other, the beetles cease their theatrics and pause in mid-flight, forthwith reversing course and returning to the island, weary and hungry but glad to be amongst familiar trees again, called home by the keeper of their kind.

Martyrs of the Upshot Knothole

I sit in the comfort of my easy chair, the cat on my lap, the world at my command. With my right index finger I press the button, and seconds later the hydrogen bomb explodes.

The videocassette in question is *Trinity and Beyond*, a documentary comprising two hours of restored footage shot in full color by the U.S. Air Force's 1352nd Motion Picture Squadron, aka the Atomic Cinematographers. I am watching the detonation of February 28, 1954: Castle Bravo, fifteen megatons, in its day the largest atmospheric thermonuclear test ever conducted on planet Earth.

Red as the sun, the implacable dome of gas and debris expands outward from ground zero, suggesting at first an apocalyptic plum pudding, then an immense Santiago pilgrim's hat. The blast front flattens concrete buildings, tears palm trees out by the roots, and draws a tidal wave from the Pacific. Now the filmmakers give us a half-dozen shots of the inevitable mushroom cloud. I gaze into the roiling crimson mass, reading the entrails of human ingenuity.

"You're free of cancer" and "You're the lover I've been looking for my whole life" are among the most uplifting sentences a person will ever hear, and it so happened that both declarations came my way during the same week. An optimist at heart, I took each affirmation at face value, so naturally I was distressed when the speakers in question began backpedaling.

No sooner had Dr. Joshua Pryce told me that the latest lab report indicated no malignant cells in my body, not one, than he hastened to add, "Of course, this doesn't mean you're rid of it forever."

"You think it'll come back?" I asked.

"Hard to say."

"Could you hazard a guess?"

Dr. Pryce drew a silk handkerchief from his bleached lab coat and removed his bifocals. "Let me emphasize the positive." In a fit of absentmindedness, the oncologist repocketed his glasses. "For the moment you're cancer-free. But the disease has a will of its own."

In the case of the man who called me his ideal lover — Stuart Randolph, the semi-retired NYU film historian with whom I've shared a bohemian loft over-looking Washington Square for the past eighteen years — I logically expected that his subsequent remarks would concern the institution of marriage. But instead Stuart followed his declaration by arguing that there were two kinds of commitment in the world: the contrived commitment entailed in the matrimonial contract, and the genuine commitment that flowed from the sort of "perfect rapport and flawless communication" that characterized our relationship.

"If we enjoyed perfect rapport and flawless communication, we wouldn't be having this discussion," I said. "I want to get married, Stu."

"Really?" He frowned as if confronting a particularly egregious instance of postmodern film criticism. Stuart's an auteurist, not a deconstructionist.

"Really."

"You truly want to become my fourth wife?"

"As much as I want you to become my fifth husband."

"Why, dear?" he said. "Do you think we're living in sin? Senior citizens can't live in sin."

"*Imitation of Life* is a lousy movie, but I like it anyway," I said. "Marriage is a bourgeois convention, but I like it anyway."

"Should the cancer ever return, dearest Angela, you'll be glad you've got a committed lover by your side, as opposed to some sap who happens technically to be your husband."

Stuart was not normally capable of bringing romance and reason into such perfect alignment, but he'd just done so, and I had to admire his achievement.

"I cannot argue with your logic," I told him. And I couldn't. All during my treatments, Stuart had been an absolute prince, driving me to the hospital a hundred times, holding my head as I threw up, praising the doctors when they did their jobs properly, yelling at them when they got haughty. "Checkmate."

"Love and marriage," he said. "They go together like a horse and aluminum siding."

Have no fear, gentle reader. This is not a story about what I endured at the hands of Western medicine once its avatars learned I'd developed leukemia. It's not about radiation treatments, chemotherapy, violent nausea, suicidal depression, paralyzing fear, or nurses poking dozens of holes in my body. My subject, rather, is the last performance ever given by an old colleague of mine, the biggest box-office star of all time, John Wayne — a performance that was never committed to celluloid but that leaves his Oscar-winning Rooster Cogburn gagging in the dust.

It would be inaccurate to say that Duke and I hated each other. Yes, I detested the man — detested everything he stood for — but my loathing was incompletely requited, for at some perverse level Duke clearly relished my companionship. Our irreconcilable philosophies first emerged when we appeared together in the 1953 survival melodrama, *Island in the Sky*, and ever since then our political clashes, too uncivilized to be called conversations or even debates, provided Duke with a caliber of stimulation he could obtain from no other liberal of his acquaintance. Throughout his career he routinely convinced the front office to offer me a marginal role in whatever John Wayne vehicle was on the drawing board, thereby guaranteeing that the two of us would briefly share the same soundstage or location set, and he could spend his lunch hours and coffee breaks reveling in the pleasurable rush he got from our battles over what had gone wrong with America.

As I write these words, it occurs to me that any self-respecting actress would have spurned this peculiar arrangement — a kind of love affair animated by neither love nor physical desire but rather by the male partner's passion for polemic. No public adulation or peer recognition could possibly accrue to the parts Duke picked for me. There is no Oscar for Best Performance by an Actress Portraying a Cipher. But solvency and an Actors' Equity membership are by no means synonymous, and so over a span of nearly twenty years I periodically found myself abandoning my faltering Broadway career, flying to Hollywood, and accepting good money for reciting bad dialogue.

In 1954 I played a fading opera diva trapped aboard a crippled airliner in *The High and the Mighty*, which Bill Wellman directed with great flair. Next came my portrayal of Hunlun, mother of Genghis Khan, *né* Temujin, in *The Conqueror*, probably the least watchable of the films produced by that eccentric American aviator and storm trooper, Howard Hughes. Subsequent to *The Conqueror* I essayed a middle-aged Comanche squaw in *The Searchers*, the picture on which Duke started referring to me, unaffectionately, as "Egghead." Then came my blind wife of a noble Texan in *The Alamo*, my over-the-hill snake charmer in *Circus World*, and my pacifist Navy nurse in *The Green Berets*. Finally, in *Chisum* of 1970, I was once again cast as Duke's mother, although my entire performance ended up in the trim bin.

It was Stuart who first connected the dots linking John Wayne, myself, and nearly a hundred other cancer victims in a fantastic matrix of Sophoclean terror and Kierkegaardian trembling. Six weeks after Dr. Pryce had labeled me cancer-free, Stuart was scanning the *New York Times* for March 15, 1975, when he happened upon two ostensibly unrelated facts: the Atomic Energy Commission was about to open its old nuclear-weapons proving ground in Nevada to the general public, and former screen goddess Susan Hayward had died the previous day from brain cancer. She was only fifty-six. Something started Stuart's mind working on all cylinders, and within twenty-four hours he'd made a Sherlock Holmesian deduction.

"*The Conqueror*," he said. We were having morning tea in our breakfast nook, which is also our lunch nook and our dinner nook. "*The Conqueror*— that's *it*! You shot the thing in Yucca Flat, Nevada, right?"

"An experience I'd rather forget," I said.

"But you shot it in Yucca Flat, right?"

"No, we shot it in southwest Utah, the Escalante Desert and environs— Bryce Canyon, Snow Canyon, Zion National Park . . ."

"Southwest Utah, close enough," said Stuart, shifting into lecture mode. "*The Conqueror*, 1956, Cinemascope, Technicolor, the second of Dick Powell's five lackluster attempts to become a major Hollywood director. In the early sixties, Powell dies of cancer. A decade or so later, you're diagnosed with leukemia. Somewhere in between, John Wayne has a cancerous lung removed, telling the press, 'I licked the Big C.' And now the female lead of *The Conqueror* is dead of a brain tumor."

The epic in question had Susan playing a fictitious Tartar princess named Bortai (loosely based on Genghis Khan's wife of the same name), daughter of the fictitious Tartar chief Kumlek (though the screenwriter was perhaps alluding to the real-life Naiman chief Kushlek), who slays Temujin's nonfictitious father, Yesukai, off-screen about fifteen years before the movie begins. "The curse of *The Conqueror*," I muttered.

"Hell, there's no *curse* going on here, Angela." Stuart used a grapefruit spoon to retrieve his ginseng tea bag from the steaming water. "This is entirely rational. This is about gamma radiation."

According to the *Times*, he explained, the military had conducted eleven nuclear tests on the Nevada Proving Ground in the spring of 1953, an operation that bore the wonderfully surrealistic name Upshot Knothole. The gamma rays were gone now, and civilians would soon be permitted to visit the site, but during the Upshot Knothole era anyone straying into the vicinity would have received four hundred times the acceptable dose of radiation. The last detonation, "Climax," had occurred on the fourth of June.

"And one year later, almost to the day, the *Conqueror* company arrives in the Escalante Desert and starts to work," I said, at once impressed by Stuart's detective work and frightened by its implications.

My lover exited the breakfast nook, removed the cat from our coffee-table atlas, and opened to a two-page spread comprising Utah and Nevada.

"You were maybe only a hundred and thirty miles from the epicenter. Eleven A-bombs, Angela. If the winds were blowing the wrong way on some days . . ."

"Obviously they were," I said. "And the Atomic Energy Commission now expects *tourists* to show up?"

"Never underestimate the power of morbid curiosity."

A quick trip through the back issues of *Film Fan Almanac* was all Stuart needed to reinforce his theory with two additional Upshot Knothole casualties. Unable to cope with his cancer any longer, Pedro Armendariz, who played Temujin's "blood brother" Jamuga, had shot himself in the heart on June 18, 1963. Exactly eight years later — on June 18, 1971 — cancer deprived the world of Thomas Gomez, who portrayed Wang Khan, the Mongol ruler whom Temujin seeks to usurp (thereby bestowing a throne on himself and a plot on the movie). Like Susan, Tom was only fifty-six.

"We are the new *hibakusha*," I mused bitterly. The *hibakusha*, the "explosion-affected persons," as the Hiroshima survivors called themselves. "Me, Duke, Dick, Susan, Pedro, and Tom. The American *hibakusha*. The Howard Hughes *hibakusha*. I'd never tell Duke, of course. Irony makes him mad."

Our obligation was manifest. We must contact the entire *Conqueror* company — stars, supporting players, camera operators, soundmen, lighting crew, costume fitters, art director, special-effects technician, hair stylist, makeup artist, assistant director — and advise them to seek out their doctors posthaste. And so we did. For five months Stuart and I functioned as angels of death, fetches of the Nuclear Age, banshees bearing ill tidings of lymphoma and leukemia, and by the autumn of 1976 our phone calls and telegrams had generated two catalogues, one listing eighty *Conqueror* alumni who were already dead (most of them from cancer), the other identifying one hundred forty survivors. Of this latter group, one hundred sixteen received our warning with graciousness and gratitude, three told us we had no business disrupting their lives this way and we should go to hell, and twenty-one already knew they had the disease, though they were astonished that we'd gleaned the fact from mere circumstantial evidence.

John Wayne himself was the last person I wanted to talk to, but Stuart argued that we had no other choice. We'd been unable to locate Linwood Dunn, who did the on-location special effects, and Duke might very well have a clue.

I hadn't spoken with the old buzzard in nine years, but our conversation was barely a minute underway before we were trading verbal barrages. True to form, this was not a fond sparring-match between mutually admiring colleagues but a full-blown war of the *Weltanschauungen*, the West Coast patriot versus the East Coast pink, the brave-heart conservative versus the bleeding-heart liberal. According to Duke's inside sources, President Jimmy Carter was about to issue a plenary pardon to the Vietnam War draft evaders. Naturally I thought this was a marvelous idea, and I told Duke as much. John Wayne — the same John Wayne who'd declined to don a military uniform during World War II, fearing that a prolonged stint in the armed forces would decelerate his burgeoning career — responded by asserting that once again Mr. Peanut Head was skirting the bounds of treason.

Changing the subject, I told Duke about my leukemia ordeal, and how this had ultimately led Stuart to connect the Nevada A-bomb tests with the *Conqueror* company's astonishingly high cancer rate. Predictably enough, Duke did not warm to the theory, with its implicit indictment of nuclear weapons, the Cold War, and other institutions dear to his heart, and when I used the phrase "Howard Hughes *hibakusha*," he threatened to hang up.

"We need to find Linwood Dunn," I said. "We think he's at risk."

In a matter of seconds Duke located his Rolodex and looked up Linwood's unlisted phone number. I wrote the digits on the back of a stray *New Republic*.

"Well, Egghead, I suppose it can't hurt for Lin to see the medics, but this doesn't mean I buy your nutty idea," said Duke. "Howard Hughes is a true American."

He should have said Howard Hughes *was* a true American, because even as we spoke the seventy-year-old codeine addict was dying of kidney failure in Houston.

"You may have just saved Lin's life," I said.

"Possibly," said Duke. "Interesting you should get in touch, Egghead. I was about to give you a call. I'm thinking of shooting a picture in your neck of the woods next year, and there's a real sweet part in it for you."

I drew the receiver away from my ear, cupped the mouthpiece, and caught Stuart's attention with my glance. "He wants me in his next movie," I said in a coherent whisper.

"Go for it," said Stuart. "We need the money."

I lifted my hand from the mouthpiece and told Duke, "I'll take any role except your mother."

"Good," he said. "You'll be playing my grandmother." He chuckled. "That's a joke, Egghead. I have you down for my mentor, a retired schoolteacher. We finish principal photography on *The Shootist* in two weeks, and then I'm off to New York, scouting locations. We'll have dinner at the Waldorf, okay?"

"Sure, Duke."

Later that day, Stuart and I telephoned Linwood Dunn.

"You folks may have saved my life," he said.

I'm probably being unfair to Duke. Yes, his primitive politics infuriated me, but unlike most of his hidebound friends he was not a thoughtless man. He enjoyed a certain salutary distance from himself. Of his magnum opus, *The Alamo*, he once told a reporter, "There's more to that movie than my damn conservative attitude," and I have to agree. Beneath its superficial jingoist coating, and beneath the layer of genuine jingoism under that, *The Alamo* exudes an offbeat and rather touching generosity of spirit. The freedom-loving frontiersmen holding down the fort do not demonize Santa Anna's army, and at one point they praise their enemy's courage. I think also of Duke's willingness to appear in a 1974 public forum organized by the editors of the *Harvard Lampoon*. When a student asked him where he got the "phony toupee," he replied, "It's not phony. It's real hair. Of course, it's not mine, but it's real." Another student wanted to know whether Mr. Wayne's horse had recovered from his hernia now that the superstar was dieting. "No, he died," Duke answered, "and we canned him, which is what you're eating at the Harvard Club."

This refreshing streak of self-deprecation surfaced again when we met in New York at the Waldorf-Astoria. As we dug into our steaks and baked potatoes, Duke told me his idea for an urban cop picture, which he wanted to call *Lock and Load*. He'd seen Clint Eastwood's first two Harry Callahan movies, *Dirty Harry* and *Magnum Force*, and he was beguiled by both their vigilante ethos and their hefty profits. "If a liberal like Eastwood can make a fascist film," said Duke with a sly smile, "imagine what a fascist like me could do with that kind of material."

I laughed and patted him on the arm. "You'll make Harry Callahan look like Adlai Stevenson."

It was obvious to both of us that there would probably never be a John Wayne picture called *Lock and Load*. We were eating not in the hotel restaurant but in his room, so that the general public wouldn't see what a wreck he'd become. Maybe Duke had licked the Big C in 1964, but thirteen years later it was back for a rematch. He breathed only with the help of a sinister-looking portable inhaler, and he had a male nurse in permanent attendance, a swarthy Texan named Sweeney Foote, forever fidgeting in the background like a Doberman pinscher on guard.

"You look terrific, Egghead," he said. He was wearing his famous toupee, as well as a lush Turkish bathrobe and leather slippers. "I'm sure you gave the Big C a knockout punch."

"The doctors aren't that optimistic."

Duke worked his face into a sneer. "Doctors," he said.

I glanced around the suite, appointed with tasteful opulence. Sweeney

Foote sat hunched on the mattress, playing solitaire. I'd never been in the Waldorf-Astoria before, and I wondered if Duke had selected it for its symbolic value. When the Hollywood Ten's highly publicized appearance before the House Un-American Activities Committee started going badly (not only were the Ten actual by-God former Communists, they didn't seem particularly ashamed of it), the heads of the major studios called an emergency meeting at the Waldorf. Before the day was over, the money men had agreed that unemployment and ostracism would befall any Hollywood actor, writer, or director who defied a Congressional committee or refused to come forward with his or her non-Communist credentials.

"Tell me about *Lock and Load*," I said.

"Hell of a script," said Duke. "Jimmy's best work since *The Alamo*. I'm Stonewall McBride, this maverick police captain who likes to do things his own way."

"Novel concept," I said dryly.

"Stonewall has stayed in touch with his fifth-grade teacher, kind of a mother-figure to him, regularly advising him on how to get along in a dog-eat-dog world."

"I've always enjoyed Maria Ouspenskaya."

Duke nodded, smiled, and gestured as if tipping an invisible Stetson, but then his expression became a wince. "I'll be honest, Egghead." He popped an analgesic pill and washed it down with beer. "I'm not here just to scout locations. Fact is, the Big C has me on the ropes. The medics say it's in my stomach now, as if I didn't know."

"I'm sorry, Duke."

"Back in L.A. I kept meeting folks who're into herbal medicines and psychic cures and such, and they advised me to go see this swami fella, Kieran Morella of the Greater Manhattan Heuristic Healing Center."

"Southern California at your fingertips, and you had to come to *New York* to find a hippie guru flake?"

"You can laugh if you want to, Egghead, but I hoofed it over to Kieran's office the instant I stepped off the plane, and what he said made sense to me. Sure, it's an unconventional treatment, but he's had lots of success. He uses a kind of hypnotism to send the patient back to the exact moment when some little part of him turned cancerous, and then the patient imagines his immune system rounding up those primal malignant cells the way a cowboy rounds up steers."

"Steers? Hey, this is the cure for you, Duke."

"Next the patient tries to tune in these things called quantum vibrations, and before long the space-time continuum has folded back on itself, and it's as if he'd never developed cancer in the first place."

"'Unconventional' is a good word here, Duke."

He swallowed another analgesic. "To help the patient get the proper pictures flowing through his mind — you know, images of his lymphocytes corralling the original cancer cells — Kieran shows him clips from *Red River*. Kinetotherapy, he calls it."

"Jesus, he must have been thrilled to meet you," I said. *Red River* is one of the few John Wayne westerns that Stuart and I can watch without snickering.

"He almost creamed himself. Now listen tight, Egghead. You might think I'm just talking about me, but I'm also talking about you. All during my flight east, I kept thinking about that American *hibakusha* business, and eventually I decided maybe your theory's not so crazy after all."

"Howard Hughes has nuked us, Duke. Your fellow John Bircher has pumped us full of gamma rays."

"Let's leave Howard out of this. Here's the crux. The minute I told Kieran about this possible connection between *The Conqueror* and the Big C, and how the Cinemascope lenses may have captured the very moment when the radiation started seeping into me — how it's all up there on the silver screen — well, he got pretty damn excited."

"I can imagine."

"He kept saying, 'Mr. Wayne, we must get a copy of this film. Find me a print, Mr. Wayne, and I'll cure you.'"

Duke snapped his fingers. Taking care not to disturb his matrix of playing cards, Sweeney Foote rolled off the bed. He went to the closet, reached into a valise, and drew out an object that looked like a Revell plastic model of the cryptic black monolith from *2001: A Space Odyssey*, a movie that Duke had refused to see on general principles.

"*The Conqueror* arrived this morning, special courier, along with the necessary hardware," said Duke. He took the little monolith from Sweeney, then passed it to me. "Brand new technology, Jap thing called Betamax, a spool of half-inch videotape in a plastic cassette. Sony thinks it'll be the biggest thing since the Crock-Pot."

The Betamax cassette featured a plastic window offering a partial view of both the feed core and the take-up spindle. Somebody had written "The Conqueror" on a piece of masking tape and stuck it across the top edge. "Ingenious," I said.

"It's all very well to wring your hands over Hiroshima, but if you ask me the Japs have done pretty well for themselves since then, especially the Sony people. My first kinetotherapy treatment occurs in two days and — you know what, Angela? — I'd like you to come along. You could help me concentrate, and you might even get a healing effect yourself."

"I couldn't afford it."

"I'll pay for everything. You're not out of the woods yet."

"I'm not out of the woods," I admitted ruefully.

"Monday afternoon, two o'clock, the Heuristic Healing Center, 1190 West 41st Street near Tenth Avenue. There's a goddamn mandala on the door."

"Let me talk it over with Stuart."

"With the Big C, you're never out of the woods."

I pour myself a glass of sherry, rewind *Trinity and Beyond*, and press Play. As before, the fiery mushroom cloud from the Castle Bravo explosion fills my television screen, shot after shot of billowing radioactive dust, and for a fleeting instant I experience an urge to bow down before it.

How beautiful art thou, O Mighty Fireball. How fair thy countenance and frame. Give me coffers of gold, O Great One, and I shall heap sacrifices upon thy altar. Give me silken raiment and shining cities, and I shall wash thy graven feet with priceless libations.

Stuart and I decided that as long as Duke was picking up the tab I should indeed give kinetotherapy a try, and so on Monday afternoon I took the N Train to Times Square. Ten minutes later I marched into the foyer of the Heuristic Healing Center, its walls hung with Hindu tapestries, its air laden with patchouli incense, and announced myself to the receptionist, a stately black woman wearing a beige Nehru jacket. The nameplate on her desk read JON-QUIL. Duke was waiting for me, outfitted in blue denims, a checked cotton shirt, a red bandanna, and tooled-leather cowboy boots. Sweeney Foote lurked near the coatrack, Duke's inhaler slung over his shoulder, a large crush-proof envelope tucked under his arm like a private eye's holster.

Duke and I had barely said hello when Kieran Morella, a pale slender man — white caftan, orange beads, silver-gray ponytail, salt-and-pepper goatee — sashayed out of his office, all smiles and winks. He gave us each a hug, which didn't go over well with Duke, then took the envelope from Sweeney and ushered us into Treatment Salon Number Three, a velvet-draped chamber suggesting an old-style Hollywood screening room. At the far end two brown, tufted, vinyl recliner chairs faced a television set connected to a squat device that I took to be a Betamax videocassette recorder.

As Sweeney slunk into the shadows, Kieran produced a coffee tin crammed with neatly rolled joints, presenting the stash to us as a hostess might offer her bridge club a box of chocolates. Getting stoned was optional, the therapist explained, but it would help us reach a "a peak of relaxed concentration."

"Hey, Doc, I've never smoked that Timothy Leary stuff in my life, and I'm not about to start now," said Duke. "Don't you have any drinking whiskey around here?"

"I could send Jonquil out for something," said Kieran.

"Jack Daniels, okay?"

"Tennessee's finest" — Kieran issued a nervous laugh — "endorsed by Davy Crockett himself."

Duke and Kieran spent the next twenty minutes talking about their favorite John Wayne movies. They were both keen on the so-called Cavalry Trilogy that Duke made under John Ford's direction: *Fort Apache, She Wore a Yellow Ribbon, Rio Grande* — three pictures that leave me cold. (I much prefer Duke and Ford in Irish mode: *The Quiet Man, The Long Voyage Home*.) At last Jonquil appeared with a quart of Jack Daniels and a shot glass. Kieran guided us into the recliner chairs and removed *The Conqueror* from Sweeney's envelope. He fed the cassette into the Betamax, flipped on the TV, and bustled about the room lighting incense and chanting under his breath.

"Your job is simple, Mr. Wayne." Kieran seized a remote control connected to the Betamax by a coaxial cable. "Each time you appear out there in the Escalante Desert, I want you to imagine a kind of psychic armor surrounding your body, filtering out the gamma rays. Ms. Rappaport, you have exactly the same task. During every shot you're in" — he handed me a box of wooden matches — "you must imagine a translucent shield standing between yourself and the radioactivity. If you folks can get the right quantum vibrations going, your screen images will acquire visible protective auras."

"We'll really see *auras*?" said Duke, impressed.

"There's a good chance of it," said Kieran.

Duke poured himself a slug of whiskey. I took a joint from the coffee tin, struck a match, and lit up. Kieran positioned himself behind our chairs, laying a soothing hand on each of our heads.

"This is going to be fun," I said, drawing in a puff of magic smoke.

"Concentrate," said Kieran.

I held my breath, slid the joint from my lips, and passed it to Kieran. He took a toke. The credits came on, a roll call of the dead, the doomed, and the fortunate few, this last category consisting mainly of people who didn't have to sweat under the Utah sun to get their names on the picture: the associate producer, the writer, the film editor, the sound editor.

As the movie unspooled in all its pan-and-scan glory—the film-chain operator had astutely decided that the original anamorphic images would not prosper on the average TV screen—it occurred to me that my running feud with Duke encapsulated the history of the Cold War. During the making of *The High and the Mighty*, we fought about the imminent electrocution of the "atomic spies," Julius and Ethel Rosenberg. While shooting *The Searchers*, we nearly came to blows concerning the Senate's recent decision to censure Joseph McCarthy. ("Old Joe will have the last laugh," Duke kept saying.) *The Alamo* found us at odds over the upcoming presidential election, Duke insisting that there would be jubilation in the Kremlin if Jack Kennedy, the likely Democratic contender, beat Richard Nixon, the shoo-in for the Republican nomination. Between takes on *Circus World*, we nearly drew blood over whether the Cuban missile crisis obliged the superpowers to start taking disarmament seriously or whether, conversely, it meant that America should ratchet up her arsenal to a higher level of overkill. On the sets of both *The Green Berets* and *Chisum*, the Vietnam War inevitably got us going at each other hammer and tongs.

And what about *The Conqueror* itself? What issue fueled our hostility during that benighted project? Believe it or not, our bone of contention was atomic testing, even though we knew nothing of Upshot Knothole and the radioactive toxins seething all around us. Fear of Strontium-90—like Strontium-90 itself—was in the air that year. *Fallout* had become a household word. Each night after we were back at the Grand Marquis Hotel in St. George, our base of operations during the *Conqueror* shoot, most of the cast and crew would stand around in the lobby watching Walter Cronkite, and occasionally there'd be a news story about a politician who believed that unlimited on-continent testing of nuclear devices would eventually make lots of Americans sick, children especially. (Strontium-90 was ending up in the milk of dairy cows.) One such report included the latest figures on leukemia cases attributable to Hiroshima and Nagasaki.

"Poor old Genghis Khan," I said to Al D'Agostino, the art director. "He had to spend *weeks*, sometimes *months*, bringing down a city."

"Whereas Paul Tibbets and his B-52 managed it in the twinkling of an eye," said Al, who in those days was almost as far to the left as I.

"Poor old Genghis Khan," echoed the assistant director, Ed Killy. Ed was likewise a lefty, though he usually kept it under wraps, thereby maintaining his friendship with Duke.

"You people seem to forget that Hiroshima and Nagasaki kept our boys from having to invade Japan," said Duke. "Those bombs saved thousands of American lives."

"Well, Temujin," I said, sarcasm dripping from every syllable, "I guess that settles the matter."

The Conqueror had been on Kieran's TV barely ten minutes when I decided that it wasn't a costume drama after all. It was really yet another John Wayne western, with Tartars instead of Comanches and the Mongol city of Urga instead of Fort Apache. But even the feeblest of Duke's horse operas — *The Lawless Range* comes to mind, also *Randy Rides Alone* — wasn't nearly this enervated. None of those early Republic or Monogram westerns had Duke saying, before the first scene was over, "There are moments for wisdom, Jamuga, and then I listen to you. And there are moments for action, and then I listen to my heart. I feel this Tartar woman is for me. My blood says, 'Take her!'"

"Concentrate," Kieran exhorted us, returning the joint to my eager fingers. "Repulse those gamma rays. Bend the fabric of space-time."

"I'm tryin', Doc," said Duke, downing a second slug of Jack Daniels.

"Why would anybody want to make a movie celebrating a demented brute like Temujin?" I asked rhetorically. I'd read the *Encyclopedia Britannica*'s account of Genghis Khan the night before, baiting my hook. "Bukhara was one of medieval Asia's greatest cities, a center of science and culture. At Temujin's urging, his army burned it to the ground, all the while raping and torturing everybody in sight."

"Ms. Rappaport, I must ask you not to disrupt the healing process," said Kieran.

"When the citizens of Herat deposed the governor appointed by one of Temujin's sons, the retaliatory massacre lasted a week," I continued. "Death toll, one million six hundred thousand. Genghis Khan was a walking A-bomb."

"Let's not get too high and mighty, Egghead," said Duke. "Hunlun wasn't exactly Florence Nightingale, but as I recall you didn't run screaming from the part. You picked up your paycheck along with the rest of us."

Duke had me on both counts, historical and ethical. Shortly after Temujin became the titular Mongol ruler at age thirteen, Hunlun emerged as the power behind the throne, and she ruled with an iron hand. When a group of local tribes turned rebellious, Hunlun led an expeditionary force against the obstreperous chiefs, and eventually she brought over half of them back into the fold.

"Please, people, let's focus," said Kieran. "This won't work unless we focus."

Screenwriter Oscar Millard had given my character three major scenes. In the first, Hunlun sternly reprimands her son for abducting the nubile Bortai from her fiancé, a Merkit chief named Targatai — not because it's wrong to treat women as booty, but because Bortai's father murdered Hunlun's husband. "Will you take pleasure with the offspring of your father's slayer?!" Hunlun asks Temujin. "She will bring woe to you, my son, and to your people!" In Hunlun's second major scene, she bemoans the Mongol casualties that attended both Temujin's initial seizure of Bortai and Targatai's attempt to reclaim her. "And what of *your* dead, those who died needlessly for this cursed child of Kumlek's?!" Hunlun's final sequence is her longest. While applying healing leaves and ointments to Temujin's arrow wound, Hunlun takes the opportunity to tell him that, thanks to his obsession with Bortai, he is losing track of his destiny. "Did I not hold our tribe together and raise you with but one thought — to regain your father's power and avenge his death?!"

I hadn't seen my work in *The Conqueror* since the world premiere, and I hated every frame of it. It took a full measure of willpower to ignore this embarrassing one-note performance and concentrate instead on conjuring an anti-radiation aura around my pan-and-scan form.

Despite all the encouragement from Kieran and the marijuana, I failed to build the necessary shield, and Duke didn't have any luck either. From the first shot of Temujin (our hero leading a cavalry charge) to the last (the Mongol emperor standing beside his bride as they proudly survey their marching hordes), Duke's Betamax simulacrum never once acquired anything resembling psychic armor. The actor made no effort to hide his disappointment.

"Doc, I think we're pissing in the wind."

"Kinetotherapy takes time," said Kieran. "Can you both come back tomorrow at two o'clock?"

"For grass of such quality, I'd watch this piece of crap every day for a year," I said.

"Make sure you've got plenty of Jack Daniels on the premises," said Duke.

The instant Kieran activated his television on Tuesday afternoon, the picture tube burned out, the image imploding like a reverse-motion shot of an A-bomb detonation. It's not difficult, however, to purchase a new TV set in New York City, and Jonquil accomplished the task with great efficiency. Our second kinetotherapy session started only forty minutes late.

As Kieran got the cassette rolling, Sweeney assumed his place in the shadows, Duke poured himself a shot of Jack Daniels, and I inhaled a lungful of pot. Today's weed was even better than yesterday's. Kieran might be a nutcase and a charlatan, but he knew his euphorics.

"Want to know the really scary thing about the Upshot Knothole tests?" I said. I'd spent my evening reading *The Tenth Circle of Hell*, Judith Markson's concise narrative of the Nevada Proving Ground. "By this point in history such devices were considered *tactical*—not strategic, *tactical*."

"Take it easy, Egghead," said Duke.

"Time to watch the movie," said Kieran.

"The monster that killed seventy thousand Hiroshima civilians is suddenly a fucking *battlefield weapon*!" I passed the joint to Kieran. "Isn't that *sick*? They even fired a Knothole bomb out of an *artillery cannon*! They called it 'Grable'—from Betty Grable, no doubt—fifteen kilotons, same as the Hiroshima blast. A goddamn artillery cannon."

As the screen displayed the opening logo, Kieran drew some illegal vapor into his body, then gave me back the joint.

AN RKO RADIO PICTURE FILMED IN CINEMASCOPE.

"Focus, my friends," said Kieran. "Tune in the quantum vibrations."

HOWARD HUGHES PRESENTS . . . THE CONQUEROR . . . STARRING JOHN WAYNE . . .

"Then there was 'Encore,' dropped from a plane." I sucked on the joint, inhaled deeply, and, pursing my lips, let the smoke find its way to my brain. "They suspended another payload from a balloon, dropped another from a steel tower."

SUSAN HAYWARD . . . CO-STARRING PEDRO ARMENDARIZ . . . WITH ANGELA RAPPAPORT . . . THOMAS GOMEZ . . . JOHN HOYT . . . WILLIAM CONRAD . . .

"Battlefield atomic bombs." I gave the joint to Kieran. He took a toke and handed it back. "What barbarous insanity."

WRITTEN BY OSCAR MILLARD . . . ASSOCIATE PRODUCER RICHARD SOKOLOVE . . . MUSIC BY VICTOR YOUNG . . .

"Your opinion's been noted, Egghead," said Duke.

PRINT BY TECHNICOLOR . . . DIRECTOR OF PHOTOGRAPHY JOSEPH LA SHELLE . . . PRODUCED AND DIRECTED BY DICK POWELL.

And then the movie came on: Temujin abducting Bortai from the Merkit caravan (a kind of medieval wagon train) . . . Hunlun criticizing her son's choice in sex objects . . . Targatai attempting to steal Bortai back . . . Hunlun denouncing the bloodshed that has accrued to Temujin's infatuation . . . Temujin traveling to Urga and allying with Wang Khan . . . our hero falling to the Mongol arrow and hiding in a cave . . . Bortai returning to her depraved Tartar father . . . Jamuga inadvertently leading Kumlek's henchmen to his blood brother . . . Temujin struggling beneath the weight of an ox-yoke as his captors march him toward Kumlek's camp (an image that inspired one of Stuart's students, in a paper that received a B-minus, to call Wayne's character a Christ figure) . . . our hero standing humbled before the Tartar chief . . . Bortai becoming conscious of her love for Temujin and forthwith aiding his escape . . . Temujin arriving half-dead in the Mongol camp . . .

At no point in this cavalcade of nonsense did either Temujin or his mother acquire a perceptible shield against the omnipresent radiation. But then, as my third major scene hit the screen — Hunlun treating her son's wound — something utterly amazing occurred. A rainbow aura, glowing and pulsing like Joseph's coat of many colors, materialized on Hunlun's head and torso as she uttered the line, "Would that I could cure the madness that possesses you!"

It's the pot, I told myself. I'm high on hemp, and I'm seeing things.

"Good God!" I gasped.

"You've done it, Ms. Rappaport!" shouted Kieran.

"I see it too!" cried Duke. "She's got a damn rainbow around her!"

"Wang Khan — he will betray you into disaster," insisted Hunlun, "or rob you of your spoils in victory."

But then, to my dismay, the crone's anti-radiation suit started to dissolve.

"Concentrate!" cried Kieran

My cloak continued to fade.

"Focus, Egghead!" demanded Duke.

I stared at the screen, concentrating, concentrating.

Hunlun insisted, "Were you not blinded by lust for this woman — "

"Lust?!" echoed Temujin. "You, too, are blind, my mother — blinded by your hatred for her."

"Shields at maximum, Ms. Rappaport!" shouted Kieran. "We're going to make you well!"

In a full-spectrum flash, red to orange to yellow to green to blue to indigo to violet, Hunlun's aura returned. "Daughter of Kumlek!" she sneered.

"Way to go, Ms. Rappaport!" exclaimed Kieran.

"Congratulations!" cried Duke.

"Even if you were right about Wang Khan, yet I would venture this unaided," said Temujin. Sealed head to toe in her luminous armor, Hunlun glowered at her son. "For I will have Bortai," he continued, "though I and all of us go down to destruction."

The scene ended with a dissolve to Jamuga riding through the gates of Urga, whereupon Kieran picked up the remote control and stopped the tape. It would be best, he explained, to quit while my triumph was at its zenith and the quantum vibrations were still folding back into the space-time continuum.

"Sounds reasonable to me," said Duke.

"Soon it will come to pass that the gamma rays never even penetrated your body." Kieran ejected the cassette. "Ms. Rappaport, I must applaud you. By reweaving the cosmic tapestry, you have conquered your past and reshaped your future."

"That aura wasn't real," I said, wondering whether I believed myself. "It was an illusion born of Jack Daniels and marijuana."

"That aura was more real than the bricks in this building or the teeth in my jaw," said Kieran.

Duke caught my eye, then waved his shot glass in Kieran's direction. "Told you this guy's a pro. Most swamis don't know their higher planes from a hole in the ground, but you're in good hands with Doc Morella."

"I hope you're not jealous, Duke," I said. "There was no aura. It was just the booze and the dope."

"I've had a full life, Egghead."

For the third time in a week I contemplate the Castle Bravo explosion while drinking a glass of sherry.

The mushroom cloud, I realize, is in fact a Nuclear Age inkblot test, a radioactive Rorschach smear. In the swirling vapors I briefly glimpse my has-been diva from *The High and the Mighty* as she speculates that nobody will miss her if the airliner goes into the drink. Next I see my *Alamo* character, the insufferably selfless Blind Nell, giving her husband permission to enter into a suicide pact with the boys instead of wasting his life taking care of her. And now I perceive the schoolteacher in *Lock and Load*, telling Duke to be the best obsessive-compulsive loose-cannon police captain he can be.

Slowly the quotidian seeps into my consciousness: my TV set, my VCR, my sherry, the cat on my lap — each given form and substance by my dawning awareness that the film called *Lock and Load* does not exist.

Was it just the booze and the dope? I simply couldn't decide, and Stuart had no theories either. Despite his unhappiness with postmodern scorched-earth relativism, despite his general enthusiasm for the rationalistic worldview, he has always fancied himself an intellectually vulnerable person, open to all sorts of possibilities.

"Including the possibility of a mind-body cure," he said.

"A mind-body cure is one thing, and Kieran Morella's deranged quantum physics is another," I replied. "The man's a goofball."

"So you're not going back?" asked Stuart.

"Of *course* I'm going back. Duke's paying for the weed. I have nothing to lose."

Kieran normally spent his Wednesdays downtown, teaching a course at the New School for Social Research — Psychoimmunology 101: Curing with Quarks — and Thursdays he always stayed home and meditated, so Duke and I had to wait a full seventy-two hours before entering Treatment Salon Number Three again. In a matter of minutes we were all primed for transcendence, Duke afloat on a cloud of Jack Daniels, Kieran and me frolicking through a sea of grass. Our therapist announced that, before we tried generating any more quantum vibrations, we should take a second look at Tuesday's breakthrough.

"Whatever you say, Doc," said Duke.

"It was all a mirage," I said.

"Seeing is believing," said Kieran.

I retorted with that favorite slogan of skeptics, "And believing is seeing."

Kieran fast-forwarded the *Conqueror* cassette to Hunlun treating Temujin's wound. He pressed Stop, then Play.

Against my expectations, Hunlun's aura was still there, covering her like a gown made of sunflowers and rubies.

"Thundering Christ!" I said.

This time around, I had to admit the aura was too damn intricate and splendid — too existentially *real* — to be a mere pothead chimera.

"It's a goddamn miracle!" shouted Duke.

"I would join Mr. Wayne in calling your gamma-ray shield a miracle, but I don't think that's the right word," said Kieran, grinning at me as he pressed the rewind button. " 'Miracle' implies divine intervention, and you accomplished this feat through your own natural healing powers. How do you feel?"

"Exhilarated," I said. Indeed. "Frightened." Quite so. "Grateful. Awestruck."

"Me too," said Duke.

"And angry," I added.

"Angry?" said Duke.

"Mad as hell."

"I don't understand."

"Anger has no place in your cure, Ms. Rappaport," said Kieran. "Anger will kill you sooner than leukemia."

As with our first two sessions, Duke's third attempt at kinetotherapy got him nowhere. Temujin went through the motions of the plot — he seized Bortai, speared Targatai, met with Wang Khan, suffered the Tartar arrow, endured imprisonment by Kumlek, won Bortai's heart, fled Kumlek's camp, conspired with Wang Khan's soothsayer, captured the city of Urga, appropriated Wang

Khan's forces, led the expanded Mongol army to victory against the Tartars, and slew Kumlek with a knife — but at no point did Duke's celluloid self acquire any luminous armor.

My character, on the other hand, was evidently leading a charmed life. No sooner did Hunlun admonish Temujin for courting his father's murderer than, by Kieran's account at least, I once again molded reality to my will, sheathing the crone's body against gamma rays. When next Hunlun entered the film, lamenting the pointless slaughter Temujin's lust has caused, she wore the same vibrant attire. Her final moments on screen — treating her son's wound while criticizing his lifestyle — likewise found her arrayed in an anti-radiation ensemble.

"Duke, I'm really sorry this hasn't gone better for you," I said.

The late Jamuga, now transformed into Temujin's spiritual guide, spoke the final narration, the one piece of decent writing in the film. "And the great Khan made such conquests as were undreamed of by mortal men. Tribes of the Gobi flocked to his standard, and the farthest reaches of the desert trembled to the hoofs of his hordes . . ."

Saying nothing, Duke set down his whiskey bottle, rose from his recliner, and shuffled toward the Betamax.

"At the feet of the Tartar woman he laid all the riches of Cathay," said Jamuga. "For a hundred years, the children of their loins ruled half the world."

Duke depressed the Eject lever. The cassette carriage rose from the recorder console and presented *The Conqueror* to the dying actor.

"Maybe you'll get your aura next week," I said. I took a toke, approached Duke, and squeezed his arm. "Never say die, sir. Let's come back on Monday."

"We lost in Vietnam." Duke pulled the cassette free of the machine. He removed his bandanna, mushed it together, and coughed into the folds. "Nixon signed a SALT agreement with the Russians." Again he coughed. "The Air Force Academy is admitting women. The phone company is hiring flits. Peanut Head" — he gasped — "is bringing the draft dodgers" — and gasped — "home."

Duke lurched toward me, tipped his invisible Stetson, and, still gripping the cassette, collapsed on the carpet.

Inhaler at the ready, Sweeney bounded across the room. Falling to his knees, he wrapped his arms around the supine superstar and told Kieran to apply the plastic mask to Duke's nose and mouth. It was a familiar tableau — we had just seen it on the screen: Bortai cradling the wounded Temujin as she comes to understand that this particular egomaniacal sociopathic warlord is a real catch. ("He has suffered much," says Bortai to her servant. And the servant, who knows subtext when she hears it, responds, "Deny not the heart.") Kieran handled the oxygen rig with supreme competence, and in a matter of seconds the mask was in place and Duke had stopped gasping.

"You want another shot of whiskey?" I asked, kneeling beside Duke.

"No thanks." He pressed the cassette into my hands and forced himself into a sitting position. "I know when I'm licked, Egghead," he rasped. "It's not my America anymore."

"You aren't licked," I said.

"You must have faith," said Kieran.

Sweeney proffered an analgesic pill. Duke swallowed it dry. "I've got plenty of faith," he said. "I've got faith running out my ears. It's strength I'm lacking, raw animal strength, so I figured I should hoard it for Egghead."

"For me?" I said.

"I projected all my quantum vibrations onto Hunlun," he said.

"You mean . . . you augmented Ms. Rappaport's shield?" Kieran bent low, joining our pietà.

"Augmented?" said Duke. "Let's talk plain, Doc — I made it *happen*. I threw that bubble around old Hunlun like Grant took Richmond. I blocked that radiation till hell wouldn't have it again." He set a large, sweating hand on my shoulder. "The Big C conquered John Wayne a long time ago, but you've still got a fighting chance, Egghead."

"Duke, I'm speechless," I said.

"I've never bent the space-time continuum for anybody before, but I'm glad I did it in your case," said Duke.

"I'm touched to the core," I said.

"Why does the aura make you angry?" he asked.

It took me several seconds to formulate an answer in my head, and as I started to speak the words, Duke coughed again, closed his eyes, and fainted dead away.

Before the day was over Sweeney got Duke admitted to the Sloan-Kettering Memorial Cancer Center, where they gave the old cowboy all the morphine and Jack Daniels he wanted. A week later Duke received open-heart surgery, and by the end of the month he was back home in L.A., attended around the clock by his wife, his children, and, of course, his faithful nurse.

The Big C accomplished its final assault on June 11, 1979, stealing the last breath from John Wayne as he lay abed in the UCLA Medical Center.

Duke always wanted his epitaph to read *Feo, Fuerte y Formal*, but I've never visited his grave, so I don't know what's on the stone. "Ugly, Strong, and Dignified" — a fair summary of that box-office giant, but I would have preferred either the characteristic self-knowledge of *There's More to That Movie Than My Damn Conservative Attitude* or else the intentional sexual innuendo of the eulogy he wrote for himself while drinking scotch during the *Chisum* wrap party: *He Saw, He Conquered, He Came*.

Hunlun's aura still angers me. Kinetotherapy still makes me see red. "If Kieran Morella is on to something," I told Stuart, "then the universe is far more absurd than I could possibly have imagined."

A Japanese city has been reduced to radioactive embers? No problem. We can fix that with happy thoughts. The Castle Bravo H-bomb test has condemned a dozen Asian fisherman to death by leukemia? Don't worry. Just pluck the quantum strings, tune in the cosmos, and the pennies will trickle down from heaven.

"The miracle is the meanest trick in God's repertoire," I told Stuart. "God should be ashamed of himself for inventing the miracle."

Next Tuesday I'm going to the polls and casting my vote for Bill Clinton: not exactly a liberal but probably electable. (Anything to deprive that airhead plutocrat George Bush of a second term.) The day after that, my eighty-first birthday will be upon me. Evidently I'm going to live forever.

"Don't count on it," Stuart warned me.

"I won't," I said.

According to today's *Times*, the Nevada Test Site, formerly the Nevada Proving Ground, is still open to visitors. They have a webpage now, www. nv.doe.gov. The tour features numerous artifacts from the military's attempts to determine what kinds of structures might withstand nuclear blast pressures. You'll see crushed walls of brick and cinder block, pulverized domes fashioned from experimental concrete, a railroad bridge whose I-beams have become strands of steel spaghetti, a bank vault that looks like a sand castle after high tide, and a soaring steel drop-tower intended to cradle an H-bomb that, owing to the 1992 Nuclear Testing Moratorium, was never exploded.

Disney World for Armageddon buffs.

Kieran let me keep the kinetotherapy cassette, but I've never looked at it, even though there's a Betamax somewhere in our closet. I'm afraid those goddamn psychedelic shields will still be there, enswathing my on-screen incarnation. Tomorrow I plan to finally rid myself of the thing. I shall solemnly bear the cassette to the basement and toss it into the furnace, immolating it like the Xanadu work crew burning Charles Foster Kane's sled. Stuart has promised to go with me. He'll make sure I don't lose my nerve.

I simply can't permit the universe to be that absurd. There are certain kinds of cruelty I won't allow God to perform. In the ringing words of Hunlun, "My son, this you cannot do."

Once again I import the Castle Bravo explosion into my living room. I drink my glass of sherry and study the Rorschachian obscenities.

This time I'm especially struck by the second shot in the mushroom-cloud montage, for within the nodes and curls of this burning satanic cabbage I perceive a human face. The mouth is wide open. The features are contorted in physical agony and metaphysical dread.

Try this at home. You'll see the face too, I promise you. It's not the face of John Wayne — or Genghis Khan or Davy Crockett or Paul Tibbets or the Virgin Mary or any other person of consequence. The victim you'll see is just another nobody, just another bit-player, another *hibakusha*, eternally trapped on a ribbon of acetate and praying — fervently, oh, so fervently — that this will be the last replay.

Auspicious Eggs

Father Cornelius Dennis Monaghan of Charlestown Parish, Connie to his friends, sets down the Styrofoam chalice, turns from the corrugated cardboard altar, and approaches the two young women standing by the resin baptismal font. The font is six-sided and encrusted with saints, like a gigantic hex-nut forged for some obscure yet holy purpose, but its most impressive feature is its portability. Hardly a month passes in which Connie doesn't drive the vessel across town, bear it into some wretched hovel, and confer immortality on a newborn whose parents have become too sickly to leave home.

"Merribell, right?" asks Connie, pointing to the baby on his left.

Wedged in the crook of her mother's arm, the infant wriggles and howls. "No — Madeleine," Angela mumbles. Connie has known Angela Dunfey all her life, and he still remembers the seraphic glow that beamed from her face when she first received the Sacrament of Holy Communion. Today she boasts no such glow. Her cheeks and brow appear tarnished, like iron corroded by the Greenhouse Deluge, and her spine curls with a torsion more commonly seen in women three times her age. "Merribell's over here." Angela raises her free hand and gestures toward her cousin Lorna, who is balancing Madeleine's twin sister atop her gravid belly. Will Lorna Dunfey, Connie wonders, also give birth to twins? The phenomenon, he has heard, runs in families.

Touching the sleeve of Angela's frayed blue sweater, the priest addresses her in a voice that travels clear across the nave. "Have these children received the Sacrament of Reproductive Potential Assessment?"

The parishioner shifts a nugget of chewing gum from her left cheek to her right. "Y-yes," she says at last.

Henry Shaw, the pale altar boy, his face abloom with acne, hands the priest a parchment sheet stamped with the seal of the Boston Isle Archdiocese. A pair of signatures adorns the margin, verifying that two ecclesiastical representatives have legitimized the birth. Connie instantly recognizes the illegible hand of Archbishop Xallibos. Below lie the bold loops and assured serifs of a Friar James Wolfe, M.D., doubtless the man who drew the blood.

Madeleine Dunfey, Connie reads. *Left ovary: 315 primordial follicles. Right ovary: 340 primordial follicles.* A spasm of despair passes through the priest.

The egg-cell count for each organ should be 180,000 at least. It's a verdict of infertility, no possible appeal, no imaginable reprieve.

With an efficiency bordering on effrontery, Henry Shaw offers Connie a second parchment sheet.

Merribell Dunfey. Left ovary: 290 primordial follicles. Right ovary: 310 primordial follicles. The priest is not surprised. What sense would there be in God's withholding the power of procreation from one twin but not the other? Connie now needs only to receive these barren sisters, apply the sacred rites, and furtively pray that the Eighth Lateran Council was indeed guided by the Holy Spirit when it undertook to bring the baptismal process into the age of testable destinies and ovarian surveillance.

He holds out his hands, withered palms up, a posture he maintains as Angela surrenders Madeleine, reaches under the baby's christening gown, and unhooks both diaper pins. The mossy odor of fresh urine wafts into the Church of the Immediate Conception. Sighing profoundly, Angela hands the sopping diaper to her cousin.

"Bless these waters, O Lord," says Connie, spotting his ancient face in the consecrated fluid, "that they might grant these sinners the gift of life everlasting." Turning from the vessel, he presents Madeleine to his ragged flock, over three hundred natural-born Catholics — sixth-generation Irish, mostly, plus a smattering of Portuguese, Italians, and Croats — interspersed with two dozen recent converts of Korean and Vietnamese extraction: a congregation bound together, he'll admit, not so much by religious conviction as by shared destitution. "Dearly beloved, forasmuch as all humans enter the world in a state of depravity, and forasmuch as they cannot know the grace of our Lord except they be born anew of water, I beseech you to call upon God the Father that, through these baptisms, Madeleine and Merribell Dunfey may gain the divine kingdom." Connie faces his trembling parishioner. "Angela Dunfey, do you believe, by God's word, that children who are baptized, dying before they commit any actual evil, will be saved?"

Her "Yes" is begrudging and clipped.

Like a scrivener replenishing his pen at an inkwell, Connie dips his thumb into the font. "Angela Dunfey, name this child of yours."

"M-M-Madeleine Eileen Dunfey."

"We welcome this sinner, Madeleine Eileen Dunfey, into the mystical body of Christ" — with his wet thumb Connie traces a plus sign on the infant's forehead — "and do mark her with the Sign of the Cross."

Unraveling Madeleine from her christening gown, Connie fixes on the waters. They are preternaturally still — as calm and quiet as the Sea of Galilee after the Savior had rebuked the winds. For many years the priest wondered why Christ hadn't returned on the eve of the Greenhouse Deluge, dispersing the hydrocarbon vapors with a wave of his hand, ending global warming with a heavenward wink, but recently Connie has come to feel that divine intervention entails protocols past human ken.

He contemplates his reflected countenance. Nothing about it — not the tiny eyes, thin lips, hawk's beak of a nose — pleases him. Now he begins the immersion, sinking Madeleine Dunfey to her skullcap . . . her ears . . . cheeks . . . mouth . . . eyes.

"No!" screams Angela.

As the baby's nose goes under, mute cries spurt from her lips: bubbles inflated with bewilderment and pain. "Madeleine Dunfey," Connie intones, holding the infant down, "I baptize you in the name of the Father, and of the Son, and of the Holy Ghost." The bubbles break the surface. The fluid pours into the infant's lungs. Her silent screams cease, but she still puts up a fight.

"No! Please! No!"

A full minute passes, marked by the rhythmic shuffling of the congregation and the choked sobs of the mother. A second minute — a third — and finally the body stops moving, a mere husk, no longer home to Madeleine Dunfey's indestructible soul.

"No!"

The Sacrament of Terminal Baptism, Connie knows, is rooted in both logic and history. Even today, he can recite verbatim the preamble to the Eighth Lateran Council's *Pastoral Letter on the Rights of the Unconceived.* ("Throughout her early years, Holy Mother Church tirelessly defended the Rights of the Born. Then, as the iniquitous institution of abortion spread across Western Europe and North America, she undertook to secure the Rights of the Unborn. Now, as a new era dawns for the Church and her servants, she must make even greater efforts to propagate the gift of life everlasting, championing the Rights of the Unconceived through a Doctrine of Affirmative Fertility.") The subsequent sentence has always given Connie pause. It stopped him when he was a seminarian. It stops him today. ("This Council therefore avers that, during a period such as that in which we find ourselves, when God has elected to discipline our species through a Greenhouse Deluge and its concomitant privations, a society can commit no greater crime against the future than to squander provender on individuals congenitally incapable of procreation.") Quite so. Indeed. And yet Connie has never performed a terminal baptism without misgivings.

He scans the faithful. Valerie Gallogher, his nephews' zaftig kindergarten teacher, seems on the verge of tears. Keye Sung frowns. Teresa Curtoni shudders. Michael Hinks moans softly. Stephen O'Rourke and his wife both wince.

"We give thanks, most merciful Father" — Connie lifts the corpse from the water — "that it pleases you to regenerate this infant and take her unto your bosom." Placing the dripping flesh on the altar, he leans toward Lorna Dunfey and lays his palm on Merribell's brow. "Angela Dunfey, name this child of yours."

"M-M-Merribell S-Siobhan . . ." With a sharp reptilian hiss, Angela wrests Merribell from her cousin and pulls the infant to her breast. "Merribell Siobhan Dunfey!"

The priest steps forward, caressing the wisp of tawny hair sprouting from Merribell's cranium. "We welcome this sinner — "

Angela whirls around and, still sheltering her baby, leaps from the podium to the aisle — the very aisle down which Connie hopes one day to see her parade in prelude to receiving the Sacrament of Qualified Monogamy.

"Stop!" cries Connie.

"Angela!" shouts Lorna.

"No!" yells the altar boy.

For someone who has recently given birth to twins, Angela is amazingly spry, rushing pell-mell past the stupefied congregation and straight through the narthex.

"Please!" screams Connie.

But already she is out the door, bearing her unsaved daughter into the teeming streets of Boston Isle.

At 8:17 p.m., Eastern Standard Time, Stephen O'Rourke's fertility reaches its weekly peak. The dial on his wrist tells him so, buzzing like a tortured hornet as he scrubs his teeth with baking soda. *Skreee*, says the sperm counter, reminding Stephen of his ineluctable duty. *Skreee, skreee*: go find us an egg.

He pauses in the middle of a brushstroke and, without bothering to rinse his mouth, strides into the bedroom.

Kate lies on the sagging mattress, smoking an unfiltered cigarette as she balances her nightly dose of iced Arbutus rum on her stomach. Baby Malcolm cuddles against his mother, gums fastened onto her left nipple. She stares at the far wall, where the cracked and scabrous plaster frames the video monitor, its screen displaying the regular Sunday-night broadcast of *Keep Those Kiddies Coming*. Archbishop Xallibos, seated, dominates a TV studio appointed like a day-care center: stuffed animals, changing table, brightly colored alphabet letters. Preschoolers crawl across the prelate's Falstaffian body, sliding down his thighs and swinging from his arms as if he is a piece of playground equipment.

"Did you know that a single act of onanism kills up to four hundred million babies in a matter of seconds?" asks Xallibos from the monitor. "As Jesus remarks in the Gospel According to Saint Andrew, 'Masturbation is murder.'"

Stephen coughs. "I don't suppose you're . . ."

His wife thrusts her index finger against her pursed lips. Even when engaged in shutting him out, she still looks beautiful to Stephen. Her huge eyes and high cheekbones, her elegant swanlike neck. "Shhh — "

"Please check," says Stephen, swallowing baking soda.

Kate raises her bony wrist and glances at her ovulation gauge. "Not for three days. Maybe four."

"Damn."

He loves her so dearly. He wants her so much — no less now than when they received the Sacrament of Qualified Monogamy. It's fine to have a connubial conversation, but when you utterly adore your wife, when you crave to comprehend her beyond all others, you need to speak in flesh as well.

"Will anyone deny that the hottest places in hell are reserved for those who violate the rights of the unconceived?" asks Xallibos, playing peek-a-boo with a cherubic toddler. "Who will dispute that contraception, casual sex, and nocturnal emissions place their perpetrators on a one-way cruise to Perdition?"

"Honey, I have to ask you something," says Stephen.

"Shhh — "

"That young woman at Mass this morning, the one who ran away . . ."

"She went crazy because it was twins." Kate slurps down her remaining rum. The ice fragments clink against each other. "If it'd been just the one, she probably could've coped."

"Well, yes, of course," says Stephen, gesturing toward Baby Malcolm. "But suppose one of *your* newborns . . ."

"Heaven is forever, Stephen," says Kate, filling her mouth with ice, "and hell is just as long." She chews, her molars grinding the ice. Dribbles of rum-tinted water spill from her lips. "You'd better get to church."

"Farewell, friends," says Xallibos as the theme music swells. He dandles a Korean three-year-old on his knee. "And keep those kiddies coming!"

The path to the front door takes Stephen through the cramped and fetid living room — functionally the nursery. All is quiet, all is well. The fourteen children, one for every other year of Kate's post-pubescence, sleep soundly. Nine-year-old Roger is quite likely his, product of the time Stephen and Kate got their cycles in synch; the boy boasts Stephen's curly blond hair and riveting green eyes. Difficult as it is, Stephen refuses to accord Roger any special treatment — no private outings to the duck pond, no second candy cane at Christmas. A good stepfather didn't indulge in favoritism.

Stephen pulls on his mended galoshes, fingerless gloves, and torn pea jacket. Ambling out of the apartment, he joins the knot of morose pedestrians as they shuffle down Winthrop Street. A fog descends, a steady rain falls: reverberations from the Deluge. Pushed by expectant mothers, dozens of shabby, canvas-cowled baby buggies squeak mournfully down the asphalt. The sidewalks belong to adolescent girls, gang after gang, gossiping among themselves and stomping on puddles as they show off their pregnancies like Olympic medals.

Besmirched by two decades of wind and drizzle, a limestone Madonna stands outside the Church of the Immediate Conception. Her expression lies somewhere between a smile and a smirk. Stephen climbs the steps, enters the narthex, removes his gloves, and, dipping his fingertips into the nearest font, decorates the air with the Sign of the Cross.

Every city, Stephen teaches his students at Cardinal Dougherty High School, boasts its own personality. Extroverted Rio, pessimistic Prague, paranoid New York. And Boston Isle? What sort of psyche inhabits the Hub and its surrounding reefs? Schizoid, Stephen tells them. Split. The Boston that battled slavery and stoked the fires beneath the American melting pot was the same Boston that massacred the Pequots and sent witchfinders to Salem. But here, now, which side of the city is emergent? The bright side, Stephen decides, picturing the hundreds of heaven-bound souls who each day exit Boston's innumerable wombs, flowing forth like the bubbles that had so recently streamed from Madeleine Dunfey's lips.

Blessing the Virgin's name, he descends the concrete stairs to the copulatorium. A hundred votive candles pierce the darkness. The briny scent of incipient immortality suffuses the air. In the far corner, a CD player screeches out Scorched Earth performing their famous rendition of "Ave Maria."

The Sacrament of Extramarital Intercourse has always reminded Stephen of a junior high prom. Girls strung along one side of the room, boys along the other, gyrating couples in the center. He takes his place in the line of males, removes his jacket, shirt, trousers, and underclothes, and hangs them on the nearest pegs. He stares through the gloom, locking eyes with Roger's old kindergarten teacher, Valerie Gallogher, a robust thirtyish woman whose incandescent red hair spills all the way to her hips. Grimly they saunter toward each other, following the pathway formed by the mattresses, until they meet amid the morass of writhing soul-makers.

"You're Roger Mulcanny's stepfather, aren't you?" asks the ovulating teacher.

"Father, quite possibly. Stephen O'Rourke. And you're Miss Gallogher, right?"

"Call me Valerie."

"Stephen."

He glances around, noting to his infinite relief that he recognizes no one. Sooner or later, he knows, a familiar young face will appear at the copulatorium, a notion that never fails to make him wince. How could he possibly explicate the Boston Massacre to a boy who'd recently beheld him in the procreative act? How could he render the Battle of Lexington lucid to a girl whose egg he'd attempted to quicken on the previous night?

For ten minutes he and Valerie make small talk, most of it issuing from Stephen, as was proper. Should the coming sacrament prove fruitful, the resultant child will want to know about the handful of men with whom his mother had connected during the relevant ovulation. (Beatrice, Claude, Tommy, Laura, Yolanda, Willy, and the others were forever grilling Kate for facts about their possible progenitors.) Stephen tells Valerie about the time his students gave him a surprise birthday party. He describes his butterfly collection. He mentions his skill at trapping the singularly elusive species of rat that inhabits Charlestown Parish.

"I have a talent too," says Valerie, inserting a coppery braid into her mouth. Her areolas seem to be staring at him.

"Roger thought you were a terrific teacher."

"No — something else." Valerie tugs absently on her ovulation gauge. "A person twitches his lips a certain way, and I know what he's feeling. He darts his eyes in an odd manner, and I sense the drift of his thoughts." She lowers her voice. "I watched you during the baptism this morning. Your reaction would've angered the archbishop — am I right?"

Stephen looks at his bare toes. Odd that a copulatorium partner should be demanding such intimacy of him.

"Am I?" Valerie persists, sliding her index finger along her large, concave bellybutton.

Fear rushes through Stephen. Does this woman work for the Immortality Corps? If his answer smacks of heresy, will she arrest him on the spot?

"Well, Stephen? Would the archbishop have been angry?"

"Perhaps," he confesses. In his mind he sees Madeleine Dunfey's submerged mouth, bubble following bubble like beads strung along a rosary.

"There's no microphone in my navel," Valerie asserts, alluding to a common Immortality Corps ploy. "I'm not a spy."

"Never said you were."

"You were thinking it. I could tell by the cant of your eyebrows." She kisses him on the mouth, deeply, wetly. "Did Roger ever learn to hold his pencil correctly?"

" 'Fraid not."

"Too bad."

At last the mattress on Stephen's left becomes free, and they climb on top and begin reifying the Doctrine of Affirmative Fertility. The candle flames look like spear points. Stephen closes his eyes, but the upshot is merely to intensify the fact that he's here. The liquid squeal of flesh against flesh becomes louder, the odor of hot paraffin and warm semen grows more pungent. For a few seconds he manages to convince himself that the woman beneath him is Kate, but the illusion proves as tenuous as the surrounding wax.

When the sacrament is accomplished, Valerie says, "I have something for you. A gift."

"What's the occasion?"

"Saint Patrick's Day is less than a week away."

"Since when is that a time for gifts?"

Instead of answering, she strolls to her side of the room, rummages through her tangled garments, and returns holding a pressed flower sealed in plastic.

"Think of it as a ticket," she whispers, lifting Stephen's shirt from its peg and slipping the blossom inside the pocket.

"To where?"

Valerie holds an erect index finger to her lips. "We'll know when we get there."

Stephen gulps audibly. Sweat collects beneath his sperm counter. Only fools considered fleeing Boston Isle. Only lunatics risked the retributions meted out by the Immortality Corps. Displayed every Sunday night on *Keep Those Kiddies Coming*, the classic images — men submitting to sperm siphons, women locked in the rapacious embrace of artificial inseminators — haunt every parishioner's imagination, instilling the same levels of dread as Spinelli's sculpture of the archangel Chamuel strangling David Hume. There are rumors, of course, unconfirmable accounts of parishioners who'd outmaneuvered the patrol boats and escaped to Québec Cay, Seattle Reef, or the Texas Archipelago. But to credit such tales was itself a kind of sin, jeopardizing your slot in Paradise as surely as if you'd denied the unconceived their rights.

"Tell me something, Stephen." Valerie straps herself into her bra. "You're a history teacher. Did Saint Patrick really drive the snakes out of Ireland, or is that just a legend?"

"I'm sure it never happened literally," says Stephen. "I suppose it could be true in some mythic sense."

"It's about penises, isn't it?" says Valerie, dissolving into the darkness. "It's about how our saints have always been hostile to cocks."

Although Harbor Authority Tower was designed to house the merchant-shipping aristocracy on whose ambitions the decrepit Boston economy still depended, the building's form, Connie now realizes, perfectly fits its new, supplemental function: sheltering the offices, courts, and archives of the archdiocese. As he lifts his gaze along the soaring facade, he thinks of sacred shapes — of steeples and vaulted windows, of Sinai and Zion, of Jacob's Ladder and hands pressed together in prayer. Perhaps it's all as God wants, he muses, flashing his ecclesiastical pass to the guard. Perhaps there's nothing wrong with commerce and grace being transacted within the same walls.

Connie has seen Archbishop Xallibos in person only once before, five years earlier, when the stately prelate appeared as an "honorary Irishman" in Charlestown Parish's annual Saint Patrick's Day Parade. Standing on the side-walk, Connie observed Xallibos gliding down Lynde Street atop an enormous motorized shamrock. The archbishop looked impressive then, and he looks impressive now — six foot four at least, Connie calculates, and not an ounce under three hundred pounds. His eyes are as red as a lab rat's.

"Father Cornelius Dennis Monaghan," the priest begins, following the custom whereby a visitor to an archbishop's chambers initiates the interview by naming himself.

"Come forward, Father Cornelius Dennis Monaghan."

Connie starts into the office, boots clacking on the polished bronze floor. Xallibos steps out from behind his desk, a glistery cube hewn from black marble.

"Charlestown Parish holds a special place in my affections," says the archbishop. "What brings you to this part of town?"

Connie fidgets, shifting first left, then right, until his face lies mirrored in the hubcap-size Saint Cyril medallion adorning Xallibos's chest. "My soul is in torment, Your Grace."

"'Torment.' Weighty word."

"I can find no other. Last Tuesday I laid a two-week-old infant to rest."

"Terminal baptism?"

Connie ponders his reflection. It is wrinkled and deflated, like a helium balloon purchased at a long-gone carnival. "My eighth."

"I know how you feel. After I dispatched my first infertile — no left testicle, right one shriveled beyond repair — I got no sleep for a week." Eyes glowing like molten rubies, Xallibos gazes directly at Connie. "Where did you attend seminary?"

"Isle of San Diego."

"And on the Isle of San Diego did they teach you that there are in fact two Churches, one invisible and eternal, the other — "

"Temporal and finite."

"Then they also taught you that the latter Church is empowered to revise its rites according to the imperatives of the age." The archbishop's stare grows brighter, hotter, purer. "Do you doubt that present privations compel us to arrange early immortality for those who cannot secure the rights of the unconceived?"

"The problem is that the infant I immortalized has a twin." Connie swallows nervously. "Her mother stole her away before I could perform the second baptism."

"Stole her away?"

"She fled in the middle of the sacrament."

"And the second child is likewise arid?"

"Left ovary, two hundred ninety primordial follicles. Right ovary, three hundred ten."

"Lord . . ." A high whistle issues from the archbishop, like water vapor escaping a teakettle. "Does she intend to leave the island?"

"I certainly hope not, Your Grace," says the priest, wincing at the thought. "She probably has no immediate plans beyond protecting her baby and trying to — "

Connie cuts himself off, intimidated by the sudden arrival of a roly-poly man in a white hooded robe.

"Friar James Wolfe, M.D.," says the monk.

"Come forward, Friar Doctor James Wolfe," says Xallibos.

"It would be well if you validated this posthaste." James Wolfe draws a parchment sheet from his robe and lays it on the archbishop's desk. Connie steals a glance at the report, hoping to learn the baby's fertility quotient, but the relevant statistics are too faint. "The priest in question, he's celebrating Mass in" — sliding a loose sleeve upward, James Wolfe consults his wristwatch — "less than an hour. He's all the way over in Brookline."

Striding back to his desk, the archbishop yanks a silver fountain pen from its holder and decorates the parchment with his famous spidery signature.

"*Dominus vobiscum*, Friar Doctor Wolfe," he says, handing over the document.

As Wolfe rushes out of the office, Xallibos steps so close to Connie that his nostrils fill with the archbishop's lemon-scented aftershave lotion.

"That man never has any fun," says Xallibos, pointing toward the vanishing friar. "What fun do you have, Father Monaghan?"

"Fun, Your Grace?"

"Do you eat ice cream? Follow the fortunes of the Celtics?" He pronounces "Celtics" with the hard *C* mandated by the Seventh Lateran Council.

Connie inhales a hearty quantity of citrus fumes. "I bake."

"Bake? Bake what? Bread?"

"Cookies, your Grace. Brownies, cheesecake, pies. For the Feast of the Nativity, I make gingerbread magi."

"Wonderful. I like my priests to have fun. Listen, regardless of the difficulties, the rite must be performed. If Angela Dunfey won't come to you, then you must go to her."

"She'll simply run away again."

"Perhaps so, perhaps not. I have great faith in you, Father Cornelius Dennis Monaghan."

"More than I have in myself," says the priest, biting his inner cheeks so hard that his eyes fill with tears.

"No," says Kate for the third time that night.

"Yes," insists Stephen, savoring the dual satisfactions of Kate's thigh beneath his palm and Arbutus rum washing through his brain.

Pinching her cigarette in one hand, Kate strokes Baby Malcolm's forehead with the other, lulling him to sleep. "It's wicked," she protests, placing Malcolm on the rug beside the bed. "A crime against the future."

Stephen grabs the Arbutus bottle, pours himself another glass, and, adding a measure of Dr. Pepper, takes a greedy gulp. He sets the bottle back on the nightstand, next to Valerie Gallogher's enigmatic flower.

"Screw the unconceived," he says, throwing himself atop his wife.

On Friday he'd shown the blossom to Gail Whittington, Dougherty High School's smartest science teacher, but her verdict had proved unenlightening. *Epigaea repens*, "trailing arbutus," a species with at least two claims to fame: it is the state flower of the Massachusetts Archipelago, and it has lent its name to the very brand of alcohol Stephen now consumes.

"No," says Kate once again. She drops her cigarette on the floor, crushes it with her shoe, and wraps her arms around him. "I'm not ovulating," she avers, forcing her stiff and slippery tongue into the depths of his mouth. "Your sperm aren't . . ."

"Last night, the Holy Father received a vision," Xallibos announces from the video monitor. "Pictures straight from Satan's infernal domain. Hell is a fact, friends. It's as real as a stubbed toe."

Stephen whips off Kate's chemise with all the dexterity of Father Monaghan removing a christening gown. The rum, of course, has much to do with their mutual willingness (four glasses each, only mildly diluted with Dr. Pepper), but beyond the Arbutus the two of them have truly earned this moment. Neither partner has ever skipped Mass or missed a Sacrament of Extramarital Intercourse. And while any act of nonconceptual love technically lay beyond the Church's powers of absolution, surely Christ would forgive them a solitary lapse. And so they go at it, this sterile union, this forbidden fruitlessness, this coupling from which no soul can come.

"Hedonists dissolving in vats of molten sulfur," says Xallibos.

The bedroom door squeals open. One of Kate's middle children, Beatrice, a gaunt six-year-old with flaking skin, enters holding a rude toy boat whittled from a hunk of bark.

"Look what I made in school yesterday!"

"We're busy," says Kate, pulling the tattered muslin sheet over her nakedness.

"Do you like my boat, Stephen?" asks Beatrice.

He slams a pillow atop his groin. "It's splendid, dear."

"Go back to bed," Kate commands her daughter.

"Onanists drowning in lakes of boiling semen," says Xallibos.

Beatrice fixes Stephen with her receding eyes. "Can we sail it tomorrow on Parson's Pond?"

"Certainly. Of course. Please go away."

"Just you and me, right, Stephen? Not Claude or Tommy or Yolanda or *anybody*."

"Flaying machines," says Xallibos, "peeling the damned like ripe bananas."

"Do you want a spanking?" seethes Kate. "That's exactly what you're going to get, young lady, the worst spanking of your whole life!"

The child shrugs elaborately and strides away in a huff.

"I love you," says Stephen, removing the pillow from his privates like a chef lifting the lid from a stew pot.

Again they press together, throwing all they have into it, every limb and gland and orifice, no holds barred, no positions banned.

"Unpardonable," Kate groans.

"Unpardonable," Stephen agrees. He's never been so excited. His entire body is an appendage to his loins.

"We'll be damned," she says.

"Forever," he echoes.

"Kiss me," she commands.

"Farewell, friends," says Xallibos. "And keep those kiddies coming!"

Wrestling the baptismal font from the trunk of his car, Connie ponders the vessel's resemblance to a birdbath — a place, he muses, for pious sparrows to accomplish their avian ablutions. As he sets the vessel on his shoulder and starts away, its edges digging into his flesh, a different metaphor suggests itself. But if the font is Connie's cross, and Constitution Road his Via Dolorosa, where does that leave his upcoming mission to Angela Dunfey? Is he about to perform some mysterious act of vicarious atonement?

"Morning, Father."

He slips the font from his shoulder, standing it upright beside a fire hydrant. His parishioner Valerie Gallogher weaves amid the mob, dressed in a threadbare woolen parka.

"Far to go?" she asks brightly.

"End of the block."

"Want help?"

"I need the exercise."

Valerie extends her arm and they shake hands, mitten clinging to mitten. "Made any special plans for Saint Patrick's Day?"

"I'm going to bake shamrock cookies."

"Green?"

"Can't afford food coloring."

"I think I've got some green — you're welcome to it. Who's at the end of the block?"

"Angela Dunfey."

A shadow flits across Valerie's face. "And her daughter?"

"Yes," moans Connie. His throat constricts. "Her daughter."

Valerie lays a sympathetic hand on his arm. "If I don't have green, we can probably fake it."

"Oh, Valerie, Valerie — I wish I'd never taken Holy Orders."

"We'll mix yellow with orange. I'm sorry, Father."

"I wish this cup would pass."

"I mean yellow with blue."

Connie loops his arms around the font, embracing it as he might a frightened child. "Stay with me."

Together they walk through the serrated March air and, reaching the Warren Avenue intersection, enter the tumbledown pile of bricks labeled No. 47. The foyer is as dim as a crypt. Switching on his penlight, Connie holds it aloft until he discerns the label *Angela Dunfey* glued to a dented mailbox. He begins the climb to apartment 8-c, his parishioner right behind. On the third landing, Connie stops to catch his breath. On the sixth, he puts down the font. Valerie wipes his brow with her parka sleeve. She takes up the font, and the two of them resume their ascent.

Angela Dunfey's door is wormy, cracked, and hanging by one hinge. The mere act of knocking swings it open.

They find themselves in the kitchen — a small musty space that would have felt claustrophobic were it not so sparsely furnished. A saucepan hangs over the stove; a frying pan sits atop the icebox; the floor is a mottle of splinters, tar paper, and leprous shards of linoleum. Valerie sets the font next to the sink. The basin in which Angela Dunfey washes her dishes, Connie notes, is actually smaller than the one in which the Church of the Immediate Conception immortalizes infertiles.

He tiptoes into the bedroom. His parishioner sleeps soundly, her terrycloth bathrobe parted down the middle to accommodate her groggy, nursing infant; milk trickles from her breasts, streaking her belly with white rivulets. He must move now, quickly and deliberately, so there'll be no struggle, no melodramatic replay of 1 Kings 3:26, the desperate whore trying to tear her baby away from Solomon's swordsman.

Inhaling slowly, Connie leans toward the mattress and, with the dexterity of a weasel extracting the innards from an eggshell, slides the barren baby free and carries her into the kitchen.

Beside the icebox Valerie sits glowering on a wobbly three-legged stool.

"Dearly beloved, forasmuch as all humans enter the world in a state of depravity," Connie whispers, casting a wary eye on Valerie, "and forasmuch as they cannot know the grace of our Lord except they be born anew of water" — he places the infant on the floor near Valerie's feet — "I beseech you to call upon God the Father that, through this baptism, Merribell Dunfey may gain the divine kingdom."

"Don't beseech *me*," snaps Valerie.

Connie fills the saucepan, dumps the water into the font, and returns to the sink for another load — not exactly holy water, he muses, not remotely chrism, but presumably not typhoidal either, the best the under-budgeted Boston Water Authority has to offer. He deposits the load, then fetches another.

A wide, milky yawn twists Merribell's face, but she does not cry out.

At last the vessel is ready. "Bless these waters, O Lord, that they might grant this sinner the gift of life everlasting."

Dropping to his knees, Connie begins removing the infant's diaper. The first pin comes out easily. As he pops the second, the tip catches the ball of his thumb. The Crown of Thorns, he decides, feeling the sting, seeing the blood.

He bears the naked infant to the font. Wetting his punctured thumb, he touches Merribell's brow and draws the sacred plus sign with a mixture of blood and water. "We receive this sinner unto the mystical body of Christ, and do mark her with the Sign of the Cross."

He begins the immersion. Skullcap. Ears. Cheeks. Mouth. Eyes. O Lord, what a monstrous trust, this power to underwrite a person's soul. "Merribell Dunfey, I baptize you in the name of the Father . . ."

Now comes the nausea, excavating Stephen's alimentary canal as he kneels before the porcelain toilet bowl. His guilt pours forth in a searing flood — acidic strands of cabbage, caustic lumps of potato, glutinous strings of bile. Yet these pains are nothing, he knows, compared with what he'll experience on passing from this world to the next.

Drained, he stumbles toward the bedroom. Somehow Kate has bundled the older children off to school before collapsing on the floor alongside the baby. She shivers with remorse. Shrieks and giggles pour from the nursery: the pre-schoolers engaged in a raucous game of blindman's bluff.

"Flaying machines," she mutters. Her tone is beaten, bloodless. She lights a cigarette. "Peeling the damned like . . ."

Will more rum help, Stephen wonders, or merely make them sicker? He extends his arm. Passing over the nightstand, his fingers touch a box of aspirin, brush the preserved *Epigaea repens*, and curl around the neck of the half-full Arbutus bottle. A ruddy cockroach scurries across the doily.

"I kept Willy home today," says Kate, taking a drag. "He says his stomach hurts."

As he raises the bottle, Stephen realizes for the first time that the label contains a block of type headed *The Story of Trailing Arbutus*. "His stomach *always* hurts." He studies the breezy little paragraph.

"I think he's telling the truth."

Epigaea repens. Trailing arbutus. Mayflower. And suddenly everything is clear.

"What's today's date?" asks Stephen.

"Sixteenth."

"March sixteenth?"

"Yeah."

"Then tomorrow's Saint Patrick's Day."

"So what?"

"Tomorrow's Saint Patrick's Day" — like an auctioneer accepting a final bid, Stephen slams the bottle onto the nightstand — "and Valerie Gallogher will be leaving Boston Isle."

"Roger's old teacher? Leaving?"

"Leaving." Snatching up the preserved flower, he dangles it before his wife. "Leaving . . ."

"And of the Son," says Connie, raising the sputtering infant from the water, "and of the Holy Ghost."

Merribell Dunfey screeches and squirms. She's slippery as a bar of soap. Connie manages to wrap her in a dish towel and shove her into Valerie's arms.

"Let me tell you who you are," she says.

"Father Cornelius Dennis Monaghan of Charlestown Parish."

"You're a tired and bewildered pilgrim, Father. You're a weary wayfarer like myself."

Dribbling milk, Angela Dunfey staggers into the kitchen. Seeing her priest, she recoils. Her mouth flies open, and a howl rushes out, a cry such as Connie imagines the damned spew forth while rotating on the spits of Perdition. "Not her, too! Not Merribell! No!"

"Your baby's all right," says Valerie.

Connie clasps his hands together, fingers knotted in agony and supplication. He stoops. His knees hit the floor, crashing against the fractured linoleum. "Please," he groans.

Angela plucks Merribell from Valerie and affixes the squalling baby to her nipple. "Oh, Merribell, Merribell . . ."

"Please." Connie's voice is hoarse and jagged, as if he's been shot in the larynx. "Please . . . please," he beseeches. Tears roll from his eyes, tickling his cheeks as they fall.

"It's not *her* job to absolve you," says Valerie.

Connie snuffles the mucus back into his nose. "I know."

"The boat leaves tomorrow."

"Boat?" Connie runs his sleeve across his face, blotting his tears.

"A rescue vessel," his parishioner explains. Sliding her hands beneath his armpits, she raises him inch by inch to his feet. "Rather like Noah's ark."

"Mommy, I want to go home."

"Tell that to your stepfather."

"It's cold."

"I know, sweetheart."

"And dark."

"Try to be patient."

"Mommy, my stomach hurts."

"I'm sorry."

"My head, too."

"You want an aspirin?"

"I want to go home."

Is this a mistake? wonders Stephen. Shouldn't they all be in bed right now instead of tromping around in this nocturnal mist, risking flu and possibly pneumonia? And yet he has faith. Somewhere in the labyrinthine reaches of the Hoosac Docks, amid the tang of salt air and the stink of rotting cod, a ship awaits.

Guiding his wife and stepchildren down Pier 7, he studies the possibilities — the scows and barges, the tugs and trawlers, the reefers and bulk carriers. Gulls and gannets hover above the wharfs, squawking their chronic disapproval of the world. Across the channel, lit by a sodium-vapor searchlight, the USS *Constitution* bobs in her customary berth beside Charlestown Navy Yard.

"What're we doing here, anyway?" asks Beatrice.

"Your stepfather gets these notions in his head." Kate presses the baby tight against her chest, shielding him from the sea breeze.

"What's the *name* of the boat?" asks Roger.

"*Mayflower*," answers Stephen.

Epigaea repens, trailing arbutus, mayflower.

"How do you spell it?" Roger demands.

"M-a-y . . ."

"F-l-o-w-e-r?"

"Good job, Roger," says Stephen.

"I *read* it," the boy explains indignantly, pointing straight ahead with the collective fingers of his right mitten.

Fifty yards away, moored between an oil tanker and a bait shack, a battered freighter rides the incoming tide. Her stern displays a single word, *Mayflower*, a name that to the inhabitants of Boston Isle means far more than the sum of its letters.

"Now can we go home?" asks Roger.

"No," says Stephen. He has taught the story countless times. The Separatists' departure from England for Virginia . . . their hazardous voyage . . . their unplanned landing on Plymouth Rock . . . the signing of the covenant whereby the non-Separatists on board agreed to obey whatever rules the Separatists imposed. "*Now* we can go on a nice long voyage."

"On *that* thing?" asks Willy.

"You're not serious," says Laura.

"Not me," says Claude.

"Forget it," says Yolanda.

"Sayonara," says Tommy.

"I think I'm going to throw up," says Beatrice.

"It's not your decision," Stephen tells his stepchildren. He stares at the ship's hull, blotched with rust, blistered with decay, another victim of the Deluge. A passenger whom he recognizes as his neighbor Michael Lotz leans out a porthole like a prairie dog peering from its burrow. "Until further notice, I make all the rules."

Half by entreaty, half by coercion, he leads his disgruntled family up the gangplank and onto the quarterdeck, where a squat man in an orange raincoat and a maroon watch cap demands to see their ticket.

"Happy Saint Patrick's Day," says Stephen, flourishing the preserved blossom.

"We're putting you people on the fo'c'sle deck," the man yells above the growl of the idling engines. "You can hide behind the pianos. At ten o'clock you get a bran muffin and a cup of coffee."

As Stephen guides his stepchildren in a single file up the forward ladder, the crew of the *Mayflower* reels in the mooring lines and ravels up the anchor chains, setting her adrift. The engines kick in. Smoke pours from the freighter's twin stacks. Sunlight seeps across the bay, tinting the eastern sky hot pink and making the island's many-windowed towers glitter like Christmas trees.

A sleek Immortality Corps cutter glides by, headed for the wharfs, evidently unaware that enemies of the unconceived lie close at hand.

Slowly, cautiously, Stephen negotiates the maze of wooden crates — it seems as if every piano on Boston Isle is being exported today — until he reaches the starboard bulwark. As he curls his palm around the rail, the *Mayflower* cruises past the Mystic Shoals, maneuvering amid the rocks like a skier following a slalom course.

"Hello, Stephen." A large woman lurches into view, abruptly kissing his cheek.

He gulps, blinking like a man emerging into sunlight from the darkness of a copulatorium. Valerie Gallogher's presence on the *Mayflower* doesn't surprise him, but he's taken aback by her companions. Angela Dunfey, suckling little Merribell. Her cousin, Lorna, still spectacularly pregnant. And, most shocking of all, Father Monaghan, leaning his frail frame against his baptismal font.

Stephen says, "Did we . . . ? Are you . . . ?"

"My blood has spoken," Valerie Gallogher replies, her red hair flying like a pennant. "In nine months I give birth to our child."

Whereupon the sky above Stephen's head begins swarming with tiny black birds. No, not birds, he realizes: devices. Ovulation gauges sail through the air, a dozen at first, then scores, then hundreds, immediately pursued by equal numbers of sperm counters. As the little machines splash down and sink, darkening the harbor like the contraband tea from an earlier moment in the history of Boston insurgency, a muffled but impassioned cheer arises among the stowaways.

"Hello, Father Monaghan." Stephen unstraps his sperm counter. "Didn't expect to find *you* here."

The priest smiles feebly, drumming his fingers on the lip of the font. "Valerie informs me you're about to become a father again. Congratulations."

"My instincts tell me it's a boy," says Stephen, leaning over the rail. "He's going to get a second candy cane at Christmas," asserts the bewildered pilgrim as, with a wan smile and a sudden flick of his wrist, he breaks his bondage to the future.

If I don't act now, thinks Connie as he pivots toward Valerie Gallogher, I'll never find the courage again.

"Do we have a destination?" he asks. Like a bear preparing to ascend a tree, he hugs the font, pulling it against his chest.

"Only a purpose," Valerie replies, sweeping her hand across the horizon. "We won't find any Edens out there, Father. The entire Baltimore Reef has become a wriggling mass of flesh, newborns stretching shore to shore." She removes her ovulation gauge and throws it over the side. "In the Minneapolis Keys, the Immortality Corps routinely casts homosexual men and menopausal women into the sea. On the California Archipelago, male parishioners receive periodic potency tests and —"

"The Atlanta Insularity?"

"A nightmare."

"Miami Isle?"

"Forget it."

Connie lays the font on the bulwark then clambers onto the rail, straddling it like a child riding a seesaw. A loop of heavy-duty chain encircles the font, the steel links flashing in the rising sun. "Then what's our course?"

"East," says Valerie. "Toward Europe. What are you doing?"

"East," Connie echoes, tipping the font seaward. "Europe."

A muffled, liquid crash reverberates across the harbor. The font disappears, dragging the chain behind it.

"Father!"

Drawing in a deep breath, Connie studies the chain. The spiral of links unwinds quickly and smoothly, like a coiled rattlesnake striking its prey. The slack vanishes. Connie feels the iron shackle seize his ankle. He flips over. He falls.

"Bless these waters, O Lord, that they might grant this sinner the gift of life everlasting . . ."

"Father!"

He plunges into the harbor, penetrating its cold hard surface: an experience, he decides, not unlike throwing oneself through a plate-glass window. The waters envelop him, filling his ears and stinging his eyes.

We welcome this sinner into the mystical body of Christ, and do mark him with the Sign of the Cross, Connie recites in his mind, reaching up and drawing the sacred insignia on his forehead.

He exhales, bubble following bubble.

Cornelius Dennis Monaghan, I baptize you in the name of the Father, and of the Son, and of the Holy Ghost, he concludes, and as the black wind sweeps through his brain, sucking him toward immortality, he knows the peace that passes all understanding.

The Iron Shroud

Jonathan Hobbwright cannot discourse upon the formic thoughts that flicker through the minds of ants, and he is similarly ignorant concerning the psyches of locusts, toads, moles, apes, and bishops, but he can tell you what it's like to be in hell. The abyss has become his fixed abode. Perdition is now his permanent address.

Although Jonathan's eyes deliver only muddy and monochromatic images, his ears have acquired an uncommon acuity. Encapsulated head-to-toe in damnation's carapace, he can hear the caw of a raven, the scrabblings of a rat, the throbbing of a lizard's heart.

Not only is the abyss acoustically opulent, it is temporally egalitarian. In this place every second is commensurate with a minute, every minute with an hour, every hour with an aeon. Has he been immured for a fortnight? A month? A year? Is he reciting to himself the twentieth successive account of his incarceration? The hundredth? The thousandth?

Listen carefully, Jonathan Hobbwright. Attend to every word emerging from the gossamer gates of your phantom mouth. Perhaps on this retelling you will discover some reason not to abandon hope. Even in hell stranger things have happened.

It is at the funeral of his mentor and friend, the illustrious Alastair Wohlmeth, that Jonathan meets the woman whose impeccable intentions are to become the paving-stones on his road to perdition. By the terms of Dr. Wohlmeth's last will and testament, the service is churchless and austere: a graveside gathering in Saint Sepulchre's Cemetery, Oxford, not so very far from Wadham College, where Wohlmeth wrought most of his scientific breakthroughs. Per the dead man's prescription, the party is limited to his one true protégé — Jonathan — plus his valet, his beloved but dull-witted sister, his three most promising apprentices, and the Right Reverend Mr. Torrance.

As the vicar mutters the incantation by which an Englishman once again becomes synonymous with ashes and dust, the mourners contemplate the corpse. Dr. Wohlmeth's earthly remains lie within an open coffin suspended above the grave, its oblong form casting a jagged shadow across the cavity like the gnomon on an immense sundial. The inscription on the stone is singularly spare: A. F. WOHLMETH, 1803–1881.

To assert that Alastair Wohlmeth was a latter-day Prometheus would not, in Jonathan's view, distort the truth. Just as the mythic Titan stole fire from the gods, so did Wohlmeth appropriate from nature some of her most obscure principles, transforming them into his own private science, the nascent sphere of knowledge he called vibratology. This new field was for its discoverer a fundamentally esoteric realm, to be explored in a manner reminiscent of the ancient Pythagoreans practicing their cultish geometry. Of course, when the outside world realized that Wohlmeth's quest had yielded a practical invention — a tuning fork capable of cracking the thickest crystal and pulverizing the strongest metal — the British Society of Engineers urged him to patent the device and establish a corporation dedicated to its commercial exploitation. One particularly aggressive B.S.E. member, a demolitions expert named Cardigan, wanted to market the Wohlmeth resonator as "an earthquake in a satchel-case," a miraculous implement auguring a day when "the dredging of canals, the blasting of mines, the shattering of battlements, and the moving of mountains will be accomplished with the wave of a wand." To Dr. Wohlmeth's eternal credit, or so Jonathan constructed the matter, he resisted all such blandishments. Until the day he died, Wohlmeth forbade his disciples to discuss the resonator in any but the most opaque mathematical terms, confining the conversation to quarterlies devoted solely to theoretical harmonics. The technical periodicals, meanwhile, remained as bereft of articles about the tuning fork as they did of lyric poetry.

Contrary to Wohlmeth's wishes, a ninth mourner has appeared at the service, a parchment-skinned crone in a black-hooded mantle. Her features, Jonathan notes, partake as much of the geological as the anatomical. Her brow is a crag, her nose a promontory, her lower lip a protuberant shelf of rock. With impassive eyes she watches whilst the sexton, a nimble scarecrow named Fautley, leans over the open coffin and, in accordance with the deceased genius's desires, lays a resonator on the frozen bosom, wrapping the stiff fingers about the shank, so that in death Dr. Wohlmeth assumes the demeanor of a sacristan clutching a crucifix the size of a shovel. An instant later the sexton's assistants — the blockish Garber and the scrawny Osmond — set the lid on the coffin and nail it in place. Fautley works the windlass, lowering Wohlmeth to his final resting place. Taking up their spades, Garber and Osmond return the dirt whence it came, the clods striking the coffin lid with percussive thumps, even as the crone approaches Jonathan.

"Dr. Hobbwright, I presume?" she says in a viscous German accent. "Vibratologist *extraordinaire?*"

"Not nearly so *extraordinaire* as Alastair Wohlmeth."

Reaching into her canvas sack, the crone produces the January, April, and July issues of *Oscillation Dynamics* for 1879. "But you published articles in all these, *ja?*"

"It was a good year for me," Jonathan replies, nodding. "No fewer than five of my projects came to fruition."

"But 1881 will be even better." The crone's voice suggests a corroded piccolo played by a consumptive. "Ere the month is out, you will bring peace and freedom to a myriad unjustly imprisoned souls." From her sack she withdraws a leather-bound volume inscribed with the words *Journal of Baron Gustav Nachtstein.* "I am Countess Helga Nachtstein. Thirty years ago I gave birth to the author of this confession, my beloved Gustav, destined for an untimely end — more untimely, even, than the fate of his father, killed in a duel when Gustav was only ten."

"My heart goes out to you," says Jonathan.

The Countess sighs extravagantly, doubling the furrows of her crenellated brow. "The sins of the sons are visited on the mothers. Please believe me when I say that Gustav Nachtstein was as brilliant a scientist as your Dr. Wohlmeth. Alas, his investigations took him to a dark place, and many innocent beings have consequently spent the past eleven years locked in an earthly purgatory. Just when I'd begun to despair of their liberation, I happened upon my son's collection of scientific periodicals. The fact that the inventor of the Wohlmeth resonator is no longer amongst the living has not dampened my expectations, for I assume you can lay your hands on such a machine and bear it to the site of the tragedy."

"Perhaps."

"As consideration I can offer one thousand English pounds." The Countess presses her son's diary into Jonathan's uncertain grasp. "Open his journal to the entry of August the sixth, 1870, and you will find an initial payment of two hundred pounds, plus the first-class railway tickets that will take you from London to Freiberg to the village of Tübinhausen — and from there to Castle Kralkovnik in the Schwartzwald. May I assume that a week will suffice for you to put your affairs in order?"

Cracking the spine of the Baron's journal, Jonathan retrieves an envelope containing the promised banknotes and train tickets. "I must confess, Countess, I'm perplexed by your presumption." He glances toward the grave, noting that the crater has been filled. The mourners linger beside the mound, locked in contemplations doubtless ranging from cherished memories of Dr. Wohlmeth, to apprehension over who amongst them will next feel the Reaper's scythe, to curiosity about the location of the nearest public-house. "Does it not occur to you that I may have better things to do with my time than rectifying your son's misdeeds?"

By way of reply, the Countess produces from her sack a tinted daguerreotype of a young woman. "I am not the only one to experience remorse over Gustav's transgressions. My granddaughter Lotte is also in pain, tormented by her failure to warn her father away from his project. Having recently extricated herself from an ill-advised engagement, she presently resides at the castle. The thought of meeting the renowned Dr. Hobbwright has fired her with an anticipation bordering on exhilaration."

Jonathan spends the remainder of the afternoon in the Queen's Lane Coffee-House, perusing the Baron's confession. Shortly after four o'clock he finishes reading the last entry, then slams the volume closed. If this fantastic chronicle can be believed, then the evil that Gustav Nachtstein perpetrated was so profound as to demand his immediate intervention.

He will go to the Black Forest, bearing a tuning fork and collateral voltaic piles. He will redeem the damned souls of Castle Kralkovnik. But even if their plight had not stirred Jonathan, the case would still entail two puissant facts: £1,000 is the precise sum by which a competent vibratologist might continue Dr. Wohlmeth's work on a scale befitting its importance, and never in his life has Jonathan beheld a creature so lovely as Fräulein Lotte Nachtstein.

15 March 1868

After many arduous years of research into the dubious science of spiritualism, I have reached six conclusions concerning so-called ghosts.

1. There is no great beyond — no stable realm where carefree phantoms gambol whilst awaiting communiqués from turban-topped clairvoyants sitting in candlelit parlors surrounded by the dearly departed's loved ones. Show me a medium, and I'll show you a mountebank. Give me a filament of ectoplasm, and I'll return a strand of taffy.

2. There is life after death.

3. Once a specter has elected to vacate its fleshly premises, no ordinary barrier of stone or metal will impede its journey. A willful phantom can easily escape a pharaoh's tomb, a potentate's mausoleum, or a lead casket buried six feet underground.

4. With each passing instant, yet another quantum of a specter's incorporeal substance scatters in all directions. Once dissipated, a ghost can never reassemble itself. The post-mortem condition is evanescent in the extreme, not to be envied by anyone possessing an iota of joie de vivre.

5. Despite the radical discontinuity between the two planes, a specter may, under certain rare circumstances, access the material world prior to total dissolution — hence the occasional credible account of a ghost performing a boon for the living. A deceased child places her favorite doll on her mother's dresser. A departed suitor posts a letter declaring eternal devotion to his beloved. A phantom dog barks one last time, warning its master away from a bridge on the point of collapse.

6. In theory a competent scientist should be able at the moment of death to encapsulate a person's spectral shade in some spiritually impermeable substance, thus canceling the dissipation process and creating a kind of immortal soul. The question I intend to explore may be framed as follows. Do the laws of nature permit the synthesis of an alloy so dense as to trap an emergent ghost, yet sufficiently pliant that the creature will be free to move about?

17 May 1868

For the past two months I have not left my laboratory. The music of science surrounds me: burbling flasks, bubbling retorts, moaning generators, humming rectifiers. Von Helmholtz, Mendeleyev, and the rest — my alleged peers — will doubtless aver that my quest partakes more of a discredited alchemy than a tenable chemistry. When I go to publish my results, they'll insist with a sneer, I would do better submitting the paper to the *Proceedings of the Paracelsus Society* than to the *Cambridge Journal of Molecularism*. Let the intellectual midgets have their fun with me. Let the ignoramuses scoff. Where angels fear to tread, Baron Nachtstein rushes in — and one day the dead will extol him for it.

If all goes well, by this time tomorrow I shall be holding in my hand a lump of the vital material. I intend to call it bezalelite, in honor of Judah Löew ben Bezalel, the medieval rabbi from Prague who fashioned a man of clay, giving the creature life by incising on its brow the Hebrew word EMETH — that is, truth.

Although Judah Löew's golem was a faithful servant and protector of the ghetto, the rabbi was obliged to prevent it from working on the Sabbath, a simple matter of effacing the first letter of EMETH, the Aleph, leaving Mem and Taw, characters that spell METH — death. But one fateful Friday evening Löew forgot to disable his brain-child. In consequence of this inadvertent sacrilege, the golem ran amok all day Saturday, and so, come Sunday, the heartsick rabbi dutifully ground the thing to dust.

I shall not lose control of my golems. From the moment they come into the world, they will know who is the puppet and who the puppeteer, who the beast and who the keeper, who the slave and who the master.

9 July 1868

At long last, following a deliriously eventful June, I have found time to again take pen in hand. Not only did I fashion the essential alloy, not only did I learn how to produce it in quantities commensurate with my ambitions, but I have managed to coat living tissue with thin and malleable layers of the stuff. Naturally I first tested the adhesion process on animals. After many false starts and innumerable failures, I managed to electroplate a wasp, a moth, a dragonfly, a frog, a serpent, a tortoise, and a cat, successfully trapping their spirits as the concomitant suffocation deprived them of their lives.

In every case, the challenge was to find an optimum rate at which to replenish the bezalelite anode with fresh quantities of the alloy. If I introduced too many positively charged atoms into the bath, then the cathode — that is, the experimental vertebrate or invertebrate — invariably suffered paralysis. Too few such ions, and the chrysalis became so porous as to allow the soul's egress.

I was pleased and surprised by how quickly a plated specter learns to move. Within hours of its emergence from the electrolyte solution, each subject variously flew, hopped, slithered, crawled, or ran as adeptly as when alive. To the best of my knowledge, a ghost's condition entails only one deficit. Because the olfactory sense is actually heightened by the procedure, the creature will undergo an unpleasant interval whilst its former corporeal host decays within the chrysalis. Once decomposition is complete, however, the encapsulated phantom is free to revel in its immortality.

Finding an experimental subject of the species *Homo sapiens* posed no difficulties. Three months ago my manservant Wolfgang was diagnosed with a cancer of the stomach. His anguish soon proved as unimaginable as the physicians' palliatives proved useless. The instant I proposed to sever his tormented soul from his ravaged flesh, he surrendered himself to my science.

I shall not soon forget the sight of Wolfgang's glazed body rising from the wooden vat — eyeless, noseless, mouthless, hairless: the solution had plated all his features, much as an enormous candle burning atop a bust will, drip by drip, sheath the face in wax. In a single deft gesture I removed the breathing-pipe and, taking up a permanent bezalelite plug, stoppered the ventilation hole, so that death by asphyxiation occurred in a matter of minutes. Even as the waters of Wolfgang's rebirth sluiced along his arms and cascaded down his chest, he began teaching his phantom limbs to animate the chrysalis, his phantom eyes to pierce the translucent husk, and so he climbed free of the tar-lined tub without misadventure. The gaslight caught the hardened elixir, causing cold sparks to flash amongst the bulges and pits. A naïve witness happening upon my golem would have taken him for a knight clad in armor fashioned from phosphorescent brass and polished amber.

"The pain is gone," the ghost reported.

"I have disembodied you," I replied. "Henceforth your name is Nonentity 101."

"I can barely see," he moaned.

"A necessary and — as you will soon realize — trivial side effect."

"I feel buried alive. Set me free, Herr Doktor Nachtstein."

"Take heart, Nonentity 101. You are the harbinger of a new and golden race. Welcome to Eden. Ere long hundreds of your kind will inhabit this same garden, arrayed in immortal metal, sneering at oblivion."

"Let me out."

"Do not despair. In the present Paradise, the lethal Tree of Knowledge is nowhere to be found. This time around, my dear Adam, you will eat only of the Tree of Life."

The abbreviated train that brings Jonathan Hobbwright eastward from the tiny village of Tübinhausen to the outskirts of Castle Kralkovnik comprises a lone passenger carriage hauled by a decrepit switch-engine. Shortly after six o'clock *post meridiem*, he arrives at a forlorn clapboard railway station, terminus of a spur line created solely to service the late Baron Nachtstein's estate.

As Jonathan wanders about the platform, a thunderstorm arises in the Schwartzwald, the harsh winds flogging his weary flesh. The station offers no refuge, being as tightly sealed as Dr. Wohlmeth's grave, its door secured with a padlock as large as a teapot. For a half-hour the vibratologist huddles beneath the drizzling eaves and leaky gutters, until at last a humanoid figure comes shambling through the tempest, gripping a kerosene lantern that imparts a coppery glow to its bezalelite skin.

"Good evening, Dr. Hobbwright," says the golem in a kettle-drum voice.

"Actually, it's a deplorable evening."

"I am called Nonentity 157. My race, you will hardly be surprised to learn, regards you as the new Moses, come to set us free." The ghost heaves the vibratologist's steamer trunk onto his massive shoulders. "Judging from its weight, I would surmise that herein lies the mechanism of our deliverance."

"A thousand-ampere Wohlmeth resonator plus an array of voltaic piles."

Nonentity 157 leads Jonathan down the sodden platform and across the glistening tracks. Peering through the gale, the vibratologist discerns a stout and stationary coach, hitched to a pair of electroplated horses. Nonentity 157 lofts the steamer trunk atop the roof, securing it with ropes, then opens the door and guides Jonathan into the mercifully dry passenger compartment. Climbing into the driver's box, the golem urges his team forward.

By the time the conveyance reaches its destination, the storm has subsided, the curtains of rain parting to reveal a gibbous moon. The silver shafts strike Castle Kralkovnik, limning a complex that is less a fortress than a walled hamlet, the whole mass surmounting a hill so bald and craggy as to suggest a skull battered by a mace. The phantom horses trot through a gateway flanked by stone gargoyles and begin negotiating a labyrinth of cobblestoned streets.

Golems are everywhere on view, skulking along the puddle-pocked alleys, clanking across the bridges, rumbling through the tunnels, huddling beneath the gothic arches. In this city of the ambulatory dead, every citizen seems to Jonathan a kind of renegade pawn, recently escaped from a tournament whose rules, though ostensibly those of chess, are in fact known only to Lucifer.

The coach halts beside the veranda of the main château. Jonathan alights, and two golems appear, giving their names and offering their services. Whilst Nonentity 201 takes charge of the steamer trunk, Nonentity 337 leads the vibratologist upward along the graceful curve of the grand staircase to a private bedchamber. A note rests on the pillow. Countess Nachtstein wants Jonathan to join her and Lotte for supper at eight o'clock. When the trunk arrives, he changes into dry clothing: a wholly benevolent carapace, he decides, as opposed to the malign husks in which the Baron's progeny are imprisoned.

Returning to the first floor, Jonathan employs his olfactory sense — his nose is almost as keen as a golem's — in finding the dining hall. The Countess and her granddaughter are seated at a ponderous banquet table, sipping Rhenish.

"Welcome, Dr. Hobbwright," says the Countess. "Do you prefer white wine or red?"

"Red, please."

"Will burgundy suffice?"

"Yes, thank you."

Owing to the daguerreotype, Lotte Nachtstein seems to Jonathan a familiar presence. Like the reputation of a famous personage, her high cheekbones, supple mouth, and flashing green eyes have preceded her. He soon learns, however, that her nature is as harsh as her features are fair. Whilst a cadre of golems serves the dinner — a veritable feast predicated on an entire roast boar — it becomes apparent that gentle words rarely fall from this Fräulein's generous lips.

"Evidently I've become something of a legend amongst your father's experimental subjects," says Jonathan, savoring his wine. "They see me as the source of their salvation."

"My father never regarded the golems as mere experimental subjects," Lotte says in an acerbic tone. "If you'd read his journal more carefully, you would have grasped that fact."

"Nevertheless, his project went beyond the pale."

"For a man of Gustav Nachtstein's genius, there are no pales," Lotte insists. "You are not the first prospective savior to visit us, Dr. Hobbwright. In recent months my grandmother and I have consulted with experts from all over England and the Continent. Every imaginable remedy has been tried and found wanting: acids, chisels, hacksaws, steam drills, welding torches, explosives."

"But Dr. Hobbwright is our first vibratologist," the Countess reminds Lotte, then turns to Jonathan and says, "My granddaughter and I believe that the right sort of specialist has finally come to Castle Kralkovnik."

"Speak for yourself, Mother," says Lotte. "You were convinced that Dr. Orloff's silver bullets would free the golems, likewise Dr. Edelman's caustic butter, not to mention your misplaced faith in Dr. Callistratus, who wasted six days attempting to deplate the cat."

Jonathan helps himself to a second glass of burgundy. "Might I presume to ask how Baron Nachtstein met his end?"

"Violently," says Lotte.

"His creatures assassinated him," says the Countess with equal candor. "The details are unpleasant."

"My father died even more horribly than my mother, who suffered a fatal hemorrhage giving birth to me," says Lotte. "Just as the Baroness Nachtstein's fertility destroyed her, so did Baron Nachtstein's brilliance occasion his downfall."

"Your father was prodigiously gifted, but his journal also reveals a man obsessed," says Jonathan.

Lotte sips her Rhenish and glowers at the vibratologist. "It's the *golems* who are obsessed, incapable of seeing beyond their *idée fixe* about damnation. I ask you, Dr. Hobbwright, does not the fact that they declined to plate my father argue for the essential benevolence of the procedure? If their condition is as intolerable as they maintain, they would have inflicted it on their creator instead of simply murdering him."

"In that case, perhaps I should return to Oxford," says Jonathan, sensing that in defending the Baron so vociferously Lotte has overstepped the bounds of her actual beliefs. "Given that your father's creatures are such incurable dissemblers, I see no point in helping them."

"No, please — you must stay," says Lotte, her voice now filled with a pragmatic amity. "Perhaps my father was mistaken. If the golems insist their situation is unendurable, it behooves us to give them the benefit of the doubt."

13 January 1869

Nonentity 157 and his bezalelite brethren are adamant on one point. They insist that a wandering soul's burning need is to venture forth from its cadaverous habitat and dissipate, occasionally favoring its survivors with a benevolent gesture *en passant*. By tampering with this process, I have plunged the golems into an irremediable despair. Indeed, I have dispatched them to hell.

My instincts tell me to ignore these complaints. Creatures in such a metaphysically unprecedented state are wont to indulge in hyperbole. Like the vast majority of sentient beings, my golems are unreliable narrators of their own lives.

As it happens, their illusion of damnation is useful to my purposes. By promising to return them to the electrolyte bath any day now, subsequently reversing the plating process and dissolving their husks, I retain a remarkable measure of control over their minds. I cannot speak for the whole of Creation, but here in the Schwartzwald law and order enjoy a proper hegemony over anarchy and chaos.

Judging from my latest series of animal experiments, I would have to say that, alas, bezalelite plating can occur in one direction only. I would do well to sequester that unhappy fact in the pages of this journal. Were the golems to comprehend the immutability of their situation, they would suffer unnecessary distress.

To date I have brought forth one hundred and thirteen electroplated souls, most of them terminal consumptives and cancer patients from Freiberg, Pforzheim, Reutlingen, and Stuttgart. With each such parturition I come closer to perfecting my methods. To help maintain a constant ion level, I have learned to add potassium cyanide to the bath, along with salts of the bezalelite itself. Conductivity can be further enhanced with carbonates and phosphates. As it happens, if the golem-maker first deposits a layer of pure silver on the subject's epidermis, no more than one-tenth of a micrometer thick, total adhesion of the alloy to the protein substrate is virtually guaranteed. Finally, if the experimenter wishes to hasten the process by means of high current densities, he should employ pulse-plating to prevent erratic deposition rates. In the case of human subjects, the ideal cycle is fifteen seconds on followed by three seconds off. To ensure a wholly homogeneous chrysalis, the golem-maker will want to vary the direction of the electricity flowing from the rectifier. In density the reverse pulse should exceed the forward pulse by a factor of four, whilst the width of the forward pulse must be three times that of the reverse.

6 August 1870

I must confess, though with a certain understandable reluctance, that I have found in the Franco-Prussian War a catastrophe of enormous convenience. Approach a man who has just been blown apart by an artillery shell, his viscera spilling forth like turnips from a torn sack, and propose to translate him into a domain where his agony will vanish and his soul endure forever, and he will invariably assent. If you kneel beside a soldier recently trampled during a cavalry charge and offer to sign him up for an eternity of painless existence, he will forthwith beg for a contract and a pen.

This afternoon my creatures and I landed in the Alsatian town of Fröschwiller, where earlier in the day Marshall Patrice de Mac-Mahon's French brigades had clashed with a combined force of Prussians, Bavarians, Badeners, Württembergers, and Saxons. Perhaps historians will ultimately frame the Battle of Fröschwiller as the cradle of a unified German state, but what I beheld on that ghastly field was not so much a cradle as a mass grave. Each side, I would estimate, lost at least ten thousand men to instant death or irremediable wounds.

Crossing the bloody terrain with a large convoy of tumbrels, the golems collected over five hundred candidates for bezalelite immortality. Thanks to humankind's affection for mayhem, I shall soon have an army of my own.

3 October 1870

Immediately after the necessary plans and diagrams arrived from Prague, along with a team of master builders, I embarked on a colossal endeavor. Here in the heart of the Schwartzwald we have razed my ancestral manor and begun to assemble in its stead a structure of stupefying splendor. My new abode will replicate the Bohemian castle of Kralkovnik wall for wall, gate for gate, plaza for plaza, and spire for spire.

Amongst their many virtues, my golems are extraordinarily diligent laborers. Already the first, second, and third courtyards have been paved. Tomorrow a crew of three hundred and fifty will start erecting Poelsig Tower, even as the remaining seven hundred and twenty-five lay the foundations of the principal château.

A man's home, it has been remarked, is his castle. By analogy, a man's castle is his kingdom and his kingdom his dominion. I intend to administer my empire in a manner befitting the first scientist to weld the carnal plane to its spectral counterpart — that is, with a firm but enlightened hand. As Lotte told me this morning, "When the golems undertake to compose their epics, they will sing their creator's praises in rapturous words, borne by the most sublime music yet heard in heaven or on earth."

At first light Jonathan Hobbwright rises from his canopied bed and, venturing beyond the castle walls, begins his quest for a suitable site on which to stage the golems' salvation. From seven o'clock until noon he roams the fields and woods, eventually happening upon a clearing so wide it could accommodate a circus act featuring a troupe of elephants. The vibratologist returns to the castle, seeks out Nonentity 157, and enlists its aid in transporting the apparatus to the place where, God willing, he will redeem the Baron's creatures.

After Nonentity 157 departs, Jonathan bears the Wohlmeth resonator to the center of the circle. Coils of fog sinuate across the ground like phantom serpents. Meticulously he deploys the tuning fork, prongs pointed upwards in a configuration evoking the Devil's own trident bursting through the crust of the earth. Next he places the voltaic piles a full hundred yards from the resonator, fearing that without this margin the vibrations will shatter not only the bezalelite husks but the battery array itself, thus terminating the golems' deliverance *in medias res*.

At this juncture Countess Nachtstein's icily beautiful granddaughter appears, dressed in a bright scarlet cloak, so that her emergence from the fog suggests the Red Death exiting a white tent. In the moist but congenial glow of morning, Lotte seems a rather different person from the high-minded moralist who dominated the previous night's dinner conversation, and she addresses Jonathan in tones that betray genuine contrition.

"Please accept this lunch along with my apology for scolding you last night," she says, handing over a sack containing cold meat, warm bread, two apples, and a flask of burgundy. "My father did monstrous things. I would deny that fact only at my peril."

"In most contexts, honoring one's parents is a laudable endeavor," says Jonathan. "I cannot blame you for defending Baron Nachtstein, injudicious as his project may have been."

"The man who would expiate my father's sins is not only a great scientist but a paragon of graciousness."

When Lotte squeezes his arm and suggests that she help him finish installing the resonator, Jonathan can discern no ulterior motive. During the subsequent hour they connect a long rubber-sheathed wire to the positive terminals of the voltaic piles, then attach a second such strand to the negative terminals, subsequently running the insulated copper filaments to the fork and wrapping them about the outer prongs. Returning to the piles, Jonathan fastens the wires to a pair of chronometers, the first enabling him to determine how many minutes will elapse ere the blade of the concomitant knife-switch descends, the second allowing him to fix the interval between the initial vibrations and the termination of the circuit.

"I see no reason not to move quickly," says Lotte. Suddenly her imperious aspect is ascendant. It seems she has taken command of the experiment, a situation to which Jonathan is expected to acquiesce. "We shall switch on the resonator at three o'clock. Is that acceptable to you?"

"What if it were unacceptable?"

Lotte makes no reply but instead points to the rheostat. "I assume that, given bezalelite's extreme density, we should run the apparatus for at least an hour—and at full power."

"I would advise against it. To drive a Wohlmeth resonator beyond eight hundred amperes would be to create an acoustic cyclone. My preferred parameters would be four hundred amperes for twenty minutes."

"We shall compromise," Lotte informs Jonathan. "Six hundred amperes for forty minutes. After setting the chronometers, we shall retreat to the safety of the castle. We needn't worry about the golems' welfare. After all, they're already dead."

3 November 1877

When I embarked on this project, I fully anticipated the pleasure I would experience whilst watching the golems prepare our meals, make our beds, brew our beer, plow our fields, and harvest our crops. But I had no inkling of the delights one could derive from observing them engage in meaningless tasks.

Come to Castle Kralkovnik, ladies and gentlemen. Behold the living dead playing croquet in the moonlight using petards instead of balls, ka-boom, ka-boom, ka-boom (explosions to which the carapaces prove immune). Watch the tethered spirits build a tower to heaven on an inviolable order from Yahweh, then tear it down in response to an equally sacrosanct command. Bear witness to my metal phantoms as they plan and rehearse seven separate productions of *Macbeth*, each to unfold three seconds out of phase with both its antecedent and its successor, then stage multiple command performances for their favorite baron.

On the whole, it is wrong for a person to spawn a race of artificial beings and demand their unquestioning obedience. Godhead too easily goes to one's head. From time to time, however, the world is blessed with an individual so wise that he may play the part of locally situated deity without any attendant corruption to his character.

12 February 1878

Last month I made a momentous discovery. No matter how much he may be adored, worshiped, and feared, a man in my position will not be satisfied until his progeny come to blows over how best to interpret their creator's will. We demiurges cannot rest until a great quantity of violence has occurred on our behalf. If I am to enjoy genuine peace of mind, my adherents must go to war.

In keeping with the scenario I wrote for them, the orthodox golems — the Singularists, lead by Nonentity 741 — believe in a unitary deity. The Quadripartists, under Nonentity 899, insist that I am of a piece with a pantheon that includes my mother, Helga, my daughter, Lotte, and my alter ego, Rabbi Judah Löew ben Bezalel. Both sides employ incineration as their principal method for punishing incorrect understandings of my unknowable essence. Once a heretic has been tried and convicted, he is chained to a stake, engulfed by mounds of kindling, and put to the torch. Of course, unlike most victims of religious persecution, Singularist and Quadripartist heretics actually wish to be treated in this brutal fashion, for they imagine that the flames might prove hot enough to melt their shells: a physical impossibility, but desperate specters will not be reconciled to the laws of nature.

This same expectation of deliverance undergirds the theological wars that periodically ravage the Schwartzwald. The sight of a thousand golems falling upon one another with claymores, cudgels, and battle-axes is as exhilarating a spectacle as a deity could ever hope to witness. Needless to say, the carapaces always remain intact. Like the golems themselves, my bezalelite is essentially a supernatural phenomenon, impervious to the ambitions of the quick and the desires of the dead.

12 August 1879

Today I endured one of the most distressing events of my life. Shortly after Nonentity 316 and Nonentity 214 appeared at the breakfast table, the former serving my morning eggs and sausage, the latter bringing me my newspaper, Nonentity 667 strode into the dining hall, looming over me whilst I attempted to read an article detailing how the spiritualism fad has come to Vienna.

"You are blocking my light," I told the golem.

"Rather the way you have occluded our enlightenment," Nonentity 667 replied. "We have read your journal, Herr Doktor Nachtstein. You have deceived us. The procedure cannot be undone."

"Nonsense. You have misinterpreted the relevant entry. I now have in hand the knowledge by which you will transcend your alloys. Allow me two more experiments, three at the most, and I shall bless you all with oblivion."

"Perhaps we shall exact our retribution tomorrow, perhaps the next day, perhaps a year from now. But know that our vengeance is coming."

"You cannot frighten me," I said, though in truth I was terrified. "For Singularists and Quadripartists alike, I am the only possible source of salvation."

"*Fiat justitia, ruat caelum,*" said Nonentity 667. "Let justice be done, though the heavens may fall."

Heavy of heart, unquiet of mind, Jonathan paces Castle Kralkovnik's highest point, the roof of Poelsig Tower. His path is an ellipse, its eastern focus marked by Countess Nachtstein, the western by Lotte, the center by a telescope pointing towards the clearing. He wishes he'd never agreed to run the resonator at six hundred amperes. Conceivably Lotte's directive sprang from some intuitive insight into her father's recondite alloy, but more likely it bespoke only a mania to cleanse his legacy.

Pausing before the telescope, Jonathan presses his right orb to the eyepiece. He adjusts the tubes, making the image crisp. The golems stand in three concentric circles about the tuning fork, a tableau suggesting a tossed pebble raising rings in a pond. A palpable serenity has descended upon the creatures. They are patience personified. Having waited so many years for their freedom, they can endure whatever interval remains ere the blade drops.

"One month after they stole my father's journal and learned that the plating is seemingly permanent," says Lotte, "a mob of golems, two dozen at least, appropriated every dagger, hatchet, and sword in the castle."

"With military precision — most of them were soldiers — they disassem-bled my son," says the Countess. "Each bore away a different piece of him and buried it in the forest."

"It speaks well of your Christian generosity that you would seek to liberate the Baron's murderers," says Jonathan, stepping away from the telescope.

"Our project has less to do with compassion than with self-preservation," the Countess replies. "Upon consummating their plot against Gustav, the golems gave Lotte and myself to know that they intended to destroy us, too. Only after they realized we were taking every conceivable step to free them, hiring one metallurgist, galvanicist, and molecularist after another, did they become as compliant as when my son first brought them into being."

A white-hot bead of rage burns through Jonathan's breast. If the present experiment fails, he will surely become entangled in whatever lethal plans the golems draw against Lotte and the Countess. How dare these women presume to put him in such jeopardy? But before he can articulate his anger, he hears the sharp electric report of the chronometer blade snapping into place.

Jonathan again avails himself of the telescope. Already the trident had become a humming, wailing, incandescent blur, each prong oscillating like the pendulum of some demonic inverted clock. At the edge of the circle, poplars and beeches shiver in the aural storm. The trunks fracture, and the trees crash to the forest floor, even as scores of owls, rooks, larks, foxes, hares, hedgehogs, and deer flee the cataclysm. On all sides of the resonator, jagged crevasses open in the earth.

So great is the pain in Jonathan's head that he abandons the telescope, shuts his eyes, and massages his throbbing temples. His tendons tremble like harp strings plucked by invisible hands. Were the tower nearer to the fork by as few as ten yards, he calculates, his eardrums would rip, his heart burst, and his bones turn to powder.

Fighting his way through the crashing waves of sound, Jonathan returns to the telescope. Everywhere he looks, fault lines zigzag across the golems' metal flesh. Their faceless heads resemble ancient vases, cracked and battered by his-tory's vicissitudes. Like an ancient mosaic shedding its tiles, the creatures molt bit by bit. Bezalelite fragments drop from their phantom arms, legs, and tor-sos, revealing the moldering skeletons beneath. Momentarily mastering his fear and transcending his astonishment, Jonathan takes satisfaction in know-ing that — given the intensity of the tremors — the fork is probably freeing not only the human golems but also the Baron's experimental insects, reptiles, and mammals.

"*Mirabile dictu!*" cries the Countess.

"The specters are hatching!" shouts Lotte.

"It's not safe here!" screams Jonathan, urging the women toward the stairwell. "Run!"

Despite her advanced age, the Countess negotiates the steps two at a time, as do Jonathan and Lotte, so that everyone reaches the ground floor within three minutes. No sooner does Jonathan start charging down the corridor than the ceiling disintegrates, squalls of plaster cascading into his path. Frantically he sidles and weaves amidst the plummeting timbers and errant chunks of masonry, but his athleticism proves useless before the force he has unleashed. As he reaches the door to the conservatory, a wayward chandelier, luminous with gas, lands squarely atop his skull. The bright bludgeon plunges him into darkness, but not before he notices that the hall now swarms with a thousand phantoms, each a disquieting shade of red and all wearing strangely despondent expressions, utterly unbefitting of persons recently released from the bottomless pit.

At first Jonathan assumes he has fallen prey to a nightmare. How else might he explain the scene now stretching before him? Heaped with kindling, two wooden obelisks rise from the central courtyard, each holding a Nachtstein woman, bound, gagged, and blindfolded. The plaque above Lotte's head reads *Singularist*. Countess Nachtstein's stake is labeled *Quadripartist*.

Jonathan has become one with the wall. Cold and dazed, naked, he stretches to full height, straining against the granite niche into which his captors have wedged him. He shivers in the Schwartzwald wind, goose bumps erupting on his bare skin like rivets, even as his cranium aches with the aftermath of his encounter with the chandelier. Vapor-faced phantoms throng across the plaza, their visages twisted by an inscrutable sadness. As if ignorant of the laws of actuality, the former golems attempt to prolong their purchase on the world. They flex their nonmuscles, tense their nonligaments, curl their nonfingers.

"Surely you don't mean to burn these women," says Jonathan. "They rescued you. You owe them everything."

"We mean to burn them — as surely as we mean to electroplate you," says a crimson specter in a fluttering voice.

"That makes no sense."

"True," says a scarlet specter. "We understand your frustration. You want your ghosts to be outré but not perverse, weird but not recondite, occasionally sublime though never ridiculous. So sorry, Herr Doktor. We are avatars of the abyss. Coherence is not our business."

Jonathan watches helplessly as a vermilion ghost applies a firebrand to the fagots encircling the Countess's stake. As the flames climb the fleshly ladder of the victim's form, a carmine specter flourishes a Wohlmeth resonator — the very fork, Jonathan realizes, that gave the golems their freedom — and hurls it into the burgeoning conflagration.

"The dead don't lack for foresight," a maroon ghost avers. "In a matter of minutes the fork will become a charred ruin, thus canceling any hopes you might entertain of liberation by a passing Samaritan."

Now a ruby specter sets Lotte's pyre aflame, but not before jamming the Baron's journal into the fagots.

"Set her free!" Jonathan screams.

Yanking him free of the niche, a band of phantoms drags Jonathan out of the plaza and down a maze of stairways to the Baron's subterranean laboratory, a cavernous space dominated by the electrolyte vat. Although they've never done this before, his captors act with great efficiency, ramming a breathing-pipe down his throat, dumping him into the solution, chaining his naked body to the cathode column.

Ignoring his pleas for mercy, a magenta specter connects the rectifier to the anode, agleam with the Baron's alloy. Countless positively charged bezalelite atoms drift through the bath and accumulate on Jonathan's flesh. Atom by atom, molecule by molecule, the metal embraces the helpless vibratologist, each instance of adherence like the sting of a microscopic hornet.

Within one hour the process is complete, leaving him encapsulated, immobile, and half-blind. A gurgling reaches his ears. The phantoms are draining the vat. A searing pain rips though his chest as a ghost pulls the breathing-pipe from his trachea. An instant later another specter seals the airhole with an immortal bezalelite plug.

Mummified by the exotic alloy, the prisoner is soon deprived of oxygen, and then of life itself. He is also deprived of death. Now and forever he will be the ghost of Jonathan Hobbwright — vibratologist *extraordinaire* become solitary golem — chained to the cathode pillar of Baron Nachtstein's infernal machine. Some day, perhaps, when entropy has dismantled the universe, he will be a free man, but for now he must reconcile himself to the unendurable, the interminable, and the endlessly absurd.

Jonathan Hobbwright cannot discourse upon the formic thoughts that flicker through the minds of ants, and he is similarly ignorant concerning the psyches of locusts, toads, moles, apes, and bishops, but he can tell you what it's like to be in hell. His imagination affords him only fleeting respites. Each time he dreams himself free of his bezalelite coffin — passing through the portals of the abyss, striking out for *terra incognita* — Satan's angels give chase, and they inevitably track him down.

Come back, Dr. Hobbwright. Return to perdition. Tell your story for the tenth time, the hundredth, the thousandth. The more frequently you give voice to the wretched chronicle of your life, death, and damnation, the longer you will forestall your descent into madness.

And whilst your reason remains, you might take heart in recalling that the progenitor of your race is dead and gone. In the aeons to come, you will not be made to laud Gustav Nachtstein in song or build an altar to his glory. Cold comfort, to be sure, but in the bottomless pit one seizes upon whatever pleasures lie to hand.

Against the odds and in defiance of his circumstances, Jonathan's most recent recitation culminates in a miracle: a minor such phenomenon, to be sure, a mediocre miracle, but impressive all the same. For it happens that on certain rare occasions, despite the essential incompatibility between the human plane and the spectral — it's all in the Baron's journal — a disintegrating ghost will perform a philanthropic act. Jonathan remembers the passage in question. The words are etched on his transient soul. And so it happens that, when a fresh barrage assaults Castle Kralkovnik, roaring through the Baron's laboratory like a tornado, reducing the walls to rubble as it cracks the prisoner's chrysalis, Jonathan is not entirely surprised.

Sloughing off his husk, abandoning his corpse, the vibratologist floats free of the cathode, then fixes on Lotte's crimson ghost. "How long was I entombed?" he asks.

"Ten days," she replies.

"It felt like forever."

"Hell knows nothing of clocks."

"Where did you obtain the fork?" asks Jonathan.

"From Alastair Wohlmeth," replies Countess Nachtstein's scarlet specter. "The task we set ourselves was grueling. In our given tenure Lotte and I had to reach Oxford, unseal the grave, open the coffin, steal the resonator, and return to the castle."

"I am deeply grateful."

"We have no need of your gratitude," says the Countess. "Nor do you have need of ours."

"And now we must take eternal leave of you," says Lotte as her misty form dissolves. "Oblivion beckons."

"Farewell, Dr. Hobbwright." The Countess has become as transparent as the surrounding air. "Please know that it was never my intention to occasion your death."

It suddenly occurs to Jonathan that he desperately wants to enlighten humanity concerning the destiny of the dead. So tenuous is the spectral plane, so ultimately meaningless, he greatly desires to share this knowledge with his former fleshly confederates. The Baron's journal having been reduced to specks of carbon, Jonathan alone can tell the world about the appalling insipidity of ghosts.

"I wish to perform a philanthropic act of my own," he declares. "Bring me pen and ink and paper."

"Whatever for?" asks the invisible Lotte.

Even as the answer forms on Jonathan's airy lips, he realizes that his aspiration is futile. There is no time to collect the implements. Already he is less than ashes. Already he is a brother to dust.

Wrenching sobs burst from the vibratologist's ethereal throat. Briny droplets roll down his ephemeral cheeks. For an infinitesimal instant Jonathan Hobbwright is seized by an infinite remorse, but then his sorrow evaporates — like rain, like dew, like sweat, like the last and least of his tears.

Fixing the Abyss

Language speaks. If we let ourselves fall into the abyss denoted by this sentence, we do not go tumbling into emptiness. We fall upward, to a height. Its loftiness opens up a depth. The two span a realm in which we would like to become at home, so as to find a residence, a dwelling place for the life of man.
— Martin Heidegger

To this day no one can say precisely why a remorseless and reified nihilism visited itself upon Western civilization in the second decade of the twenty-first century. Being neither a trained philosopher nor a credentialed historian, but merely a creator of depleting and socially irresponsible horror films, I cannot hold forth authoritatively on the coming of the abyss. As a member of that cadre of accomplished pessimists deputized to explore the belly of the beast, however, I believe that my recollections are worth setting down — to say nothing of my therapist's conviction that, if I fail to complete this memoir, my dreams will never be devoid of demons again.

The most viable theory of the rift's origins attributes it to a conjunction of five disparate events. I allude not only to the wholesale abandonment of reason, under cover of Jesus, by several major political parties in the industrialized democracies of Europe and North America, not only to the ballooning of thermonuclear-weapon stockpiles in the United States and Russia following a convulsion of nostalgia for the Cold War, but also to the realization by the priestly caste that they could once again impose their carnal requirements on nonconsenting children without running afoul of the civil courts, as well as to the ontological transmogrification of suicide bombing — from despicable terrorist act to rarefied genre of performance art — by the hipper sectors of the Islamic blogosphere. Finally, of course, we must factor in the delivery by Dr. Dudley Yarborough, comparative literature professor at the Pennsylvania State University, of his three-hundredth stand-up lecture titled "Mutually Assured Deconstruction," keyed to his professionally lucrative and intractably tenured conviction that morality, truth, beauty, and knowledge are illusory notions at best, overthrown in the previous century by perspectivism, relativism, hermeneutics, and France.

We do know that the beast first stretched its jaws in proximity to Dudley. No sooner had he finished saying, "As Baudrillard has noted, it is no longer relevant to say that the real world 'exists,'" than a fault line opened down the middle of Room 102 in the Willard Building. Although no earthquake stronger than 3.7 on the Richter scale had struck central Pennsylvania since the late Cretaceous, the class naturally assumed they were witnessing a seismic event, but when cobra-size flagella emerged from the rupture, along with rivulets of a tar-like substance that was certainly not lava, plus a stench suggestive of Dover Beach at low tide, everyone realized that the phenomenon would not be easily named. Yarborough himself proved unequal to the crisis. According to his students, he simply stared dumbfounded at the gulf, a stick of chalk pressed against his mustache and a frown coalescing around his wire-rimmed glasses.

Luckily, the situation was redeemed by a returning-ed student, Brenda Lutz, a thirty-four-year-old divorcée who'd resolved to get her B.A. despite juggling two jobs and the responsibilities of single motherhood. Brenda had the presence of mind to organize an evacuation of the entire building and then alert the administrators in Old Main that an abyss had arrived and they might want to look into it. "Though no one should presume to discuss the event coherently," Brenda informed President Clapham's one and only reachable plenipotentiary, "for logocentrism is dead, and we have lost all fixed vantages from which to make sense of the world, or so Professor Yarborough, following Derrida, tells us." Before the day was out, the entire campus population had been relocated to the outskirts of town with the loss of only one life, the victim in question being Lewis Thornhill, a romantically inclined sophomore who fancied himself a latter-day Young Werther and, *mutatis mutandis*, hurled himself into the void.

While the recrudescent religiosity of the West's secular republics certainly contributed to the cataclysm, as did the renaissance of the arms race, the institutionalization of clerical rape, and the aestheticization of suicide bombing, I must lay most of the blame at Yarborough's feet. It's all very well for a scorched-earth, skepticism-squared ethos to enrapture Ivy League humanities departments, but when *épistémologie noire* comes to America's land-grant universities, we know we're all in a lot of trouble. In my view Sheila Kittman's Senate Subcommittee on Postmodern Irruptions was well within its rights to deny Yarborough a place on our team. He'd done enough damage already.

You will recall that, shortly after the coming of the widening gyre, Governor Abelard arranged for the Pennsylvania National Guard to lower into its gullet a live videocamera and concomitant floodlight, the whole arrangement connected to a twenty-mile length of coaxial cable. Although the void soon proved hostile to this probe, pulverizing the camera with a flagellum shortly after the cable had paid out, the broadcast lasted long enough to afford the world a three-second glimpse of an amoeboid something-or-other lying at the bottom of the pit. The PBS commentator floridly described the beast as "the Minotaur of our disordered zeitgeist, raging at the nexus of a vertical labyrinth," but the public never warmed to that epithet. The label that stuck issued from Drexel Sprite of the Nowhere Network, who dubbed the amoeba Caltiki, after the mucilaginous monster featured in that classic 1959 Eurotrash feature, *Caltiki il Mostro Immortale*, co-directed by Riccardo Freda and an uncredited Mario Bava, the supreme master of Italian horror cinema. Let me hasten to note that my presence on the exploration team had nothing to do with my unauthorized *Caltiki* sequels and everything to do with the fact that, in the words of Boing Boing blogger Justin Felix, my oeuvre suggests "the sorts of irredeemably meaningless movies Vladimir and Estragon might have made if they'd had a 16mm Eclair at their disposal."

Slowly, inexorably, the rift expanded, growing at the rate of thirty meters per day. By Thanksgiving a dozen evacuated communities had plummeted into the gulf, including State College, Lemont, Boalsburg, and Pine Grove Mills. Although there were predictable instances of severe melancholics interacting fatally with the phenomenon, inevitable suicide pacts by cliques of clinically depressed adolescents, and unavoidable casualties among homeless persons, farm animals, and woodland creatures, it claimed remarkably few lives. (Fortunately the void did not manifest itself in Utah, Nevada, or some other state with a high suicide rate.) Still, there was no question that Caltiki had to be stopped before FEMA ran short of resources and humanity ran out of places to hide.

Although the catastrophe was obviously metaphysical in nature, I can hardly fault the U.S. Army Corps of Engineers for attempting a technological fix. Not only did they have the manpower, to say nothing of a three-billion-dollar appropriation from Senator Kittman's subcommittee, they were also receiving advice around the clock from BP, a corporation that, having successfully capped the Deepwater Horizon oil well in the spring of 2010 after despoiling the Gulf of Mexico for over a hundred days, could boast of considerable experience in these matters. Impressed by the Army's assets, several prominent technocrats went on record with predictions that the abyss would be sutured shut within a month. But Caltiki was having none of it. The flagella snapped the web of steel girders like matchsticks, leaving the monster free to pursue its enigmatic agenda.

I felt equally hopeful when I learned from CNN that President Trilby, exercising her authority under the Unitary Executive War Powers Act, had implemented a policy of "strategic neutralization." The principle was perfectly sound. We all know from high-school chemistry that a pool of sulfuric acid may be rendered inert by adding sodium hydroxide to create an exothermic reaction whose end products are sodium sulfate and water, that is, $H_2SO_4 + 2NaOH \rightarrow Na_2SO_4 + 2H_2O$. It seemed logical to suppose, therefore, that Caltiki might be paralyzed through copious applications of sentimentality, to wit, Nihilism + Schmaltz $\rightarrow$ Insipidity + Tears. And so it was that countless Smurfs and Care Bears were thrown into the pit by preschool children bussed in from every state in the Union, even as their parents dumped wheelbarrow loads of garden gnomes, Charles Dickens novels, and Mother's Day cards, along with ten thousand emergency DVD transfers of Shirley Temple movies. When this gesture proved futile, Disney World was dismantled *in toto*, shipped to central Pennsylvania on flatcars, and surrendered in an epic gesture of propitiation, despite raucous protests from the Florida tourism industry. Plans were underway for sacrificing the Alamo stone by stone when President Trilby declared that her administration was abandoning its appeasement policy, a decision that occasioned jubilation throughout the state of Texas.

Shortly after the ingestion of Bellefonte, Senator Kittman's subcommittee arranged for a vanguard of Navy SEALs to reconnoiter the first two miles of the shaft. They returned bearing a fount of useful information. Rappelling gear would not be necessary, for the void boasted a narrow footpath spiraling ever downward like grooves in a rifle barrel. Besides hiking boots, utility belts, Kevlar jumpsuits, and thermal long-johns, our exploration team would also do well to wear pith helmets, as the overhanging crags were continually releasing what one scout described as "gobbets of incandescent oatmeal." The outriders found that they could palliate the omnipresent stench by donning face masks of the sort used by Muscovites during the peat-fire season. As for laptops, digital cameras, iPads, cell phones, and other portable electronic devices, we might as well leave them at home. There was no Wi-Fi in the abyss, and the amoeba made a point of using its psychokinetic abilities to fry any lithium batteries that came within a hundred yards of its domain.

On the night before our scheduled descent, the members of our intrepid quartet got to know one another over pints of Yuengling in the saloons of Altoona, a metropolis that, lying a mere nine miles from the gulf's leading edge, was scheduled for evacuation over the next seventy-two hours. Barhopping across the bewildered city, traveling incognito to avoid interrogation by the news media, hauling packs jammed with clean socks, flashlights, sleeping bags, MREs, and potable water, we soon realized that none of us fully understood how the idea of negotiating with Caltiki had first come about. I opened my CosmoBook and trolled the Internet, soon satisfying our collective curiosity. Although President Trilby wanted the world to believe that the policy had originated with her staff, even as a liberal think tank called the Montesquieu Institute likewise attempted to claim credit, it turned out that the godmother of our adventure was one Rhonda Scoursby, a Unitarian Universalist minister from Nashua, New Hampshire, whose YouTube video had gone so promiscuously viral that it came to the attention of the White House.

"My intuition tells me that the beast does not intend to be causing so much damage," said Reverend Scoursby, speaking into her fourteen-year-old son's digital camera. "This is almost certainly a case of cross-cultural misunderstanding. The proper plan of action is clear. We must assemble a team of crack nihilists and send them on a journey to the center of the void, their goal being to communicate with the amoeba and find out what it wants."

At the last minute Dudley Yarborough attempted to join our fellowship, no doubt seeking expiation for his sins, but the rest of us quickly agreed that, when it came to playing hardball with the abyss, he simply wasn't in our league. To the end we remained a community of four — spindly Egon Spackle, lead vocalist of the notorious *métal hurlant* band Shit Sandwich; brilliant Helga Arnheim, prominent public intellectual and author of *Das Nichts*, a Brechtian play about Josef Mengele's career at Auschwitz-Birkenau; elfin Myron Solomon, avant-garde mathematician and inventor of that distressing set of hypothetical numbers known as "division-by-zero resultoids"; and my overweight self, Jerome Mallow, perpetrator of such deplorable instances of cinematic Grand Guignol as *The Blood-Brain Barrier, Entrails, Entrails II, AtroCity, Teleology Lost, The Heat Death of the Universe, Ragnarök,* and *Ragnarök: the Sequel,* not to mention my five smash-hit homages, *Disillusionment of Caltiki, Resentment of Caltiki, Dionysian Revels of Caltiki, Bitter Wisdom of Caltiki,* and *Caltiki Fucks the World.*

Typical moment from a Jerome Mallow film: near the beginning of the third act of *AtroCity,* a freckle-faced adolescent walks into a McDonald's restroom, takes a piss, washes up, and avails himself of the blow-dryer — thereby triggering a blast of heat that melts the flesh from his hands. Ligaments seared away, the little finger-bones fall to the tiled floor with a crisp tinkling sound. We worked very hard on the Foley track. You can understand why the team needed me.

Our journey began on the twentieth of October. I must confess I was hoping we'd be home by Halloween, when I was scheduled to give a live prime-time interview on the Nausea Channel in conjunction with a forty-eight-hour marathon of films by horror auteurs Herschell Gordon Lewis, George Romero, David Cronenberg, and, yes, Jerome Mallow. The audience, I feared, would not regard my service on the expedition as a sufficient excuse for a no-show, since most of them had sided with the rift and didn't want to see it healed. But I had no control over the situation, each pair of coordinates on Caltiki's gullet marking a point of no return, and I resolved to put self-promotion out of my mind and concentrate on the odyssey at hand.

The first two days passed uneventfully, albeit unpleasantly, our descent haunted by the foul odor of the amoeba's breath and the percussive ploppings of the incandescent globules on our pith helmets. Although our flashlights shone brightly enough to guide our footsteps, the gloom grew so thick it became a palpable presence, an entity that feasted on light and excreted dung of infinite mass. The gelatinous walls glistened with an ectoplasmic excrescence, like the skin of an immense snail, even as the path mysteriously acquired an asphalt paving. With our every downward tread, the flagella increased in number and thickness, and by the morning of day three these undulating extrusions had so proliferated as to suggest a plantation of sea anemones thriving at the bottom of the Mariana Trench.

Day four brought an unexpected sight: a Swiss chalet embedded in the sticky walls, its front porch extending far enough to provide a platform for a wooden crossing-gate. Had the horizontal barrier not been on fire, we could have easily climbed over it, but as things stood we were stymied, the flames soaring upward to form an impassable rampart — and yet, paradoxically, the red tongues did not consume their fuel.

A fiftyish man with rheumy eyes, pallid skin, and feral hair hobbled onto the balcony of the chalet. His moustache was as broad and thick as the paintbrush he might have used to touch up the gingerbread ornamentation hanging from the eaves. He radiated unwellness, remaining upright only with the aid of a cane.

"I am the guardian of the first gate!" he screamed. "Be gone, decadent mortals!"

"Good God, it's Friedrich Nietzsche!" gasped Egon, who knew a thing or two about philosophy, having dropped out of Harvard before dropping out of Western civilization. "Zarathustra himself, everybody's favorite Antichrist — the one who foresaw Caltiki's coming!"

"Prescient I was when alive, and prescient I am today!" cried Nietzsche, corroborating Egon's praise. His chunky German accent evoked the way Werner Krauss would have sounded in *The Cabinet of Dr. Caligari* had it been a talkie. "In my own immortal words, 'Man would sooner have the void for his purpose than to be void of purpose'!"

"Please quench the fire," said Helga. "We're on a vital mission."

"Truths are illusions whose illusory nature has been forgotten!" proclaimed Nietzsche.

"The whole world is counting on us," noted Myron.

"Our metaphors have been worn smooth like guineas effaced by too much handling! Our words now function as mere metal and no longer as coins!"

"Leave this dude to me," Egon whispered to the rest of us. "January the third, 1889, Turin, the Piazza Carlo Alberto, Herr Doktor Nietzsche witnessing a coachman savagely beating his horse."

"I've heard that anecdote," said Helga. "Nietzsche hugs the poor animal and weeps like a motherless child."

"Go for it," I told Egon.

"Take no prisoners," said Myron.

Stepping as close to the fire as he could without igniting his long hair, the lead vocalist of Shit Sandwich held his flashlight like a microphone, cleared his throat, threw back his shoulders, and, fixing on the philosopher, sang with an intensity of feeling such as I'd not experienced since Alanis Morissette covered "Fever Dream" over the credits of *Entrails II*. As far as I could tell, Egon performed all three stanzas without a whiff of irony or one iota of irreverence.

Oh Danny boy, the pipes, the pipes are calling
From glen to glen, and down the mountain side
The summer's gone, and all the flowers are dying
'Tis you, 'tis you must go and I must bide.

But come ye back when summer's in the meadow
Or when the valley's hushed and white with snow
'Tis I'll be here in sunshine or in shadow
Oh Danny boy, oh Danny boy, I love you so.

And if you come, when all the flowers are dying
And I am dead, as dead I well may be
You'll come and find the place where I am lying
And kneel and say an "Ave" there for me.

The effect on Nietzsche was immediate and dramatic. His lower lip trembled uncontrollably. Tears squirted from his eyes like jets from a child's water pistol. His sobs reverberated off the walls of the rift, which for all their pulpiness produced a credible echo.

Like a wizard wielding his staff, Nietzsche raised his cane high, then aimed it at the flaming crossing-gate. Instantly the fire went out, and the arm flew upward, assuming a forty-five-degree angle.

"If you reach the monster, please don't reveal that I let you pass without a fight," said Nietzsche, wiping his tears with his sleeve. "Tell it that, after a ferocious battle, the four of you wrestled me to the ground. Once I realized I was defeated, I insisted that you crucify me on the balcony of my chalet."

"As you wish," said Egon.

"Assure the beast that I still regard pity as the most pathetic of emotions," the philosopher begged us. "Say nothing of 'Danny Boy.'"

We nodded synchronously.

"Perhaps you'd like to come along," Helga suggested. "We could use a man of your formidable intellect."

"What better ambassador to the abyss than Friedrich Nietzsche?" said Myron.

"Zarathustra does not desert his post!" the philosopher declared. "Now and forever, I shall remain true to my Kantian duty, even if Kant himself was a *schnorrer!*"

Marching forward, we passed beneath the raised gate without mishap, whereupon it dropped back into place. Before continuing on our way, we faced Nietzsche and permitted him to set us straight about a thing or two.

"Harken, Jerome Mallow, from whose *Bitter Wisdom of Caltiki* I have derived much aesthetic satisfaction!" shouted Nietzsche, gesturing toward the gate with his cane. The arm once again burst into flames. "To you I say, 'He who fights with monsters should look to it that he himself does not become a monster!' Hear me, Helga Arnheim, who has pondered the dark heart of the devil Mengele! To you I say, 'When you gaze into the abyss, take care that the abyss does not gaze into you!' Listen, Egon Spackle, troubadour of unpalatable truths! To you I say, 'It's all very well to make music, but now I challenge you to turn your own life into a work of art, as I have done!' Exiting the balcony, the philosopher slipped into the gloom of his chalet. "Heed my words, Professor Solomon, mathematician *extraordinaire!*" he called from out of the shadows. "To you I say, 'Your lust for knowledge is in truth a yearning for hell! Once you have exhausted all of nature with your science, you will next seduce damnation itself — a conquest that will leave you as hungry as ever, begging the universe for just one more crumb!'"

The four of us exchanged complex scowls whose meaning, *pace* Derrida, was unequivocal. Nietzsche might be a bona fide genius, but he was also a bit of a windbag, if not a megalomaniac. It was probably just as well he'd elected to remain behind.

Collectively we drew forth our kerchiefs, wiping the sweat of the circum-scribed inferno from our brows. We slaked our thirst with swigs from our can-teens, extended our walking poles, and, with the fire at our backs and Caltiki still to come, continued on our way.

What animal goes on four legs in the morning, on two legs at noon, and on three legs in the evening? Doubtless you recall the Riddle of the Sphinx. Surely you remember that the solution is Man. Yes, correct, *nolo contendere*: but then there are those animals that travel on six legs at all times, morning, noon, and evening — and also in the dead of night.

Can you guess what particular hexapodal creature presided over the second barrier on the black-brick road to Caltiki? Cineasts will immediately think of the quintessential 1950s giant-insect movie, *Them!*, which found Edmund Gwenn and James Whitmore coping with a colony of immense ants, but that is not the right answer. Litterateurs might say T.S. Eliot, who famously desired to be a pair of ragged claws scuttling across the floors of silent seas — and yet that reply must also be disqualified, crabs being ten-legged. This leaves only one possible solution.

The instant I clamped eyes on the immense vermin, over five feet long from head to rectum, I knew who he was. Ever since acquiring the movie rights to *The Metamorphosis* from Kurt Wolff Verlag — a major headache, let me tell you — I'd felt an intense rapport with this insect. And, indeed, I was the abys-sonaut to whom he first spoke.

"Jerome Mallow, we meet at last!" cried the cockroach in a voice evocative of the creaking diabolical mechanism that graced the climax of Roger Cor-man's *The Pit and the Pendulum*. "I want you to know I'm one of your most devoted aficionados. That said, I cannot let you pass."

This time our way was blocked by a ferocious helix of steel wire, its razor-sharp barbs grinning in the beams of our flashlights. The insect sentinel lay crouched atop his dwelling-place: a battered, corroded Quonset hut protrud-ing from the surrounding membrane like a rusty nail holding a blintz to a dartboard. His segmented antennae moved up and down with the rhythmic alternations of a timpanist working his mallets.

"We have an appointment with the void," I said. "Kindly remove your wire."

"Nowhere in the cinema of pessimism does *Disillusionment of Caltiki* find its equal," said the insect. "I'm sorry you never found funding for *The Meta-morphosis*. You would've done me proud. Please go away."

"Is that who I think it is?" asked Helga Arnheim, pointing toward the ver-min. "*Als Gregor Samsa eines Morgens aus unruhigen Träumen erwachte —*"

"One and the same," I said.

"I want you all to depart this instant," Gregor Samsa declared.

"You want us to depart — and you desire something else as well," I said.

The cockroach's antennae stopped twitching. He fixed me with both compound eyes. "And what might that be?"

"You know, my dear Gregor."

"Do I?"

"Climb down!" I commanded.

Limb by spindly limb, the vermin scrabbled from the roof of the Quonset hut to the ground. At one point his abdomen crashed against the corrugated tin shell, sending forth reverberations suggesting a bell calling pilgrims to some incomprehensible rite.

The instant Gregor attained his front yard, I threw myself upon him. Wrapping my arms around his carapace, I accorded the insect an impassioned embrace. He smelled of decaying eggs and festering fish heads. Gagging, I pressed my lips to his thorax, his mouthparts, his many-lensed eyes. I kissed the symbolic apple that his father, in an act of inordinate cruelty, had lodged in his back. At first my colleagues simply stood and stared, simultaneously appalled and appreciative — but then they, too, lavished affection on Gregor, tenderly stroking his every mound and crevice. For the better part of an hour, caresses were bestowed and reciprocated, moans exuberantly traded, bodily fluids luxuriantly exchanged.

"Until you four came down the road, my life was utterly barren," the cockroach told us. "How can I ever repay you?"

We told him how, and there followed an event so remarkable that I hope to put it in a movie one day. With surprising aplomb Gregor clamped his mouthparts around one end of the steel wire and began drawing it into his body, inch by inch, foot by foot, an image suggesting nothing so much as a reverse-motion shot of a spider releasing a filament of silk from her spinneret. A harsh and bitter meal, to be sure — and yet Gregor seemed to thrive on it: a ringing vindication, I decided, of Nietzsche's assertion that we are strengthened by every ordeal short of annihilation. As we tramped past the Quonset hut and continued on our way, the insect reared back, balanced himself adroitly on his cloaca, and, having assumed a posture evocative of multi-armed Kali, waved at us with all six of his legs.

"Farewell, Gregor!" I cried, glancing toward the gesticulating cockroach. "We'll explain to Caltiki that you didn't let us go without a fight!"

"No — don't!"

"No?"

"Tell the beast the truth — tell him I wouldn't let you go without a kiss!" Gregor insisted. "Godspeed, Jerome Mallow! I hope we get to make our movie sooner rather than later!"

As our fellowship continued its descent, fissures appeared beneath our feet, and soon the asphalt sheathing dissolved into chunks resembling the lowest grades of bituminous coal. Even as our path crumbled, it also narrowed, until we found ourselves walking along a precarious ledge, hemmed by the membrane on one side and open air on the other: a seven-mile drop to Caltiki's brow or brain or whatever dorsal aspect it presented to the world. Egon Spackle and I advanced with particular caution, fearful that, having made our contributions to the quest — the beguiling of Nietzsche, the seduction of Gregor Samsa — we were now considered expendable by whatever arcane powers lay behind the abyss.

We rounded a corner. A bungalow appeared, plated in gold and studded with gemstones. The dazzling edifice spanned the lane and extended into the void, defying gravity by means of foundational flying buttresses. The sign on the front door read, *Enter of Your Own Free Enterprise*, which is exactly what we did, forthwith finding ourselves in a room opulently appointed with a Persian rug, Tiffany lamps, and a suede sofa of such apparent softness it suggested a therapeutic mud-bath.

Seated at a poker table swathed in green baize, our host made lucid pantomimic gestures, inviting us to assume the four empty chairs. He was a vigorous man in middle age, with a costly tan and an auburn toupee. We sat down as instructed, whereupon our host, still saying nothing, provided each of us with a thousand dollars in blue, red, and white chips. Silently he dealt a game of five-card draw, then opened for eighty dollars. Everyone stayed in. Myron requested one card. Egon, Helga, and I each drew three. The dealer stood pat, subsequently wagering his entire stack of chips. I dropped out, having no faith in my pair of eights. Helga likewise left the game, as did Egon. Myron matched the dealer's extravagant investment.

Speaking for the first time, our host said, "Take today's lesson to heart, gentlemen," then showed his hand: a ten-high straight. "Gamble only with other people's money, but keep the winnings for yourself."

"Although in this particular instance," noted Myron, revealing his diamond flush, "the winnings are moving in an unexpected direction."

Our host scowled and snorted. "The rear door to my cottage is locked, and I've hidden the key where you'll never find it. Try climbing over the fucking roof, and I'll push the ejector button, hurtling you into the void. In short, I'm the best and brightest of the rift's guardians. You might as well turn around and head back to Altoona."

"Not before we learn who you are," said Myron, raking in his pot.

"Roscoe Prudhomme. You've never heard of me. I'm not in the same fucking pantheon with your Nietzsche or your Kafka or your Marquis de Sade, but as the principal architect of the most insidious and socially useless financial products of all time, I can say I've made my contribution to nihilism's ascent."

Prudhomme went on to explain how, way back in 1994, he and two dozen of his fellow JPMorganers were enjoying an off-site weekend in Boca Raton when — everyone having tired of the yacht parties, bikini-model parades, and $3,000 double magnums of Cristal — the conversation turned to the U.S. Government's pesky requirement that a bank must keep billions of inert dollars on hand in case its clients, be they corporations or countries, began defaulting on their loans en masse. Inevitably the JPMorganers posed a challenge to themselves. Might they design a financial product certain of protecting them from the slings and arrows of unreliable borrowers even as it freed up vast quantities of capital?

"And suddenly I had it!" cried Prudhomme. "An unprecedented sort of third-party contract that would allow us to erase all risk of unpaid loans from our books and put it on the ledgers of nonfinancial institutions such as indemnity companies and pension funds!"

"I don't know what you're talking about," I said.

"Neither do I," said Egon.

"Neither does anyone else," said Prudhomme. "That's the fucking beauty of it."

"But you were a *bank*," said Helga. "You were *supposed* to have risk on your books."

"I'll never forget that sunny day in Boca Raton," said Prudhomme, ignoring Helga's admonishment. "The excitement was electric. It was like working on the fucking Manhattan Project. They should put a plaque on the wall, like the one at the University of Chicago commemorating the first self-sustaining nuclear chain reaction. 'In this conference room the credit-default swap was born.'"

"But you forgot to ask a crucial question," Myron insisted. "What if one of those compliant third parties doesn't have the money to pay up? Obviously this would create — dare I say it? — a chain reaction, one default leading to another, with investors bailing out left and right. You should have foreseen that, Roscoe."

"Actually we did foresee it, but we went ahead and started selling our swaps anyway — how's *that* for state-of-the-art cynicism?"

"If you're such a hotshot financier, why aren't you on Wall Street right now, making a million dollars a day?" asked Helga. "Why do you waste your time down here?"

"Because I'm fucking *dead*, that's why," Prudhomme replied. "Not long after the crash of 2008, my conscience got the better of me. I decided I'd created a Frankenstein monster, guaranteed to increase the sum of misery in the world, so I put a bullet through my brain. In recent months I've come to regret that decision. My guilt has all but evaporated. Knowing he'll be hanged in the morning wonderfully concentrates a man's mind, but the abyss does an even better job."

"Unlike my friends, I *do* know something about derivatives," Myron told our host. "It happens that you're talking to the inventor of division-by-zero resultoids. You want my advice? Forget your pathetic little investment strategies. Forget swaps, futures, options, hedge funds, arbitrage, endorsements in blank, collateralized debt obligations, marked-to-market assets, and securitizing your grandmother." The mathematician unfurled his fingers and patted the breast pocket of his jumpsuit. "I happen to be carrying a blueprint for the most lucrative financial instrument since the popes were peddling their eschatological insurance policies back in the Middle Ages."

"Myron Solomon, am I right?" said our host, his astonished jaw swinging open. "I read about you in *Discover*! It's a pleasure to meet you, sir" — the banker seized the mathematician's hand, shaking it vigorously — "a pleasure and a privilege!"

"I detested that *Discover* profile," said Myron. "The reporter was some sort of Trotskyite."

"Dr. Solomon, you'll be interested to know that, before too long, the poker tournament of the millennium will occur at this table." Prudhomme tapped the baize with his index finger. "Fifteen successive days of Dallas Balls-to-the-Wall, a five-hundred-million-dollar buy-in, no limits on bets or raises. The late, great Ken Lay of Enron is in the rec room right now, playing Pac-Man and raring to go. We're still waiting for the incomparable Keating to die — Charlie Keating of that gorgeous savings-and-loan swindle — likewise the inimitable Madoff. Bernie's son hanged himself awhile back — maybe you heard, terrible tragedy — so Mark would be the logical fifth, but he's lousy at cards and knows it. Do you understand what I'm offering you, Dr. Solomon? Your friends must go home, but you can have a piece of the action."

"I don't want a piece of your damn action. I want — "

"I know what you want. All right, Myron. Very well. Give me the blueprint, and I'll give you the key to the back door."

"Give me the key to the back door," retorted Myron, "and I'll give you the blueprint." From his vest pocket he produced a business envelope, dangling it in front of Prudhomme like a felinophile tempting a domestic shorthair with a catnip mouse. "You know about pyramid schemes, Roscoe, including the innovations wrought by your friend Madoff. My device is three times as lucrative, four times as sustainable, and five times more difficult to regulate. It's called a tesseract scheme."

"A tesseract scheme?" said Prudhomme, rising from his chair. "As in the famous four-dimensional hypercube?"

"I'm impressed with your knowledge of higher mathematics," said Myron.

"When the credit-default swap emerged from my brow, I was the smartest guy in the room," said Prudhomme.

Approaching a particle-board bookcase, the financier withdrew an ostensible Ronald Reagan biography, then flipped back the cover to reveal that it was in fact a cedarwood receptacle. From the compartment he removed a gold key, then pressed it into Myron's palm. Casting me a freighted glance, Myron indicated with his eyes that I should vacate my seat and sidle toward the back door. Nonchalantly I repositioned myself as my fellow explorer had requested.

Prudhomme rubbed his hands as if lathering a bar of soap. He retrieved the envelope, broke the seal, and removed a single sheet of paper. "This had better be good," he said, unfolding the page.

"Now!" cried Myron, delivering the key into my possession with a deft lateral pass.

I jammed the implement into the hole, rotated my wrist, pulled open the door. Helga leaped out of her chair and sprinted through the jamb, followed by Egon, Myron, and myself.

"Wait a minute!" shouted Prudhomme. "This doesn't look like a tesseract scheme! This looks like a goddamn chess problem!"

"It *is* a goddamn chess problem!" cried Myron as the four of us raced along the path.

"Come back here, you generation of vipers! You fucking velociraptors! You scumbag Bolsheviks!"

"So long, sucker!" replied Myron. "We'll give your regards to Caltiki!"

For a full half-hour we frantically pursued the twisting bore of the void, our boots pounding the crumbling asphalt, our flashlights etching silvery veins on the throbbing walls. Only after the last echo of Prudhomme's curses died away did we dare decelerate, our mad dash becoming a steady jog and then a brisk walk.

The following day — weary and hungry, dazed and bewildered — we arrived at the bottom of the abyss. Huddling together in Caltiki's mammoth shadow, drawing what solace we could from one another's company, we strove to project a manifest deference toward the object of our quest. As large as Gregor Samsa's Quonset hut, the thing was indeed an amoeba: a quivering, gunky, funky, one-celled spheroid of protoplasm, evocative of the very mass of cow intestines from which Freda and Bava had fashioned their original *Mostro Immortale*. A dozen tentacle-like pseudopods radiated from the amoeba's great blobby core. Its food vacuole held an unlit marijuana joint as large as a canoe.

"You may address me as 'Your Lordship,'" said the behemoth in a thunderous voice, its power to intimidate diminished only slightly by an endearing lisp. "I shall address you however I see fit."

"We are honored to be in Your Lordship's presence," I said.

"You are surely among the greatest and most powerful beings in the galaxy," said Helga.

"If not the universe," said Egon.

"Cut the bullshit," said Caltiki.

"Yes, Your Lordship," Egon, Helga, and I replied in unison.

"I apologize for all the mess topside," the monster continued. "There was probably an easier way to get your attention than devouring a college town and the adjacent communities, but I couldn't think of one."

"The damage estimates begin at around three billion dollars," noted Myron.

"So sue me."

"We wouldn't dream of it, Your Lordship," I said.

"You obviously have much to teach us," said Helga.

"Stop it," Caltiki admonished us, igniting the spliff with a firebrand. "Sycophancy does not become you. Don't hide your lights under a bushel, O my guests. You got past Nietzsche, an accomplishment worth bragging about. Allow me to salute you." The monster proceeded to do just that, gesturing respectfully with all twelve of its pseudopods. "You circumvented the cockroach. Very resourceful. You outfoxed Roscoe Prudhomme. Most impressive. In short, you have proven yourselves worthy of an audience with the abyss. Shall I tell you why your species is in so much trouble?"

"Oh, yes," I said.

"Indeed," said Egon.

"Please do," said Myron.

"You have our complete attention," said Helga.

Caltiki sucked in a profligate portion of cannabis smoke. "We'll begin with a history lesson. For the past twenty-five hundred years, every time a great sage was born into your world, the same three mystics mounted their camels and rode to the nativity site bearing gold, frankincense, and myrrh. But who, really, were these magi? They were Zoroastrians, that's who, Persian astrologers, keepers of a philosophic tradition tracing all the way back to 600 B.C. — and the proprietors of the single worst idea your human race has ever devised."

"The single worst?" echoed Helga, transfixed.

"I refer to the notion that all sentient souls can be neatly sorted into the saved and the lost — the enlightened and the benighted, the virtuous children of Ormazd and the vicious adherents of Ahriman." Caltiki took another toke. "The gold, frankincense, and myrrh were simply a ruse for getting past the midwives and reaching the cradles of Plato, Christ, and the rest. In every case, Balthazar, Caspar, and Melchior bent over the newborn infant and whispered their poisonous dichotomy into his little ear. 'Ormazd versus Ahriman, Ormazd versus Ahriman, Ormazd versus Ahriman . . .'"

"The argument gets resurrected in the third century A.D. as Manichaeism," Helga explained to our fellowship.

"The sands of time make their inexorable descent," said Caltiki. "The babies become adults, strutting one by one onto the stage of history. Plato and his students, tidily dividing the population of Athens into clever Socratics and clueless Sophists. Jesus and his apostles, deftly separating eternity-bound sheep from eternally damned goats. Mohammed and his followers, blithely pitting believers against infidels. Descartes and his disciples, coolly sundering the biosphere, thinking humans on one side, unfeeling animals on the other. Marx and his coterie, confidently cleaving *Homo sapiens* into a capitalist bourgeoisie and its proletarian victims. Need I go on? O my guests, from an amoeba's perspective it's an intolerably bizarre way to look at the world — and by the evidence of your history it's a bloody-minded way as well. If Nietzsche had appreciated what Zoroaster was *really* about, he would never have chosen him as his mouthpiece. Thus spake Caltiki."

Silence settled over the abyss, a quietude so complex and dense it fully befitted the magisterial amoeba before whose throne we stood. At last Helga spoke.

"It would appear that we find ourselves at a crossroads," she told our fellowship.

"Somehow we must progress past dualism," I said, realizing for the first time that I was in love with Helga.

"Sign me up," said Egon.

"Hear, hear!" said Myron. "Though I cannot imagine how we'll go about it."

"I would invite you to ponder the material cause of your sickness," said the monster. "An effective cure normally requires a correct diagnosis. Look at your own naked bodies in the mirror. What do you see? A radical form of bilateral symmetry, that's what. Dualistic arms, legs, ears, nipples, buttocks. Submit yourself to an autopsy, and it's the same story. Dualistic lungs, kidneys, auricles, ventricles, cerebral hemispheres. Thus spake Caltiki."

"No *wonder* we're all Manichaeans at heart," said Helga, heaving a sigh. "It's bred into our bones. What a brilliant analysis, Your Lordship!"

"Don't patronize me."

"I'm not," said Helga. "I really believe you're onto something."

"Even if we accept your conclusion, I don't see what we can do about it," I said. "We can't turn ourselves into asymmetrical invertebrates like you."

Myron said, "Though when I consider recent breakthroughs in genetic engineering, I sense that something along those lines might be arranged."

"The ingenuity of humans never ceases to amaze me," said Caltiki. "Still, you won't be going monolateral anytime soon, and meanwhile the abyss is gaining on you. If you're serious about climbing out of your hole, you might start by attempting some cognitive restructuring vis-à-vis your local giant amoeba from hell."

"I'm sure I speak for the whole group when I say we're willing to give it a try," said Helga.

"You think of me as a creature apart — am I right?" said Caltiki. "An anomalous monster, possibly malign, possibly benevolent in a *Star Trek* sort of way, but always a monster. Horse manure. Grow up, people. There are no creatures apart. There are no monsters. Read your Darwin. I'm an amoeba, for Christ's sake. A particularly large amoeba, but still an amoeba. Tunnel deep into the earth, and you'll discover my living relatives. Study the fossil record, and you'll come upon my extinct ancestors. My line is legitimate. Domain, *Eukaryota*. Kingdom, *Amoebozoa*. Phylum, *Tubulinea*. Genus and species, *Amoeba proteus*. My pedigree is entirely in order — and so is yours. In fact, if you look back far enough into the mists of antiquity, you'll find that amoebas, people, petunias, and all other creatures are intimately and materially and perhaps even spiritually connected, though I've never really liked that word, 'spiritually.' Every time I hear it, I see another dualism on the wing."

"Caltiki means to say we're all DNA-bearing eukaryotes under the skin," Myron explained to me, as if I didn't know, which I didn't. "Now, I suppose one *could* argue for a primal dichotomy between eukaryotes and prokaryotes, but at the end of the day even *they're* on the same continuum."

"As for my epithet, *mostro immortale* — what an absurdity!" wailed Caltiki. "When it comes to eluding death, O my guests, I'll have no greater success than you." The amoeba inhaled a cloud of euphoriant. "And that is all I know. Thus spake Caltiki. This interview is over."

"Just one more question, Your Lordship," said Myron. "As we march back to the surface, will we have to deal with the three guardians again?"

"You won't have to *march* at all," Caltiki replied, lifting up three pseudo-pods to reveal a hole about the diameter of the wishing well in my most erotic movie, *Snow White and the Seven-Year Latency Period*. "Have your forgotten your Heidegger? Go ahead, O my guests. Take the plunge. You can trust me."

We hesitated for a protracted interval, our vociferous debate punctuated by periods of nonverbal fretting. In the end we decided the amoeba was telling the truth, and so we held hands, closed our eyes, and made the leap.

The rest of the story is not mine to tell, except in the most trivial sense — yes, we did fall upward, returning to Altoona unharmed, and, yes, I did get back in time for my live appearance on the Nausea Channel. But now the narrative belongs to *Homo sapiens* per se. The ball is in our collective court. We'd better not take the Manichaean bait again. The moving pseudopod writes and, having writ, moves on.

Ever since the great gulf sealed itself, we four explorers have been fighting the good fight on behalf of asymmetry. I have nothing but praise for Myron Solomon's best-seller, *What To Do Until the Amoeba Comes: A Personal Inquiry into the Modern Malaise, with Answers in the Back of the Book*. No less impressive are Egon Spackle's recent efforts. After dissolving Shit Sandwich and reforming the band as Cheerful Despair, he produced a hit album, *Krapp's Penultimate Tape*, including a half-dozen songs that invite the listener to apprehend the world from an amorphous invertebrate's perspective. But I must reserve my supreme encomiums for the encyclopedic, three-part, nine-hour anti-dualism play written by my new bride, Helga Arnheim-Mallow. Winner of the Pulitzer Prize, *Fixing the Abyss* is a thoughtful and nuanced celebration of that rare bird, the genuine monist, a breed of thinker that historically includes, by Helga's reckoning, Epicurus, Isaac Newton, Percy Bysshe Shelley, the fourteenth Dalai Lama, and nobody else. Rumor has it that Dudley Yarborough, the scholar who brought us the void, has just incorporated *Fixing the Abyss* into his syllabus.

As for my own answer to the amoeba's challenge, I am pleased to report that my film adaptation of *The Metamorphosis*, music by Egon Spackle, is cleaning up at the box office. If this trend continues, the profits will be sufficient to underwrite *Caltiki in the Most Plausible of All Possible Worlds*, which I believe is my best script ever. True, the critics savaged my decision to give Gregor Samsa's story an obliquely happy ending, but I believe that Kafka — who had a better sense of humor than most movie reviewers — would forgive me.

Before dropping dead, Gregor meets one of his contemporaries, Raymond Dart, the South African anatomist who discovered the first *Australopithecus* fossils, those unequivocal links between human beings and extinct anthropoid apes. Thanks to Professor Dart, Gregor learns that he isn't quite as alienated as he believed. Domain, *Eukaryota*. Kingdom, *Animalia*. Phylum, *Arthropoda*. Class, *Insecta*. Order, *Blattaria*. And so on.

"So you see," says Dart, anticipating what Caltiki will tell our expedition one hundred years later, "there are no creatures apart. There are no monsters. You are not alone."

"Cold comfort, that," says Gregor.

"Do you think you're the only entity on earth to experience existential dread?" says the anatomist to the insect. "Do you think you're the sole being in the Western world who's had an encounter with nothingness? Get over yourself, Gregor. Yes, what I'm dishing up is cold comfort, but that's better than nobody giving you any sort of comfort! I'm making an effort here!"

For some reason, these remarks strike Gregor Samsa as hysterically funny, and Raymond Dart starts laughing as well. Soon the insect and the anatomist are hugging, kissing, and guffawing up a storm. A veritable deluge of salt water spills from the dying cockroach's eyes, flowing forth into the theater — *The Metamorphosis* is being exhibited in 3-D and Tactiloscope — an event that initially proves disconcerting to the audience. But in time they realize there's no cause for fear and trembling. It's only a movie. Even the most nihilistic filmmaker would not drown his own patrons. And so they sit back and relax, bathed in an unfathomable sadness while swimming in a river made of Gregor's enigmatic tears, until at long last the strange currents bear everyone safely home.

The Wisdom of the Skin

Even as I hauled his shivering body from the river and dragged it onto the pier, examining his ancient face as a numismatist might scrutinize a rare coin, I did not recognize him. He was supposed to be dead, after all — killed along with his wife when their rental Citroën transmuted into a fireball following its collision with a concrete wall in Florence. Not until he'd stopped wheezing, lifted his head, and placed a kiss of gratitude on my cheek did I understand that the newspaper accounts of his incineration had been false. This was surely Bruno Pearl. I'd been privileged to rescue the genius who'd given his audiences *Sphinx Recumbent*, *Flowering Judas*, and a dozen other masterpieces of copulation.

Just as musical comedy eclipsed operetta — just as silent movies killed vaudeville, talkies usurped the silents, and television reduced radio drama to a prolix mockery of itself — so did the coming of the Siemanns plasmajector spell the demise of the sex artists, whose achievements today survive largely in the memories of aging aficionados. I shall always regret that I never saw a live concert. How enthralling it must have been to enter a public park during the last century knowing that you might witness a pair of high-wire sensualists, avant-garde couplers, or Viennese orgasmeisters. It was an age of giants. Sara and Jaspar. Quentin and Alessandra. Roger and Dominic. The anonymous Phantoms of Delight. Teresa and Gaston, also known as the Portions of Eternity. Marge and Annette, who styled themselves Enchanted Equinox. You might even find yourself in the legendary presence of Bruno and Mina Pearl.

During my student days at the New England School of Art and Design, I was shrewd enough to take Aesthetics 101: Metaphysics of the Physical, taught by the benignly deranged Nikolai Vertankowski. Thanks to Vertankowski's extensive collection of pirate videos and bootleg DVDs, his students experienced tantalizing intimations of the medium in which Bruno Pearl and his wife discovered such transcendent possibilities. We learned of the couple's chance meeting at the audition for Trevor Paisley's defiant presentation of *Oedipus Rex* (it began with Antigone's conception), as well as their early struggles on the eros circuit and their eventual celebrity. At the height of the lovers' fame nobody came close to matching their carnal sorcery, their lubricious magic, that bewitchment for which there is no name. Vertankowski also taught us about Bruno and Mina's uncanny and unaccountable decline: the inexplicable fact that, when their Citroën exploded, they hadn't given a memorable performance in over two years.

Throughout the workweek I cross the Hudson twice a day, riding the ferry back and forth between the unfocused city of Hoboken, where I live, and the cavernous reaches of lower Manhattan, where I ply my trade. A decade ago my independent film company, Kaleidoscope Productions, received an Oscar nomination for *The Rabble Capitalists*, a feature-length documentary about the unlicensed peddlers of Gotham, those dubious though ambitious folk you see selling fake Rolexes, remaindered books, and sweatshop toys on street corners and in subway stations. Alas, my success was fleeting, and I eventually resigned myself to a career in cranking out instructional videos (tedious and talky shorts intended to galvanize sales forces, inspire stockholders, and educate dentists' captive audiences). One of these days I'm going to sell the business and return to my former life as the SoHo bohemian who signed her oil paintings "Boadicea," though my name is really Susan Fiore.

The night I delivered Bruno Pearl from death, my mood was not far from the syndrome explicated in the Kaleidoscope video called *Coping with Clinical Depression*. At the beginning of the week I'd broken up with Anson, a narcissistic though talented sculptor for whom I'd compliantly aborted a pregnancy one month earlier. As always occurs when I lose a lover, I'd assumed a disproportionate share of the blame, and I was now engaged in a kind of penance, pacing around on the ferry's frigid upper level as the wind cut through my fleece jacket and iced my bones. Despite my melancholy, I took note of the old man, the only other passenger on the weather deck. He was leaning over the stern rail, a skeletal septuagenarian in a tweed overcoat, his face as compacted as a hawk's, his nose supporting a pair of eyeglasses, one lens held in place by a ratty pink Band-Aid. He stared at the Statue of Liberty, an intense gaze, far-reaching, immune to the horizon. My forlorn companion, it seemed, could see all the way to Lisbon.

Glancing north, I fixed on the brightly lit George Washington Bridge, each great sagging cable gleaming like a rope of luminous opals. Anson believed that our descendants will regard suspension bridges with the same admiration we ourselves accord cathedrals and clipper ships, and tonight I understood what he meant. I turned back to the Statue of Liberty. The gentleman with the broken glasses was gone. In his place — a void: negative space, to use one of Anson's favorite terms.

I peered over the rail. If suicide had been the old man's aim, he'd evidently thought better of the decision; he was thrashing about amid the ferry's widening wake with a desperation indistinguishable from panic. For a fleeting instant the incongruity transfixed me — the lower Hudson, an aquatic wasteland, a place for concrete quays and steel scows but not this fleshy jetsam — and then I tossed aside my rucksack, inhaled sharply, and jumped.

Anyone who has ever studied under Nikolai Vertankowski knows better than to equate performance intercourse with displays of more recent vintage. Today's amateur exhibitionists and open-air stunt fuckers, the professor repeatedly reminded us, are not carrying on a tradition; they are desecrating it. For the true sex artist, all was subtext, all was gesture and grace. In revealing their skin to the world, the classical copulationists achieved not pornographic nudity but pagan nakedness. When Bruno and Mina ruled the eros circuit, they shed each garment so lissomely, planted each kiss so sublimely, and applied each caress so generously that the spectators experienced this tactile cornucopia no less than the lovers themselves.

Then, of course, there was the conversation. Before and after any overt hydraulics, Bruno and Mina always talked to each other, trading astute observations and reciting stanzas of poetry they'd composed especially for the occasion. Sensitive women wept at this linguistic foreplay. Canny men took notes. But the connections themselves remained the sine qua non of each concert. By the time they were famous, Bruno and Mina had perfected over a dozen acts, including not only *Sphinx Recumbent* and *Flowering Judas* but also *Fearful Symmetry*, *Sylph and Selkie*, *Chocolate Babylon*, *Holy Fools*, *Menses of Venus*, *Onan in Avalon*, *Beguiling Serpent*, *Pan and Syrinx*, and *Fleur de Lis*. When their passions were spent, their skins sated, and their reservoirs of post-coital verse exhausted, Bruno and Mina simply got dressed and watched approvingly as the spectators dropped coins and folding money into their gold-hinged mahogany coffer.

Performance copulators lived by a code, a kind of theatric chivalry, its nuances known only to themselves. None had an agent or manager. They never published their touring schedules or distributed press kits. Souvenir mongering was forbidden. Videotaping by spectators was tolerated but frowned upon. The artists always arrived unexpectedly, without fanfare, like a goshawk swooping down on a rabbit or a fox materializing in a henhouse. Naturally they favored the major venues, appearing frequently in Golden Gate Park, Brussels Arboretum, Kensington Gardens, and Versailles, but sometimes they brought their brilliance to the humblest of small-town greens and commons. Quixotic tutelaries. Daemons of the flesh. Now you saw them, now you didn't.

Although I had never before attempted the maneuvers illustrated in the Kaleidoscope video called *Deep Water Rescue*, my relationship with that particular short was so intimate that, upon entering the Hudson, I spontaneously assumed a backstroke position, placed one hand under the drowning man's chin, bade him relax, and, kicking for motive power, towed him to Jersey. The instant I levered him onto the derelict wharf, his teeth started chattering, but he nevertheless managed to explain that his eyeglasses had slipped from his face and how in grabbing for them he'd lost his balance and tumbled over the rail. He chastised himself for never learning to swim. Then came the kiss on the cheek — and then the flash of recognition.

"You're Bruno Pearl," I told him.

Instead of acknowledging my assertion, he patted his pants, front and back, soon determining that his wallet and keys had survived the misadventure. "Such a wonderfully courageous, a *foolishly* courageous young woman." His teeth continued to vibrate, castanets in the hands of a lunatic. "Tell me your name, dear lady."

"Susan Fiore."

"Call me John."

"You're Bruno Pearl," I informed him again. When you've just saved a person's life, a certain impertinence comes naturally. "You're Bruno Pearl, and the world believes you're dead."

He made no response, but instead rubbed each arm with the opposite hand. "In my experience, lovely Susan," he said at last, "appearances are deceiving."

Whether this was Bruno Pearl or not, my obligation to him clearly had not ended. My beneficiary's most immediate problem was not his lost eyeglasses — though he said he was functionally blind without them — but the threat of hypothermia. When the gentleman revealed that he lived in north Hoboken, near the corner of Willow Avenue and 14th Street, I proposed that we proceed directly to my apartment, a mere two blocks from the wharf.

He readily assented, and so I took him by the hand and led him into the nocturnal city.

By the time we reached my apartment he'd stopped shivering. Supplying him with a dry wardrobe posed no challenge: although my ex-lovers are a heterogeneous bunch, they share a tendency to leave their clothes behind. That night Bruno received Warren's underwear, Jack's socks, Craig's dungarees, and Ken's red polo shirt. I actually had more difficulty replacing my own soggy attire, but eventually I found a clean blouse and presentable khakis.

While Bruno got dressed, I spread the contents of his wallet — money, credit cards, an ancient snapshot of Mina — across the kitchen counter to dry. Next I telephoned the ferry terminal: good news — not only had some admirable soul turned in my abandoned rucksack, the dispatcher was willing to hold it for me. Before Bruno emerged from the bedroom, I managed to feed my cat, Leni, an affectionate calico with a strong sense of protocol, and prepare hot tea for the artist and myself. The instant he appeared in the kitchen, I handed him a steaming mug of oolong, seeking to elevate both his spirits and his core temperature.

"I had a college professor once, Nikolai Vertankowski, your most devoted fan," I told him as, tea mugs in hand, we moved from my cramped kitchen to my correspondingly miniscule parlor. "We spent most of Aesthetics 101 watching Bruno and Mina tapes, especially the Boston Common concerts."

He settled into my wing chair, fluted his lips, and at long last drew a measure of liquid warmth into his body. He frowned. "Mina and I never authorized any recordings," he muttered, acknowledging his identity for the first time. "Your professor trafficked in contraband."

"He knew that," I replied. "The man was obsessed. Probably still is."

Leni jumped into Bruno's lap, tucked her forelegs beneath her chest, and purred. "Obsessed," he echoed, taking a second swallow of tea. He brushed Leni's spine, his palm smoothing her fur like a spatula spreading frosting on a cake. "Obsession is something I can understand — obsession with thanatos, obsession with the élan vital. Speaking of life, I owe you mine. In return, I shall grant you any favor within my capabilities."

"Talk to me."

"A great sex artist is celebrated for his conversation," he said, nodding.

"Talk to me, Bruno Pearl. Tell me the truth about yourself."

"There was a bullet," he said.

There was a bullet. But before the bullet, there was a triumphant performance in Philadelphia. On only two previous occasions had Mina and Bruno accomplished *Fleur de Lis* plus *Holy Fools* in a single afternoon. The Fairmount Park concert had elicited raucous cheers, rapturous sighs, and thunderous applause.

To celebrate their success, the artists treated themselves to a lobster dinner in their hotel room, followed by a stroll along the Delaware. At some undefined moment they crossed an indeterminate boundary, moving beyond the rehabilitated sector of Front Street, with its well-lighted walkways and quaint restaurants, and entering the warehouse district, domain of illegal transactions in flesh and pharmaceuticals. Under normal conditions the artists might have noted their seedy surroundings, spun around in a flurry of self-preservation, and headed south, but they were too intoxicated by their recent success: *Fleur de Lis* and *Holy Fools* — both in the same concert!

The bullet came from above, flying through a window on the second floor of a gutted factory and subsequently following its evil and inexorable trajectory downward. Bruno would later remember that the shot was the first in a series. A heroin deal gone wrong, he later surmised, or possibly a violent altercation between a prostitute and her pimp.

Spiraling toward Mina, the bullet drilled through the left side of her head, drove bits of skull into her cerebral cortex, entered her midbrain, and lodged in her cerebellum.

"Oh, my God," I said.

"Those were my exact words," said Bruno. " 'Oh, my God!' I screamed."

"Did she die?"

Bruno pleasured my cat with his long delicate fingers. "The odds were against her," he replied cryptically.

Mina, delirious, collapsed in Bruno's arms, blood geysering from the wound. He laid her on the asphalt. It was surprisingly warm. Somehow he remained sane enough to administer first aid, tearing off his shirt and bandaging her leaking head. He carried her one block west and hailed a cab. The driver, a Mexican, ten years behind the wheel, had seen worse, much worse, and without a breath of hesitation he drove them to Thomas Jefferson Memorial Hospital. Twenty minutes after her arrival in the emergency room, Mina lay beneath two halogen lamps, hovering on the cusp of oblivion as a surgical team struggled to reassemble her shattered brain.

A soothing and attractive Pakistani nurse directed Bruno down the hall to an ecumenical chapel — a dark place, soft, small, stinking of lilies and candle wax. He was the only patron. Religious music of unknown origin and protean denomination wafted through the air. The artist believed in neither God, Jesus, Allah, nor Krishna. He beseeched them all. He solicited divine intervention more devoutly than when, at age ten, he still knew, absolutely knew, that God always came through for you in the end, that it was just a matter of waiting.

"After I finished praying, I held my hand over a candle flame." Bruno showed me his right palm. The pale, fibrous scar had pulled the skin into a shape resembling a Star of David. "To this day, I'm not sure why I did it. A kind of oblation, I suppose. I felt nothing at first. A tickle. I actually smelled my burning flesh before I apprehended the pain."

Near dawn a bulky man in a white smock waddled into the chapel and introduced himself as Gregor Croom, chief among the surgeons who'd operated on Mina. Dr. Croom was perhaps the most physically unappealing person Bruno had ever met. A great mass of superfluous tissue clung to his upper spine, forcing him into a stoop. Mounds of overlapping flab drooped from the sides of his face, so that his tiny black eyes suggested raisins embedded in a pudding.

The surgeon spoke clinically, phlegmatically. They'd stopped the bleeding, he said, internal and external, and her vital signs were stable — but she'd lost massive quantities of irreplaceable neural matter. It was doubtful that she would ever again move her limbs of her own volition. In all likelihood the bullet had excised her ability to speak.

"I wept," said Bruno, finishing his tea. Leni's errant tail slapped his knee. "I wept like a baby."

"My poor Mr. Pearl," I said.

Dr. Croom's demeanor underwent an abrupt transformation. His manner grew gentle, his voice mellifluous. Locking a gnarled hand around Bruno's wrist, he confessed that he was as steadfast an apostle as the sex artists would ever know, proud owner of ninety-eight Bruno and Mina tapes of dubious provenance. His failure to foresee and attend that afternoon's concert in Fairmount Park would haunt him for years to come.

"Please know I shall do all within my power to return Mina to the eros circuit," Dr. Croom told the despairing Bruno. "My expertise lies wholly at your disposal, free of charge."

"Are you saying . . . there's hope?"

"More than hope, Mr. Pearl. A cure."

As the anemic light of dawn washed over Philadelphia, Dr. Croom told Bruno how he had recently perfected a new, audacious, auspicious — and untested — method of rehabilitating victims of neural trauma. He freely revealed that his colleagues had no faith in the technique, and he admitted that it lay outside the bounds of orthodox medical practice. The pioneering experiment would occur in Croom's private laboratory, which he maintained in the basement of his Chestnut Hill mansion.

"The doctor proposed to employ a unique genetic-engineering technology," Bruno told me, massaging Leni with extravagant strokes that began at her nose and continued to the end of her tail. "His desire was to create an embryo bearing Mina's precise genetic heritage. He would then accelerate the fetus's development through hormonal manipulation, so that it would become an infant within seven days, an adolescent within five weeks, and a woman of thirty-six years — Mina's age — in a matter of months. The result, he promised me, would be an exact biological duplicate of my wife."

"But it would *not* be a duplicate," I protested. "It would have none of her experiences, none of her memories."

"You may be sure that I presented this objection to Dr. Croom. His answer astonished me."

The doctor told Bruno about a heuristic computer, the JCN-5000-X. Among the machine's several spectacular functions was an ability to scan a person's cerebrum, encode the totality of its electrochemical contents, and insert these byzantine files into the tabula rasa that is the nervous system of a genetically engineered, hormonally accelerated human replica. In Croom's view, a complete restoration of Mina was entirely feasible, for the bullet had damaged her brain's motor and autonomic areas only — the very motor and autonomic areas that the hypothetical duplicate would boast in full. With the exceptions of certain trivial skills and some useless bits of nostalgia, the doppelgänger Mina would enjoy a selfhood identical to that possessed by the original before the bullet arrived.

"Look at me, Mr. Pearl," said Dr. Croom. "Contemplate my ugliness. What woman would have this walrus for her lover? And yet, thanks to you and your wife, I have known many a sybaritic satisfaction."

Bruno grew suddenly aware of the pain throbbing in his palm. "This person you're proposing to create . . . would it truly be Mina — Mina restored, Mina reborn — or would it be . . . somebody else?"

"I'm not a philosopher," Dr. Croom replied. "Neither am I a theologian nor a sage. I'm a cyberneurologist with a mission. Sanction this procedure, I beg you. For the sake of art — for the sake of all the world's freaks and Quasimodos — allow me to resurrect your wife."

Bruno requested a second serving of tea. I retired to the kitchen, brewed the oolong, and, upon handing him his replenished mug, voiced my opinion that the duplicate Mina Pearl and the original Mina Pearl would be exactly the same person.

He scowled.

"You disagree?" I said.

"Imagine, sweet Susan, that you have faithfully recorded your every memory, belief, dream, hope, and habit in some massive journal. Call it *The Book of Susan*. Each time you finish making the day's entry, you store the volume on a high shelf in your private library. After your death, the executor of your will — a cousin, let's say — decides to browse among your bookshelves. She spies *The Book of Susan*, stretches for it, dislodges it. Suddenly the volume falls heavily on her head, rendering her unconscious. Five hours later, the executor awakens — as a total amnesiac. She notices the open book in front of her and immediately starts to read it. Her empty mind is like a sponge, absorbing every one of your recorded experiences. Now, dear Susan. Here's the question. At the precise moment when your cousin finishes reading the book and rises from the library floor, have you been reborn?"

"Reborn?"

"Take all the time you want," he said.

"Of *course* I haven't been reborn," I said.

"*Quod erat demonstrandum.*"

"And so you refused to let Dr. Croom carry out his experiment?"

"No," he said.

"No?"

Bruno scratched Leni behind the ears. "I told him he could proceed — proceed with my blessing . . . provided he acceded to one condition. He must also make a duplicate of me, someone to look after the original Mina, nourishing her, cleaning her, caressing her, while my real self again joined the circuit."

"And Croom agreed?"

Bruno nodded. "The man was a romantic."

Like most other Bruno and Mina enthusiasts, I had often wondered about the one-year hiatus in their career. Had they become ill? Grown weary of the circuit? Now the riddle was solved. Throughout his absence Bruno had occupied a motel on the outskirts of Philadelphia — the first time he'd ever settled in one place for more than a week — caring for his frightened, aphasic, and largely paralyzed wife.

He fed her three meals a day, changed her diapers faithfully, and spent many hours reading poetry and fiction aloud in her presence. Despite the lost neurons, Mina retained a modicum of control over her dominant hand, and she managed to compose, at least twice a week, a letter filled with ardor and appreciation. The effort depleted her, and her script bordered on the illegible, but it was obvious from these exchanges that the primal Mina was no zombie. She knew what had happened to her. She understood that her doppelgänger was growing in a Chestnut Hill basement. She realized that a duplicate Bruno would soon replace the loving husband who attended her, so that he might go forth and again practice his art.

"Did Mina approve?" I asked.

"She said she did," Bruno replied. "I was skeptical, naturally, but her letters evinced no feelings of betrayal. Whenever I suggested that she was telling me what I wanted to hear, she became angry and hurt."

Nine months after the bullet ruined Mina's brain, Dr. Croom summoned Bruno to his ramshackle laboratory and presented him not only with a facsimile of the artist's wife but also with his own artificial twin.

"I can't tell you which phenomenon amazed me more" — Bruno finished his second mug of tea — "seeing and speaking with Mina's replica, or interviewing my second self."

"Credible copies?" I asked.

"Perfect copies. And yet I kept wondering: if this was Mina, then who was that person back in my hotel room? I wholly admired the duplicate. You might even say I cherished her. Did I love her? Perhaps. I don't know. My mind was not on love that day."

And so Bruno hit the road once more, coupling with the forged Mina in forty-two parks — famous and obscure, metropolitan and suburban, Old World and New — over the course of a full year. It was one of their most successful tours ever, drawing unqualified accolades from the critics even as audiences presented the artists with vast quantities of applause, adulation, and cash.

"But the new Mina — the Mina duplicate — what did she make of all this?" I asked.

"She didn't like to talk about it. Whenever I broached the subject, she offered the same reply, 'My life is my art,' she said. 'My life is my art.'"

While Bruno and the new Mina pursued the eros circuit, their shadow half — the doppelgänger Bruno and the damaged Mina — journeyed to the south of France, moving into a farmhouse outside of Nîmes. No member of this odd quartet took much joy in the arrangement, but neither did anyone despair. Never before in human history, Bruno speculated, had irreversible brain injury been so cleverly accommodated.

"But cleverness, of course, mere cleverness — it's an ambiguous virtue, no?" Bruno said to me. "After pursuing Dr. Croom's ingenious scheme a mere fourteen months, I felt an overwhelming urge to abandon it."

"Because it was clever?"

"Because it was clever and not beautiful. Everything I knew, everything I held dear, had become false, myself most especially. *The Book of Bruno* had lost its poetry, and instead there was only correct punctuation, and proper spelling, and subjects that agreed with their verbs."

Bruno Pearl, the falsest thing of all, or so he imagined himself: a man with glass eyes, a nylon heart, neoprene muscles, plastic viscera. He could enact his passion for Mina, but he could not experience it. He could enter her body, but not inhabit it. The flawless creature in his arms, this hothouse orchid, this unblemished replica who wore his wife's former face and spoke in her previous voice — nowhere in her flesh did he sense the ten million subtle impressions that had accrued, year by year, decade by decade, to their collective ecstasy.

"The skin is wise," he told me. "Our tissues retain echoes of every kiss and caress, each embrace and climax. Blood is not deceived. Do you understand?"

"No," I said. "Yes," I added. "I'm not sure. Yes. Quite so. I understand, Mr. Pearl."

I did.

Shortly after a particularly stunning concert in Luxembourg Gardens, Bruno and the duplicate Mina drove down to Nîmes, so that the four of them might openly discuss their predicament.

The artists gathered in the farmhouse kitchen, the primal Mina resting in her wheelchair.

"Tell me who you are," the primal Bruno asked the counterfeit.

"Who am I?" said the forged Bruno.

"Yes."

"I ponder that question every day."

"Are you I?" asked the primal Bruno.

"Yes," the forged Bruno replied. "In theory, yes — I am you."

"I was not created to be myself," noted the facsimile Mina.

"True," said the primal Bruno.

"I was created to be someone else," said the facsimile Mina.

"Yes," said the primal Bruno.

"If I am in fact you," asked the forged Bruno, "why do I endure a meaningless and uneventful life while the world lays garlands at your feet?"

"I need to be myself," said the facsimile Mina.

"I hate you, Bruno," said the forged Bruno.

The primal Mina took up a red crayon and scrawled a tortured note. SET THEM FREE, she instructed her husband.

"The right and proper course was obvious," Bruno told me. "My twin and I would trade places."

"Naturally," I said, nodding.

"I told my doppelgänger and the duplicate Mina that if they wished to continue the tour, I would respect and support their decision. But I would never do *Sphinx Recumbent* or any other act in public again."

Bruno was not surprised when, an hour before their scheduled departure from Nîmes, the replicas came to him and said that they intended to resume the tour. What *else* were they supposed to do? Performance intercourse was in their bones.

For nearly five years, the duplicates thrived on the circuit, giving pleasure to spectators and winning plaudits from critics. But then the unexpected occurred, mysterious to everyone except Mina and Bruno and their doubles —

though perhaps Dr. Croom comprehended the disaster as well. The ersatz copulators lost their art. Their talent, their touch, their raison d'être — all of it disintegrated, and soon they suffered a precipitous and irreversible decline. Months before the automobile accident, audiences and aestheticians alike had consigned these former gods to history.

"Inevitably one is tempted to theorize that the Citroën crash was not an accident," Bruno said.

"The despair of fallen idols," I said.

"Or, if an accident, then an accident visited upon two individuals who no longer wished to live."

"I guess we'll never know," I said.

"But if they deliberately ran their car into that concrete wall, I suspect that the reason was not their waning reputation. You see, lovely Susan, they didn't know who they were."

A fat, sallow, October moon shone into my apartment. It was nearly ten o'clock. Bruno rose from my wing chair, prompting Leni to bail out, and requested that I lead him home. Naturally I agreed. He shuffled into the kitchen, reassembled his wallet, and slid it into his back pocket.

Gathering up Bruno's clothes, still damp, I dumped them into a plastic garbage bag. I told him he was welcome to keep Craig's dungarees, everything else too. I gave him Anson's sheepskin coat as well, then escorted him to the door.

"How do you feel?" I asked.

"Warm," he said, slinging the plastic bag over his shoulder. Leni pushed against Bruno's left leg, wrapped herself around his calf. "Restored."

Retrieving my motorcycle jacket from the peg, I realized that I still felt protective toward my charge: more protective, even, then when I'd first pulled him from the Hudson. As we ventured through the city, I insisted on stopping before each red traffic light, even if no car was in sight. Noticing an unattended German shepherd on the sidewalk ahead, I led us judiciously across the street. Finally, after a half-hour of timid northward progress, we reached 105 Willow Avenue.

Removing his keys from Craig's dungarees, Bruno proceeded to enact a common ritual of modern urban life — a phenomenon fully documented in the Kaleidoscope video called *Safe City Living*. Guided by my fingertips, he ascended the stoop, disengaged the bolt on the iron gate, unlocked the door to the building, climbed one flight of stairs, and, aided by a third key, let himself into his apartment.

"Darling, I want you to meet someone," Bruno said, crossing the living room.

Mina Pearl sat in a pool of moonlight. She wore nothing save a wristwatch and a jade pendant. Her bare, pale skin gleamed like polished marble. A fan-back wicker chair held her twisted body as a bamboo cage might enclose a Chinese cricket.

"This is Susan Fiore," Bruno continued. "As unlikely as it sounds, I fell off the ferry tonight, and she rescued me. I lost my glasses."

Mina worked her face into the semblance of a smile. She issued a noise that seemed to amalgamate the screech of an owl with the bleating of a ewe.

"I'm pleased to meet you, Mrs. Pearl," I said.

"Tomorrow I'm going to sign up for swimming lessons," Bruno averred.

As I came toward Mina, she raised her tremulous right hand. I clasped it firmly. Her flesh was warmer than I'd expected, suppler, more robust.

She used this same hand to gesture emphatically toward Bruno — a private signal, I concluded. He opened a desk drawer, removing a sheet of cardboard and a felt-tip marker. He brought the implements to his wife.

THANK YOU, Mina wrote. She held the message before me.

"You're welcome," I replied.

Mina flipped the cardboard over. PAN AND SYRINX, she wrote.

For the second time that evening, Bruno shed all his clothes. Cautiously, reverently, he lifted his naked wife from the wicker chair. She jerked and twitched like a marionette operated by a tipsy puppeteer. As her limbs writhed around one another, I thought of Laocoön succumbing to the serpents. A series of thick, burbling, salivary sounds spilled from her lips.

Against all odds, Mina and Bruno connected. It took them nearly an hour, but eventually they brought *Pan and Syrinx* to a credible conclusion. Next came a forty-minute recital of *Flowering Judas*, followed by an equally pro-tracted version of *Sphinx Recumbent*.

The lovers, sated, sank into the couch. My applause lasted three minutes. I said my good-byes, and before I was out the door I understood that no mat-ter how long I lived or how far I traveled, I would never again see anything so beautiful as Bruno and Mina Pearl coupling in their grimy little Willow Avenue apartment, the pigeons gathering atop the window grating, the traffic stirring in the street below, the sun rising over Hoboken.

The Raft of the Titanic

15 April 1912
LAT. 40°25' N, LONG. 51°18' W

The sea is calm tonight. Where does that come from? Some Oxbridge swot's poem, I think, one of those cryptic things I had to read in school — but the title hasn't stayed with me, and neither has the scribbler's name. If you want a solid education in English letters, arrange to get born elsewhere than Walton-on-the-Hill. "The sea is calm tonight." I must ask our onboard litterateur, Mr. Futrelle of Massachusetts. He will know.

We should have been picked up — what? — fourteen hours ago. Certainly no more than sixteen. Our Marconi men, Phillips and Bride, assure me that Captain Rostron of the *Carpathia* acknowledged the *Titanic*'s CQD promptly, adding, "We are coming as quickly as possible and expect to be there within four hours." Since the Ship of Dreams sailed into the Valley of Death, sometime around 2:20 this morning, we have drifted perhaps fifteen miles to the southwest. Surely Rostron can infer our present position. So where the bloody hell is he?

Now darkness is upon us once again. The mercury is falling. I scan the encircling horizon for the *Carpathia*'s lights, but I see only a cold black sky sown with a million apathetic stars. In a minute I shall order Mr. Lightoller to launch the last of our distress rockets, even as I ask Reverend Bateman to send up his next emergency prayer.

For better or worse, Captain Smith insisted on doing the honorable thing and going down with his ship. (That is, he insisted on doing the honorable thing and shooting himself, thereby guaranteeing that his remains would go down with his ship.) His gesture has left me *en passant* in command of the present contraption. I suppose I should be grateful. At long last I have a ship of my own, if you can call this jerry-built, jury-rigged raft a ship. Have the other castaways accepted me as their guardian and keeper? I can't say for sure. Shortly after dawn tomorrow, I shall address the entire company, clarifying that I am legally in charge and have a scheme for our deliverance, though that second assertion will require of the truth a certain elasticity, as a scheme for our deliverance has not yet visited my imagination.

I count it a bloody miracle that we got so many souls safely off the founding liner. The Lord and all His angels were surely watching over us. So far we have accumulated only nineteen corpses: a dozen deaths during the transfer operation — shock, heart attacks, misadventure — and then another seven, shortly after sunrise, from hypothermia and exposure. Grim statistics, to be sure, but far better than the thousand or so fatalities that would have occurred had we not embraced Mr. Andrews's audacious plan.

Foremost amongst my immediate obligations is to keep a record of our tribulations. So here I sit, pen in one hand, electric torch in the other. By maintaining a sort of captain's log, I might actually start to feel like a captain, though at the moment I feel like plain old Henry Tingle Wilde, the Scouser who never got out of Liverpool. The sea is calm tonight.

16 April 1912
LAT. 39°19' N, LONG. 51°40' W

When I told the assembled company that, by every known maritime code, I am well and truly the supreme commander of this vessel, a strident voice rose in protest: Vasil Plotcharsky from steerage, who called me "a bourgeois lackey in thrall to that imperialist monstrosity known as White Star Line." (I'll have to keep an eye on Plotcharsky. I wonder how many other Bolsheviks the *Titanic* carried?) But on the whole my speech was well received. Hearing that I'd christened our raft the *Ada*, "after my late wife, who died tragically two years ago," my audience responded with respectful silence, then Father Byles piped up and said, so all could hear, "Right now that dear woman is looking down from Heaven, exhorting us not to lose faith."

My policy concerning the nineteen bodies in the stern proved more controversial. A contingent of first-cabin survivors led by Colonel Astor insisted that we give them "an immediate Christian burial at sea," whereupon my first officer explained to the aristocrats that the corpses "may ultimately have their part to play in this drama." Mr. Lightoller's prediction occasioned horrified gasps and indignant snorts, but nobody moved to push these frigid assets overboard.

This afternoon I ordered a complete inventory, a good way to keep our company busy. Before floating away from the disaster site, we salvaged about a third of the buoyant containers Mr. Latimer's stewards had tossed into the sea: wine casks, beer barrels, cheese crates, bread boxes, footlockers, duffel bags, toilet kits. Had there been a moon on Sunday night, we might have recovered this jetsam *in toto*. Of course, had there been a moon, we might not have hit the iceberg in the first place.

The tally is heartening. Assuming that frugality rules aboard the *Ada* — and it will, so help me God — she probably has enough food and water to sustain her population, all 2,187 of us, for at least ten days. We have two functioning compasses, three brass sextants, four thermometers, one barometer, one anemometer, fishing tackle, sewing supplies, baling wire, and twenty tarpaulins, not to mention the wood-fueled Franklin stove Mr. Lightoller managed to knock together from odd bits of metal.

Yesterday's attempt to rig a sail was a fiasco, but this afternoon we had better luck, fashioning a gracefully curving thirty-foot mast from the banister of the grand staircase, then fitting it with a patchwork of velvet curtains, throw rugs, signal flags, men's dinner jackets, and ladies' skirts. My mind is clear, my strategy is certain, my course is set. We shall tack towards warmer waters, lest we lose more souls to the demonic cold. If I never see another ice-floe or North Atlantic growler in my life, it will be too soon.

18 April 1912
LAT. 37°11' N, LONG. 52°11' W

Whilst everything is still vivid in my mind, I must set down the story of how the *Ada* came into being, starting with the collision. I felt the tremor about 11:40 p.m., and by midnight Mr. Lightoller was in my cabin, telling me that the berg had sliced through at least five adjacent watertight compartments, possibly six. To the best of his knowledge, the ship was in the last extremity, fated to go down at the head in a matter of hours.

After assigning Mr. Moody to the bridge — one might as well put the sixth officer in charge, since the worst had already happened — Captain Smith sent word that the rest of us should gather posthaste in the chartroom. By the time I arrived, at perhaps five minutes past midnight, Mr. Andrews, who'd designed the *Titanic*, was already seated at the table, along with Mr. Bell, the chief engineer, Mr. Hutchinson, the ship's carpenter, and Dr. O'Loughlin, our surgeon. Taking my place beside Mr. Murdoch, who had not yet reconciled himself to the fact that my last-minute posting as chief officer had bumped him down to first mate, I immediately apprehended that the ship was lost, so palpable was Captain Smith's anxiety.

"Even as we speak, Phillips and Bride are on the job in the wireless shack, trying to raise the *Californian*, which can't be more than an hour away," said the Old Man. "I am sorry to report that her Marconi operator has evidently shut off his rig for the night. However, we have every reason to believe that Captain Rostron of the *Carpathia* will be here within four hours. If this were the tropics, we would simply put the entire company in life-belts, lower them over the side, and let them bob about waiting to be rescued. But this is the North Atlantic, and the water is twenty-eight degrees Fahrenheit."

"After a brief interval in that ghastly gazpacho, the average mortal will succumb to hypothermia," said Mr. Murdoch, who liked to lord it over us Scousers with fancy words such as *succumb* and *gazpacho*. "Am I correct, Dr. O'Loughlin?"

"A castaway who remains motionless in the water risks dying immediately of cardiac arrest," the surgeon replied, nodding. "Alas, even the most robust athlete won't generate enough body heat to prevent his core temperature from plunging. Keep swimming, and you might last twenty minutes, probably no more than thirty."

"Now I shall tell you the good news," said the Old Man. "Mr. Andrews has a plan, bold but feasible. Listen closely. Time is of the essence. The *Titanic* has at best one hundred and fifty minutes to live."

"The solution to this crisis is not to fill the lifeboats to capacity and send them off in hopes of encountering the *Carpathia*, for that would leave over a thousand people stranded on a sinking ship," Mr. Andrews insisted. "The solution, rather, is to keep every last soul out of the water until Captain Rostron arrives."

"Mr. Andrews has stated the central truth of our predicament," said Captain Smith. "On this terrible night our enemy is not the ocean depths, for owing to the life-belts no one — or almost no one — will drown. Nor is the local fauna our enemy, for sharks and rays never visit the middle of the North Atlantic in early spring. No, our enemy tonight is the temperature of the water, pure and simple, full stop."

"And how do you propose to obviate that implacable fact?" Mr. Murdoch inquired. The next time he used the word *obviate*, I intended to sock him in the chops.

"We're going to build an immense floating platform," said Mr. Andrews, unfurling a sheet of drafting paper on which he'd hastily sketched an object labeled *Raft of the Titanic*. He secured the blueprint with ashtrays and, leaning across the table, squeezed the chief engineer's knotted shoulder. "I designed it in collaboration with the estimable Mr. Bell" — he flashed our carpenter an amiable wink — "and the capable Mr. Hutchinson."

"Instead of loading anyone into our fourteen standard thirty-foot lifeboats, we shall set aside one dozen, leave their tarps in place, and treat them as pontoons," said Mr. Bell. "From an engineering perspective, this is a viable scheme, for each lifeboat is outfitted with copper buoyancy tanks."

Mr. Andrews set his open palms atop the blueprint, his eyes dancing with a peculiar fusion of desperation and ecstasy. "We shall deploy the twelve pontoons in a three-by-four grid, each linked to its neighbors via horizontal wooden beams. Our masts are useless — mostly steel — but we're hauling tons of oak, teak, mahogany, and spruce."

"With any luck, we can affix a twenty-five-foot beam between the stern of pontoon A and the bow of pontoon B," said Mr. Hutchinson, "another such bridge between the amidships oarlock of A and the amidships oarlock of E, another between the stern of B and the bow of C, and so on."

"Next we'll cover the entire matrix with jettisoned lumber, securing the planks with nails and rope," said Mr. Bell. "The resulting raft will measure roughly one hundred feet by two hundred, which technically allows each of our two-thousand-plus souls almost nine square feet, though in reality everyone will have to share accommodations with foodstuffs, water casks, and survival gear, not to mention the dogs."

"As you've doubtless noticed," said Mr. Andrews, "at this moment the North Atlantic is smooth as glass, a circumstance that contributed to our predicament — no wave broke against the iceberg, so the lookouts spotted the bloody thing too late. I am proposing that we now turn this same placid sea to our advantage. My machine could never be assembled in high swells, but tonight we're working under conditions only slightly less ideal than those that obtain back at the Harland and Wolff shipyard."

Captain Smith's moustache and beard parted company, a great gulping inhalation, whereupon he delivered what was surely the most momentous speech of his career.

"Step one is for Mr. Wilde and Mr. Lightoller to muster the deck crew and have them launch all fourteen standard lifeboats — forget the collapsibles and the cutters — each craft to be rowed by two able-bodied seamen assisted where feasible by a quartermaster, boatswain, lookout, or master-at-arms. Through this operation we get our twelve pontoons in the water, along with two roving assembly craft. The ABs will forthwith moor the pontoons to the *Titanic's* hull using davit ropes, keeping the lines in place until the raft is finished or the ship sinks, whichever comes first. Understood?"

I nodded in assent, as did Mr. Lightoller, even though I'd never heard a more demented idea in my life. Next the Old Man waved a scrap of paper at Mr. Murdoch, the overeducated genius whose navigational brilliance had torn a three-hundred-foot gash in our hull.

"A list from Purser McElroy identifying twenty carpenters, joiners, fitters, bricklayers, and blacksmiths — nine from the second-cabin decks, eleven from steerage," Captain Smith explained. "Your job is to muster these skilled workers on the boat deck, each man equipped with a mallet and nails from either his own baggage or Mr. Hutchinson's shop. For those who don't speak English, get Father Montvila and Father Peruschitz to act as interpreters. Use the electric cranes to lower the workers to the leeward side, where Mr. Andrews and Mr. Hutchinson will be constructing the machine."

The Old Man rose and, shuffling to the far end of the table, rested an avuncular hand on his third officer's epaulet.

"Mr. Pitman, I am charging you with provisioning the raft. You will work with Mr. Latimer in organizing his three hundred stewards into a special detail. Have them scour the ship for every commodity a man might need were he to find himself stranded in the middle of the North Atlantic: water, wine, beer, cheese, meat, bread, coal, tools, sextants, compasses, small arms. The stewards will load these items into buoyant coffers, setting them afloat near the construction site for later retrieval."

Captain Smith continued to circumnavigate the table, pausing to clasp the shoulders of his fourth and fifth officers.

"Mr. Boxhall and Mr. Lowe, you will organize two teams of second-cabin volunteers, supplying each man with an appropriate wrecking or cutting implement. There are at least twenty emergency fire-axes mounted in the companionways. You should also grab all the saws and sledges from the shop, plus hatchets, knives, and cleavers from the galleys. Team A, under Mr. Boxhall, will chop down every last column, pillar, and post for the crossbeams, tossing them to the construction crew, along with every bit of rope they can find, yards and yards of it, wire rope, Manila hemp, clothesline, whatever you can steal from the winches, cranes, ladders, bells, laundry rooms, and children's swings. Meanwhile, Team B, commanded by Mr. Lowe, will lay hold of twenty thousand square feet of planking for the platform of the raft. Towards this end, Mr. Lowe's volunteers will pillage the promenade decks, dismantle the grand staircase, ravage the panels, and gather together every last door, table, and piano lid on board."

Captain Smith resumed his circuit, stopping behind the chief engineer.

"Mr. Bell, your assignment is at once the simplest and the most difficult. For as long as humanly possible, you will keep the steam flowing and the turbines spinning, so our crew and passengers will enjoy heat and electricity whilst assembling Mr. Andrews's ark. Any questions, gentlemen?"

We had dozens of questions, of course, such as, "Have you taken leave of your senses, Captain?" and "Why the bloody hell did you drive us through an ice field at twenty-two knots?" and "What makes you imagine we can build this preposterous device in only two hours?" But these mysteries were irrelevant to the present crisis, so we kept silent, fired off crisp salutes, and set about our duties.

19 April 1912
LAT. 36°18' N, LONG. 52°48' W

Still no sign of the *Carpathia*, but the mast holds true, the spar remains strong, and the sail stays fat. Somehow, through no particular virtue of my own, I've managed to get us out of iceberg country. The mercury hovers a full five degrees above freezing.

Yesterday Colonel Astor and Mr. Guggenheim convinced Mr. Andrews to relocate the Franklin stove from amidships to the forward section. Right now our first-cabin castaways are toasty enough, though by this time tomorrow our coal supply will be exhausted. That said, I'm reasonably confident we'll see no more deaths from hypothermia, not even in steerage. Optimism prevails aboard the *Ada*. A cautious optimism, to be sure, optimism guarded by Cerberus himself and a cherub with a flaming sword, but optimism all the same.

I was right about Mr. Futrelle knowing the source of "The sea is calm tonight." It's from "Dover Beach" by Matthew Arnold. Futrelle has the whole thing memorized. Lord, what a depressing poem. "For the world, which seems to lie before us like a land of dreams, so various, so beautiful, so new, hath really neither joy, nor love, nor light, nor certitude, nor peace, nor help for pain." Tomorrow I may issue an order banning public poetry recitations aboard the *Ada*.

When the great ship *Titanic* went down, the world was neither various and beautiful, nor joyless and violent, but merely very busy. By forty minutes after midnight, against all odds, the twelve pontoons were in the water and lashed to the davits. Mr. Boxhall's second-cabin volunteers forthwith delivered the first load of crossbeams, even as Mr. Lowe's group supplied the initial batch of decking material. For the next eighty minutes the frigid air rang with the din of hammers, the clang of axes, the whine of saws, and the squeal of ropes locking planks to pontoons, the whole mad chorus interspersed with the thumps of lumber being lowered to the construction team, the steady splash, splash, splash of provisions going into the sea, and exhortatory cries of "Stay out of the drink!" and "Only the cold can kill us!" and "Twenty-eight degrees!" and "*Carpathia* is on the way!" It was all very British, though occasionally the Americans pitched in, and the emigrants proved reasonably diligent as well. I must admit, I can't imagine any but the English-speaking races constructing and equipping the *Ada* so efficiently. Possibly the Germans, an admirable people, though I fear their war-mongering Kaiser.

By 2:00 a.m. Captain Smith had successfully shot himself, three-fifths of the platform was nailed down, and the *Titanic's* bridge lay beneath thirty feet of icy water. The stricken liner listed horribly, nearly forty degrees, stern in the air, her triple screws, glazed with ice, lying naked against the vault of Heaven. For my command post I'd selected the mesh of guylines securing the dummy funnel, a vantage from which I now beheld a great mass of humanity jammed together on the boat deck: aristocrats, second-cabin passengers, emigrants, officers, engineers, trimmers, stokers, greasers, stewards, stewardesses, musicians, barbers, chefs, cooks, bakers, waiters, and scullions, the majority dressed in life-belts and the warmest clothing they could find. Each frightened man, woman, and child held onto the rails and davits for dear life. The sea spilled over the tilted gunwales and rushed across the canted boards.

"The raft!" I screamed from my lofty promontory. "Hurry! Swim!" Soon the other officers — Murdoch, Lightoller, Pitman, Boxhall, Lowe, Moody — took up the cry. "The raft! Hurry! Swim!" "The raft! Hurry! Swim!" "The raft! Hurry! Swim!"

And so they swam for it, or, rather, they splashed, thrashed, pounded, wheeled, kicked, and paddled for it. Even the hundreds who spoke no English understood what was required. Heaven be praised, within twelve minutes our entire company managed to migrate from the flooded deck of the *Titanic* to the sanctuary of Mr. Andrews's machine. Our stalwart ABs pulled scores of women and children from the water, plus many elderly castaways, along with Colonel Astor's Airedale, Mr. Harper's Pekingese, Mr. Daniel's French bulldog, and six other canines. I was the last to come aboard. Glancing about, I saw to my great distress that a dozen life-belted bodies were not moving, the majority doubtless heart-attack victims, though perhaps a few people had gotten crushed against the davits or trampled underfoot.

The survivors instinctively sorted themselves by station, with the emigrants gathering at the stern, the second-cabin castaways settling amidships, and our first-cabin passengers assuming their rightful places forward. After cutting the mooring lines, the ABs took up the lifeboat oars and began to stroke furiously. By the grace of Dame Fortune and the hand of Divine Providence, the *Ada* rode free of the wreck, so that when the great steamer finally snapped, breaking in two abaft the engine room, and began her vertical voyage to the bottom, we observed the whole appalling spectacle from a safe distance.

22 April 1912
LAT. 33°42' N, LONG. 53°11' W

We've been at sea a full week now. No *Carpathia* on the horizon yet, no *Californian*, no *Olympia*, no *Baltic*. Our communal mood is grim but not despondent. Mr. Hartley's little band helps. I've forbidden them to play hymns, airs, ballads, or any other wistful tunes. "It's waltzes and rags or nothing," I tell him. Thanks to Wallace Hartley's strings and Scott Joplin's syncopations, we may survive this ordeal.

Although no one is hungry at the moment, I worry about our eventual nutritional needs. The supplies of beef, poultry, and cheese hurled overboard by the stewards will soon be exhausted, and thus far our efforts to harvest the sea have come to nothing. The specter of thirst likewise looms. True, we still have six wine-casks in the first-cabin section, plus four amidships and three in steerage, and we've also deployed scores of pots, pans, pails, kettles, washtubs, and tierces all over the platform. But what if the rains come too late?

Our sail is unwieldy, the wind contrary, the current fickle, and yet we're managing, slowly, ever so slowly, to make our way towards the thirtieth parallel. The climate has grown bearable — perhaps forty-five degrees by day, forty by night — but it's still too cold, especially for the children and the elderly. Mr. Lightoller's Franklin stove has proven a boon for those of us in the bow, and our second-cabin passengers have managed to build and sustain a small fire amidships, but our emigrants enjoy no such comforts. They huddle miserably aft, warming each other as best they can. We must get farther south. My kingdom for a horse latitude.

The meat in steerage has thawed, though it evidently remains fresh, an effect of the cold air and the omnipresent brine. Ere long I shall be obligated to issue a difficult order. "Our choices are clear," I must tell the *Ada*'s company, "fortitude or refinement, nourishment or nicety, survival or finesse — and in each instance I've opted for the former." Messrs. Lightoller, Pitman, Boxhall, Lowe, and Moody share my sentiments. The only dissenter is Murdoch. My chief officer is useless to me. I would rather be sharing the bridge with our Bolshevik — Plotcharsky — than that fusty Scotsman.

In my opinion an intraspecies diet need not automatically entail depravity. Ethical difficulties arise only when such cuisine is practiced in bad faith. During my one and only visit to the Louvre, I became transfixed by Théodore Géricault's *Scène de naufrage*, "Scene of a Shipwreck," that gruesome panorama of life aboard the notorious raft by which the refugees from the stranded freighter *Medusa* sought to save themselves. As Monsieur Géricault so vividly reveals, the players in that disaster were, almost to a man, paragons of bad faith. They ignored their leaders with insouciance, betrayed their fellows with relish, and ate one another with alacrity. I am resolved that no such chaos will descend upon the *Ada*. We are not orgiasts. We are not beasts. We are not French.

4 May 1912
LAT. 29°55′ N, LONG. 54°12′ W

At last, after nineteen days afloat, the *Ada* has crossed the thirtieth parallel. We are underfed and dehydrated but in generally good spirits. Most of the raft's company has settled into a routine, passing their hours fishing, stargazing, card-playing, cataloguing provisions, bartering for beer and cigars, playing with the dogs, minding the children, teaching others their native languages, repairing the hastily assembled platform, and siphoning seawater from the pontoons (to stabilize the raft, not to drink, God knows). Each morning Dr. O'Loughlin brings me a report. Our infirmary — the area directly above pontoon K — is presently full: five cases of chronic *mal de mer*, three of frostbite, two of flux, and four "fevers of unknown origin."

Because the *Ada* remains so difficult to pilot, even with our newly installed wheelhouse and rudder, it would be foolish to try tacking towards the North American mainland in hopes of hitting some hospitable Florida beach. We cannot risk getting caught in the Gulf Stream and dragged back north into frigid waters. Instead we shall latch onto every southerly breeze that comes our way, eventually reaching the Lesser Antilles or, failing that, the coast of Brazil.

As darkness settled over the North Atlantic, we came upon a great mass of flotsam from an anonymous wreck: a poaching schooner, most likely, looking for whales and seals but instead running afoul of a storm. We recovered no bodies — life-belts have never been popular amongst such scalawags — but we salvaged plenty of timber, some medical supplies, and a copy of the *New York Post* for 17 April, stuffed securely into the pocket of a drifting mackintosh. At first light I shall peruse the paper in hopes of learning how the outside world reacted to the loss of the *Titanic*.

The dry wood is a godsend. Thanks to this resource, I expect to encounter only a modicum of hostility whilst making my case next week for what might be called the *Medusa* initiative for avoiding famine. "Only a degenerate savage would consume the raw flesh of his own kind," I'll tell our assembled company. "Thanks to the Franklin stove and its ample supply of fuel, however, we can prepare our meals via broiling, roasting, braising, and other such civilized techniques."

5 May 1912
LAT. 28°10' N, LONG. 54°40' W

I am still reeling from the *New York Post*'s coverage of the 15 April tragedy. Upon reaching the disaster site, Captain Rostron of the *Carpathia* and Captain Lord of the *Californian* scanned the whole area with great diligence, finding no survivors or dead bodies, merely a few deck chairs and other debris. By the following morning they'd concluded that the mighty liner had gone down with all souls, and so they called off the search.

The *Ada*'s company greeted the news of their ostensible extinction with a broad spectrum of responses. Frustration was the principal emotion. I also witnessed despair, grief, bitterness, outrage, amusement, hysterical laughter, fatalistic resignation, and even — if I read correctly the countenances of certain first-cabin and amidships voyagers — fascination with the possibility that, should we in fact bump into one of the Lesser Antilles, a man might simply slip away, start his life anew, and allow his family and friends to count him amongst those who'd died of exposure on day one.

If the *Post* report may be believed, our would-be rescuers initially thought it odd that Captain Smith had neglected to order his passengers and crew into life-belts. Rostron and Lord speculated that, once the *Titanic*'s entire company realized their situation was hopeless, with the Grim Reaper making ready to trawl for their souls within a mere two hours, a tragic consensus had emerged. As Stanley Lord put it, "I can hear the oath now, ringing down the *Titanic*'s companionways. 'The time has come for us to embrace our wives, kiss our children, pet our dogs, praise the Almighty, break out the wine, and stop resisting a Divine Will far greater than our own.'"

Thus have we become a raft of the living dead, crewed by phantoms and populated by shades. Mr. Futrelle thought immediately of Samuel Taylor Coleridge's "The Rime of the Ancient Mariner." He muttered a stanza in which the cadaverous crew, their souls having been claimed by the skull-faced, dice-addicted master of a ghost ship (its hull suggestive of an immense rib-cage), return to life under the impetus of angelic spirits: "They groaned, they stirred, they all uprose, nor spake nor moved their eyes. It had been strange, even in a dream, to have seen those dead men rise." And when we all come marching home to Liverpool, Southampton, Queenstown, Belfast, Cherbourg, New York, Philadelphia, and Boston — that, too, will be awfully strange.

9 May 1912
LAT. 27°14′ N, LONG. 55°21′ W

This morning the Good Lord sent us potable water, gallons of it, splashing into our cisterns like honey from Heaven. If we cleave to our usual draconian rationing, we shall not have to take up the Ancient Mariner's despairing chant — "Water, water everywhere, nor any drop to drink" — for at least two months. Surely we shall encounter more rain by then.

Predictably enough, my directive concerning the steerage meat occasioned a lively conversation aboard the *Ada*. A dozen first-cabin voyagers were so scandalized that they began questioning my sanity, and for a brief but harrowing interval it looked as if I might have a mutiny on my hands. But in time more rational heads prevailed, as the pragmatic majority apprehended both the utilitarian and the sacramental dimensions of such a menu.

Reverend Bateman, God bless him, volunteered to oversee the rite — the deboning, the roasting, the thanksgiving, the consecration — a procedure in which he was assisted by his Catholic confrères, Father Byles and Father Peruschitz. Not one word was spoken during the consumption phase, but I sensed that everyone was happy not only to have finally received a substantive meal but also to have set a difficult precedent and emerged from the experience spiritually unscathed.

14 May 1912
LAT. 27°41′ N, LONG. 54°29′ W

Another wreck, another set of medical supplies, another trove of cooking fuel — plus two more legible newspapers. As it happened, the *Philadelphia Bulletin* for the 22nd of April and the *New York Times* for the 29th carried stories about the dozens of religious services held earlier in the month all over America and the United Kingdom honoring the *Titanic*'s noble dead. I explained to our first-cabin and second-cabin passengers that I would allow each man to read about his funeral, but he must take care not to get the pages wet.

Needless to say, our most illustrious voyagers were accorded lavish tributes. The managers of the Waldorf-Astoria, St. Regis, and Knickerbocker Hotels in Manhattan observed a moment of silence for Colonel John Jacob Astor. (Nothing was said about his scandalously pregnant child-bride, the former Madeleine Force.) The rectors of St. Paul's Church in Elkins Park, Pennsylvania, commissioned three Tiffany windows in memory of the dearly departed Widener family, George, Eleanor, and Harry. Senator Guggenheim of Colorado graced the *Congressional Record* with a eulogy for his brother, Benjamin, the mining and smelting tycoon. President Taft decreed an official Day of Prayer at the White House for his military advisor, Major Butt. For a full week all the passenger trains running between Philadelphia and New York wore black bunting in honor of John Thayer, Second Vice-President of the Pennsylvania Railroad. During this same interval the flags of all White Star Line steamers departing Southampton flew at half-mast in memory of the company's president, J. Bruce Ismay, even as the directors of Macy's Department Store in Herald Square imported a Wurlitzer and arranged for the organist to play each day a different requiem for their late employer, Isidor Straus. The Denver Women's Club successfully petitioned the City Council to declare a Day of Mourning for Margaret Brown, who'd done so much to improve the lot of uneducated women and destitute children throughout the state.

On the whole, our spectral community took heart in their epitaphs, and I believe I know why. Now that our deaths have been duly marked and lamented, the bereaved back home can begin, however haltingly, to get on with the business of existence. Yes, throughout April the mourning families knew only raw grief, but in recent weeks they have surely entered upon wistful remembrance and the bittersweet rewards of daily life, wisely heeding our Lord's words from the Gospel of Matthew, "Let the dead bury their dead."

18 June 1912
LAT. 25°31' N, LONG. 53°33' W

To reward our steerage passengers for accepting the *Medusa* initiative with such élan, I made no move to stop them when, shortly after sunrise, they killed and ate Mr. Ismay. I could see their point of view. By all accounts, from the moment we left Cherbourg, Ismay had kept pressing the captain for more steam, so that we might arrive in New York on Tuesday night rather than Wednesday morning. Evidently Ismay wanted to set a record, whereby the crossing-time for the maiden voyage of the *Titanic* would beat that of her sister ship, the *Olympic*. Also, nobody really liked the man.

I also went along with the strangling and devouring of Mr. Murdoch. There was nothing personal or vindictive in my decision. I would have acquiesced even if we didn't detest each other. Had Murdoch not issued such a bone-headed command at 11:40 p.m. on the night of 14 April, we wouldn't be in this mess. "Hard a-starboard!" he ordered. So far, so good. If he'd left it at that, we would've steamed past the iceberg with several feet to spare. But instead he added, "Full astern." What the bloody hell was Murdoch trying to do? Back up the ship like a bloody motorcar? All he accomplished was to severely compromise the rudder, and so the colossus slit us like a hot knife cutting lard.

When it came to Mr. Andrews, however, I drew the line. Yes, before the *Titanic* sailed he should have protested the paucity of lifeboats. And, yes, when designing her he should have run the bulkheads clear to the brink, so that in the event of rupture the watertight compartments would not systematically feed one another with ton after ton of brine. But even in his wildest fancies Mr. Andrews could not have imagined a three-hundred-foot gash in his creation's hull.

"Let him amongst you who has designed a more unsinkable ship than RMS *Titanic* cast the first stone," I told the mob. Slowly, reluctantly, they backed away. Today I have made an eternal friend in Thomas Andrews.

5 December 1912
LAT. 20°16' N, LONG. 52°40' W

Looking through my journal, I am chagrined to discover that the entries appear at such erratic intervals. What can I say? Writing does not come easily for me, and I am forever solving problems more pressing than keeping this tub's log up to date.

Since getting below the Tropic of Cancer, we have endured one episode of becalming after another. Naturally Mr. Futrelle supplied me with an appropriate stanza from Coleridge. "Down dropt the breeze, the sails dropt down — 'twas sad as sad could be, and we did speak only to break the silence of the sea." And yet we are much more than the poet's painted ship upon a painted ocean. The *Ada* abides. Life goes on.

In August, young Mrs. Astor gave birth to her baby, faithfully attended by Dr. Alice Leader, the only female physician on board. (Mother and child are both thriving.) September's highlights included a spellbinding public recitation by Mr. Futrelle of his latest "Thinking Machine" detective story, which he will commit to paper when we reach dry land. (The plot is so devilishly clever that I dare not reveal any particulars.) Last month our resident theatre company staged a production of *The Tempest*, directed by Margaret Brown and featuring our fetching movie-serial actress Dorothy Gibson as Miranda. (The shipwreck scene provoked unhappy memories, but otherwise we were enchanted.) And, of course, each dawn brings a plethora of birthdays to celebrate. Mr. Futrelle informs me of the counterintuitive fact that, out of any group of twenty-three persons, the chances are better than fifty-fifty that two will share a birthday. I couldn't follow his logic, but I'm not about to question it.

On the romantic front, I've been pleased to observe that our young wire-less operator, Harold Bride, has set his cap for a twenty-one-year-old Irish emigrant named Katie Mullen. (Though Mr. Bride has not been pleased to observe me observing him.) In June, Mr. and Mrs. Straus marked their forty-first wedding anniversary. (Mr. Lightoller arranged a candlelit dinner for them above pontoon F.) In July, Mr. Guggenheim and his mistress, Mme. Léotine Aubert, finally got married, Rabbi Minkoff officiating. (They passed their honeymoon in the gazebo above pontoon D.) Sad to say, last month Mr. and Mrs. Widener decided to get divorced, despite the protests of Father Byles and Father Montvila. The Wideners insist that their decision has noth-ing to do with the stress of the shipwreck, and everything to do with their disagreements over women's suffrage. I personally don't understand why the gentler sex wishes to sully its sensibility with politics, but if ladies really want the vote, I say give it them.

7 July 1913
LAT. 9°19' N, LONG. 44°42' W

For reasons that defy my powers of analysis, a steady cheerfulness obtains aboard the *Ada*. Despite our isolation, or perhaps because of it, we've become quite attached to our crowded little hamlet. Notwithstanding the occasional doldrums, literal and figurative, our peripatetic tropical isle remains a remark-ably congenial place.

I am aided immeasurably by the incompetence of captains who came before me. Thanks to the superfluity of wrecks, and our skill in plundering the flotsam and jetsam, we are blessed with a continual supply of fresh meat, good ale, novel toys for the children, *au courant* fashions for the first-cabin women, lumber for new architectural projects, rigging to improve our maneuverability, firearms to discourage pirates, and lambskin sheaths to curb our population. Drop by the *Ada* on any given Saturday night, and you will witness dance marathons, bridge tournaments, poker games, lotto contests, sing-alongs, and amorous encounters of every variety, sometimes across class lines. We are a merry raft.

Even our library is flourishing. This last circumstance has proved espe-cially heartening to young Harry Widener, our resident bibliophile, who needs bucking up after his parents' divorce. Jane Austen is continually in circulation, likewise Charles Dickens, Anthony Trollope, Conan Doyle, and an epic Polish novel, at once reverent and earthy, called *Quo Vadis*. We also have *The Oxford Book of English Verse*, compiled in 1900 by Arthur Quiller-Couch, so now I need no longer turn to Mr. Futrelle when I wish to ornament my log with epigraphs.

At least ten weeks have passed since anybody has asked when we're going to reach the Lesser Antilles. How might I account for this cavalier attitude toward our rescue? I suspect that the phenomenon traces in part to the special editions of the *New York Herald-Tribune* and the *Manchester Guardian* that we salvaged last May. In both cases, the theme of the issue was "The *Titanic* Catastrophe: One Year Later." Evidently the outside world has managed to extract a profound moral lesson from the tragedy. Man, our beneficiaries have learned, is a flawed, fallible, and naked creature. Our pride is nothing of which to be proud. For all our technological ingenuity, we are not gods or even demiurges. If a person wishes to be happy, he would do better planting his garden than polishing his gaskets, better cultivating his soul than multiplying his possessions.

Given the ethos that now obtains throughout North America, Europe, and the British Empire, how can we blithely go waltzing home? How dare we disillusion Western civilization by returning from the dead? I've consulted with representatives from steerage, amidships, and the aristocracy, and they've all ratified my conclusion. Showing up now would amount to saying, "Sorry, friends and neighbors, but you've been living in a Rousseauian fantasy, for the *Titanic's* resourceful company defeated Nature after all. Once again human cleverness has triumphed over cosmic indifference, so let's put aside all this sentimental talk of hubris and continue to fill the planet to bursting with our contrivances and toys."

To be sure, we also have certain personal — you might even say selfish — reasons to keep the *Ada* as our address. Colonel Astor, Mr. Widener, and Mr. Guggenheim note, with great exasperation, that according to our salvaged newspapers the American Treasury Department intends to levy a severe tax on people at their level of income. Reverend Bateman and Father Byles aver that their castaway flocks have proven a hundred times more attentive to the Christian message than were their congregations on dry land. At least half our married men, regardless of class, confess that they've grown weary of their wives back home, and many have started courting the nubile colleens from steerage. Surprisingly, many of our unescorted married women admit to analogous sentiments. Consider the case of Margaret Brown, our Denver suffragette and rabble-rouser, who avers that her marriage to J. J. Brown lost its magic many years ago, hence her proclivity for throwing herself at me in a most shocking and, I must say, exciting manner.

And, of course, we continue to expand our material amenities. Last week we put in a squash court. This morning Mr. Andrews showed me his plans for a Turkish bath. Tomorrow my officers and I shall consider whether to allocate our canvas reserves to a canopy for the emigrants, analogous to the protection enjoyed by our second-cabin and forward residents. All in all, it would appear that, as captain of this community, I am obligated to defer our deliverance indefinitely, an attitude with which the vivacious Mrs. Brown heartily agrees.

11 December 1913
LAT. 10°17' S, LONG. 32°52' W

Looking back on Vasil Plotcharsky's attempt to foment a socialist revolution aboard the *Ada*, I would say that it was all for the best. Just as I suspected, the man is besotted with Trotsky. At first he confined his political activities to organizing marches, rallies, and strikes amongst the steerage passengers and former *Titanic* victualing staff, his aim being to protest what he called "the tyrannical regime of Czar Henry Wilde and his decadent courtiers." Alas, it wasn't long before Mr. Plotcharsky and his followers broke into the arms locker and equipped themselves with pistols, whereupon they started advocating the violent overthrow of my regime.

But for the intervention of our resident logic-meister, Mr. Futrelle, who can be as quick-witted as his fictional Thinking Machine, Plotcharsky's exhortations might have led to bloodshed. Instead, Futrelle explained to the Trotsky-ites that, per Karl Marx's momentous revelation, the land of collectivist milk and classless honey is destined to rise only from the rubble of the Western imperialist democracies. The Workers' Paradise cannot be successfully organized within feudal societies such as contemporary Russia or, for that matter, the good ship *Ada*. In due time, with scientific inevitability, the world's capitalist economies will yield to the iron imperatives of history, but for now even the most ardent Bolshevik must practice forbearance.

Mr. Plotcharsky listened attentively, spent the following day in a brown study, then canceled the revolution. To tell you the truth, I don't think his heart was in it.

Of course, not all of Vasil Plotcharsky's partisans were happy with this turn of events, and one of them — a Southampton butcher named Charles Barrow — argued that we should forthwith institute a democracy aboard the *Ada*, as an essential first step towards a socialist utopia. Initially I resisted Mr. Barrow's argument, whereupon he introduced his cleaver into the conversation, and I assured him that I would not stand in the way of progress.

And so a bright new day has dawned aboard the *Ada*. Mr. Andrews's astounding machine is now considerably more than a raft, and I am now considerably less than her captain. On 13 October, by a nearly unanimous vote, Mr. Plotcharsky and Colonel Astor abstaining, we became the People's Republic of Adaland. Our constitutional convention, drawing representatives from the aristocracy, the second-cabin precincts, and steerage, dragged on for two weeks. George Widener, John Thayer, and Sir Cosmo Duff-Gordon were scandalized by the resulting document, mostly because it forbade the establishment of a state church, instituted a unitary parliament oblivious to class distinctions, and — owing to the tireless efforts of Margaret Brown and her sorority of suffragettes — enfranchised every adult female citizen. I keep trying to convince Widener, Thayer, and Duff-Gordon that certain concessions to modernity are better than the Bolshevik alternative.

On 13 November I was elected Prime Minister of our republic in a landslide, thereby vindicating the platform of my Egalitarian Party and giving pause to Father Peruschitz's Catholic Workers Party, Sir Cosmo's Christian Entrepreneurs Party, Thomas Andrews's Technotopia Party, and Vasil Plotcharsky's Communist Party. Two days after my triumph at the polls, I asked Maggie Brown to marry me. She'd done a splendid job as my campaign manager, attracting over eighty percent of the female vote to our cause, and I knew she would make an excellent wife as well.

17 April 1914
LAT. 13°15' N, LONG. 29°11' W

The week began with an extraordinary stroke of luck. Shortly after noon, poking through the wreck of a frigate called the *Ganymede*, we happened upon a wireless set, plus a petrol engine to supply it with power. In short order John Phillips and Harold Bride got the rig working. "Once again I have the ears of an angel," enthused a beaming Phillips. "I can tell you all the gossip of a troubled and tumultuous world."

Woodrow Wilson has been elected the 28th President of the United States. The Second Balkans War has ended with a peace treaty between Serbia and Turkey. Mahatma Gandhi, leader of the Indian Passive Resistance Movement, has been arrested. Pope Pius X has died, succeeded by Cardinal della Chiesa as Pope Benedict XV. Ernest Shackleton is headed for the Antarctic. The feisty suffragette Emmeline Pankhurst languishes in prison after attempting to blow up Lloyd George. Nickelodeon audiences have fallen in love with a character called the Little Tramp. A great canal through the Isthmus of Panama is about to open. The second anniversary of the *Titanic* disaster occasioned sermons, speeches, editorials, and religious observances throughout the Western world.

Good Lord, has it been two years already? It seems only yesterday that I watched Mr. Andrews unfurl his blueprint in the chartroom. So much has happened since then: the launching of the *Ada*, the consumption of Ismay and Murdoch, the reports of our collective demise, our decision to remain water-borne for the nonce, the birth of this republic — not to mention my marriage to the redoubtable Maggie.

Adaland continues to ply the Atlantic in a loop bounded on the north by the Tropic of Cancer and on the south by the Tropic of Capricorn. We last crossed the equator in late February. Mrs. Wilde marked the event by organizing an elaborate masquerade ball reminiscent of the fabled Brazilian *Carnaval*. The affair was a huge success, and we shall probably do the same thing three months hence when we hit the line again.

At least once a week we find ourselves within hailing distance of yet another pesky freighter or presumptuous steamer. By paddling furiously and hoisting all sails — our spars now collectively carry ten thousand square feet — we always manage to outrun the intruder. In theory, thanks to our wireless rig, we have endured the last of these nerve-wracking chases, for Phillips and Bride can now sound the alarm well before we become objects of unwanted charity.

2 September 1914
LAT. 25°48' S, LONG. 33°16' W

Against the dictates of reason, in defiance of all decency, with contempt for every Christian virtue, the world has gone to war. According to our wireless intercepts, a Western Front stretches a staggering four hundred and seventy-five miles across northern France, the Boche on one side, the Allies on the other, both armies dug in and defending themselves with machine guns. In my mind's eye I see the intervening terrain: a no-man's-land presided over by Death, now on holiday from Coleridge's skeletal ship and reigning over a king-dom of muck, blood, bone, mustard gas, and barbed wire, whilst Life-in-Death combs her yellow locks, paints her ruby lips, and sports with the boys in the trenches. Between 4 August and 29 August, Phillips informs me, two hundred and sixty thousand French soldiers died the most wretched, agonizing, and pointless deaths imaginable.

"I was under the impression that, since the *Titanic* allegedly went down two years ago, self-delusion had lost favor in Europe," remarked Mrs. Wilde. "How does one account for this madness?"

"I can't explain it," I replied. "But I would say we now have more reason than ever to remain aboard the *Ada*."

Although the preponderance of the butchery is occurring thousands of miles to the northeast, the British and Germans have succeeded in creating a nautical war zone here in the tropics. Mr. Phillips has inferred that a swift and deadly armored fleet, under the command of Admiral Craddock aboard HMS *Good Hope*, has been prowling these waters looking for two German cruisers, the *Dresden*, last seen off the Brazilian state of Pernambuco, and the *Karlsruhe*, recently spotted near Curaçao, one of the Lesser Antilles. If he can't catch either of these big fish, Craddock will settle for one of the Q-ships — merchant vessels retrofitted with cannons and pom-poms — that the Germans have deployed in their efforts to destroy British commercial shipping around Cape Horn. In particular Craddock hopes to sink the *Cap Trafalgar*, code name *Hilfskreuzer B*, and the *Kronprinz Wilhelm*, named for the Kaiser himself.

We are monitoring the Marconi traffic around the clock, eavesdropping on Craddock's relentless patriotism. Two hours ago Mr. Bride brought me a report indicating that the *Kronprinz Wilhelm* is being pursued by HMS *Carmania*, one of the British Q-ships that recently joined Craddock's cruiser squadron. Bride warns me that the coming fight could occur near our present location, about two hundred miles south of the Brazilian island of Trindade. We would be well advised to sail far away from here, though in which direction God only knows.

14 September 1914
LAT. 22°15′ S, LONG. 29°52′ W

A dizzyingly eventful day. Approaching Trindade, we were abruptly caught up in the Great War, bystanders to a furious engagement between the *Carmania* and the *Kronprinz Wilhelm*. There is blood on our decks tonight. Bullets and shells have shredded our sails. From our infirmary rise the moans and gasps of a hundred wounded German and British evacuees.

I had never witnessed a battle before, and neither had any other Adaland citizens save Major Butt and Colonel Weir, who'd seen action in the Philippines during the Spanish-American War. "Dover Beach" came instantly to mind. The darkling plain, the confused alarms, the ignorant armies clashing by night, or, in this case, by noon.

For two full hours the armed freighters pounded each other with their 4.1-inch guns, whilst their respective supply vessels — each combatant boasted a retinue of three colliers — maintained a wary distance, waiting to fish the dead and wounded from the sea. On board the *Ada*, the children cried in terror, the adults bemoaned the folly of it all, and the dogs ran in mad circles trying to escape the terrible noise. With each passing minute the gap separating the *Carmania* and the *Kronprinz Wilhelm* narrowed, until the two freighters were only yards apart, their sailors lining the rails and exchanging rifle shots, a tactic curiously reminiscent of Napoleonic-era fighting, quite unlike the massed machine-gun fire now fashionable on the Western Front.

At first I thought the *Carmania* had gotten the worst of it. Fires raged along her decks, her bridge lay flattened by artillery shells, her engines had ceased to function, and she'd started to lower away. But then I realized the *Wilhelm* was fatally injured, her hull listing severely, her crew launching lifeboats, her colliers drawing nearer the fray, looking for survivors. Evidently some shells had hit the *Wilhelm* below her waterline, rupturing several compartments. A North Atlantic iceberg could not have sealed her doom more emphatically.

Owing to the relentless explosions, the proliferating fires, the rain of bullets, and the general chaos, nearly three hundred sailors — perhaps three dozen from the *Carmania*, the rest from the *Wilhelm* — were now in the water, some dead, others wounded, most merely dazed. Fully half the castaways swam for the colliers and lifeboats of their respective nationalities, but the others took a profound and understandable interest in the *Ada*. And so it happened that our little republic found itself in need of an immigration policy.

Unlike the *Titanic*, the *Wilhelm* did not break in two. She simply lurched crazily to port, then slowly but inexorably disappeared. Throughout the sinking I consulted with the leaders of Parliament, and we reached a decision that, ten hours later, I am still willing to call enlightened. We would rescue anyone, British or German, who could climb aboard on his own hook, provided he agreed to renounce his nationality, embrace the founding documents of Adaland, and forswear any notion of bringing the Great War to our waterborne, sovereign, neutral country. As it happened, every sailor to whom we proposed these terms gave his immediate assent, though doubtless many prospective citizens were simply telling us what they knew we wanted to hear.

Being ill-equipped to deal with the severely maimed, we had to leave them to the colliers, even those unfortunates who desperately wanted to join us. I shall not soon forget the bobbing casualties of the Battle of Trindade. Even Major Butt and Colonel Weir had never seen such carnage. A boy — and they were all boys — with his lower jaw blasted away. Another boy with both hands burned off. An English lad whose severed legs floated alongside him like jettisoned oars. A German sailor whose sprung intestines encircled his midriff like some grisly life-preserver. The pen trembles in my hand. I can write no more.

29 October 1914
LAT. 10°35' S, LONG. 38°11' W

Every day, fair or foul, the Great War chews up and spits out another ten thousand mothers' sons, sometimes many more. Were the *Ada*'s scores of able-bodied Englishmen, Irishmen, Welshmen, and Scotsmen to sail home now and repatriate themselves, the majority would probably wind up in the trenches. The beast needs feeding. As for those hundreds of young men who boarded the *Titanic* intending to settle in New York or Boston or perhaps even the Great Plains — they, too, are vulnerable, since it's doubtless only a matter of months before President Wilson consigns several million Yanks to the Western Front.

And so it happens that a consensus concerning the present cataclysm has emerged amongst our population. I suspect we would have come to this view even without our experience of naval warfare. In any event, the Great War is not for us. We sincerely hope that the participating nations extract from the slaughter whatever their hearts desire: honor, glory, adventure, relief from ennui. But I think we'll sit this one out.

Yesterday I held an emergency meeting with my capable Deputy Prime Minister, Mr. Futrelle, my level-headed Minister of State, Mr. Andrews, and my astute Minister of War, Major Butt. After deciding that the South Atlantic is entirely the wrong place for us to be, we set a northwesterly course, destination Central America. I can't imagine how we're going to get through the canal. Mrs. Wilde assures me we'll think of something. Lord, how I adore my wife. In January we're expecting our first child. This happy phenomenon, I must confess, caught us completely by surprise, as Mrs. Wilde is forty-six years old. Evidently our baby was meant to be.

15 November 1914
LAT. 7°10' N, LONG. 79°15' W

Mirabile dictu — we've done it! Thanks to Mrs. Astor's diamond tiara, Mrs. Guggenheim's ruby necklace, and a dozen other such gewgaws, we managed to bribe, barter, and wheedle our way from one side of the Isthmus of Panama to the other. Being a mere 110 feet side to side, the lock chambers barely accommodated our machine, but we nevertheless squeaked through.

The *Ada* is heading south-southwest, bound for the Galápagos Islands and the rolling blue sea beyond. I haven't the remotest notion where we might end up, luscious Tahiti perhaps, or historic Pitcairn Island, or Pago Pago, or Samoa, and right now I don't particularly care. What matters is that we are rid of both the Belle Époque and the darkling plain. Bring on the South Pacific, typhoons and all.

Night falls over the Gulf of Panama. By the gleam of my electric torch I am reading the *Oxford Book of English Verse*. Three stanzas by George Peele seem relevant to our situation. In the presence of Queen Elizabeth, an ancient warrior doffs his helmet, which "now shall make a hive for bees." No longer able to fight, he proposes to serve Her Majesty in a different way. "Goddess, allow this aged man his right to be your beadsman now, that was your knight." The poem is called "Farewell to Arms," a sentiment to which we Battle of Trindade veterans respond with enthusiastic sympathy, though not for any reasons Mr. Peele would recognize. Farewell, ignorant armies. Auf Wiedersehen, dreadful *Kronprinz Wilhelm*. Adieu, fatuous *Good Hope*. Hail and farewell.

I am master of a wondrous raft, and soon I shall be a father as well. Over two thousand pilgrims are in my keeping, and at present every soul is safe. Strange stars glitter in a stranger sky. Colonel Astor's Airedale and Mr. Harper's Pekingese howl at the bright gibbous moon. The sea is calm tonight, and I am a lucky man.

Acknowledgments

"Arms and the Woman" copyright © 1991 by James Morrow. First appeared in *Amazing Stories* (July 1991).

"Auspicious Eggs" copyright © 2000 by James Morrow. First appeared in *The Magazine of Fantasy & Science Fiction* (October/November 2000).

"Bible Stories for Adults, No. 17: The Deluge" copyright © 1988 by James Morrow. First appeared in *Full Spectrum* (New York: Bantam Books, 1988).

"Bible Stories for Adults, No. 31: The Covenant" copyright © 1989 by James Morrow. First appeared in *Aboriginal Science Fiction* (November/December 1989).

"Bigfoot and the Bodhisattva" copyright © 2009 by James Morrow. First appeared in *Conjunctions: 52* (Spring 2009).

"The Cat's Pajamas" copyright © 2001 by James Morrow. First appeared in *The Magazine of Fantasy & Science Fiction* (October/November 2001).

"Daughter Earth" copyright © 1991 by James Morrow. First appeared in *Full Spectrum 3* (New York: Bantam Books, 1991).

"Fixing the Abyss" copyright © 2011 by James Morrow. First appeared in *Conjunctions: 56* (Spring 2011).

"The Iron Shroud" copyright © 2011 by James Morrow. First appeared in *Ghosts by Gaslight* (New York: HarperCollins, 2011).

"Known But to God and Wilbur Hines" copyright © 1991 by James Morrow. First appeared in *There Won't Be War* (New York: Tor Books, 1991).

"Lady Witherspoon's Solution" copyright © 2008 by James Morrow. First appeared in *Extraordinary Engines* (Nottingham, UK: Solaris, 2008).

"Martyrs of the Upshot Knothole" copyright © 2004 by James Morrow. First appeared in *Conqueror Fantastic* (New York: DAW Books, 2004).

"The Raft of the Titanic" copyright © 2010 by James Morrow. First appeared in *The Mammoth Book of Alternate Histories* (London: Robinson, 2010).

"Spinoza's Golem" copyright © 2014 by James Morrow. First appeared in *Tales in Firelight and Shadow* (Markham, ON: Double Dragon, 2014).

"The Vampires of Paradox" copyright © 2010 by James Morrow. First appeared in *Is Anybody Out There?* (New York: DAW Books, 2010).

ABOUT THE AUTHOR

James Morrow is the author of ten novels, three stand-alone novellas, and several dozen short stories. Although his obsessions are wide-ranging, he frequently writes in a satiric-theological mode. He has twice received the World Fantasy Award and twice the Nebula Award, as well as the Prix Utopia, the Grand Prix de l'Imaginaire, and the Theodore Sturgeon Memorial Award. He lives in State College, Pennsylvania, with his wife, Kathryn Morrow, and two professional dogs.